UNRAVELING THE THREADS

KNOTS SAGA, BOOK 2

BY SUSAN GARZON

Printed in the United States of America
Print ISBN: 9781951490805
E-Book ISBN: 9781951490812

Canoe Tree
Press

4697 Main Street
Manchester Center, VT 05255

Canoe Tree Press is a division of DartFrog Books.

For all those writers
whose craft sustains them
through the hard times

CONTENTS

CHAPTER ONE

January 20, 1978, New Bergen, Iowa

The phone rang. "Not now," Patricia grumbled. After a long day at the clinic, she needed a hot meal followed by love-making, not a drive over icy roads in a frigid car. Hank flashed her a sympathetic look. He'd just taken a bubbly chicken casserole out of the oven, and its aroma filled her kitchen.

She lifted the receiver off the wall phone. "Hello. Dr. Baldt speaking."

"Ay, Patricia, I have sad news," a woman said in Spanish, her voice shaky. "Your father has died."

"Mama?" It had taken a moment to recognize that this fragile-sounding woman was her mother. Judging from the static on the line, she must be calling from Guatemala.

"Of course. Who else would I be?" Eugenia snapped, sounding more like herself. "Your father died of a massive stroke. In case you're interested."

"Oh my God." Patricia vaguely remembered a note her mother had sent her months before saying her father was ill. As usual,

Patricia hadn't responded. Why should she? Her father meant nothing to her, not since the night twenty-four years earlier when she had watched him set fire to the highland Indian town of Chayaka and shoot a man who tried to escape. It wasn't the kind of thing one could easily forget.

And now her father was gone. Patricia felt a weight lift from her, followed by a hollow sadness. The man she had called "Papa" was dead. Her mind filled with a vision of him dancing with her at her fifteenth birthday party, guiding her in a smooth two-step. How beautiful she had felt, how protected and admired in the arms of her tall, handsome father.

"I'm a widow now," Eugenia said between sniffles. Patricia wondered how much her mother was really grieving. After all, Eugenia had devoted a good deal of her life to dealing with her husband's dark, erratic moods and angry outbursts. Now that was over. Still, she would have to adjust, after spending all her adult years as the wife of Otto Baldt, owner and manager of their large coffee plantation.

"Patricia, did you hear me?" her mother asked.

"Yes, yes. I'm sorry, Mama. This must be hard for you."

"The funeral will be Tuesday."

The funeral? Surely her mother didn't expect her to be there. In fact, Patricia hadn't set foot in Guatemala since she was eighteen and had hurtled off a cliff in her car. On its way down the mountainside, the car door had flung open, pitching her onto a rocky ledge. She woke up in a hospital room, where the doctor informed her that her cheek bone was smashed and her jaw was broken, as were her left hip, her sternum, and several ribs. It was a miracle, everyone said, that she had survived. She'd spent months recovering, first in Guatemala City and later in Chicago, where she had undergone plastic surgery.

"Let me know when you're arriving," Eugenia said, "and I'll have someone meet you at the airport."

"Oh no, Mama. I can't possibly attend. Not on such short notice. I have patients and...I can't be there. I'm sorry."

"What are you talking about? Everyone will ask about you. They'll wonder why Otto's daughter is not here."

"You'll think of something to tell them," Patricia said. Her mother would come up with a plausible story, and her friends and relatives would sympathize and pretend to believe her. Patricia told her mother to take care of herself, and a moment later they hung up.

Hank stood beside the kitchen counter, his weathered face creased in concern.

"My father is dead," Patricia blurted and suddenly, absurdly, began to cry.

"I'm sorry, honey," Hank said. He gathered her into his arms, her face resting against his chest, her tears moistening his soft flannel shirt.

"I don't know why I'm crying," she said as the sobs subsided. "We weren't close."

"A father is a father," he said. "You only get one."

She straightened and took a deep breath, slowly exhaling the shock and grief. "Let's eat," she said, although she had lost her appetite.

Hank grabbed pot holders and placed the casserole on the kitchen table, while Patricia removed a jar of applesauce from the refrigerator and spooned chunks into dessert bowls. She and Hank's sister Margit had canned two dozen jars of applesauce the previous fall, and Patricia was proud of her row of quart jars.

They sat down at the table, where she had set out white plates on red Norwegian place mats. Patricia helped herself to a spoonful of Hank's five-can casserole. He'd learned to cook several years earlier, when his wife Bonnie was dying from leukemia. The meals he made mostly came from Campbell's Soup recipes in *Better Homes and Gardens* advertisements. Bland but filling. She kept a bottle of Tabasco sauce on the table.

Patricia and Hank had started going out five years earlier, and now they spent most weekends together. He would arrive on Friday night and start supper if she was running late, which she often was. Hank was fifty-three, eleven years older than her forty-two, and it had not escaped Patricia's attention that he was one of very few men of his generation who would cook a meal for a woman.

They ate silently for several minutes, Patricia's news casting a pall over the meal. "How was your day?" she asked finally.

"Not bad. The Hendrickson brothers dropped by. They're thinking to replace their old tractor and combine. Wanted some advice." Winter was Hank's slow time. He was an agricultural extension agent, equally adept at getting along with the local farmers and with the Iowa State professors who shared their research with him.

"How are things at the clinic?" Hank asked.

"Busy," she said. "Mostly flu and GI tract stuff. Oh, and poor Mrs. Rasmussen fell again. This time getting down from a step ladder. Anita doesn't think she should be living alone." Anita was Patricia's trusted nurse as well as Hank's eldest daughter.

"Yep. That son of hers needs to get back here and take care of things." Hank had grown up in New Bergen and raised two daughters there. He knew everyone.

They started in on the chunky applesauce, pink from the apple peels and sweetened with cinnamon sticks. Usually Patricia loved it, but tonight she just nibbled while Hank polished his off.

"I stopped at the travel agency," he said, pulling a pamphlet out of his shirt pocket and setting it on the table. In a little under a month, they would be heading for a seafront resort on Barbados.

"I'll leave this here," he said. "You can take a look at it later...see if you still want to go."

"Of course I want to go," Patricia said. She could hardly wait for the week in the Caribbean, away from the bitter cold. Sub-freezing temperatures had started right after Christmas and stayed there for week after dreary week. Hank's usual idea of a vacation was to go farther north, to Minnesota or Wisconsin, where they could ski or snowshoe in a place where the wintry beauty was even more striking and austere than in Northern Iowa. But this time Patricia had prevailed, opting for warmth and a greener, more exuberant beauty. "What does the brochure say?"

Hank scanned the paper. "There's a list of places to visit and things to do. Here are a couple. Take a romantic stroll along white sandy beaches."

"Mm. Sounds marvelous."

"Next, snorkel to a coral reef teeming with tropical fish."

"Also good." She glanced up at the clock on the wall. Nearly seven-thirty. It felt much later. She yawned.

Hank gazed at the bedroom. "You in the mood?" he asked hesitantly.

"How about tomorrow?"

"Good enough." He cocked his head. "But I could stay for a while if you like, keep you company. Watch some TV?"

"No. You go ahead. Your pals will be expecting you." Hank lived in a farmhouse a couple of miles outside New Bergen with two affectionate dogs and three semi-feral cats.

They got up to clear the table.

"When's the funeral?" Hank asked as he stacked plates in the dishwasher.

"Tuesday. But I'm not going. I have too much to do."

He stared at her, aghast. "Patty, it's your dad's—"

"I'm not going. And don't look at me like that. It's not as if my mother will be alone. My brother Carlos will be there. And my Aunt Claudia. And a zillion other people."

He opened his mouth as if to object, then seemed to change his mind. "Well, it's your life." She accompanied him to the front door, where he pulled on his boots, then his parka and gloves. He kissed her good-bye, and a minute later, she heard his Ford truck revving in the driveway.

Patricia wandered to the living room and sank listlessly onto her lumpy, dove gray sofa, a garage sale find she'd picked up when she first arrived in New Bergen as a new doctor, many years earlier. She pulled an afghan crocheted in shades of red and blue onto her lap.

How could Hank possibly understand her unwillingness to attend her father's funeral? His own father had been a hard-working farmer who insisted that his three kids get a college education. A few years ago, she'd attended his memorial service, after which dozens of neighbors and kin had packed into the fellowship hall in the basement of Big Canoe Lutheran Church. They'd reminisced about Aksel Dalgaard's many acts of quiet generosity and about his hardiness, splitting firewood when he was in his late seventies and striding across his land in all weather, trailed by his large, scar-faced cat, Al.

In contrast, Patricia's father had been an angry, violent man, who had struck out at anyone who opposed him, including his own children. She was sorry if she seemed hard-hearted to Hank, but she couldn't mourn her father. Now he was dead, and whatever remaining influence he might have had over her life was at an end.

On Tuesday morning, Patricia thought of her father's funeral as she was assembling a tuna sandwich for her lunch bag. She pictured her family gathered at the large Catholic Church in San Felipe, in the company of the other plantation owners. Everyone would be in black, her mother veiled. First there would be Mass, then Holy Communion. Her mother would see to that, even though her father was never religious, at least not when Patricia was growing up.

But there was no time to dwell on thoughts of her family. She had a full day of work ahead of her. And in fact, she didn't think of her father again until that evening, when she felt only relief that the funeral would now be over and her father interred.

By Friday evening, Patricia had put her father's death out of her mind. Once again, she and Hank were in the kitchen, preparing chili together this time. She was chopping an onion when the phone rang. Hank answered it, listened for a minute, then covered the receiver with his hand.

"I think it's your mother," he said.

"Tell her I'm not here. Tell her: No está."

He shot her a cut-the-nonsense look, and Patricia rinsed her hands and took the phone. "Mama?"

"At last you're home," Eugenia said. "Who was that man who answered the phone?"

"A friend." As if it were her mother's business. "How was the funeral? Did it go well?"

"It was well attended, of course. Everyone asked about you afterwards. I told them you were devastated that you couldn't be with us. And your brother invited his ruffian friends. Other than that, it was fine."

"I'm glad," Patricia said. She was curious about the ruffian friends but didn't want to draw her mother further into conversation. "Is there a reason you called?"

"Yes. In fact, it's a matter of urgency. I've met with Amilcar, our lawyer. Your father has left you an inheritance. You need to come home and take care of it."

It couldn't be much, Patricia thought. She hadn't seen her father in over twenty years, and they weren't on good terms when she left. "Whatever Papa left me, you and Carlos can split it. I'll write to the attorney."

"It's not that easy."

"I don't see why not. Who inherited the finca? Carlos?" Her brother must be in his mid-thirties, more than old enough to run Finca Baldt.

"No, but he wants it. He's being very ugly. You have to come home."

So, it was her mother who had inherited the estate. Poor Carlos. She could see why he would be upset. Her father hadn't approved of him when he was a boy. Maybe they had never warmed up to each other. "I'm sorry, Mama, but you're going to have to deal with Carlos yourself. He certainly isn't going to listen to me after all these years. And he's your son, after all."

"You don't understand, *hija*. Your father left the estate to you."

"What?" Patricia raised her hand to her temple, her mind reeling. This made no sense at all. "But why?"

"It's complicated. You need to come home, and I'll explain."

Patricia groaned. There was no way she was going to get dragged into a dispute between her mother and brother. "Look. I'm going to renounce my inheritance."

"No, you will not. If you do, it will be left to a judge to decide who inherits the finca. And my old friend, Judge Hernandez, has retired. Now there's a new judge, a younger fellow. I know what will happen. He'll side with Carlos and give him the finca. And Carlos is incompetent. He will leave the place in ruins."

"Then you can help him run the place. Anyway, it's not my concern." Carlos had been an unpleasant child, and it sounded like he hadn't matured well. Too bad, but her mother was resourceful. After all, she'd handled her husband all those years. "Who's your lawyer? Amilcar Villanueva? Isn't that his name?"

A mumbled response.

"Mama, is that his name?"

"Yes."

"What's his address? I'm going to write him."

"He's on...Calle Salazar. 600 Calle Salazar. Zone 4."

"Office number?"

"110."

Patricia wrote it on a note pad by the telephone. "Listen, Mama. I'm going to tell Villanueva that I renounce my inheritance. And you and Carlos are going to have to work this out."

"Very well," her mother said icily.

They mumbled a good-bye. Patricia hung up and stared at the phone in disbelief.

"What did your mother have to say?" Hank asked.

"It appears that I've inherited the family finca."

"No kidding. I guess you'll be making a trip to Guatemala after all."

"Not a chance. I'm going to Barbados. With you."

CHAPTER TWO

February 3, Oak Park, Illinois

Meg carried two steaming mugs of coffee into the living room, where her father sat on the faded blue sofa, his fingers tapping on his fine wool slacks. She hadn't seen him look this distressed since four years earlier, when her mother died of breast cancer. What in the world could be the matter now? He'd been evasive on the phone when he'd called to tell her he was driving down, and it wasn't like him to venture out on such a cold day, with sloppy roads. At eighty, her father was becoming frail.

Meg set the mugs on the coffee table before sitting down next to him. "So, what brings you here on this nippy afternoon?"

Jonathan took a cheap blue envelope out of his jacket pocket and cleared his throat. "This came in the mail day before yesterday," he said. "It's from Guatemala. I had it translated, so I know what it says." He shook his head. "I wasn't sure I should even show it to you. But well, it's for you."

She raised her bifocals from the chain around her neck and took the envelope. The name on the front tugged at her heart. It wasn't her name, but her mother's—Señora Evelyn Cabell. The address had been typed on an old manual typewriter by an inexpert typist. Capital letters flew drunkenly above the line, and some of the letters were darker than others. The typed sheet that she withdrew had the same defects, and she began reading aloud, translating into English as she went.

"Esteemed Señora Fuente," she read. "Oh," she said, looking up, "it is for me." It had been many years since anyone had called her Mrs. Fuente, certainly not since she married Charlie and became Mrs. Reid sixteen years earlier.

She continued reading. "It is my great desire that you and your family find yourselves content and in good health. Without further particulars, I wish to inform you that your son Juan José is alive and well."

Her breath caught. A wild jolt of hope turned into a searing stab of pain. Juan José—her J.J.—was buried next to his father in the cemetery outside Lake Forest.

"Meg..."

"No, it's okay," she said. "Just give me a second." She took a long breath and stared blankly out the picture window toward the barren branches of their maple tree. What in the world was this all about? Her mind plunged back to the old house at Los Ancianos, to the smoke-filled bedroom and the flaming hallway where her husband Pablo had collapsed and died, trying to reach J.J.'s room. She had shouted desperately to her son, but there had been no response. None at all. She raised her fingers to her throat, remembering the searing heat. J.J. could not have survived that fire. Her own rescue was due to a worker's act of selfless courage and to lucky timing.

She looked back at the letter. "He signs it 'un amigo'—a friend. A male friend."

"Some friend," her father muttered. "There's no name and no return address, so we have no way of knowing who the guy is. I'd say it's some kind of hoax."

"Yes, a cruel one. Or maybe some horrible misunderstanding."

"I'm sorry, Meg. I should never have brought it to you."

"Don't be silly, Dad. You were right to show it to me."

She gazed down at the letter, frowning. "Who in the world would write such a thing?"

"You got me," her father said. "Must be somebody who knows us, or at least knows who we are. And somehow he came by the Lake Forest address. But the guy certainly isn't up to date. He isn't aware that Evelyn passed away or that you've remarried."

Meg picked up the envelope. There was a blurred postmark. January 25, 1978, ten days earlier. And the location: San Felipe.

San Felipe. She hadn't thought of the place for ages. It was the nearest town to Los Ancianos, her husband Pablo's coffee plantation. For almost three years, she'd driven to the town once a week to shop and pick up mail. The last year, 1954, she'd spent many hours at a café where she'd talked politics with the members of a revolutionary labor party. She had also been teased by an activist named Ernesto Guevara, who later became known as Che. And San Felipe was the town where she and Sergio had made love under the shadow of impending disaster, knowing that Sergio would be in grave danger if the Arbenz government fell. It collapsed not long after that, but by then, Meg was back in the United States, her husband and small son dead. Looking back, that intense, terrifying, ultimately tragic period felt to Meg like a different lifetime.

"I guess I should show the letter to Charlie," she said. Her husband was a labor organizer, accustomed to dealing with difficult individuals. She'd met him when he represented the union in negotiations at her father's manufacturing plant, and she had sat in on the sessions. She and Charlie had learned to respect each other, and the respect had eventually turned into something deeper. He was seven years younger than she was, but it didn't seem to matter, at least not now when he was forty-six and she fifty-three. They had twelve-year-old twin daughters, both with their father's coppery hair.

"I don't suppose that husband of yours is in town," Jonathan mumbled. He had a grudging respect for Charlie but didn't approve of all his son-in-law's traveling.

"As a matter of fact, he'll be home for dinner."

"Better show him the letter, then." Jonathan said. "See what he makes of it."

She examined the envelope again. "Who used to write to Mother from Guatemala?"

"Just Eugenia Baldt, as far as I know."

Patricia's mother. "So," Meg said, "the writer was probably someone who had contact with the Baldts, who could have gotten the address from Eugenia. But that doesn't tell us much. He could be a friend, a neighbor, a servant, even a member of the family, I suppose."

Jonathan nodded slowly. "Makes sense. Do you think we should tell Patricia about this?"

"I don't know." Her friend Patricia avoided discussions of the events leading up to her car accident, including the fire at Los Ancianos. Since the letter's claim seemed to have no basis in fact, it was probably better not to bring it up. "Let's not mention the letter to her," Meg said finally.

She looked across the room to a framed family photograph standing on the side table. There they were, she and Charlie, with the girls sitting between them, both wearing brand new sweater vests. The photograph portrayed them pretty accurately, Meg thought. A loving and generally happy family. And didn't all families have shadows in their pasts? Fate had been generous enough to bring Charlie into her life, and then the girls, not to mention Meg's father and Charlie's mother, who provided loving support. "You know what I think?" Meg said. "We should just forget the letter."

"I agree. It's not worth thinking about. I'll dispose of it."

Meg slipped the letter into the envelope and began to hand it to him, then stopped. "Never mind," she said. "I'll get rid of it."

An hour later, Meg sat at her desk in the upstairs room that she used as an office. It was crowded with her mother's cherry desk and chair, an electric typewriter on a table, a bookcase filled with medical reference books and style guides for writers, and a single bed where Neffie, her tortoiseshell cat, was now sleeping.

Most days, Meg found her job editing a medical journal only moderately challenging, but today it seemed impossible. The article on a recent advance in cardiac care was written by an author with decent writing skills, but Meg hadn't gotten through the first two lines before she was thinking about J.J. That blasted letter! What sort of demented person would raise such an impossible hope?

She pictured her four-year-old son standing proudly in front of his tree house, and her body ached for him, as it had thousands of times before. She tried to resist the impulse to re-read the letter but finally gave in and pulled it out from the bottom of her desk drawer, where she'd buried it. The words were already engraved in her mind: "Your son Juan José is alive and well."

Leaning back in the chair, she closed her eyes and wrapped her arms around her body. She could still feel J.J.'s heartbeat inside her.

What if he was alive? Was it possible? He'd be twenty-eight, an adult. What wouldn't she give to see her boy again! To hear his voice, to hold him in her arms. Even just to see him across the street, to know he was alive. She heard a chirpy meow at her feet, and Neffie leapt onto her lap, then settled in a soft pile.

"It's okay," Meg said to the cat, stroking the silky fur. She eyed the letter. That way madness lies, she thought as she dropped it back in the desk drawer. After looking briefly at the cardiac care article, she slid it into a file folder. Her deadline for completion wasn't for a few days yet, thank heavens.

Spaghetti sauce. She'd cook that up. It was active work and wouldn't require a lot of concentration. Neffie jumped down and followed her to the bathroom, where Meg splashed water on her face and ran a comb through her short, layered hair, a number of gray strands mixed in with the blond. Twice, people had mistaken her for the twins' grandmother.

She and the cat went downstairs to the kitchen, where Meg peeled a garlic clove and started mincing it on the pig-shaped chopping block that her daughter Laura had given her as a birthday present.

Questions assailed her. The Guatemalan police had found J.J.'s remains in the ruins of the house. But how did they know it was J.J.? Identification must have been difficult. Could there have been some mistake? She had been in the hospital, heavily sedated due to burns and smoke inhalation at the time, but her parents had been in touch with the Embassy official who oversaw everything. She looked at the wall clock. 3:45. Maybe she'd call her father. He should be home by now. She washed the garlic off her hands and headed for the phone in the living room.

"Dad, I've been thinking," she said when Jonathan picked up.

"About that letter? Me too."

Of course. Had she really thought they could put it out of their minds? "How were Pablo and J.J. identified? I was too dopey on pain medication to take it all in."

A pause at the other end. "They weren't identified exactly. I saw the remains briefly before the coffins were sealed. Just an assortment of charred bones really."

An image of bones, small and forlorn, filled Meg's mind. She felt sobs rising and pressed her hand against her mouth.

"Meg? You there?"

She took a long, ragged breath. "Just thinking. So, how did the police know it was Pablo and J.J.?"

"They found the remains of two bodies at the house site. A man and a child. So, they just assumed...we all did. Who else would they be?"

"And no one else was reported missing?"

"No. We specifically asked. I don't think the police saw any reason to explore other possibilities. What are you thinking, Meg? That J.J. might be alive?"

"No, not really. Well, I did consider it. I mean...that letter makes you wonder, doesn't it?"

"Yes," he said, "but the writer didn't provide one shred of evidence. And he wasn't even willing to identify himself."

"I know."

"I have to admit, at one point, your mother and I thought about hiring a detective and starting our own investigation into the fire."

"You did?" They'd never mentioned such a thing. She felt the hair on her arms rise. "Did you think J.J. might be alive?"

"No, nothing like that. But there were some things that seemed fishy. Like, why did Patricia's father claim that one of Pablo's workers was the arsonist, when Patricia insisted that he couldn't be? And what about Pablo's gift of the valley to the Indian town? Did it have anything to do with the fire?"

So, her parents had wanted more answers. "Why didn't you go ahead with the investigation?"

"For one thing, the Embassy advised against it. They thought it would go nowhere, especially with war about to break out. Everybody was in a lather about that. Besides, our first priority was to make sure you got home safe and sound."

She took a deep breath. "Dad, do you think there's any chance that J.J. might be alive?"

A long pause. "No, Meggie. I think he died in the fire. If I'd had any inkling that J.J. might be alive—any evidence at all—I wouldn't have left Guatemala."

"I know that, Dad. I just needed to hear you say it." Her father was right. There was nothing to be gained by torturing herself with an impossible hope. She needed to set this matter to rest.

"It was hard at the time," Jonathan said, "not being able to properly identify Pablo and J.J. But your mother and I both felt strongly that we had to accept reality. We all needed to move forward with our lives. And you did that, Meg, in your own time. We were proud of you."

She heard the voices of young children shouting outside. School must be out. The girls would be home soon. "Well, I'm sorry to have bothered you."

"No bother. The same questions have been going through my head. That note stirred up a lot. I'm just glad Evelyn isn't here to deal with it."

"Mother would have been okay," she said. "She would have knitted her way through it."

Her father chuckled. "I guess that's right."

But Meg couldn't help wondering what her mother would have said. Would she have told Meg to follow up on the letter? To look for J.J. no matter how impossible it seemed?

Laura and Amy announced their arrival home from school with a vigorous stomping of boots on the mat outside the front door. As a rush of frigid air invaded the house, Meg called hello from the kitchen as cheerily as she could.

"Mom, you won't believe this," Amy said, entering the kitchen.

"It's the worst," said Laura. "Jane Rogen is moving to St. Louis!"

Meg mumbled something sympathetic. It was too bad for the girls, but she wouldn't miss Jane's mother, who always weaseled out of PTA and Girl Scout duties. Meg set out glasses, and the girls helped themselves to milk and oatmeal cookies.

"We should have a slumber party before Jane leaves," Amy said. She and her sister both eyed Meg hopefully.

Meg was about to reply that she would think about it, but the words that came out were "Sure. Why not."

The girls cheered, then tromped upstairs to their rooms, discussing the slew of farewell activities they would soon be launching.

In the kitchen, Meg continued browning a pound of ground beef, but her mind kept returning to the letter, and before long, a smoky odor rose to let her know she'd scorched the bottom of the pan. Oh well. The girls would be "grossed out," but her husband wouldn't mind a little char in his spaghetti sauce. He'd been traveling in Indiana most of the week, and he would be happy to sit down to a home-cooked meal, regardless of its shortcomings.

Charlie arrived a little after six and perched on the high kitchen stool with a can of Miller Lite, his jaw stubbled with a coppery five o'clock shadow. His green eyes creased happily. He'd just gotten off the phone with a machinist in a plant near Indianapolis where the workers were ready to unionize.

Meg put on water to boil for the spaghetti and told him shakily about the message from the anonymous writer.

Charlie frowned. "Did the guy ask for money? Dollars in exchange for information? Anything like that?"

"No."

"Well, that's good, at least." He paused. "Do you think there could be anything to his claim?"

"How could there be?" But it was more of a wail than a question, and her eyes glazed with tears. He took her in his arms, and she melted against him. He was a couple of inches taller than she was and had the muscle tone of a guy who had played baseball in high school and college and could still send a ball soaring. "Dad and I think it's a hoax," she said. "Or something like that."

"Sorry, hon," he said. "That's got to be tough. Hey. If we find the jerk who wrote the letter, I know a couple of guys who will be glad to go down there and eliminate him."

She half-smiled. "I'll keep it in mind." Charlie was always ready to fix things—change a washer in the faucet, clean out the eaves. She wasn't sure he would actually come through with the hit man, but under the right circumstances, she might not put it past him.

At dinner, the girls talked on and off about their week and who they might invite to their slumber party, and Charlie glanced from time to time at Meg, who ate little.

Meg carried out her usual Friday evening routine as if she were moving between two worlds—her comfortable, safe home in Oak Park and a far-away place where she had lived with Pablo and her son. She did the dishes, then made popcorn at the stove, shaking an old pan over the burner as the kernels popped against the lid, first in single explosions, then in a torrent. J.J. had loved popcorn.

She poured two loads into a big Tupperware bowl, then drizzled melted butter over the top. After filling a red enamel bowl with popcorn and preparing a glass of 7-Up on ice, she headed to the dining room, where Charlie was writing up notes from a meeting.

"How's it going?" she asked, setting down his snack.

"It would be faster if I could read my own handwriting." He tossed a popcorn kernel in the air and opened his mouth to let it fall in. Her coordinated husband.

In the living room, she deposited the Tupperware bowl between the girls, who were sitting cross-legged in front of the TV, watching *Wonder Woman*, their bright coppery hair falling to their shoulders.

"Did you put on enough butter?" Amy asked, grabbing a handful of popcorn without looking away from the screen.

"Enough for me," Meg said. She'd have to soak the popcorn in butter to satisfy her daughters.

She sat on the sofa, arranging her nubby pullover sweater over her beige slacks. Neffie jumped up and settled onto her lap, which had become increasingly ample over the last year. In spite of aerobics classes at the community center, Meg's clothing size had crept up from twelve to fourteen. Neffie began to purr, and soon, the TV noises faded from Meg's mind, and she thought again of Patricia and wondered what she would have made of the letter.

A little after ten, Meg locked up the house. Charlie had gone to bed early, worn out from his trip, and she had said good night to the girls, wishing them sweet dreams. Meg threw a couple of Neffie's cloth mice into her toy box and headed for the kitchen. She was tired but still felt off-kilter, so she filled the tea kettle and put it on the stove to boil, then dropped a peppermint tea bag into a mug. She sat at the small table and waited for the water in the teapot to start bubbling.

Suddenly, a memory jolted her. The waif!

There had been a child in the woods at Los Ancianos. They used to leave food for him. A child who might have come up to the house and sought refuge in some hidden corner, easy enough when no one was around. If so, he could have been trapped by the fire. And if he'd died, no one would have reported him missing.

Meg stood, her breath coming quickly. There was a chance—a small chance—that the bones that were discovered in the ashes belonged to the wild child, not to J.J. The kettle began to shriek, and she turned off the knob on the stove. Then, half-dazed, she climbed the stairs to her office, retrieved the anonymous letter, and walked back down to the living room. There, she sat on the chair by the phone and glanced at her watch. Ten fifteen. A bit late for a phone call, but maybe not too late. She lifted the receiver and dialed Patricia's number.

CHAPTER THREE

New Bergen, Iowa

Patricia had just changed into her red flannel pajamas when the phone on the nightstand rang. She picked up the receiver, collecting herself to deal with some patient's late-night emergency.

"It's Meg. I have news." Her voice sounded strained.

"Meg, are you okay?" Patricia asked, seating herself on the edge of the bed. "What is it?"

"Look. I know this sounds strange, but...there's a possibility that J.J. is alive."

"What?" Had Meg gone crazy?

"I can explain." Meg read the anonymous letter out loud, describing the typewritten script and the San Felipe postmark.

Patricia hesitated, and the scene of the fire flashed before her, as it had so many times—the demonic flames shooting up, the house crashing in on itself, and the knowledge that Pablo and J.J. were inside. Dead. "Look, Meg—"

"I know what you're thinking, that it's impossible. But maybe it isn't. Listen. There was a child who hid out in the ravine near our house. I never saw him up close, but we used to put out food for him."

Patricia searched her memory. "I vaguely recall J.J. talking about a wild kid."

"He didn't look very old, maybe six or so. And the bones that the police found in the house were badly damaged in the fire. They could have belonged to that child. Not to J.J. It's possible, don't you think?"

"I don't know, Meg. J.J. was four, wasn't he? That's quite a bit younger."

"Yes, but the...the remains were in bad shape. Everybody just assumed they were J.J.'s. They couldn't really be identified."

Patricia hesitated, unsure of what to say. As a doctor, she had sometimes dealt with parents of dying children. Many were incapable of facing reality. Their belief in the child's survival was a seemingly immutable force, sometimes extending far beyond any reasonable hope. Was this something similar? On the basis of a sketchy letter and the memory of a child in the ravine, Meg seemed to be creating a whole new scenario, one in which her son survived.

"I have no choice," Meg said. "I'm going to San Felipe to look for J.J."

Patricia considered. The following day was Saturday. "I'll drive over tomorrow morning. We can discuss it then."

Patricia and Hank left New Bergen early the next morning in Hank's Ford Ranger pick-up. He'd been planning to finish work on a cradle that he was building for his youngest daughter, who was eight months pregnant.

"The cradle can wait," he'd said over the phone without hesitation.

Patricia wasn't really surprised. Hank was fond of Meg. On their first meeting, they had discussed his work with farmers and had ended up talking at length about Norman Borlaug, a Norwegian-American who had radically changed agriculture around the world. Since then, they had engaged in many spirited conversations, often about farming in third world countries.

Hank had offered to pick up Patricia this morning, which was fine with her, although she recognized that his gentlemanly offer stemmed in part from his doubts about her driving. She had to admit that earlier that winter, her car had slid off an icy country road and ended up in a ditch. She wasn't injured, and the car was fine, but the experience had revived frightening memories, and she had still been shaken up when she talked to Hank afterwards. Plus, the first time that she and Hank slept together, she had explained that her many scars were the result of driving a car off a cliff. He had not forgotten.

They had left before dawn, and now, as they drove east over the snow-packed two-lane highway, the winter sun hovered below the rolling hills, rimming the snowy landscape with golden light. In the distance, sturdy farmhouses became increasingly visible, with smoke spiraling up from their chimneys into the chilly air. While Hank steered the car around slick curves, Patricia talked about the fire at Los Ancianos, dredging up the painful details. Hank knew that Meg had lost her first husband and son in a fire, but until now he hadn't heard the specifics. "Gosh. Poor Meg," he said.

At Dubuque, Hank steered the pick-up onto the bridge spanning the Mississippi. Today it was covered by a broad, leaden sheet of ice, bordered by the low cliffs on the opposite side. Below them, a man in a navy parka skated down the river in long, powerful strides.

A moment later, they were across the bridge and into Illinois, where the countryside flattened out and extended for miles, corn stubble peeking above the snow. Patricia peered out the window. She still felt like an alien in this Midwestern world with no mountains and with a climate that swung between sticky heat and frigid cold.

Her unlikely arrival in New Bergen had its origins fourteen years earlier. She'd just finished medical school at Northwestern when she discovered that New Bergen was willing to pay the bills for a one-year internship in exchange for a commitment to practice medicine in the town for three years. The Cabells had paid for Patricia's medical school, but she didn't like to continue relying on their generosity, so she had arranged for an interview. It was a long shot. She knew the town was looking for an American man, not a foreign woman. But she assured the three-man interview committee that she would stay for the full three years and would not marry during that time, so they didn't need to worry about her following a husband to another place or getting pregnant. For some reason—a shortage of other candidates probably—they had offered her the contract.

At first, New Bergen had felt like the end of the earth. It was a two-stoplight town with a movie theater and a café. Social life revolved around the four churches—two Lutheran ones and two smaller Baptist and Catholic ones. But slowly, Patricia had adjusted to the place, and she stayed on past her three-year commitment. Long past.

In truth, her contentment was due partly to Danny, a good-natured ophthalmologist she'd met in medical school, who lived in an apartment in an artsy neighborhood in Chicago. He was fun to be with, and like her, he was uninterested in marriage. Once a month, Patricia drove three hours to see him. They would have light-hearted sex, then take in a movie—often a foreign one that would never make it to New Bergen—or visit a museum or art gallery. Or they would walk around one of Chicago's many ethnic neighborhoods.

Dinner was usually something spicy and exotic. The next day, she would stop in to see the Cabells on her way home.

Her relationship with Danny wasn't one that she would ever have imagined for herself, but it seemed to work—that is, until five years earlier, when Danny announced one Sunday morning over coffee that he was engaged to the daughter of a real estate broker. He'd offered to continue his get-togethers with Patricia, but when she shot him a dirty look, he laughed. "Just kidding," he said.

Patricia was not devastated by Danny's defection. Theirs had never been a love match. And by that time, she had carved out a comfortable niche for herself in New Bergen. She knew everyone in town and rarely went into a business without being drawn into conversation with the clerk or proprietor. Although she worked long hours, she made time to join three single women—the librarian, the pharmacist, and a retired high school teacher—for coffee at the café or for pizza and a movie. They had all grown up outside New Bergen and enjoyed laughing at the in-grown oddities of the town. But without Danny, Patricia was starting to feel cut off from the larger world, and she began searching for openings for general practitioners around Chicago and in cities farther south, places with milder winters.

Anita, Patricia's nurse, was mostly silent about Patricia's plan to leave the clinic. However, one day she made a suggestion as they sat in the lunch room, eating sandwiches and drinking soup from thermoses. "You know, Patricia, you really need to learn to cross-country ski. And I know the best teacher in the county. My dad."

That Saturday, Hank had arrived at Patricia's house with two pairs of cross-country skis, poles, and a pair of boots that Anita had found for her. Patricia climbed into Hank's truck with some trepidation. Not only had she never skied, but Hank was handsome, his blond good looks reminding Patricia uncomfortably of her father. This changed, however, after they spent a few hours on skis, swooshing around the hills surrounding New Bergen. Hank was kind, patient, and quick to laugh at himself. In short, he was nothing like Otto Baldt. Finally, after all her time living in the Upper Midwest, Patricia learned to appreciate winter, and she also got to like her ski instructor. Soon, she had stopped looking for other jobs.

But this winter had been a challenge. With temperatures that kept dipping below zero, nearly every trip outdoors was an ordeal of getting into bulky layers of clothes and trudging across slippery sidewalks and parking lots. Patricia's old injuries ached, and even breathing was difficult in the searing cold.

Patricia's attention shifted back to the present as Hank's truck slowed on the highway. They were gaining on a semi, its huge wheels spewing slush. Hank accelerated and passed it, their vision blocked momentarily by the watery mess. Patricia clutched the armrest until they were safely in front.

"You know," Hank said after a moment, "Meg's idea about her son has a few holes. If the boy escaped the fire, why didn't he appear later? Wouldn't someone have found him and taken him to the police or a church or...someplace?"

"You'd think so."

"And nobody even knew that Meg's family was at home, right? That seems to make a kidnapping unlikely. But let's say the boy was abducted. Wouldn't the kidnappers have asked for ransom? Jonathan Cabell is a rich man."

"I know. There are lots of reasons to believe that J.J. died in the fire. But Meg isn't thinking very logically." In fact, Patricia thought, her friend might be a little bit crazed.

It was mid-morning when Hank's truck entered the thickening stream of traffic moving toward the Chicago suburbs, and Patricia roused herself from the drowsiness that miles of Illinois cornfields always brought on. A bright sun reflected off the cars that raced along the highway, which was now lined with heaps of gritty snow. Hank turned off at the Oak Park exit, and they drove past a mix of one and two-story houses visible through bare tree branches. A few yards sported snowmen. Soon, Meg's house came into view, a trim two-story colonial, painted white with cobalt blue shutters.

Meg met them at the front door, dressed in a loose-fitting sweater and navy pants. Based on their conversation the night before, Patricia half expected her friend to be in a manic state, so she was relieved to see that Meg seemed composed, although dark shadows underlined her eyes.

"It's so good of you to come," Meg said as she helped them off with their coats and hats. "And on such short notice."

"We wanted to be here," Patricia said.

"Dad has already arrived," Meg said, lowering her voice. "And he has taken charge." She led them down the hall. "Oh, and Charlie went out on a kolache run earlier," Meg said over her shoulder. "So we're well supplied."

"Great," Hank said. Meg knew he was a kolache fan.

They followed Meg to the dining room, where Jonathan Cabell was sitting at the head of the polished maple table, clad in a herringbone sports jacket. A notebook and attaché case lay in front of him.

"Hi there," Patricia said.

Jonathan looked up, and his solemn expression brightened. "Well, hello. It's good to see you two."

For the last several years, Jonathan had been slowing down, but as he stood, Patricia noticed that he had his old air of authority.. He came around the table, where five places were set with legal pads, a pen and a pencil. Jonathan kissed Patricia on the cheek and shook hands with Hank.

The aroma of coffee filled the room, and Patricia filled mugs for herself and Hank from a carafe on the sideboard. Meg slipped into the kitchen and appeared a moment later, carrying a tray of kolaches, crackers, cheese, and grapes. She pointed to the kolaches. "These have a poppy seed filling, those have cream cheese, and the rest have cherry."

They seated themselves around the table, with Meg on the far side and Patricia and Hank facing her. "Good coffee," Patricia said, as its rich warmth spread through her. She reached for a pastry. A hasty breakfast and the cold morning air had given her an appetite.

"Charlie will be here shortly," Meg said. "We decided we didn't want the girls to know anything about this, at least not yet, so he's dropping them off at his mother's house." A minute later they heard the sound of the front door opening and of boots in the front hall.

Charlie appeared in the doorway, dressed in faded jeans and a forest green flannel shirt. Patricia was aware of his commanding presence, not so different from his father-in-law's. Charlie startled noticeably when he saw Jonathan sitting at the head of the table, but he recovered quickly and greeted everyone. "The girls are settled for the day," he said and sat next to Meg.

"Then let's begin, shall we?" Jonathan said. "We're all familiar with the letter and with the background information, I presume." He looked at Hank, who nodded. "Good. I understand, as you all do, that there may be little to the letter writer's claim. But we are going to proceed with the assumption that it could have some merit. We— that is, Meg, Charlie, and I—have decided on four lines of inquiry."

Patricia had supposed they would discuss the letter, but the group had clearly moved beyond that.

Jonathan clasped his age-spotted hands. "First, at Meg's suggestion, we've decided to exhume J.J.'s—that is—the boy's body. I viewed the bones briefly many years ago. As I recall, they were in pretty bad shape. But a forensic pathologist may be able to get some idea of the child's size and age. If it turns out that the bones are from an older child, then they might belong to the boy from the ravine. That would lend support to the idea that J.J. could have survived the fire." He paused. "Of course, the examination might reveal that the bones are J.J.'s. In that case, we will halt our search."

Patricia glanced at Meg, whose mouth was set in a hard line. It must have been a tough decision to have the boy's body exhumed. "Are there dental records?" Patricia asked.

"Unfortunately, no," Meg said. "We took J.J. to the dentist once, but he didn't have x-rays taken or any dental work done."

"Any idea how long it will all take?" Patricia asked.

"I have a couple of friends among the city commissioners," Jonathan said. "I think they can expedite the process."

Patricia felt something warm moving against her lower leg and looked down to see Meg's tortoiseshell cat, Neffie, swishing past her.

"In the meantime," Jonathan said, "we're going to begin the second line of inquiry. Our plan is to run a series of personal ads in the Guatemalan newspapers. We'll ask the writer to contact us at a post office box in the capital."

"There are a couple of national newspapers," Patricia said, "both widely read."

"How do you want the ad to read?" Hank asked.

"We thought we'd consult Patricia about that," Jonathan said. "We'll probably cite the date of the letter and say something like,

'We request that the friend of Margaret Fuente contact her at such and such a post office box.'"

"We were also wondering about a reward," Meg said. "Maybe offer compensation if the person can lead us to J.J.—without mentioning his name, of course. We want to offer an incentive but not mobilize any treasure hunters."

"That sounds reasonable," Patricia said. "We can work out the exact language later. Who will place the ads and collect the responses?"

"I thought I'd contact our old attorney, Bernabé Muñoz," Meg said. "He must be in his late sixties or seventies by now. I'm hoping that he'll take charge of the project."

Jonathan turned to Patricia. "You knew him, as I recall." She nodded. Bernabé Muñoz. Ceci and Arturo's father. Patricia could feel the threads of her old life starting to reconnect.

"I'll have my assistant find the phone number for his law firm," Jonathan said. "Assuming he's still practicing. Patricia, could you make the call?"

"Of course." The threads were pulling tighter.

"I'd do it myself," Meg said, "but I'm afraid my Spanish is pretty rusty. Something I intend to work on."

The doorbell rang. "Probably the neighbor kid," Meg said as she hastened out of the dining room.

"Let's take a break," Jonathan said, rising and heading out of the room.

Hank leaned back in his chair. "You worked fast," he said to Charlie. "When did you find out about this? Last night?"

"Meg told me about the letter last night, but I didn't hear about the kid in the ravine until this morning. When I came down to breakfast, Meg was sitting at the kitchen table scribbling away in her notebook."

"So, these lines of inquiry are Meg's ideas?" Patricia asked.

"Mostly." He cracked a smile. "Jonathan and I are basically her flunkies."

"What do you think of the anonymous letter?" Hank asked.

"The guy's probably a crackpot. But who knows?"

Patricia wrapped her hands around her coffee mug. "I'm afraid for Meg."

"So am I," Charlie said. "If it turns out this is all a hoax..."

Meg will be devastated, Patricia thought. How could she live through the loss of her child twice? She fetched the carafe from the sideboard and topped off everyone's coffee, while Hank reached for another kolache. A moment later, Meg and Jonathan returned.

"And now," Jonathan said, "Meg will explain the third line of action."

She leaned forward, folding her hands on the table. "I'm making reservations to fly to Guatemala City on Sunday, February 20. That's a little over two weeks from now. Charlie's planning to be home that week, so I can leave the girls with him." She paused. "Of course, I would cancel the trip if we found proof that J.J....that he died in the fire."

"I offered to go with her," Jonathan said, his CEO demeanor slipping, "but she said I'd be in the way."

"That's not what I said, Dad. And anyway, you know we need you here to coordinate things." Meg addressed the group, her blue eyes steady and her voice firm. "So, here's my plan. When I get to Guatemala, I interview everyone who was near Los Ancianos the night of the fire—anyone who might have seen a child or even heard a rumor about one."

"That would include most of my father's workers," Patricia said. "I'm sure my mother can help you locate them."

"That's what I was thinking," Meg said. "I'd also like to know who might have my mother's address. As you know, it was her name on the envelope that Dad received. I'll ask your mother about that too."

"Patricia said you returned home unexpectedly on the night of the fire," Hank said. "Was anyone there at the time?"

"Just the watchman." Meg shook her head. "I have no idea what happened to him. I've been trying to remember his name, but for the life of me I can't think of it. He was from Chayaka. I'm sure of that. Anyway, I'll look for him as well."

Jonathan cleared his throat. "We've discussed one other possibility. J.J. might have been put up for adoption, maybe on the international market. I'm going to check into adoption agencies with links to Guatemala. Groups who were there in 1954 and the following years. I'll see if any of them placed a child with a description similar to J.J.'s."

"Will they volunteer information?" Patricia asked.

"I'll pull some strings among my legislative buddies," Jonathan said. "I think they'll help me with the agencies."

"I don't know," Hank said. "Is adoption even a possibility? I mean, wouldn't the boy have told someone about his real family? A worker in the adoption agency? Or his adoptive parents?"

"He might," Patricia said, "but then it's hard to know what a traumatized four-year-old would do. And at that age, a child might forget quickly." She glanced at Meg, who was staring downward. The thought of J.J. being put up for adoption was excruciating. But it might actually be the best of the possible scenarios.

Charlie placed his hand over Meg's, and it occurred to Patricia that this ordeal could have an impact on their marriage. Charlie was supportive of Meg, but he must be affected by her single-minded pursuit of her son by another man. Patricia hoped for everyone's sake that J.J.'s fate would be resolved soon.

"I guess that's about everything," Jonathan said and closed the meeting.

Patricia looked across the table to Meg. This discussion had been intense, and she wondered how her friend was doing. Meg's eyes met hers.

"Don't worry," Meg said. "Way will open." Patricia recognized the Quaker saying that expressed a faith in the active presence of the Spirit. If some action had a rightness to it, the way would open. Not immediately, perhaps, but in good time. Meg said that it was an idea that supported Friends in the midst of difficulty, even when there appeared to be no path forward.

Patricia nodded. Let the way open for Meg, she thought, and soon.

CHAPTER FOUR

Patricia called the Muñoz law firm during her lunch break on Monday, dialing the long string of numbers that connected her to Guatemala City. Then she braced herself for a plunge into her past. If Muñoz was there, she would keep her interaction brief and professional. The line crackled and a woman answered in cultivated Spanish, identifying the attorneys Muñoz & Muñoz.

"Good afternoon," Patricia replied. "I'm calling on behalf of Señora Margaret Fuente. I'd like to speak with Licenciado Bernabé Muñoz."

"Just a moment," the secretary said, and put Patricia on hold. A minute later, a familiar male voice came on the phone.

"Señora Fuente, what a pleasure," the man said in slow, careful Spanish, no doubt for Meg's benefit. "But I'm afraid I have bad news. My father retired last year. I wonder if I might help you. I am his son, Arturo Muñoz."

Arturo. Patricia gulped. His voice was familiar, but mellower and more authoritative than she remembered. Warmth flooded her, followed by alarm. He knew her too well, knew her family too well. She had a sudden vision of their midnight race across the valley to

Chayaka, followed by crouching on the hillside as the town went up in flame, then the drive to the capital. She steadied herself.

"Mrs. Fuente?" Arturo said. "Shall I speak in English? It's better, no?"

"No, it isn't necessary. Actually, this is Patricia Baldt Contreras speaking." She heard a sharp intake of breath on the other end.

"Patricia, is it really you? I can't believe it, after all these years. How are you? Are you well?"

"Yes. I'm fine, thank you. And you?"

"Very well. An attorney, as you see. *Ay*, Patricia, I can't tell you how good it is to hear your voice. I heard you were a doctor. Is it true?"

"That's right." She couldn't help smiling. Arturo might be an established attorney, but he had not lost his boyish eagerness. "I should explain. I'm calling on behalf of Margaret Fuente. That is, Margaret Reid now." She explained Meg's situation and their need for a newspaper ad.

"Of course," Arturo said. "I'll handle the advertisement personally. Anything for Señora Fuente. Pardon me—for Señora Reid. My father was very fond of the Fuentes. And of course, I am always at your service."

A few minutes later, they had concluded their arrangements, wished each other well, and hung up. It could have been worse, Patricia thought. In fact, Arturo had been rather sweet. She might have asked about his personal life, but she hadn't. He was probably married by now, to a woman from some politically progressive family. But really, there was no need to get personal, not on a business call. And it was safer that way.

She got up and removed a can of Dr. Pepper from the lunch room fridge. After taking a few swigs, she called Meg, who answered on the second ring.

"Did you get hold of the attorney?" Meg asked after they exchanged greetings.

"Yes. His son, that is. He's taken over the practice." She explained that she and Arturo's sister were school mates and described their conversation concerning the newspaper ad. "Arturo is looking forward to your arrival. And you should feel free to call him any time."

"Can we count on him to be discreet?" Meg asked. "We need someone we can trust."

"Yes, I believe so," Patricia said. She had relied on him all those years ago, and as far as she knew, he hadn't told anyone about their exploits.

"Good," Meg said. "I'm glad that you and Arturo know each other. That will make everything easier."

As if anything could make her trip easy, Patricia thought. Poor Meg. If only she had someone to go with her.

Patricia froze. Anyone but her. Especially now, when her mother was poised to drag her into the family turmoil.

The only other time she'd even considered going to Guatemala was two years earlier, when the 7.5 magnitude earthquake hit the country. Horror had filled her as information trickled in—a steadily rising death toll eventually reaching over 20,000 with tens of thousands more injured or homeless. She'd thought about offering her medical services there, but she realized that even if she kept a low profile, sooner or later, someone would identify her. She would no longer be Patricia Baldt, M.D., but would return to being the tragically scarred daughter of the wealthy and ruthless Otto Baldt. In the end, she had worked long hours to collect donations among friends and colleagues and to send medical supplies. It was enough, she had told herself.

"Thank you for making the phone call," Meg said. "By the way, I found a couple of novels in Spanish at the library. I'm hoping I can revive my Spanish quickly."

"Good idea. I'm sure it will come back." They said good-bye a minute later, and Patricia sat back on her chair. Meg will be fine, she told herself. She's lived in Guatemala, and she knows how to get around. Arturo will certainly assist her, as will others. The people there love children, and they will help a mother looking for her long-lost son.

Meanwhile, Patricia thought, in a little over two weeks, she and Hank would be on their way to Barbados.

The following Saturday afternoon, Patricia made a batch of spicy chili and Jiffy corn bread, then pulled on her long johns, jeans, and two sweaters in preparation for a trip to Hank's farmhouse. He liked to keep his thermostat at a bone-chilling sixty-six degrees—to save on the heating bill, he said, but she suspected he liked it that way. Twenty minutes later, she got out of the car, and Hank's two dogs rushed to greet her—a silky collie and a small, energetic mutt that appeared to be mostly terrier. They accompanied her to the frame house, where wood-scented smoke rose up from the chimney.

Inside, Patricia planted herself on Hank's double bed, cross-legged, a scratchy blanket around her, while he sorted through piles of clothes to find something to wear on their trip. It wasn't easy, since even in the summer, he spent his free time in jeans, raggedy shirts, and a shabby pair of sneakers. Fortunately, he had one pair of faded swim trunks.

"Don't worry," she said. "Once we get to the island, we can buy you some beach clothes."

Hank grimaced. "No Hawaiian shirts. And I'm not wearing shorts. I'll just look stupid."

"No problem." Actually, she suspected that shorts or no shorts, Hank's Nordic good looks would turn the heads of many mature ladies.

On Tuesday evening, the phone rang while Patricia was on the sofa reading a *Time* magazine article on Trudeau's problems with Quebec. The caller was Meg, her voice subdued. The child's body had been exhumed and they already had the report from the pathologist's examination.

"The bottom line is, we can't say for certain if it's J.J. or not," Meg said. "The bones are malformed from the fire, and actually, a lot of them are missing. The police in San Felipe did a shoddy job of collecting them."

"Could the pathologist tell you anything useful?" Patricia asked.

"He said that the child was probably between 42 and 44 inches tall and between four and seven years old. J.J. fit into the low end of that range, and the wild child probably fit into the higher end."

"Well, it was worth a try."

"Yes. I'm disappointed, of course. So are Dad and Charlie. We were hoping we'd learn something decisive. But at least it's one line of inquiry completed. And now I know that I'll be going to Guatemala."

"Any news from Arturo?" Patricia asked.

"Oh yes. He called this morning. The ad is in the Guatemalan newspapers. He said to be patient, though. It might take a while for a response to make its way through the postal system, especially if the writer is living outside the capital. Like in San Felipe.

"I think I'll like working with Arturo," she continued. "He seems competent and friendly. Oh, and he offered to call your mother and tell her I was coming. I've already heard back. She's going to meet me at the airport. I hate to inconvenience her that way, but she insisted. It will be nice to see a familiar face. And she offered to drive me to San Felipe."

"She loves going to the airport," Patricia said. "I remember, she and her friends always liked to meet their friends who were flying in or out. It was a social occasion."

Patricia visualized her mother behind the wheel of her black Buick. Of course, she was probably driving something different now. Especially with her husband dead. If there was money, she could have sprung for a sports car, which was what she had always wanted. "Maybe you should think twice about traveling to San Felipe with Mama. She drives like a maniac."

Meg laughed, then sobered. "I put my life in your mother's hands once before," she said. "I can do it again. And who knows? Maybe she's mellowed with age."

"Possibly," Patricia said without much conviction.

"Oh, and guess what else Arturo told me. There's a decent hotel in San Felipe now. He's going to make reservations for me there. For a week. And we'll see what happens after that."

Meg reported that Charlie was currently out of town, but he would be back on Thursday, in plenty of time to go to the girls' dance recital on Saturday. He would also take Meg to O'Hare on Sunday for her eleven o'clock flight.

"No kidding," Patricia said. "My flight leaves at ten. Maybe Hank and I will run into you at the airport."

Patricia waited until Thursday night to check in again with Meg. She made the call curled up on her living room sofa.

"I'm so glad you called," Meg said. "We finally sat down with the girls and explained what's been going on. They'd suspected something was afoot. We didn't tell them everything. They knew I'd been married before, so we told the girls that I'm going to look for a young relative of Pablo's. They can hardly wait to meet him."

"I hope they understand that you may not find him," Patricia said gently. And I hope *you* understand too, she thought. She distrusted the optimistic lilt in her friend's voice.

"We told them, but I'm not sure they took it in. They're too excited." A pause on the line. "I am too, I guess. Dad keeps telling me to keep my expectations low. I know my chances of finding J.J. are small. Even if he's alive, he could be anywhere. And it's not as if he'll remember me. At best, I'll be some hazy memory. But none of that matters. You see that, don't you? I have to look for him."

"I know."

"In a way," Meg said, "it would be enough just to know he survived, even if I never found him. Just to know that he has had a life. But to actually see him one more time—I would give anything for that."

At noon the next day, Anita read the clinic's thermometer and announced that the temperature had risen to a balmy thirty-six degrees. Outside, the skies were a deep blue. But Patricia noted that the radio was forecasting snow for that evening as well as dropping temperatures. Again.

Ominous gray storm clouds began moving in around four, and snowflakes fell on Patricia's car as she was driving home. After that, the snow came down in a thick curtain for several hours. On the KWWL ten o'clock news, the weatherman reported that eight inches of snow had fallen before the storm moved east, on its way to Illinois.

The next morning, Patricia awoke to a brilliant white world. Snow covered roofs and porches, outlined tree limbs, bent shrub branches nearly to the ground, and blanketed yards in smooth, white icing. Patricia dressed and began digging out her driveway. The snow plow must have arrived in the early hours, because a wall of snow was heaped at the bottom of her drive. A couple of bundled-up kids pulled their sleds down the street, chattering happily, heading toward a steep hill nearby. Lucky kids.

Her shovel grated against concrete as she dug under the snow, lifted, and heaved the load onto the four-foot-high wall of snow that already bordered the drive. She stopped to stretch her back, unsure if the pain and stiffness were the result of her long-ago injuries or the beginnings of arthritis, or both. The neighbor boy who used to do her yard work had gone off to college, and she had foolishly not made the effort to find a replacement.

By the time she went inside, her feet were icy from snow that had dropped into her boots, and her hair was plastered to her head with sweat. As she showered, she consoled herself that in three days she'd be on a Caribbean beach.

She made a ham sandwich, then drove to the clinic, the car fish-tailing as she braked at two intersections. Fortunately, the snow plows had cleared the roads, and a section of the parking lot behind the clinic was dug out. She was alone in her office and starting to make headway with a stack of paperwork when calls started coming in, and soon she had patients. A housewife had fallen and sprained her ankle while walking down her icy back steps, and a ten-year-old boy had fractured his arm playing in the snow. A farm wife brought in her elderly neighbor, who'd sounded confused over the phone and proved to have hypothermia.

At lunch, Patricia washed down her sandwich with a can of Dr. Pepper, opened a bag of Fritos, and called Meg, who reported that the storm had left over a foot of snow in the Chicago area. But work crews were out, and officials were optimistic that traveling conditions would be normal by later that day. So they should have no problem driving to O'Hare the next day.

"I was hoping the girls' recital would be canceled," Meg said, "but it's still scheduled for four this afternoon. I was supposed to take two dozen hors d'oeuvres, but Charlie's mother, bless her heart, offered to make her special meatballs." She sighed. "All that leaves me is laundry, cleaning, cooking, and packing."

"You sound a little frazzled."

"Exhausted is more like it," Meg said.

"Other than that, how are you doing? Emotionally, I mean."

"To tell you the truth, I'm not sure. I'm excited, of course. You know, I picture myself walking down a street in San Felipe. I turn a corner, and...there is my son. A grown man, handsome like his father." Her voice cracked on "his father," and she paused. "But I'm also terrified. I'm afraid that I'll get off the plane in Guatemala and be overcome by memories. And what if I fail?"

Patricia shifted in her seat. What could she say to her friend, who was returning to face a place of terrible tragedy? "Listen, Meg. I know you. You'll be okay. You have a list of things to do. Just follow them one step at a time. Don't look forward or back. Keep your focus on what's right in front of you. That's what I learned in medical school. It still saves me from freezing up when I'm faced with more than I can handle."

"You're right. I can do that. But there's something else that's worrying me. You know, it's been three weeks since the writer mailed the letter. What if I've waited too long?"

"Meg, it's been twenty-four years since the fire. A few more days can't make much difference."

"I'm not so sure," Meg said, her voice shaky. "What if there was some kind of urgency about contacting me now? Some kind of problem we don't know about? Maybe the writer was dying, and it was his last chance to tell me. I could be too late."

"Meg, please, this is wild speculation. You know that, right? We're doing everything we can. Once you get to Guatemala, you and Arturo can sort things out. With a little luck, this will become clearer soon." For better or worse. "Look, I'll call you from Barbados."

"No, don't be silly," Meg said, sounding a little calmer. "You and Hank should just go and enjoy the beach and sun. You deserve it." They talked for a few more minutes before saying good-bye.

A thought occurred to Patricia after she set down the receiver. What if, in fact, J.J. was kidnapped all those years ago? Whoever took him must have had a compelling reason for doing it. And he would have an equally compelling reason for keeping the truth hidden now. Meg could be heading into danger.

From the sidewalk outside came the muffled sound of men's voices in conversation, no one Patricia recognized. She sat back and tried to clear her head. What was she thinking? The chances that J.J. was alive were practically nil. Somehow she had to find a way to support Meg emotionally without getting swept up into her friend's fantasies.

At two o'clock, Dr. Arne Bergit, Patricia's temporary replacement, showed up for a tour. The year before, he had retired from practicing cardiology at the Mayo Clinic and moved to New Bergen, to be close to his wife's elderly father. Patricia had been relieved when he agreed to spend half days at the clinic while she was gone. Arne was short, with big ears and a wrinkled face that made him look like a friendly gnome, and she was happy to see that he seemed at home in the clinic.

By four-thirty, Patricia had finished up her paper work. She hurried to the parking lot, the low sun casting long shadows across the pavement. As she sat in her car, letting the engine warm up, she took a deep breath, then smiled. At this time tomorrow, she'd be in warm, sunny Barbados.

CHAPTER FIVE

Patricia stared into the fridge, trying to figure out how to combine a bunch of leftovers into some kind of dinner. The wall phone rang, and she was surprised to hear Charlie, Meg's husband, at the other end. He was calling from the hospital in Oak Park, and his news was bad. Meg was in the emergency room with a broken leg. She'd slipped on an icy patch of sidewalk while carrying a tray of meatballs from her mother-in-law's house to the car.

"Oh no. What kind of fracture is it? What did the doctor say?"

"A tibial shaft fracture," Charlie said, enunciating carefully, as if he were reading the words. "Apparently just below the knee. The doctor said there doesn't seem to be any displacement. They'll perform surgery tomorrow. We're just waiting for a room now."

"How is she doing otherwise? Is she all right?"

"She's furious at herself for falling. She can't bear the thought of missing her flight tomorrow."

"I can imagine. You know, I hate to tell you this, but I don't think Meg will be taking any trips for a while, not with a break like that." It could be months if her leg was in a cast.

"That's what the ER doctor said. Look, Patricia, could you call your mother and tell her Meg won't be arriving tomorrow? She's concerned about that."

"Of course."

Charlie promised to call back when Meg was settled into her room, and they hung up.

Patricia started to dial the Finca Baldt number, then stopped. If her mother was planning to pick up Meg tomorrow, she would probably be in the capital by now, probably staying with her sister. What was that phone number? Patricia let her mind go blank until the digits popped into her head, then dialed her aunt's house. When the maid answered, Patricia identified herself and asked if her mother was there. A minute later Eugenia's voice came on the line.

"*Hija.* What a marvelous surprise. Have you changed your mind? Are you coming with Meg?"

Her mother never gave up. "Listen, Mama, Meg has had an accident." She summarized the details.

"Ay, poor Meg," Eugenia said. "She doesn't deserve such bad luck."

"I know. She's terribly disappointed about the trip. But thank you for offering to look after her. That was kind of you."

"Evelyn was a dear friend," Eugenia said. "I would do anything to help her daughter. But *hija*, in this case, it's better that Meg isn't coming. Just think of it—the poor woman running around, looking for a boy who died over twenty years ago. Everyone would think she was crazy."

"Maybe."

"But you, Patricia, you must come home. Your brother is sending me to my grave with his outrageous demands—"

"I have to go now, Mama. I have other calls to make. We'll talk later." She hung up.

It was after seven, and Patricia took a wedge of Cheddar cheese and half a bottle of White Zinfandel out of the fridge. She needed the wine but didn't want to drink on an empty stomach, so she sat at the kitchen table and sliced a piece of cheese, then poured herself a glass. She was warm enough in jeans, fleece-lined slippers, and her New Bergen Vikings sweatshirt, but she would be glad to exchange them for shorts and a sleeveless shirt tomorrow.

After a glass of wine, Patricia decided that maybe her mother was right. It was just as well that Meg wasn't going to Guatemala. While Meg convalesced in Oak Park, they would all wait to see if the classified ads in the Guatemalan newspapers brought any leads. If so, Arturo could follow up on them. If the anonymous writer didn't respond, that would be the end of it.

After cleaning up her snack, Patricia called Hank and told him about Meg.

"Do you want to cancel our trip?" he asked.

She hated leaving the country when Meg was in the hospital, but a broken leg wasn't life-threatening, and Patricia had been looking forward to this trip for what seemed like forever. "No. Meg is in good hands. And they have telephones in Barbados. I can call from there."

"Okay," he said. "I'll be at your house at four-thirty tomorrow morning."

Patricia finished packing her suitcase and set it by the kitchen door. In the morning, she would throw a few last-minute things in her carry-on, and she'd be set to go. But her happy anticipation was muted. Meg's accident had cast a pall over everything. That would change, Patricia assured herself, once she and Hank were at the beach. With the warm sand under their feet, winter and all other unpleasantness would soon fade into the background.

She dropped onto the sofa in the living room, drawing her

colorful afghan onto her lap. That damn anonymous letter. It had made everybody crazy to one extent or another. She pictured the postmark on the envelope. January 25. A disquieting thought rose up in her mind, and she roused herself and headed to the kitchen, where she reached for the calendar hanging on a nail next to the phone. She lowered February's scenic island photograph to reveal the month of January, with all its scribbled events and appointments. When had her mother called to let her know about her father's death? It had been on a Friday. That would make it the twentieth. The writer had posted his letter five days later, on the day after her father's funeral. A chill crept up her spine.

What if Meg was right? What if the letter's timing was important? Not because of a crucial event in J.J.'s life, but because it was linked to the death of Patricia's father. Lots of people had probably not mourned Otto Baldt's passing. Had one of them been waiting for her father to die, so that he could tell Meg that her son was alive?

Patricia flipped the January page up and hung it on the nail, so that she faced February once more, with "Barbados" inked in for the whole week, starting the next day. Sighing, she sank onto the chair at the end of the kitchen table.

Her father had been in a fury on the night of the fires, but even so, she had no doubt that he would have been overjoyed to learn that J.J. was alive. And so would his workers, many of whom had children of their own. If J.J. had lived, why would anyone have wanted to keep that information from her father? It made no sense.

The wine bottle was still on the table, and she poured a little more wine into her glass. As she sipped, a chilling thought came to her. Was it possible there was an arsonist at Los Ancianos that night? Not an Indian, but someone else. An arsonist who was also a kidnapper, whether or not he had planned to be. If so, the letter writer might have known the guy and realized what he'd done. Or maybe the writer and the arsonist were the same person. Later, he felt remorse and wanted to tell Meg that her son had lived. But he saw Otto Baldt as an obstacle.

But why? Out of fear, most likely. A fear of attracting Otto's wrath. Or maybe her father was involved in the crime in some way. Was it possible? Perhaps he and the letter writer shared some kind of secret that connected them to the fire at Los Ancianos. God, she hoped not.

Patricia stared into the rose-colored wine remaining in her glass. This was insane. It wasn't like her to give in to such wild musings. Still, there was so much she didn't know about that night. It was as if she had seen only the surface events and had remained unaware of all the underlying ones—why the fire had started and what parts different people had played in the unfolding horror.

Patricia gazed blankly through the window over the sink, where a red cedar tree was just visible in the moonlight. She sighed. For years, she had distanced herself from her father, telling herself that his transgressions had nothing to do with her. But now, sitting here in a house in a small Iowa town, she realized she had to face up to the truth. She and her father were tied together, linked indelibly by blood and shared history. Like it or not, she was Otto Baldt's daughter, and even in death, his life would continue to impact her own.

She took one last swallow of wine and set down the glass. If her father had any connection to J.J.'s life or death—any connection at all—she had to get to the bottom of it. And one thing was certain. She wouldn't get any answers lounging on the beach in Barbados or sitting around New Bergen.

Hank was the first person she called. She listened to the phone ring several times, wishing she didn't have to break the disappointing news. He too had been looking forward to the trip. "I have bad news," she said when he picked up. "I'm going to Guatemala tomorrow, to look for J.J. Meg thought it might be important not to lose any more time. I decided she could be right." There was a moment of silence over the line.

"Well, that's fine," Hank said. "While you're looking for the boy, you'll have a chance to reconnect with your family."

"I'm sorry about our trip," she said. "I suppose it's too late to get a refund."

"Afraid so." They'd each paid half, so at least neither would lose the full amount. She expected him to say not to worry, that they would go later after she got back.

"Well, I have the week off work," he said. "And I don't want to lose all that money. I guess I'll just go by myself."

She was stunned. "Sure. Why not," she said finally.

"I'll miss you," he said.

Charlie called twenty minutes later from Meg's hospital room. He passed the phone to Meg, who cried at Patricia's decision to go to Guatemala. "Thank you, thank you, thank you," Meg said between sobs.

"It's okay," Patricia said. In the face of Meg's gratitude, Patricia wondered how she had even considered not going.

Jonathan, Meg's father, took the phone next. "Let me guess. You're going to Guatemala," he said.

"Any chance I can leave tomorrow? My bags are packed."

"I should be able to get Meg's plane reservation switched over to you. She was taking the eleven o'clock Pan Am flight through Miami. And you know, of course, that I'll pick up the bills."

"Okay. And another thing. Do you have any pictures of J.J.? Just to remind myself of what he looked like as a boy."

"He wasn't one for sitting still," Jonathan said. "We were going to have a family portrait taken that summer, but...anyway, Evelyn kept a scrapbook. I'll see what I can find."

They agreed to meet at ten o'clock by the Pan Am desk.

Patricia had one last phone call, one she wasn't looking forward to. But her mother would find out fast enough that she was in Guatemala.

"I'm arriving tomorrow, Mama," she said. "I'll be on Meg's former flight, Pam Am from Chicago through Miami."

Eugenia gasped. "My prayers are answered. I'll meet you at the airport."

After they hung up, Patricia was amazed to feel an odd sense of calm. She was returning home, she reminded herself, not as the wounded teenager she'd been when she left, but as a mature woman, a physician. And the task ahead of her was challenging, but not impossible. She would do everything in her power to find J.J., but if it appeared certain that he had died in the fire, then she could at least put their doubts to rest.

Patricia hauled her suitcase from the back door to her bedroom and prepared to replace beach wear with clothing suitable for February in highland Guatemala. She'd need a sweater but no rain gear, since it would be the dry season. And she would probably have to wear a skirt in public, unless people had become less con-servative over the years—which was possible.

After removing her swimsuit and shorts from the bag, she fold-ed in two more sleeveless blouses, three softly flared skirts, kha-ki-colored slacks, and her tomato-red blazer. On top, she placed her black sleeveless dress with a bolero jacket. In the corners of the suitcase, she stuffed a pair of low black pumps to accompany the sandals that she'd already packed. Finally, for the drive to the airport, she would wear a wool skirt, a long-sleeved white blouse, and her cream-colored cardigan sweater, as well as her comfortable walking shoes. She could leave her wool coat in the car. She dropped a gold chain and matching earrings into an inside pocket of her shoulder bag, then straightened.

There was one good thing about this trip. It would give her a chance to find out what had happened to Demetrio and his family. She pictured him as he'd looked when they worked together at the dig—young and fit and energetic. He would be older now, probably married with children. And his little sister, Noemi, would be grown up too. If they had survived the earthquake two years before, that is. Thousands had died in the highlands, she knew. And many more had lost their homes.

When the disaster hit, Patricia had tried to find out how Demetrio's family was faring. But her inquiries to the Red Cross and a doctor working in the region revealed that communications to the rural areas, which had never been good, were now abysmal. A letter that she sent to the Quespe family was never answered, and she imagined it simply disappeared in the chaos. Now she could look for Demetrio in person. She cringed at the thought of driving the steep, winding road to Chayaka, but she could figure out something later.

She clicked shut her suitcase and hauled it to the door once more. Hank would be making last minute preparations too, if he wasn't already in bed. By tomorrow night, he would be in Barbados, drinking rum cocktails and chatting with bronzed women in bathing suits. She realized she would have to keep busy in Guatemala if she didn't want to spend her time brooding. She would station herself in San Felipe, as Meg had planned to do, since that's where the letter had come from, and the town was close to Los Ancianos. But she could only spend so much time interviewing people who were at the long-ago fire and waiting for the writer to reply to the newspaper ad.

Then it occurred to her that she could probably volunteer at a clinic or hospital. It would give her a home base. She could work part time, meet some people, get a feel for what was going on in San Felipe.

After paging through her address book, she found the phone number for an agency she'd used that set up medical trips for physicians. It was nine o'clock on a Saturday night, but she remembered that the agent worked from home, so she called. The woman was cheerful over the phone. She remembered Patricia and promised to start looking for a volunteer opportunity in San Felipe first thing Monday morning. Patricia opened her suitcase and stuffed a few white clinic coats into it.

Hank picked her up at the house at four-thirty the next morning, just as they'd arranged when they were both planning to fly to Barbados. They drove along in the darkness, saying little, although after they crossed the Mississippi River into Illinois, Hank started whistling one of Harry Belafonte's calypso songs. Day-o, daaay-o. He was in a cheerful mood, which irked her, given that she wouldn't be going with him. By the time the sun rose golden over the snow-covered corn fields, they were approaching the outer Chicago suburbs. At last, they arrived at the exit for O'Hare, and a few minutes later, Hank pulled up his truck outside the Pan Am departure gate. They unloaded Patricia's baggage, then stood on the walkway and embraced.

"You'll be okay," he said.

"I know."

"Well, I'd better go park," he said. "My flight will be boarding soon."

Our flight, she thought. "Have a good time," she said, trying to sound cheerful.

He kissed her on the cheek. "Next time we'll go together."

Once inside the terminal, Patricia found a baggage cart and hoisted on her suitcase and medical bag, setting her shoulder bag on top. She trudged to the Pan Am terminal, pushing the cart. When she approached the airline counter, she spotted Charlie, with his unmistakable copper hair, slumping on a bench against the wall. He looked fatigued. She sat down beside him, and he straightened.

"Patricia. Good to see you."

"How is Meg?"

"Doing well. She was in the recovery room when I left. Jonathan is still there." He reached down and opened Jonathan's monogrammed attaché case. He handed her a Pan Am envelope containing her plane ticket.

"That was fast work."

"I tell you, that assistant of Jonathan's is a magician. He also sent this." It was an envelope containing two thousand dollars in hundred-dollar bills and a typed letter requesting her to tell him when he should wire her more. It also informed her that she had reservations for two nights at the Ritz Continental in Guatemala City, along with the street address and phone number. Below that was a phone number for Arturo Muñoz and for a few officials at the American Embassy. In a hand-written note at the bottom, Jonathan promised to send her and Hank on a vacation anywhere in the world when she returned. That eased the disappointment a little.

Charlie pulled a manila envelope out of the case. "And there's one more thing." Inside the envelope, she found three grainy photos, one of J.J. as a toddler eating ice cream with messy abandon, and another of him playing in the sand with a shovel and pail. Finally, there was a picture of J.J. as she remembered him, around the age of four. In the photo, he was decked out in a makeshift pirate's costume, with a bandanna tied around his forehead and what looked like a toy knife tucked into his belt. On his face was a fierce scowl, apparently the appropriate pirate's response to a photo request. Her chest ached. Could he possibly be alive?

"Cute kid, huh?" Charlie said. "Did you know him?"

"Oh yes." She remembered the softness of his small hand in hers as he'd escorted her to see small treasures he'd found—smooth, river-worn pebbles; twisted wood; and once, a fragment of engraved metal that turned out to be part of a Spanish piece of eight. She'd taken him for a few short drives in her Bel Air, a car he had deeply admired. A car that was probably now a rusted hulk lying at the bottom of a chasm.

"Jonathan said to take any of the pictures you want," Charlie said. "He has the negatives."

Patricia slipped the first two photos into the envelope and handed it back to Charlie. "I'll take this one with me," she said, taking another look at J.J.'s pirate picture. His facial features were distorted by the scowl, but she could see his dark hair, light brown eyes, and his swashbuckling spirit.

CHAPTER SIX

Patricia boarded the plane to Miami and settled into her first-class seat, a surprise since she knew that Meg never flew first class. Jonathan must have bumped her up. It occurred to her that sitting here on the plane was the first opportunity she'd had to think in an organized way about her search for J.J. She pulled a pen and notebook out of her shoulder bag and stared at the blank page. Where to start? She wrote the words "People to Interview" at the top.

The list quickly grew, consisting of people who were at the fire at Los Ancianos: her mother, Gustavo, her father's other workers—at least, those men who were still around. Don Javier and his workers went on next, since they had also shown up at Los Ancianos. Then there was Arturo, along with his friend, the doctor who had helped to save Meg's life. And the watchman at Los Ancianos. She hoped she could avoid a trip to Chayaka to find him, but if she had to go, at least it might be an opportunity to look for Demetrio's family. Beatriz joined the list. Although she hadn't been at the fire, she knew everyone at Los Ancianos, and she might have some insights into how the fire started or what happened to the waif in the ravine.

She scanned the names on her list. She couldn't serious-ly imagine any of them being involved in J.J.'s kidnapping. Still, maybe one of them would remember something about that night or the days that followed, some overlooked but important clue to J.J.'s whereabouts.

She stowed the notebook in her bag and gazed out the window at the dull whiteness. By now, Hank would be on board his flight to Barbados. She missed him, his affection and good humor and down-to-earth judgment. If she'd asked him to come with her, to provide moral support and stability, he would undoubtedly have agreed. But it was a big favor, and she had no real claim on him. It wasn't as if they were married or even engaged.

Twice, Hank had asked her to marry him, and each time she'd said no. Marriage wasn't for her, she'd said, and offered no further explanation for her decision. In fact, she wasn't sure why she didn't want to marry Hank. It certainly would have cut down on trips be-tween her house in town and his farmhouse. It would also have put an end to the town gossip. On the other hand, Hank didn't really need a new family. He already had two married daughters and a grandchild on the way. Patricia and his daughter Anita were good friends and colleagues, but Patricia didn't want to become Anita's stepmother. And Hank's other daughter, Judy, was polite, but she was cool to the idea of anyone taking her deceased mother's place, even after eight years. The child she was expecting would be Hank and Bonnie's grandchild, not Patricia's.

But there was something more, something Patricia couldn't quite put her finger on. A vague sense that marriage to Hank just wasn't right. Well, it wasn't something she had to think about now. She closed her eyes, her mind merging with the numbing drone of the plane. Her eyes fluttered open as the plane began its decent into Miami.

The flight to Guatemala City was a different story. The plane was full, and she had a window seat in coach, where the air buzzed with the vibrant melody of Guatemalan Spanish, a sound that Patricia had hardly heard in years.

The plump, thirtyish woman sitting next to her was glowing from a successful Miami shopping run. She had stuffed the overhead bin and the space in front of her with shopping bags full of purchases, most of which she intended to sell at a nice profit in her hometown of Quetzaltenango. From her purse, Patricia pulled out a women's magazine that she'd picked up at the Miami airport. She leafed through ads for furniture and skimmed an article on how to decorate for inexpensive parties.

Two hours later, the plane began its descent. She looked out the porthole to see that they had left behind the flat expanse of water and were now flying over rounded mountains with terraced fields. The countryside was mostly brown, aside from pine trees studding steep slopes. Even so, she felt a surge of pleasure. This landscape was a part of her, imprinted during childhood. She was almost home.

The plane swooped into the Ermita Valley, and she gazed in shock at the size of the capital. Twenty-four years earlier, Guatemala City had been a large town. Now it was a real city, with neighborhoods sprawled across the valley, and a number of buildings jutting several stories into the air. In the distance, the surrounding mountains looked hazy.

The plane screeched to a halt, and passengers soon jammed the aisles. Patricia descended the steps of the plane behind her seatmate, whose arms were full of shopping bags. It was four-thirty, and she basked in the warmth of the afternoon sun as she strode to the terminal. She could already feel her bones thawing from the northern winter.

It didn't take long to get her American passport stamped with a tourist visa, and with just one suitcase, a medical bag, and a purse, she passed through Customs quickly. She had decided to travel with her American passport, as she had always done since gaining her citizenship several years earlier. But since Guatemala allowed dual citizenship, she'd kept both passports. Her Guatemalan one was tucked away in her shoulder bag, in case she needed it for resolving the inheritance issue.

At a booth in the terminal, she changed five hundred dollars into five hundred quetzales, gathered her bags, and a few moments later carried her luggage through the doors leading to the throng of families, porters, and taxi drivers.

Off to the side, she spotted a petite older woman in a stylish gray suit with a pencil skirt and high heels. Her mother. She was standing alone, her face partially covered by a matching wide-brimmed hat with a shiny black feather tucked in under the band. It was odd to see her mother in a somber color, since she had always favored rich hues—ruby, emerald, citrine. This was a mourning suit, Patricia realized. Eugenia spotted her and waved excitedly. Patricia waved back, surprised to feel a rush of affection for her mother. A moment later her mother was at her side.

"It's good to see you, Mama," Patricia said and brushed her lips against her mother's powdered cheek. Eugenia's lipstick was a luscious red, attractive with the gray suit. Her mother had always been beautiful, and she was still attractive, even at sixty or so, with crow's feet at her eyes and fine lines around her mouth. Looking at her mother's happy countenance, Patricia wondered if Eugenia was one of those fortunate widows who started to bloom after their husbands died.

"At last you're here," Eugenia said and inserted her hand in the crook of Patricia's elbow. Their short, beefy cab driver carried

Patricia's bags outside and went off to fetch his car, which pulled up a moment later.

"We have lots to talk about," her mother said after they'd climbed into the back seat. "I'm afraid our city house still has some cracks from the earthquake, so I'm staying with Claudia. It's homier anyway. Shall we go there?"

"I'd rather not," Patricia blurted out. Dealing with her mother was bad enough. There was no way she wanted to deal with her nosy aunt as well. "That is, I'm staying at the Ritz Continental. Jonathan Cabell made the reservations. Why don't we go there instead?"

"Perfect. They have a charming rooftop bar. It shouldn't be busy now. We can have a nice chat there."

As they drove from the airport, Patricia saw changes everywhere. In the outskirts of the city, gray smoke rose from factories, probably the source of the the haze surrounding the mountains. And where once there had been fields, neighborhoods had taken hold. Debris cluttered some lots, probably left over from the earthquake.

But the Avenida La Reforma was still much as she remembered it, with trees and statues dotting the median as they had twenty-four years earlier. Stately villas were still visible along side streets, but there were now more commercial buildings lining the avenue—apartment houses and offices, as well as modern-looking retail shops. The city was clearly expanding. Its population had been close to 300,000 when she left in 1954. It was reportedly now nearly a million.

"How is Carlos?" Patricia asked.

Eugenia sniffed. "Your brother. Well enough, I suppose. We'll talk about him later. But first, you must tell me about your life. I hardly know anything, especially now that Evelyn Cabell is gone. I would hardly have recognized you if she hadn't sent pictures over the years. Oh, not that I wouldn't know my own daughter." She gave Patricia's hand a small squeeze.

Eugenia had actually visited Patricia in New Bergen twelve years earlier. She had insisted on visiting during the month of July, over Patricia's strong objections. The minute her mother arrived, she had started complaining. First of all, the weather was unbearably hot and humid. And worse, Patricia had turned into a drudge, working ridiculously long hours at the clinic, then toiling like a maid at home, sweeping her own floors and washing her own dishes. What's more, the women of New Bergen lacked any sense of real style. Had Patricia noticed their clothing? And their lack of fine jewelry or stylishly coiffed hair? Why couldn't Patricia have settled in New York City? Or Miami?

At the end of the first week, Patricia had driven her sulky mother to the Cabells' house overlooking Lake Michigan. Evelyn took Eugenia shopping at Saks and Marshall Fields and to a performance of Giselle, where Eugenia could enjoy the ballet patrons milling around the lobby in their fashionable clothing. Eugenia had found this touch of elegance gratifying, according to Evelyn, who had finally put Patricia's mother on a flight back to Guatemala. But the visit had not been a total loss. Patricia had the comfort of knowing that her mother had seen New Bergen and would never return.

The taxi sped toward the older part of the city, Zone One, which Eugenia explained was now referred to by the tourists as the historic area. She bombarded Patricia with questions about Hank. What kind of work did he do? How old was he? When were they going to marry? Patricia evaded the last one and was relieved when the taxi pulled up to the hotel.

The Ritz Continental was a modern, five-story hotel. While her mother headed for the rooftop bar, Patricia checked in, then took the elevator to her fourth-floor room, where she tipped the porter who had brought her bags. The room was spacious, with an attractive beige and white decor, a comfortable bed, and a round table in one corner.

She looked out the window and saw the roof and upper floors of the National Palace. She realized with a start that she was only a few blocks away. Suddenly, she was back in June of 1954, watching the gray airplane diving low and strafing the Palace, the antiaircraft guns blazing below. It seemed like another world. Ernesto had been there too—Che, as the Cubans would call him. He had stood in the park, fearlessly watching the attack. Of course, she had followed his later life through media reports. Then, ten years ago, she had heard on the radio of Ernesto's death in Bolivia. It was 1967, and she was returning from a weekend in Chicago with Danny. The news saddened her. From what she'd read, Ernesto had maintained his revolutionary zeal, but he had turned ruthless once he came to power under Fidel Castro. Still, he had been kind to her in 1954, when she was alone and needed a friend—even if he had made fun of the mustache she'd drawn on so carefully to pass as a boy.

In her mind, she pictured the teenagers in the churchyard, the ones who had ridden out on their bicycles to chastise people whose house lights were left on, while she and Ernesto kept watch from the bell tower. She wondered what had happened to those kids. And to Sergio, Meg and Ernesto's friend. She knew that Meg had tried to contact him after the coup, without success. As long as she was in San Felipe, maybe she could find out where Sergio had ended up.

In the bathroom, she reapplied a little lipstick, then rode the elevator to the rooftop bar. It was a large room, with windows offering a panoramic view of the city, surrounded by the mountains.

Her mother was sitting at a corner table, at a distance from the few other patrons. She was half way through a pink and gold drink, a tequila sunrise from the looks of it. Patricia slipped onto the chair beside her mother and ordered a vodka tonic from the waiter who had instantly appeared.

Eugenia regarded Patricia with a benevolent gaze. "We haven't been close for many years. But I feel we can start anew, don't you think?"

"Yes. Why not?" In fact, Patricia couldn't remember ever being close to her mother, but they were both adults now. They could build a new relationship. "Let's start by being candid with one another. Tell me why Papa left me the estate. Why didn't he leave it to Carlos?" She would soon learn if her mother was prepared to be honest.

"It's a long story. Let's just say that your father didn't trust Carlos. Your brother is irresponsible." She leaned toward Patricia, her eyes steely. "That's why you must sign over the estate to me. If Finca Baldt is to survive, it can't fall into your brother's hands."

"I'm afraid it's too late for that. I sent a letter to your attorney and told him I was renouncing my inheritance. He has probably received it by now."

Eugenia's eyes turned mischievous. "I'm afraid that letter didn't reach Amilcar. It was delivered to my hairdresser."

"What?"

"Really, Patricia, you didn't expect me to give you the attorney's real address."

When had her mother turned into a naughty child? So much for a fresh start. And to think, she'd even gotten the damn letter notarized.

"I didn't want to deceive you," Eugenia said. "You forced me by your stubbornness."

Patricia's affection for her mother was waning fast. They both fell silent as the waiter served Patricia's drink before returning to the bar.

"Look, Mama, suppose we go to the attorney tomorrow. I can leave half the estate to you and half to Carlos."

"I'm afraid that's impossible," Eugenia said. "The estate must be passed on intact. Besides, if Carlos and I had to share the finca, we would be at each other's throats."

This was going to be difficult, Patricia realized. Should she just sign over the property to her mother and get it over with? But how could she cheat her brother out of his share? She had left him behind years earlier, to deal with their father's turbulent moods alone. Now she couldn't just desert him again. "Tell me more. Why didn't Papa trust Carlos?"

Eugenia sighed. "Understand, *hija*, this is not easy for me."

"I'm listening."

Eugenia looked around the room, presumably to see if anyone was nearby. Satisfied, she began, speaking in a low voice. "Over the years, your father became mentally unstable. About three years ago, he decided that I had been unfaithful to him and that Carlos was not his legitimate son." She waved a hand as if to dispel the notion. "It was preposterous, of course, but he'd always seen Carlos as weak. I suppose he couldn't stand the idea that a son of his could be so flawed."

So, it was Eugenia that her father didn't trust. Could he have had reason? The doubt must have been visible on her face, because Eugenia sent her a withering look.

"Carlos is Otto's son," she said. "Oh, I had opportunities to stray, and with some very attractive men. But I was brought up to be a faithful wife. Besides, it wasn't worth the risk." She sipped her cocktail. "Anyway, a few years ago, Otto became even more irrational. He fired workers for no good reason and sued a few unfortunate people who were supposedly cheating him. He started walking around the property every day carrying that fancy hunting rifle of his. As if someone were lurking in the shadows, ready to attack him."

"The Austrian rifle?" It was a handsome firearm, with a graceful vine and leaf pattern on the stock. Not that Patricia cared much for guns. She'd spent too much time dealing with the bloody, bone-smashing injuries they inflicted. But her father had been proud of that rifle.

"That's the one," Eugenia said. "I think he was truly hoping to shoot someone with it. I talked to a psychiatrist, and he said that Otto had the classic symptoms of paranoia."

Patricia thought of her father's wild ranting, his fear and distrust of all kinds of people: everyone at the university, socialists, his own workers, and finally his wife and son. Clearly, her father had suffered from a personality disorder. They had just lacked a label for it—or an understanding of what might be behind his destructive behavior.

A chilling thought occurred to Patricia. "Mama, do you think Papa could have had something to do with the fire at Los Ancianos?"

"You mean setting it? Certainly not. Where did you get such an idea?"

"It's just...he didn't care much for the Fuentes."

"Well, he didn't care for their politics. But he and Pablo seemed to get along well enough. Otto looked after their finca, after all."

"That's true." But it was no proof that her father wouldn't turn on Pablo. He was certainly capable of arson. She'd seen that for herself at Chayaka. "What about the boy, J.J.? Do you think Papa might have been involved in his disappearance?"

Her mother stared at her. "Really, Patricia! Now you're the one who has lost her senses."

Maybe she *had* gone too far, swept up in Meg's fantasies. "All right. But tell me about Carlos. You said he's irresponsible. What has he done?"

Eugenia took a sip of her drink. "What *hasn't* he done, that's the question. Absolutely nothing to help with the finca. All he does is drain its profits. Fortunately, coffee prices are high right now. Not like a few years ago, when they hit rock bottom. I can tell you, we suffered. But that's the way with the coffee market, isn't it? Fluctuating wildly from one year to the next. The volatility of coffee on the world market keeps me awake at night."

Patricia listened in wonder. Sometime in the last twenty-four years, her mother must have learned something about the economics of coffee production. One more surprise.

Eugenia made another quick scan of the room, then lowered her voice again. "There's something you should know about your brother. He has formed some kind of militia. These militias—they're popping up everywhere. From what I can see, they're nothing but thugs who run around attacking anyone they don't like. A perfect organization for your brother. I've met a few of his friends. They're trash."

Patricia took a long swallow of her vodka tonic. If she was lucky, it would dull her senses enough that she could tolerate this conversation.

"The fact is," Eugenia said, "I'm afraid that Carlos may be paranoid too. They say these illnesses run in families. *Gracias a dios*, you have been spared. You take after my family."

"I think men are more likely to suffer from it," Patricia said. In her case, a genetic propensity for mental illness was one more reason not to marry and have children, in addition to her advancing age and the fact that she had no husband.

A couple in their thirties sat down at a table within earshot. Eugenia looked at her watch. "It's getting late and I should leave you to unpack." She cocked her head and smiled. "Listen. There's someone I'd like you to meet. I've made reservations for seven o'clock at a lovely restaurant not far from here. We can all have dinner together. I'll pick you up a little before seven."

Patricia put the bar tab on her hotel bill, and they took the elevator to the lobby, then walked out toward the street, where Eugenia's taxi driver was waiting.

"I haven't asked, Mama. How is the finca doing?" High coffee prices were a good sign, but there could be other sources of trouble.

"As a matter of fact, it's doing well. And I can take credit for that. After Otto had his stroke last year, I had the good sense to hire a manager. An excellent one—Joaquín Santander. I can't imagine what I would have done without him." The warmth in Eugenia's voice had gone up several degrees when she spoke his name. "Joaquín is the mystery guest. You'll meet him tonight."

"I look forward to it." She stopped outside her mother's cab. One more question tugged at her. "Mama, there's something I don't understand. I can see that Papa didn't trust you or Carlos. But I made it clear that I was never coming back. Why did he leave the finca to me?"

"Because you were his darling daughter. He was convinced you'd return." She smiled with a hint of smugness. "And for once, he was right."

CHAPTER SEVEN

Patricia met her mother in the hotel lobby shortly before seven, and they took a taxi to Zone Ten. The restaurant was on a street just off the Avenida La Reforma. The Villa Herminia was a converted Spanish colonial-style house, gaily lit with colored bulbs strung below the roof. The surrounding walls brimmed with scarlet and purple bougainvilleas, the colors subdued in the fading light. Even in the dry season, flowers bloomed here. Such a contrast to New Bergen, where winter was stark in its black and white palette.

Inside, Patricia and her mother were ushered past tables set with linen and sparkling crystal. "There he is," Patricia's mother whispered as she led the way to a table in the far corner. A tall, trim man in a navy blazer and pastel blue shirt stood. His black hair was wavy, and he had an easy smile.

Eugenia introduced the fellow as "my manager, Joaquín Santander." Patricia guessed he was about forty-five, fifteen years younger than her mother. But then her mother had a bright-eyed girlishness in his presence.

Joaquín extended his hand to Patricia. "What a pleasure to meet you, Dr. Baldt. I was so glad to learn you were here."

They shook hands, and a minute later Patricia found herself perusing a selection of fresh seafood on the menu. It was such a treat. Fish in New Bergen was usually limited to Mrs. Paul's frozen filets and to lutefisk at Christmas. Eugenia recommended the sea bass, and they all ordered that with rice, assorted vegetables, and a bottle of Chablis.

"Joaquín has a degree from the University of Florida," Eugenia said.

"Really," Patricia said, looking at Joaquín. "In what?"

"Agricultural Management."

"I stole him away from the Ministry of Agriculture," Eugenia said.

"I thought people stayed in government jobs forever," Patricia said. "What made you decide to leave?"

"I was at a crossroads in my life," Joaquín said. "My job at the Ministry was frustrating. I had thought I could do some good for the country, but there were too many hurdles."

"Corruption," Eugenia mouthed. Patricia wondered if Joaquín disapproved of it or if he wasn't getting his fair share. She shouldn't be so cynical, she reminded herself. So far, the man seemed perfectly nice.

"Besides," Joaquín continued, "I'd been wanting to get out of the capital for a long time. I was born in the countryside, you see, near Cobán. So, when your mother offered me a job as manager of Finca Baldt, it sounded like a worthy challenge. I would see what I could do to bring a traditional coffee-producing estate into the modern day. It would provide me with practical, hands-on experience."

"And how do you intend to do that?"

"Through diversification, mostly. Please understand, Dr. Baldt, your father was an excellent old-style plantation owner. But times have changed, and I think I can make the estate more viable in the long term. That is, if I continue to act as manager. If your brother takes over the finca, he is unlikely to require my services."

"I hired Joaquín after your father became ill," Eugenia said. "We were heading for ruin." She lifted an accusatory eyebrow. "I had no one to turn to."

"It must have been difficult," Patricia said. The waiter served bowls of chicken bouillon, and Patricia took a sip. It was mild but flavorful. She wondered at what point her mother had become so enamored of Joaquín. Before or after she hired him? Not that it mattered. She turned to him. "And your family? Are they here with you?"

"My only family consists of a grown son who's living in the States."

So, no wife, she thought, at least none on the scene. She'd noticed that he wasn't wearing a ring, but that didn't mean much.

The salad course arrived, slices of avocado drizzled with a creamy pink sauce. The waiter poured wine, and they toasted to family reunions.

Joaquín turned to Eugenia. "Did you have a chance to talk about who will take over the finca?"

"I'm afraid it won't be me," Patricia said.

"There," Eugenia said, addressing Joaquín. "You see? Patricia has a thriving medical practice in the States. And a delightful male companion, from what she tells me. A finca in Guatemala would only complicate her life."

"Such a decision can't be made lightly," Joaquín said.

"No," Eugenia said, turning to Patricia, "but unfortunately, there isn't much time to ponder it. Your brother is about to contest the will. He claims that Otto was not of sound mind when he left the estate to you."

"It sounds like that was the case," Patricia said.

"There's no hard proof," Eugenia said, "and I certainly won't provide any. Our attorney is an old friend, and he will support me." Her eyes narrowed. "Carlos has been cultivating powerful friends, but I have them too. Once the estate is in my hands, it will be hard for him to take it away. So you see, *hija*, if we want to avoid a legal battle, you must sign over the finca to me as soon as possible. We could visit Amilcar first thing tomorrow morning. He has already drawn up the paper work. You'll just need to sign." Eugenia placed her hand on Patricia's. "Then we can drive to Finca Baldt. It's been ages since you've been home."

"Mama, I can't take any action until I talk to Carlos. I'm sure you can see that." Her mother's pout indicated she couldn't. "Besides," Patricia said, "I have an appointment tomorrow with Arturo Muñoz, Meg's attorney. He's handling the newspaper ads."

"Oh, yes, I've seen the ads," Eugenia said. "They're very mysterious, aren't they? Like something out of a spy novel."

"We didn't want to give away too much information."

"No, of course not," her mother said. "Let's see. Arturo Muñoz. It seems like I heard something about him. Something spicy. Oh, I know." She leaned toward Patricia and lowered her voice. "His wife is having an affair with an Army officer. A colonel." She clicked her tongue. "Poor Arturo, to be humiliated that way. I wouldn't wish such a thing on anyone, not even a socialist."

Patricia glanced at Joaquín, who was staring into space, his expression impassive.

The waiter arrived with the dinner entrees, a welcome reprieve from steamy gossip and the threat of a lawsuit from Carlos. They all soon agreed that the sea bass was delicious. As soon as they finished dinner, Patricia excused herself, claiming fatigue after the flight. She got into a cab, leaving her mother and Joaquín standing in front of the restaurant. She didn't even want to think about where they might go from there.

It was almost ten by the time Patricia had showered and climbed into bed, the heater humming against the chill evening air. She turned off the light, her eyes gradually adjusting to the dark hotel room. Hank was probably sitting on the porch of their seafront cabin, enjoying the soft island breezes. She wondered if he was alone. Missing her. She hoped so.

Her thoughts turned to her father—handsome, powerful Otto Baldt. The imposing sound of his footsteps, of his voice, were embedded in her very being. Growing up, she had thought he was the strongest man in the world. Yet, all the time, he must have been inspired to act not by strength but by fear. Paranoia even.

The political uproar that existed during most of her youth had probably disguised her father's condition and fed it. Looking back, her father and his friends had detested President Arévalo, the first socialist president, then loathed his successor, President Arbenz, with a passion. On the other side, the leftists reviled large landowners like her father. Maybe she hadn't recognized her father's paranoia because by the time the C.I.A.-sponsored invasion took place, a lot of the country had been living with anger and fear for a long time. Given the political climate, her father's behavior would not have stood out.

Then there was her brother Carlos. She still remembered him as a sulky ten-year-old who was only happy when he was dribbling a soccer ball. Or a football, as it was called here. She needed to talk to him as soon as possible. Then, maybe she could figure out what was going on, whether he had really turned into some kind of monster. Hopefully, her mother was exaggerating.

But none of this had anything to do with her real purpose in being there. Tomorrow she would begin her search for J.J.

CHAPTER EIGHT

The next morning was a Monday, and Patricia awoke to the happy realization that winter was far away. Her tasks were daunting, but she wouldn't have to pile on three layers of clothing to confront them.

She dressed in a navy skirt, cream-colored blouse, and her red blazer, and went downstairs to the smaller of the hotel's two restaurants, where her breakfast consisted of an egg, white farmer cheese, black beans, and tortillas—what the menu referred to as the "typical" breakfast. It was a little heavy, but it tasted like home. The coffee was aromatic but weak. She realized she'd become accustomed to stronger coffee over the years. It had certainly kept her going through medical school.

Her appointment with Arturo wasn't until nine-thirty, so she ambled along the hotel concourse past various shops—a few boutiques, a travel agency, a barber shop and hair salon, a place selling colorful Guatemalan handicrafts. The bookstore had displays of American bestsellers—'Salem's Lot and Shogun in English and Spanish translation.

Exiting the hotel complex, she was bombarded by the sights and sounds of the city street. Workers and businessmen hustled by, and the street was filled with cars, buses, trucks and taxis, accompanied by the sound of vehicle horns and the smell of diesel fumes. This wasn't the gentle pace that Patricia remembered.

She started walking toward Arturo's office building on Seventh Avenue, passing the post office, with its familiar arch. A covered army truck rattled past, the dark visages of soldiers visible from an opening in the back. A chill ran through her. This was the army that had failed to defend Arbenz, bringing about his downfall. Apparently, the generals had benefited from their decision. A couple of colleagues who knew the country well had told Patricia that the supposedly democratic government was little more than a facade, its leaders holding office at the army's discretion.

A block farther on, a group of scruffy laborers doing street repairs gazed up at her admiringly, and one of them cooed to her how *bella* she was. At least in her homeland, she didn't have to be a skinny blonde Barbie doll to be appreciated.

The offices of Muñoz & Muñoz, Attorneys at Law, were on the second floor of an old office building. A young woman with trendy, over-sized eyeglasses asked Patricia to wait in the reception room, an area with comfortable padded chairs, its walls lined with vintage black and white photographs of the city.

A moment later a tall man in a pin-striped suit appeared at the inner door. Arturo. His face brightened into a wide grin. "Patricia. How marvelous to see you." His voice was deep and resonant, his Spanish cultivated. He took her hand in a warm grasp.

"It's been a long time," she said. Maturity agreed with him. The former gawkiness was gone, and his eyes seemed less prominent now that his face had filled out.

He led her back to his office, lined on one side with shelves that mostly contained rows of identically bound law volumes. She sat on a leather chair, and he seated himself behind a well-polished dark wood desk. To one side of him were two framed photographs of children, and in front was a manila folder on top of a green blotter.

"May I offer my condolences on your father's death," Arturo said. If he had any disagreeable memories of her father, his voice and expression gave no sign of them.

"Thank you," she replied. "Meg—Mrs. Reid—sends her greetings."

He smiled. "It's a pleasure to work with her, even if it's just over the phone. My father has retired. He wanted to come back to represent her, but I asked him to let me take over. The truth is, his health isn't up to it."

"I'm sorry to hear that, but I know that Meg and her father have full confidence in you. As do I." She took a photocopy of the anonymous letter out of her shoulder bag and handed it to him. "Here's the letter I told you about."

Arturo nodded as he read. "Just as you described it," he said. He opened the folder on his desk and handed her a page of classified ads from the newspaper. A large ad was circled in red. It read, in English translation:

Mrs. Margaret Fuente requests further information from writer of letter of January 24. Reward of Q300 for assistance leading to location of individual referred to in letter. Leave message at P.O. Box 1423, Guatemala City.

"Any responses?" Patricia asked.

"Not yet, but the ad has only been appearing for about a week. It could take a while. What are your plans while you're here?"

"I'm going to San Felipe. I'll look for people who remember the fire at Los Ancianos, see if I can get any leads on what happened to J.J."

"Good idea," he said. His brows furrowed. "But be aware, once you start talking about Meg, people may connect you with the newspaper ad. They could claim to have information they don't have, hoping to get the reward."

She hadn't thought of that, but he was right. "I suppose that means I should work as quickly as possible, before people start thinking up money-making schemes." She gazed at Arturo, still trying to synchronize her memory of the awkward youth with the mature man sitting across from her. "If you don't mind, perhaps I could start my interviews with you. Ask you a few questions about that night at Los Ancianos."

"Of course. You can practice on me. I imagine our memories will be very similar, since we were together."

"That's so. Still, people sometimes notice different details. Let me get right to the crucial part. When we were at Los Ancianos, did you see or hear anything that might suggest J.J. had survived? A glimpse of him maybe, or a remark by someone?"

"I would have reported it long ago if I had. That's the difficulty, right? Any responsible person would have done so." He frowned. "You know, now that I think of it, maybe these interviews aren't such a good idea. You could be dealing with an old case of arson or kidnapping. Some people might find your questions threatening."

"Yes, that occurred to me too. But what choice do I have? I must search for leads wherever I can find them."

His lips quirked into a smile. "Your tenacity doesn't exactly surprise me. But I warn you, Patricia, you will need to be careful."

"Yes, of course."

He looked down at the file. "I made reservations for Meg at a new hotel in San Felipe. The Bella Vista. It's supposed to be clean and comfortable. Do you want to stay there? It's probably as safe a place as any."

"That sounds fine."

"And you can come back to the capital any time you need a break.

Ceci is hoping she can see you while you're here," he said. He explained that his sister, her former classmate, was married with three boys. She also taught a course in microbiology at the national university.

"I would love to see her." Patricia pointed to the pictures on his desk. "Are those your kids?"

"Yes, although they're a little older now. Alicia is fourteen, and Samuel is twelve. Alicia wants to be a dancer, and Samuel wants to be anything but an attorney."

Patricia laughed. "He could change his mind later. I remember you were disillusioned with the law when you were younger. But here you are."

"That's so. How about you? I don't see a ring on your finger."

"I have a good friend, but...we haven't gotten around to marriage."

His expression sobered. "Marriage complicates things." Patricia thought of her mother's gossip. Was Arturo's wife unfaithful?

Arturo closed the manila folder. "I suppose your brother Carlos is taking over Finca Baldt. Are all the legal matters settled?"

Her family must have prevented the inheritance information from leaking out. But it would be public knowledge soon enough if Carlos was contesting the will. "If I may speak in confidence?"

"Of course."

"Actually, I inherited the estate."

"Really?" He grinned. "Congratulations. Does that mean you'll be moving back?"

"No, I don't intend to stay," she said, then described her conversation with her mother. Arturo listened, nodding occasionally. "Mama claims that Carlos is involved with some kind of militia. Whatever that is."

He grimaced. "I'm sorry to hear that, if it's true. The militias have been around for a while, but they seem to be stepping up their activities. They call themselves anti-Communist, but they target all kinds of people—students, teachers, journalists, trade unionists. Lawyers."

"Target them?"

"Murder them, mostly. Sometimes bodies are found by the roadside. Other times the people just disappear."

She shivered. Could her brother possibly be involved in such things?

"I know. It's horrible. A lot of the militias have army connections, although the men rarely wear uniforms. There seem to be some independent groups out there too. Rogues."

"But you haven't heard anything specifically about my brother?"

"Carlos? No."

She thought of Arturo's father, the left-wing attorney. "What about you? Is your family safe?"

"For now," he said darkly. Then his expression brightened. "Look. Enough with legal matters and politics. Could I take you to lunch?" He checked his watch. "I could swing by your hotel at noon."

"That would be lovely."

Patricia returned to her hotel room, where she called the hotel operator and asked her to put through a call to the agent who handled medical trips. She hated to think what the hotel's surcharge would be, but Jonathan wouldn't think twice about paying the bill.

"I believe you're in luck, Dr. Baldt," the travel agent said. "I just got off the phone with a nurse at a clinic in San Felipe. Her name is Fiona Murray, and she works with a nonprofit voluntary agency. She seems quite friendly and will be very pleased to have you help her out for a week or two. Really, it sounds ideal for you."

Patricia thanked the agent, took down the clinic phone number, and called Fiona Murray in San Felipe.

The nurse sounded cheerful when she answered the phone, her voice warm, with a Celtic lilt. She chatted a little about the clinic and its patients.

"Do people come in from the villages around San Felipe?" Patricia asked.

"Not so many. A few come from Santa Catarina. But it's the folk from San Felipe who are my regulars," Fiona said.

"I was wondering if you ever had patients from Chayaka." Besides inquiring about Demetrio, she'd assured Meg that she'd try to contact the watchman who was at Los Ancianos the night of the fire.

"I can't say that we have. They're not keen on traveling, from what I hear. And I've had little chance to leave San Felipe. Do you know the town?"

"I used to have a friend there. I was curious how his family was doing."

"I do know a fellow from Chayaka," Fiona said. "We both study marimba at the Cultural Center. He might know about your friend. I could check, if you like."

"Yes, I'd appreciate that." Patricia explained that she'd arrive in San Felipe later that afternoon. Fiona said there was a vacant apartment next to hers. The landlady liked renters who paid in dollars, and she usually let people pay by the week. She'd check into it at lunch.

At noon, Arturo surprised Patricia by driving them to the out-skirts of the city, to a colorful seafood restaurant patronized by people dressed in trendy clothes. She and Arturo lunched on tasty shellfish soup and bread, washed down with a glass of beer. They laughed about their younger days, including Arturo's comic tale of his herculean efforts to beat the arrogant Flaco Hidalgo at tennis, causing Patricia to laugh so hard she got the hiccups.

Arturo leaned closer to her. "It is an enormous relief to see you so beautiful, to know you have done so well in your life. The fact is, I have always felt responsible for your car accident."

"Responsible?" This was a surprise. "Why should you feel responsible? You weren't even there."

"Exactly. Remember that morning? You called and asked me to drive with you to Chayaka. I turned you down. And all because I had a cold. I should have gone with you. I've always thought that if I'd been driving, you would never have gone off the cliff."

Patricia stared at him. Surely he hadn't been feeling guilty for the last two decades. "Arturo, I swear to you, I have never blamed you. It never even entered my mind. In fact, I'd forgotten I called you."

"Really?"

"Now that I think of it, you told me not to go. Which was the best possible advice. I just didn't follow it."

"I should have been more forceful."

"Don't be silly," she said. "I didn't listen to anyone in those days. You know that well enough."

"Very true," he said chuckling, then pulled out his wallet to pay. "Let's get out of here. There's something I need to tell you."

A minute later, Patricia was sitting in the passenger seat of Arturo's car as he stared at the windshield.

"Is something wrong?" she asked.

"There's no good way to say this, but...my wife has a lover—an army colonel."

So, her mother had been right. Poor Arturo. He deserved better. But then, you never knew what went on in marriages. "I'm sorry."

He glanced at her. "You knew already, didn't you?"

"Mama told me."

"I suppose everyone knows," he mumbled.

"Oh, Arturo, these things happen all the time. You're an attorney. You know that."

"Carmen says I'm boring. Utterly boring."

"Then she's wrong. Did you tell her about the time you hiked to Chayaka and warned the people they would be attacked?"

They shared a smile. "That was an amazing night, wasn't it?" he said.

"You were heroic."

"Was I? Then you must bring out the hero in me. Unlike my wife." He exhaled, his shoulders sagging. "You think I'm a coward, don't you? To stay with Carmen."

"Arturo, I assure you, I'm in no position to judge. You have lovely children, and you're successful in your work. Besides, you're a good-looking man, and your wife is a fool to let you go."

"Do you think so?" Then he grimaced. "Actually, there is one advantage to my wife's infidelity. The Colonel has connections with army security. He has assured Carmen that as long as I stay out of trouble, the militias will leave me alone." He glanced at Patricia before looking away. "It's not that Carmen cares about me, you understand. But she doesn't want our children to be fatherless."

Patricia groaned. What had her poor country come to? Arturo's life sounded like a noir-ish soap opera. A woman had an affair with an army officer, and it kept her husband from being murdered.

"I didn't mean to burden you," Arturo said, "but I imagined you would hear gossip about me. I wanted you to hear the truth first."

"I'm glad you told me," Patricia said. "Now we can put that aside and focus on our joint mission, figuring out what happened to J.J."

On the drive back to the hotel, Patricia told Arturo about her call to Fiona and explained that she might stay in an apartment in San Felipe. He agreed that would be convenient.

"Thanks for lunch," she said as he pulled up to the hotel. "I'll call you soon."

Arturo started to get out of the car.

"No, don't bother," she said, reaching for her door handle.

He leaned across and kissed her on the cheek. "I'm glad you're back," he said.

She hustled out of the car. "I'll call you when I'm settled in," she said through the window, then stepped back and waved. She sensed that she would have to maintain a little emotional distance from Arturo. He was sweet, and she trusted him to help with the search for J.J., but he had a wife, even if she was unfaithful. And she had Hank.

Back in her room, she packed her belongings, then checked out of the hotel and took a taxi to Econocars, where she rented a Toyota Land Cruiser. It was expensive, but it looked like it should stand up to Guatemalan roads, and Jonathan Cabell could afford it. She would, after all, be searching for his grandson.

CHAPTER NINE

The afternoon was warm, and Patricia drove to San Felipe in a short-sleeved blouse. On either side of the gravel road, the fields were black and smelled bitter from fires that had been set to clear off last year's growth. She thought of the rich brown soil of Iowa and Illinois and the endless rows of corn and soybeans. Farming these highland Guatemalan fields, with their poor soil and steep inclines, was hard work, but it had been accomplished by the Indians for hundreds, maybe thousands of years.

It was a little before six when Patricia arrived in San Felipe. The town looked similar to what she remembered, but it seemed busier. The main avenue bustled with traffic—cars, trucks, and buses. A motorcycle without a muffler made a sputtering racket. She saw no animal-drawn carts. Workshops and small stores lined the street, and along one curb, three old Blue Bird buses were lined up. People queued behind the last one—Indians mostly, the women in colorful *huipiles* and the men in work clothes, probably returning home to their villages at the end of the day. She passed the open-air market, where a few remaining vendors were closing up their booths.

Following Fiona's instructions, she turned onto a side street with brick paving. Houses were wedged one next to the other, their tall, shuttered windows covered with curved, wrought iron bars. She noticed jagged cracks on a few walls, but otherwise, not many signs of earthquake damage. Until, that is, she came to a corner where a Catholic church stood, one that she had visited during Holy Week one year. With dismay, she saw that the once beautiful stucco structure was teetering, with one decrepit wall supported by scaffolding.

A block later, she saw a one-story building with the sign she'd been looking for: "Clínica La Luz." The Light. She parked in front and walked up to the door, where a "Closed" sign was displayed. But the door was unlocked, and she walked into the waiting room. The molded plastic chairs that circled the room were empty.

"We open at eight tomorrow," came a youthful voice from the far end of the waiting room. The speaker was a slender, dark-haired young woman in a lime green dress, who was inserting folders into a filing cabinet. Patricia walked over and introduced herself.

"Oh, you're the visiting doctor," the woman said with a smile. She introduced herself as Leticia and said that the nurse, Fiona, would be out shortly.

Just then two people emerged from a room at the back of the clinic. One was a wizened old man and the other a short, thirtyish woman wearing a white lab coat. Her hand rested on the old man's shoulder, and they both nodded as they shared some quiet words. She had a freckled face and short, sandy hair in need of a trim. Her light coloring, which would have fit in nicely with the population of New Bergen, was striking here, amid the dark-haired, dark-skinned people of San Felipe.

The old man walked out the clinic door, and Leticia introduced Patricia to Fiona. "*Bienvenida*," Fiona said in Scots-colored

Spanish and shook Patricia's hand with a firm grip. They stood eye to eye, so Patricia realized that Fiona must be about five foot four, Patricia's own height.

Leticia said she'd finished the filing, and she promptly took off with a cheery "*Hasta mañana.*"

"Leti's boyfriend is waiting," Fiona said in explanation for the girl's fast departure. "I'm so happy you're here. The woman at the agency said you were American. And you're fluent in Spanish?" Patricia nodded. "That's super," Fiona said. "Mind if we speak English? It's been a while for me."

"Not at all."

Patricia followed Fiona on a quick tour of the clinic. Besides the long waiting room, it consisted of two examination rooms, a tiny office, a storeroom, and a bathroom, all looking clean and in reasonably good repair.

"I don't suppose you brought medical supplies," Fiona said, looking hopeful.

"I'm so sorry. I only found out last night that I was coming."

"I shouldn't have asked," Fiona said. "It's just that we're sometimes a little short. Still, I'm better off than the government clinic. The doctors there occasionally send patients to me when they run short of medicine. It's a sorry state of affairs. But we all make do."

Patricia asked if she could use the phone for a collect call, and while Fiona was closing up the clinic, she called Finca Baldt. Fortunately, her mother was there.

"Well, what did you think of Joaquín?" Eugenia asked.

"He seems charming and knowledgeable."

"I knew you'd like him. But don't get any ideas," she said teasingly. "He's mine."

"Don't worry," Patricia said, amused but also a little sad that her mother saw her as a potential rival. She informed her mother that she would be working part-time at the clinic and gave her the phone number. "And I need to get in touch with Carlos."

"Good luck with that. Only his friends—the thugs—know how to contact him. Anyway, I don't see why you insist on talking to him. I've told you everything you need to know."

"Mama, he's my brother. Plus, the sooner I see him, the sooner we can get all this inheritance stuff taken care of."

"Oh, very well," her mother said. "If Carlos shows up at the finca, I'll tell him to get in touch with you." She also agreed to arrange for Patricia to talk to those of Otto's workers who had been at the fire at Los Ancianos. She had already begun identifying the men in anticipation of Meg's arrival. After all these years, some had left, she explained, including Gustavo.

"He hasn't worked at Finca Baldt for years," Eugenia said. "I heard he was working as a mechanic somewhere. San Felipe, maybe."

She also agreed to call Alma Tapia to set up a chat with Patricia. It turned out that Javier, her husband, had died a few years earlier of cancer. Patricia was sorry he had passed away, but she hadn't been looking forward to talking to him. The last time she'd seen him was the night of the fire, when he'd been jubilant about going to Chayaka to burn down the town.

By the time Patricia hung up, Fiona had shed her lab coat, revealing a white shirt with colorful embroidery around the scoop neckline and a faded blue skirt. A woven cloth bag hung from her shoulder.

"Let's take a look at the apartment and see if you want it," Fiona said. "Then, you're welcome to join me for dinner."

They took Patricia's Land Cruiser, since Fiona had walked the three blocks to the clinic. When they arrived at El Patio Apartments, Fiona unlocked a gate leading to a gravel parking lot inside. Patricia drove in and parked her Land Cruiser next to a small white van that turned out to be Fiona's.

Patricia soon discovered that the apartments were really six cottages arranged around a tiny courtyard. The owner, Mrs. Sanchez, was a buxom woman around sixty with closely permed black hair. As Fiona had predicted, she would be happy to let Patricia rent her one available apartment.

Mrs. Sanchez unlocked the apartment door and showed Patricia in. Before her was a room furnished with a rustic wooden sofa with thin pads, a chair with a caned seat, and a small table. At the left end of the room sat a dining table and two chairs. Behind the sofa, Patricia was pleased to see a sink next to a two-burner stove and a small refrigerator. It would be nice to be able to store perishable items and do a little cooking. She walked through a doorway at the right to find a small bedroom crammed with a double bed, a chest of drawers, and a closet with a few metal clothes hangers. The room opened onto a tiny bathroom with a shower.

The apartments at El Patio didn't have phones, Mrs. Sanchez explained, although she would let Patricia use hers in an emergency. There was a government-run Guatel office a few blocks away, where she could make calls.

"That's fine," Patricia said. It was inconvenient, but the clinic had a phone. This place was clean and had a lot more space than a hotel room. Plus, it was a short walk from the clinic and right next to Fiona's home. She gave her landlady a week's rent in dollars in exchange for keys to the gate and apartment. Then she and Fiona deposited Patricia's bags in her new abode.

"I'll go put dinner together," Fiona said. "Pop over when you're settled in."

The day's warmth was giving way to the evening chill, and Patricia slipped into her cardigan sweater. After putting a few things into the chest of drawers and the bedroom closet, Patricia followed the aroma of garlic and onion to Fiona's apartment next door.

Fiona turned from the stove. "I hope you like spaghetti with marinara sauce."

"I love it."

"I have a part-time maid," Fiona said. "She gets dinner started and leaves it on the stove." A bottle of red wine sat on the counter beside two glasses, one half empty. "Help yourself," she said, pointing to the bottle, then dumped half a bag of spaghetti into a pan of boiling water.

Patricia poured herself a glass of wine and settled into a caned chair, identical to the one in her apartment. Like her own living area, this one was sparsely furnished, but Fiona had placed indigo cushions on the wooden sofa and livened it up with a few throw pillows in an ikat pattern in shades of red, green, and gold. In front of the sofa, a rustic coffee table was scattered with local newspapers, colorful woven coasters, and a paperback romance novel with an English title. On the opposite wall were two framed pictures. Patricia walked over to get a closer look. One was a professional shot of Lake Atitlán, a serenely beautiful place that Patricia had visited a couple of times as a child. The other was a charming if amateurish oil painting of a winding street bordered by cottages. Fiona explained it was the town where she'd grown up.

"I wanted to see the world," Fiona said, "so I left my town in the Scottish highlands. And where did I end up? In the Guatemalan highlands."

A few minutes later they carried the meal to the dining area. It looked out on the courtyard, which was brightened by several large potted plants, including a couple of flowering bougainvilleas in shades of magenta and purple.

While Patricia and Fiona ate the pasta, Patricia described New Bergen and her work at the clinic there, and Fiona talked about growing up as the only daughter in a family with four brothers, all of them skilled football players.

"That's soccer to the Americans, isn't it?" Fiona said. Her brothers were all staunch supporters of Inverness Caledonian Thistle Football Club.

Fiona had always wanted to be a nurse, she said, and she was delighted to find that it gave her the means to travel. She'd been working for the same British aid agency for several years, and Guatemala was her third country. She'd arrived nearly a year ago.

Fiona refilled the wine glasses. "There's a plantation, a Finca Baldt, not far from here. You wouldn't be related to the family, would you?"

Patricia explained that she was the daughter of the owners.

"I heard there was a daughter who drove off a cliff," Fiona said.

Naturally, Patricia realized, that was how she would be remembered—the daughter who went over the cliff. "That's me."

"Oh. Sorry. That was rude of me. I have a bad habit of saying the first thing enters my mind."

"It's all right. It's no secret. I was driving downhill on a narrow road, and I swerved off it to avoid plowing into a bus." She had come up with this concise explanation years earlier.

They piled their dishes in the sink and took their wine to the sofa.

"If you don't mind my asking," Fiona said, "what brings you to San Felipe?"

Patricia pondered how much she should tell Fiona. Since they were going to work and live side by side, Fiona would learn about the search for J.J. sooner or later. This might be a good opportunity to bring it up. Besides, Fiona had a warmth that felt genuine, and Patricia sensed that she could confide in her.

"Actually," Patricia said, "the reason for my being here goes back to 1954." She told about the Fuentes and the archaeological dig at Los Ancianos, then explained about the fire, and how Meg had been rescued, but Pablo and J.J. had not been. She picked up her glass and was surprised to realize that her hand was trembling.

"Are you all right?" Fiona asked, looking concerned.

"Yes. I guess that night feels close to me here. It all happened about twenty minutes away, just up the road. But you asked what brought me here, and it was a letter." She described the anonymous letter that Meg had received and the plan to look for J.J. "Meg was all set to come," she said, "then she fell and broke her leg. So here I am in her place. When I'm not working at the clinic, I'll be making inquiries of people who were here in 1954 and have connections to Los Ancianos. I'll see if I can flush out the writer."

"It's a real challenge you've taken on," Fiona said. She cocked her head. "1954. Wasn't that the year of the coup d'état? When President Arbenz was deposed?"

"Yes. The fire at Los Ancianos was in early June, not long before the coup." She remembered how fast the change of power had taken place. Once the rebel army invaded, it had taken the Guatemalan army a little over a week to abandon Arbenz and join forces with the rebels in seizing power. She had been hospitalized at the time, recovering from her car accident, her mind fuzzy from pain killers. The people who came into her room mostly talked among themselves. Some of the doctors and nurses had been happy about the coup, counting on peace and stability to follow. But she had overheard two attendants whisper about family members being arrested and taken away. And even in her semi-drugged state, she had sensed an undercurrent of sadness. The Guatemalan people had tried democracy for ten years, and it had failed.

"Actually, there was a fire at Chayaka the same night that Los Ancianos burned down," Patricia said. "And I drove off the cliff a few weeks later."

"So much misfortune," Fiona said. "And your father died recently, didn't he?"

"Yes. There are some questions about my father's will," Patricia said, "so I'll have to attend to that as well."

"It's a lot to accomplish," Fiona said. "Can I help?"

Patricia thought for a moment. "If you don't mind, I can think of one thing. There was a watchman at Los Ancianos the night of the fire. I know he was from Chayaka, but I don't know his name. I'd like to ask him if he saw or heard anything. Anything that might lead us to J.J. You said you have a friend from Chayaka. I wonder if he'd know the man."

"I can ask. But Julio is thirty-one, the same age as me. He must have been pretty young at the time of the fire. He might not remember."

"That's true," Patricia said. "But other people should know who the watchman was. Does your friend ever go to Chayaka? Maybe he could ask around, see if anyone remembers."

"I think he goes most Sundays. I'll see if he's willing. Frankly, he seems a bit private to me. A typical highlander I suppose. So I don't know what he'll say."

"I don't want to put you or your friend in an awkward position," Patricia said. She'd forgotten how closed Chayaka could be. The last time she was in the town, looking for Demetrio's family, people in the street had hurried away from her, and Demetrio's aunt had refused to talk to her.

"I'll tell Julio that you're looking for the watchman," Fiona said. "Maybe he will offer to help, and maybe he won't."

"Thanks. I appreciate it." And if she found out about the watchman, she could inquire later about Demetrio. Maybe by that time she would have worked up the courage to drive the treacherous road to Chayaka.

CHAPTER TEN

After supper Patricia headed down the street to buy a few items to stock the apartment. The grocery store on the next block had a sign saying Tienda Beatriz, and Patricia remembered that Meg had left money to Beatriz to help her open a shop. Could this be the place?

Inside, a scrawny woman with hard eyes sat behind the cash register. Definitely not Beatriz. In response to Patricia's question, she said that the shop owner was indeed Beatriz Aguilar, but she had left for the day.

Well, at least I've found her, Patricia thought. She walked down the four narrow aisles bordered by shelves piled high with canned and packaged goods. The net shopping bag that Fiona had lent her soon filled up with basic cleaning and cooking supplies as well as a package of sandwich cookies and a bag of plantain chips. In the refrigerator section in back, she picked up butter, cheese, and eggs.

Patricia was checking out when an attractive middle-aged woman appeared beside the cashier. She wore a sapphire blue dress that accentuated her curvaceous figure, and her thick dark hair was swept up and accented by silver earrings. Beatriz had matured gracefully.

"Did you wish to see me?" Beatriz asked.

Patricia introduced herself and watched as recognition flooded Beatriz's face.

"Patricia. I always thought you'd return some day." She seemed friendly, but her voice had the reserved edge that Patricia remembered.

"Do you have a few minutes to talk?" Patricia asked.

"Come," Beatriz said and escorted Patricia across the shop and through a door into her living quarters. "Let me get you a soft drink." She stepped out of the room, leaving Patricia in the living room.

The sofa and chairs were red vinyl and faced a television with a V-shaped antenna, old-fashioned rabbit ears. But one wall featured nine brightly colored pictures with carved wooden frames. Patricia walked over to one and realized the scene wasn't painted, but embroidered in intricate detail. She recognized it as an Easter procession in a small town. Men in dark suits carried a saint on a platform, followed by a crowd of men and women, many carrying lilies. The picture next to it showed an embroidered school yard with barefoot children playing and a man standing at the school house door. Both pictures were charming works of what might be called folk art.

Beatriz stood beside her. "Do you like them?"

"They're beautiful. Who is the artist?"

"I am. I'm glad they please you."

"I shouldn't be surprised at your artistry," Patricia said. "You were always skillful with a needle and thread."

"Thank you. As you see, when I stopped sewing for other people, I started sewing for myself." She motioned to the other pictures displayed on the wall. "This is what resulted."

"Where do the scenes take place?"

"Different places. These two are from Santa Catarina, the way it looked when I was growing up. See the teacher? He's my father."

"You've captured him beautifully."

"Do you think so? He died many years ago. That's when I went to work for your family. I was sixteen."

So young. But then Patricia had been a child at the time, so Beatriz had seemed like a woman. "That must have been a difficult time for you," Patricia said. If she had ever heard about Beatriz's history, she had long since forgotten.

"It was. You know, I'm having an exhibit of my embroidery at the Cultural Center. It opens a week from Saturday. You should drop by. But perhaps by then you'll be back in the United States." She'd placed two open bottles of orange soda on a table in front of the sofa where they both sat down.

Patricia took a swallow of the soda and explained that she wasn't sure how long she would be in San Felipe, probably one or two weeks. "I'm helping out part-time at the Clinic La Luz."

"I had heard rumors that you were a doctor," Beatriz said. "The little nurse does such good work there. Everyone speaks well of her. So, now there are two foreigners working at the clinic. How lucky for us."

Patricia bristled. Since when had she become a foreigner? This was her home as much as Beatriz's, even if she was carrying a U.S. passport. But there wasn't much point in getting huffy. People here would probably assume she'd turned American. That would come as a shock to the people of New Bergen, who would always see her as an outsider. Many assumed she was Mexican, as if there were no other countries south of the U.S.

Beatriz asked about Meg, explaining they had lost contact years earlier. Patricia told her that Meg was living in a town near Chicago and had a husband and two daughters.

"She is very fortunate," Beatriz said.

An odd remark, Patricia thought, to describe a woman who

had lost her first husband and only son. But then, Beatriz was no stranger to hardship.

"I've come on Meg's behalf," Patricia said. She described the anonymous letter.

Beatriz's face darkened. "Who would write such a thing? Giving false hope to poor Meg. It's a crime."

"Still, if there's any possibility that J.J.—"

"Doctora, we both know that Meg is breaking her heart for nothing. The boy couldn't have survived that fire. She should forget this foolishness and attend to her family. You must tell her that."

Patricia gulped down the last of her soda. "I'd like to find Gustavo, my father's former mechanic. Do you know where I might find him?"

"Certainly. He lives here in San Felipe." Beatriz explained that Gustavo was the proprietor of López Automotive. She drew a small map to the business for Patricia, then walked her to the front of the store, where Patricia paid for her groceries, and Beatriz directed the clerk to find a boy to carry them. A moment later a wiry kid arrived, threw the bag over his shoulder, and walked Patricia to El Patio.

Back at her apartment, she tipped the boy, then stored her new provisions in the kitchen and tiny bathroom. As she deposited a bar of soap on the ledge in the shower stall, she noticed with alarm that the electrical heater attached to the shower head tilted and had wires that were attached in a precarious manner. She wondered if Fiona's shower was in a similar condition.

Fatigue was setting in, and with it, a feeling of despair. Would all her investigations go the same way? Her mother, Arturo, and Beatriz had all emphatically denied seeing J.J. or hearing anything about him. There were still others she could question, but so much depended on the letter writer. Was he too in San Felipe? And was he even now feeling an urge to come out of the shadows?

The next morning, Patricia told Fiona she had an errand to run, and a little after eight she drove to a bustling street in a new part of town and parked the car in front of López Automotive, Gustavo's repair shop.

She halted outside the shop area, breathing in the smell of motor oil and other pungent fumes. Mechanics in coveralls were working on four cars, the closest ones an old Ford on a hydraulic lift and a newer model Chrysler at ground level with its hood up. Two grease-smudged mechanics in overalls leaned under car hoods, while one was stretched out on a dolly underneath a vehicle.

The office was next door, and Patricia stepped inside, a bell announcing her arrival. A short older man approached her from behind a counter. It was Gustavo, now looking more distinguished, with receding gray hair and additional girth.

"Don Gustavo," Patricia said, "do you remember me? You gave me lessons in car maintenance a long time ago."

He broke into a broad smile. "What a pleasure to see you, Señorita," he said, then hesitated. "But it's Doctora now, isn't it? Come in. Have a cup of coffee with me. Beatriz said I should expect you." Apparently, Beatriz had wasted no time in alerting him.

He led her through a gate by the counter and into a room that contained a scarred wooden desk with an office chair and two straight wooden chairs facing it. Shelves were filled with automotive manuals and boxes of various sizes—car parts, she assumed.

Patricia sat on a straight chair while Gustavo poured coffee from a pot on a hot plate into two mugs. He added sugar, then served them both, finally sitting behind the desk across from her. The door was open, presumably so Gustavo could watch for customers. Not a very private place for a conversation, she thought, but it would have to do.

"I am sorry for your father's death," he said. "It was a great loss."

"Thank you," she said. "So, this is your business. You've done very well."

He nodded. "Your father, may he rest in peace, loaned me the money to set up the business. That was many years ago."

"Did he? I'm glad." At least there was one person who remembered her father with fondness. It wasn't surprising. Not only had Gustavo been her father's trusted mechanic, they had also gone hunting together in wooded areas around the estate. Once, Patricia had asked her father why he didn't take her with him.

"Gustavo was in the army. He's a marksman," her father had said. "You aren't."

Patricia took a sip of her coffee. "I imagine that Beatriz told you, Meg has received an anonymous letter."

He nodded soberly. "She did."

"It was postmarked San Felipe. Do you have any idea who might have sent it?"

"No, no idea. I'm sorry."

"Don Gustavo," came a male voice behind her. Gustavo sprang up and disappeared into the front office. His haste surprised her. She wondered if he didn't trust his employees to deal with difficulties, or if he was eager to escape her questions. He returned a minute later, apologetic for his abrupt retreat. The mechanic had a question about the Chrysler, he said. A fine car, but a little temperamental.

"If you'd do me the favor," Patricia said, "I'd like to reconstruct what happened the night of the fire. It might help me figure out if there is any way that J.J. could have survived."

"I'll do what I can," he said. He took out a pack of Belmonts and offered Patricia one. She hadn't smoked in years, but she took a cigarette, remembering the times they'd sat together outside the garage sharing a smoke. He had been chatty back then, and maybe he would be open with her again. She took a drag. It seared her throat, and she barely stifled a cough. It was hard to believe she'd once smoked these things.

"You were the first to arrive from Finca Baldt," she said hoarsely. "Can you tell me what happened?"

He nodded. "I was out walking when I smelled smoke drifting in from the west, from the direction of Los Ancianos. So I took one of the trucks to check it out. I turned down the drive to the house and saw that it was in flames. I drove fast, but it was too late. The fire was out of control. I remembered hearing that the Fuentes were gone that weekend. But I got out and ran around the house to make sure nobody was there. It was then that I spotted her—Doña Meg. She was standing at a window on the second floor. Looking terrified."

Gustavo's hand shook as he picked up the coffee cup to take a drink. "Then she vanished," he said. "I was panicky, you know? But I spotted a ladder leaning against the house, and I propped it up below the window. I climbed up, praying the whole time. Somehow I managed to open the window and get Doña Meg out. By that time, the upper story was in flames. Once I climbed down, it wasn't possible to go back up." He started to cough—a smoker's phlegmy rumble.

"You know the rest," he said. "Your father and the other workers showed up and tried to control the fire. Then, by the grace of God, your mother arrived with the doctor. They drove us to the hospital. I believe that was around the time that you and your friend appeared."

His narrative had been clear and orderly, and Patricia supposed he had given it before, probably several times after the fire. "Did you see any sign of J.J.?" she asked.

He shook his head.

"What about later? Did you hear anything about a child being found?"

"No, Doctora."

It was the answer she'd expected, but it was still disappointing. She flicked ashes into a tin ashtray on the desk. "What about the watchman? An Indian from Chayaka. Did you see him?"

"No. But one of the other men did. Pancho I think. He died a few years ago." He made a sign of the cross.

Patricia winced. "I'm sorry to hear it. Look, I know it was a long time ago, but try to remember. Was anyone else around? Anyone who could have started the fire? Or who could have taken J.J.?"

He shook his head. "No one. I heard that Javier Tapia arrived to help, he and his workers. But that was after I left." He took a long drag on his cigarette. "You know, I still dream about that night."

"So do I," Patricia said. After all these years, she would occasionally—maybe twice a year—wake up in terror, having relived the fires.

"I've been thinking about the letter," Gustavo said, "ever since Beatriz told me about it. You know, maybe the writer was confused. Or maybe he just wanted to give Doña Meg some comfort, let her think that her son had survived."

"Yes, maybe." Gustavo had a soft heart. Only the most benign explanations would occur to him. It was hard to imagine him as a former soldier. She stubbed out her cigarette in the ashtray. "I'm sorry to have awakened those memories for you."

"No, Doctora, don't worry. I carry J.J. and his father in my heart."

CHAPTER ELEVEN

Patricia drove to Guatel, the government-run telephone company. She needed to call Arturo to let him know where she was, but she disliked calling collect from the clinic. When she walked in, the bench along one side of the waiting room was filled with people. On the other side, muffled conversation emanated from a row of closed telephone booths.

Patricia approached the service window to her left. Behind a small opening, a fleshy, balding man was sorting papers into piles.

"I'd like to make a call to the capital," she said.

"Fill out the form," the man mumbled without looking up. She picked up a slip of paper from a small box on her side of the window. There were blank lines for her name, address, and the phone number she wanted to call.

"How long is the wait?" Patricia asked.

He eyed her, clearly irritated. "As long as it takes."

Patricia sat down on the bench beside a voluptuous woman with heavy makeup, who was leafing through a magazine. "How long have you been waiting?" Patricia asked.

"Almost half an hour," the woman said, looking at the clock on the wall. "It shouldn't be much longer. I hope."

Patricia walked out. She'd gotten spoiled, she realized, always having easy access to a telephone. In the States, she was able to call anyone she knew, because they all had a phone at home or at work. She went out to her car and drove back to El Patio, where she parked, then walked the three blocks to the clinic. It was 9:30, and the waiting room was full of people.

She washed up, put on her white coat, and began seeing patients in one of the consulting rooms. The people were mostly good-natured, although often anxious. She treated a baby who was badly dehydrated from diarrhea and a little boy who was suffering from worms. His mother had conveniently brought in a glass jelly jar containing one of the parasites. One well-dressed woman insisted on an injection to treat her cough, and Patricia was hard pressed to convince her that an injection would do her no good, since she was suffering from a virus. The woman left in a huff.

Periodically, Patricia looked over the patients in the waiting room, to see if there were any young men in their late twenties who might conceivably be J.J. It was a long shot, but you never knew. Only one of her patients was a young man in the right age range, but he looked too Indian to be J.J. Maybe she should have checked out Gustavo's mechanics while she was there, she mused, although she wasn't sure how she would have accomplished it without appearing nosy.

At noon, she took Fiona aside and asked if she could give five hundred quetzales to the clinic in exchange for being able to make long distance phone calls. Any money that she didn't use would be Jonathan Cabell's donation to the clinic. It was an extravagant amount of money for phone expenses—five hundred dollars—but she wouldn't feel bad about using the clinic phone, and anyway,

Jonathan should be happy to support the clinic. Fiona agreed to the arrangement, already thinking aloud about supplies she could purchase. She gave Patricia a key to the side door, so she could come in after hours.

Relieved at the new arrangement, Patricia sat in the small office at the back of the clinic and called Arturo. He was out, and the secretary didn't know if he'd received any responses to the newspaper ad. Patricia left the young woman with the clinic's phone number and promised to call again later.

At a Chinese restaurant down the street, she ate a serving of chicken chow mein that was filling if a little greasy. Then she wandered along the streets, her eyes automatically drawn to young men, looking for a grown-up version of the four-year-old pirate. Unfortunately, the town was filled with men with dark brown hair and brown eyes. One fellow misinterpreted her gaze for romantic interest, and it took her a few minutes to shake him off. After that, she put on sunglasses and was careful to be discreet. She felt like a spy.

Her mother called at two o'clock, as the clinic was opening for the afternoon. If Patricia drove to Finca Baldt the following morning, she could talk to the workers, then join her mother and Joaquín for mid-day dinner. Eugenia had also made arrangements for Patricia to stop in at the Tapia finca to talk with Alma Tapia, Javier's widow.

"I spoke with Carlos," Eugenia said. "He will get in touch with you. Soon, if I'm not mistaken."

Half way through the afternoon, Leti ushered a stout, older woman from Santa Catarina into Patricia's examining room. Fiona had been monitoring her blood pressure, which was high, and Patricia checked her vitals, then told her to continue the pills Fiona had prescribed.

"Do you need a new prescription?" Patricia asked.

"It isn't necessary," the woman said. Patricia wasn't surprised. The pharmacist was unlikely to require a prescription. People had far easier access to drugs here than in the States, for better or worse.

Patricia remembered that Beatriz was from Santa Catarina and asked her patient if she would be going to the opening of Beatriz's exhibit at the Cultural Center. The woman gave a short laugh. "That Beatriz. I remember when she was a snotty-nosed little girl, running around town with the other children. Now that she's well off, she has nothing to do with us. She never comes back to visit."

Patricia thought of Beatriz's pictures of Santa Catarina. She clearly had fond memories of the place. It seemed a shame that she had cut herself off from people in her town. But then, Beatriz had a prickly personality. Maybe she'd antagonized too many people there. Or maybe the townspeople were too demanding of her. Patricia knew how such things worked. As a shopkeeper, Beatriz would have been perceived as wealthy. People might have sought her out as a source of loans or as a generous godmother for their children.

About half an hour before closing, Leti stepped into Patricia's examining room, looking nervous. "Your brother is waiting for you outside," she said. "He says his business with you is urgent."

Carlos. She looked forward to seeing him after all these years, but she was uneasy at the thought of the difficult discussion that was coming. Patricia slipped out of her white coat, washed her hands, and crossed the waiting room to the door.

Outside, her heart missed a beat. A short, darkly handsome man was leaning against an orange sports car with its top down, smoking a cigarette. He looked tan and fit in his stylish shirt and slacks. Her little brother was now a man.

As she strode toward him, he looked her over and took another drag on his cigarette. He must be over thirty, but he had the smirky look of a teenager.

"The *Vieja* said you were here," he said. *Vieja.* The old woman. The term was often used affectionately, but Carlos practically spit it out. "I thought I'd come and greet my long-lost sister."

"It's good to see you, Carlos," she said and kissed him on the cheek. He smelled of a strong cologne. She wished she could say that she'd thought of him often, but it wasn't true. She'd hardly given him a thought in years.

"You don't look too bad," he said. "Considering that you drove off a cliff. And wrecked a perfectly good car."

Still the same Carlos. She turned to the sports car. "This is impressive."

"It's British. A Triumph Spitfire."

The vehicle was handsome but had a few scrapes and dents. "Looks like it's seen some action," she said.

"That's what it was built for—action." He flicked away his cigarette and opened the passenger door. "Get in. We'll go for a drive."

Why not? she thought. Let Carlos show off his car while they talked.

She opened the passenger door and lowered herself into the seat as Carlos sauntered around to the other side and got in. "So, the old woman says you don't want the finca," he said. "Is that right?"

"Yes. My home is in the U.S. now."

"Good. Then you're going to turn over the finca to me."

"It's not that simple."

He snorted. "It is if you have any sense." He steered the car onto the street, nearly ramming an oncoming vehicle, then blasted his horn, although he was clearly at fault. They drove for several blocks, ending up in a sparsely populated neighborhood. Carlos pulled into a spot beside a long masonry wall. A weedy vacant lot was visible where rock had tumbled down. He turned off the ignition and stretched his arm across the top of her seat.

She shifted to face him. "Look, Carlos. I've talked with Mama. I know she's been looking after the estate. And doing pretty well, with the help of her manager."

"They're lovers, you know. They started before the old man was even dead. Have you seen them together? The old woman is like a bitch in heat. I stay away from the finca as much as possible."

She fumed silently. Not at the idea of her mother's affair. She was getting used to that. But at Carlos's coarseness, his lack of respect. She wanted to slap him. But she'd have to calm down, she realized, if she wanted to deal with her brother. "Yes, Mama said she didn't see you often."

"And did she tell you I'm going to challenge the old man's will in court?"

"Yes. But I'm here now, so that changes things."

He laughed shortly. "You'll hand over the finca to me. Either that, or I'll testify before a judge that the old man was senile. That's the only reason he would have left the finca to a daughter who ran away twenty-four years ago."

He was right, of course. She gazed around her, as if there were some kind of escape from this unpleasant conversation. A woman with wiry, gray hair and a black, shapeless dress was shuffling along on the other side of the street.

Carlos smirked. "So tell me, who do you think the judge will side with? The son and rightful heir, or the selfish absentee daughter? Oh, and I'll be sure to tell him that our mother was having an affair under her husband's nose. That should enhance her reputation."

Patricia stared at him. "You wouldn't."

"I will. I'll make it absolutely clear that I'm the only responsible heir. Not you. Not the old woman. Me."

"Carlos, be reasonable. If you tear down our parents' reputations, you tear down the whole family, yourself included."

"*Ay, hermanita*," he said. Little sister. "It's touching to see how concerned you are for your family, especially after deserting us all those years ago."

So that's how he saw her. A deserter. Was he right? Maybe if she'd stayed, things would have been a little easier for him. She might have interceded now and then with her father, although that would have required considerable skill, maybe more than she possessed. "Look, Carlos, I admit I haven't been a good sister to you."

"If you want to make things right," Carlos said, "sign over the finca to me. I'll forget about my lawsuit. No one will ever hear about our mother's affair or our father's senility."

"I'm not ready to do that," she said, trying to tamp down her anger.

"You're just as I remember you," he said. "Stubborn and foolish."

"Please take me back to the clinic."

"At your orders," he said in mock deference. He turned the ignition and the motor revved. A few minutes later they were in front of the clinic, and Patricia reached for the door handle.

"One more thing, *hermanita*," Carlos said. "The last time someone stood in my way, he ended up in a ditch with a bullet in his head."

"What? Are you threatening me?" The whole idea was absurd.

"I'm telling you how things are. The old man always said you were smart. Let's see if he was right."

She tried to think of some suitable rejoinder but could think of nothing. She got out of the car.

"You'll be hearing from me," Carlos said. "One way or another."

When Patricia walked into the clinic, the waiting room was nearly clear, with only a mother and child on the plastic chairs. Leti was sitting at the table at the far end of the room. She looked up from a stack of patients' folders as Patricia neared.

"Doctora, are you all right? You look pale."

"I'm fine," Patricia said. "I just need to sit for a minute." She went into the office, closed the door, and sank onto the chair behind the desk. She was trembling, but that subsided. Her despair didn't. How had Carlos become so twisted? What was wrong with her family? And why in God's name had she agreed to come back here?

She thought of Hank with his calm strength. She'd like to talk with him now, tell him all about Carlos and her mother. Not that he would understand. Her world was alien to him. She pictured him stretched out on a beach chair in his faded swim trunks. Or crashing through the waves, with his Viking enthusiasm. He was too far away to be of any real help to her.

Who else was there? It wasn't fair to burden Fiona with all her troubles. Then she thought of Arturo. He was the person she needed to talk with. He was savvy about politics, and he might have some insights into Carlos's strange behavior.

It was late now, a little after six. She called Arturo's office, but there was no answer. She found the home phone number that he had written on his card and dialed.

A maid answered the phone, and a moment later Arturo was on the line. "Patricia," he said warmly. "What a pleasure to hear from you."

"Who is it?" asked a woman in the background. Her voice was deep and a little sultry. The unfaithful wife, Carmen.

"Just a client," Arturo said. "I'll take this in my study."

Patricia heard his footsteps, then the opening and closing of a door. A phone line clicked on. "You can hang up now, Carmen," Arturo said, and the other line clicked off.

"There. That's better," Arturo said. "So, tell me, what's up in San Felipe?"

Patricia explained about working at the clinic and gave Arturo the phone number. "But there's something else I want to ask you about," she said and summarized her meeting with Carlos. "What do you think? Is my brother really as vicious as he wants me to believe?"

"Look. I made a few inquiries after I talked to you yesterday. Your brother is a member of one of the far-right political parties. He's in a militia, as you thought, and from what I've heard, the group has been connected to a kidnapping and a couple of murders."

"I was hoping he was bluffing." She twisted the phone cord around her finger. "So, you think Carlos is a murderer?" She could hardly believe she was asking the question.

"Maybe not directly. There's no reason he'd have to get his hands dirty. There are plenty of guys who are willing to kill people."

"That's not very comforting."

"Comfort is in short supply these days."

She took a deep breath. "Do you think my mother and I are in danger from Carlos?"

"I would say...probably not. The people in power usually look the other way when left-wing citizens are abducted or killed. But if someone in their own circle was harmed, well, that would be a different story. Your family is socially prominent and not even remotely left wing."

That was good to hear. Maybe her father's conservative credentials would be useful now. Violence against his widow wouldn't go down well with the other planters.

"What's more," Arturo said, "the situation is fluid here, and I suspect that Carlos is trying to work his way up in the power structure. He can't afford to look rash."

In the background, she heard a door open and the sultry voice. "Arturo, we're ready to eat."

"Start without me," he said. The door closed.

"I should let you go," Patricia said.

"Carmen can wait," Arturo said. "Right now, you are my first priority." Patricia had the distinct feeling it would suit him if his wife was kept waiting for a long time.

"If you're sure," she said. "There's something I've been meaning to ask you."

"Go ahead."

"What happened after the coup in '54? I mean, I know that the military took over. But what happened to the Arbenz supporters?"

"It's not a happy story. To begin with, the army arrested thousands of citizens. Some say tens of thousands. Many were killed."

Patricia gasped. She'd had no idea.

"Some people were lucky and managed to leave Guatemala— mostly people with money. The violence was actually worst in the countryside."

"What about the area around Finca Baldt?"

"I doubt if that area was immune. The army scoured the back country, killed or arrested anyone who they thought might oppose them."

"*Ay dios*," she murmured. She wondered if any of her father's workers were affected. Or people in the small towns in the area. "How long did it last?"

"Quite a while. By the 1960s, the opposition was broken, and things had quieted down, although there were still some guerrillas hiding out. Then, after the earthquake, everything started to heat up again. Not right away. In the first weeks after the earthquake, we had a feeling of unity, a sense that everyone was pulling together. But that didn't last. There was corruption and mismanagement everywhere."

Patricia thought of the medical supplies she'd shipped off. How many of them had made it to the people who needed them most?

He cleared his throat. "So, out of all the anger and frustration, the opposition has started to grow again. Naturally, the army feels threatened—not just by the guerrillas, but by anyone who might oppose them. From what I can see, the right-wing militias are running rampant."

"Can't the military bring them under control?"

He laughed ruefully. "If they wanted to. But the militias are useful to the people in power—the big landowners and right-wing business owners, the army. The paramilitary groups provide them with a convenient way to eliminate their enemies."

"I see," she said. She could imagine the advantages for her brother. Here was a perfect opportunity for him to indulge his fondness for violence. And maybe to gain the approval of powerful people.

"Sometimes the victims get lucky," Arturo said. "They are tipped off that they're on a death list, and they go into hiding."

"Death lists?" She moaned. Could things get any worse?

"I'm sorry to be the bearer of such bad news," Arturo said.

"No, it's all right," she said, pulling herself together. "I asked, after all. Thank you for explaining the situation. I needed to know. Now I'd better let you get back to your family."

They said good-bye, promising to keep in touch. After Patricia hung up, she sat back in the office chair. She could have found out all this information long ago, if she'd really wanted to. But it had been easier to close her eyes and cut herself off from her country's misery. Now it was her misery too—at least while she was here, which, she reminded herself, shouldn't be too much longer.

CHAPTER TWELVE

The next morning, Patricia's half-hour drive to Finca Baldt was pleasant, with cool, fresh air and views of wispy, low clouds lingering in the mountains. The trip brought back memories of returning from school at holidays, elated to be free. One year, a group of her cousins had come at Christmas, and they had enjoyed fireworks and danced to "Mr. Sandman" and "Sh-Boom," which they played on her prized record player.

She turned onto the gravel driveway leading to Finca Baldt, and the familiar line of Spanish cedars extended before her, offering cool shade. At the end lay the gated wall surrounding Finca Baldt. What would the place be like after all these years? Especially now, without her father's presence? A couple of minutes later, she parked the Land Cruiser and got out. The earthquake had left its signature, jagged lines dissecting the wall. The old gate had been replaced.

Inside, Patricia crossed the patio with its multi-colored tiles. A young Indian maid went to summon Eugenia. Patricia entered the parlor, surprised to find that the burgundy-colored drapes had been replaced by sheer, cream-colored ones. And in place of the heavy mahogany furniture were lighter pieces, including a chair and sofa upholstered with a pattern of tiny flowers against an off-white background. Her father would never have allowed such a feminine touch.

"Well? What do you think of my new decor?" her mother asked, appearing at the door.

"It's lovely, Mama."

Eugenia laid her hand lovingly on the sofa. "I think so too."

They sat and her mother explained the preparations she'd made for Patricia's visit. First, Patricia would talk to Otto's workers, who should arrive momentarily. Eugenia handed Patricia a list of the men who had gone to the fire at Los Ancianos. To the best of everyone's memories, there had been ten. Of those workers, two of the older fellows had died, and two more had left Finca Baldt, banished by her father for minor infractions. Patricia had already talked with Gustavo. That left five men.

"It's a waste of time," her mother said. "I told Meg as much. None of the workers saw J.J."

"I hope you didn't tell the men it was a waste of time."

"Of course I did. Why shouldn't I? It's the truth. But they didn't mind coming. I told them they'd be paid."

"Mama, didn't it occur to you that you might be biasing their answers?"

"You're the exalted doctor," she said. "I'm sure you'll know how to handle a bunch of simple men."

Great, Patricia thought. Well, it was her own fault for not giving her mother more detailed instructions.

"Let's see," her mother continued. "After you've talked to the men, you can drive over to the Tapia's finca and talk to Alma Tapia. She's expecting you. You should be back here in time for dinner around one. Joaquín will join us. Afterward, he'd like to discuss the finca with you. Finances mostly."

"Very well." Patricia didn't look forward to the financial discussion. It was difficult enough dealing with her clinic's money issues, without delving into the management of a coffee plantation. But if she was to make a decision about the future of the estate, she should be informed about its financial health.

When Patricia left the parlor, she found the workers already waiting in a corner of the courtyard. She greeted them, genuinely happy to see these men who had inhabited her childhood world. She asked a maid to bring coffee and cookies, and the fellows looked pleased.

Patricia conducted the interviews one by one in a corner of the dining room. The conversations went smoothly, beginning with inquiries into the health of the men's wives, children, and grandchildren. Then Patricia explained that Meg had heard that J.J. might be alive, information that was clearly not new to them. She urged the men to speak freely, explaining that no harm would come to them, no matter what they said. Meg's only wish was to find J.J., not to punish anyone.

The men's answers to her questions were virtually identical. They had ridden in the finca trucks to Los Ancianos. The house was already in flames. No one had escaped the house except for Meg. They saw and heard no sign of a child. What's more, none of them had seen the Indian who had reportedly started the fire and escaped. They thought it was one of the older, now deceased, workers who had spotted him, just as Gustavo had said.

Patricia tried to probe their memories, asking if they'd heard any unusual noises that night, seen anything odd, besides the fire. Or if they'd heard any rumors afterward about a child. But they all shook their heads. And none of them could think of anyone who would want to kidnap J.J.

She didn't ask the workers about their actions at Chayaka later. There was no point, since she could see no connection between burning down the Indian town and J.J.'s disappearance.

The last worker seemed to hesitate at the end of the interview, and Patricia suspected he might be harboring some information. But his thoughts were of the future. "Doctora, if you'll pardon my asking, the other workers and I, we would all like to know. What will happen to Finca Baldt now that Don Otto is gone?"

She wondered how much they'd heard from her mother or brother, what kinds of rumors were circulating. "I'm not sure who will inherit the finca," she said, "but I expect it to stay in the Baldt family. And I will do everything I can to see that you keep your jobs. This is your home, after all."

"Thank you, Doctora," he said, looking somewhat relieved. "I'll tell the others."

It was a half hour drive to Finca Tapia, where a maid ushered Patricia into a parlor with deep red curtains and heavy furniture. When Alma appeared, she was wrinkled and walked with a cane, and Patricia remembered that the Tapias were older than her own parents. Alma offered her condolences for Otto's death, and Patricia offered hers for Javier's death a few years earlier. While they drank coffee, Alma reported that the funeral of Patricia's father had been well attended, as would be expected for a man of his stature. Naturally, all of her children and grandchildren were there, she said. The message to Patricia was clear. She should have been at the funeral. She mumbled something about how sorry she was to be detained in the U.S.

After a little chat about everyone's health, Alma changed the subject. "I understand you have come to ask me about that poor child who died in the fire at Los Ancianos. I know nothing about him."

"Actually, I was interested in speaking with some of your workers, those who went to Los Ancianos the night of the fire."

Alma drew herself up, eyes sharp. "Are you implying that my husband's workers were involved in the boy's disappearance?"

"No, no, of course not. It's just...I'm asking everyone if they might have seen or heard anything that night. Anything unusual. Or maybe they heard some kind of rumor later, about a child turning up somewhere."

Alma clicked her tongue. "Really, Patricia, this is all nonsense, just as I told your mother. But if you insist, my son will have a word with the men tomorrow. If any of them remembers anything, I'll tell your mother. I'm sure she will pass on the information to you."

This sounded like a dead end. "That's very kind of you."

"Not at all." Alma's lips twisted into a haughty smile. "The Fuentes deserved what they got, you know. They were leftists who came to stir up trouble, even trying to give their valley to the Indians. It was too bad about the child, though."

Patricia hesitated. She didn't like to challenge the old woman, but Alma Tapia had gone too far. "Pablo Fuente was an archaeologist. He came to excavate. I should know, since I worked with him."

Alma's eyes narrowed. "If I were you, I wouldn't brag about associating with him. Or his wife either. She was a slut."

Patricia was fuming as she climbed into the Land Cruiser and headed back to Finca Baldt. She still remembered Javier's glee at the idea of burning down Indian homes. Now it seemed that his wife was nasty as well. A chill ran through her. Could the Tapias have somehow caused the fire at Los Ancianos? It was hard to imagine. She had known them since she was a child—gone to parties at their house, danced with their son. They were ordinary, rather dull people. Besides, there was a huge difference between being glad someone's house burned down and actually setting the fire yourself. But Alma's attack on Meg nagged at her.

By the time Patricia arrived back at Finca Baldt, her temper had cooled somewhat. She found her mother sitting in a shady spot in the patio, immersed in an interior design magazine.

"You're back," Eugenia said. "Did you find out anything?"

"Nothing helpful." Patricia pulled up a chair. "Mama, I have something to ask you. Alma Tapia accused Meg of being...unfaithful to Pablo. Did you ever hear of such a thing?"

Eugenia looked pensive. "There was gossip, I suppose."

"I never heard it."

"Oh, well, the rumors started after the fire. Something about a lover in the capital, or maybe San Felipe. Some socialist. I didn't pay much attention. Meg had always seemed mousy to me. Men tried to flirt with her now and then, but I never saw her respond. She didn't seem like the type to have an affair. But then, people can surprise you."

There was never a shortage of malicious gossip, Patricia decided. And either way, it was all in the distant past.

A little after one o'clock, Patricia sat down for dinner with her mother and Joaquín. The dining room was sunny, its double doors open to the courtyard. Patricia noted that her mother sat in her father's old place, at the head of the table. Behind her, the painting with the misty castle had been replaced by a colorful print by Paul Klee. Its colors were similar to those of the tiles in the courtyard.

The maid served arroz con pollo, one of Patricia's favorite dishes. The conversation soon turned to a photography exhibit that her mother and Joaquín had recently visited at the French cultural center in the capital. Patricia brought up Beatriz's upcoming show in San Felipe.

"Imagine," Eugenia said, "little embroidered scenes. How quaint. I'm glad someone appreciates them."

After they'd finished dinner and a maid had served coffee, Joaquín asked Patricia if she would like to talk about the finca's finances.

"Why not," she said, glad she had caffeine to keep her awake.

Joaquín picked up a small pile of folders from the end of the sideboard and brought them to the table. "I'll start with an overview of the last several years," he said. "As you may know, the price of coffee was low in the late 1960s and early 1970s. Even so, your father maintained good practices. He replaced coffee trees on a regular rotation and kept up the roads and other infrastructure."

"I hardly bought any new furnishings for years," Eugenia said. "Any profits went back to the finca."

Joaquín continued. "A few years ago the price of coffee began to rise. In 1975, it was seventy-one cents a pound. Then the year before the earthquake, it rose to over one quetzal. At the beginning of this year, it was over two quetzales."

"That's terrific," Patricia said.

"Yes," Eugenia said, "except that three years ago, your father's mental state began to seriously deteriorate. He holed up in his office concocting stories about all the people who were plotting against him, including Carlos and me."

"You can see evidence of this change in the financial records," Joaquín said. "After years of careful record keeping, his notes became haphazard. Finally, he stopped writing down almost anything relating to the finca."

Eugenia shook her head. "Then two years ago, the earthquake struck. Your father rallied, at least enough to deal with some of the damage and keep the plantation going. But it wasn't easy." Her eyes narrowed. "He blamed me for everything that went wrong. You would have thought I had caused the earthquake."

Patricia glanced at Joaquín, who was watching her mother with an air of concern.

"Then," Eugenia said, "just as the plantation was getting back to normal, your father had a massive stroke. He was bedridden, unable to talk intelligibly. The doctors didn't give him long to live—days or a few weeks at most, they said. That's when I wrote to you. Not that you responded."

"I'm sorry, Mama. I didn't realize things were so difficult here."

"How could you?" Eugenia snapped. "Hidden away in that miserable little town in the U.S."

Patricia said nothing. She knew from experience, it was best to let her mother's anger flow and then dissipate.

Eugenia took a sip of coffee and resumed. "The doctors were mistaken. The weeks turned into months, and your father refused either to die or to get better. And your brother, who should have been helping me, started making demands for money. Did you see his car? That wasn't cheap. And do you think he worked a minute to earn it? Then there was that awful building he erected at Los Ancianos. That's when I asked Joaquín to come and work for us. I was desperate."

"I understand. What about Los Ancianos? Who acquired it?"

"Your father, of course," Eugenia said. "It should have been ours anyway. Your father was going to buy it years ago, before Pablo Fuente showed up."

"Wasn't Pablo the rightful heir?"

Eugenia waved her hand dismissively. "Who knows? Anyway, your brother has taken over the property."

"Has he built a house there?"

"More like a bunker, made of concrete blocks. It looks hideous, at least from the outside. I haven't been invited inside, so I can't tell you how he's furnished it. Dreadfully, I'm sure. He built it on the site of the Fuentes' house."

Patricia pictured the house at Los Ancianos. It had been antiquated even before the Fuentes arrived. She'd heard Meg express her dissatisfaction with it more than once. Still, it was her friends' home. She hated to think of a concrete bunker in its place.

"Would you like to see the place?" Joaquín asked. "We could walk over there, see a little more of the plantation on our way."

"Your father built a connecting road," Eugenia said. "It's only a few minutes away."

Visit Los Ancianos? Patricia froze. It was the site of her nightmares. But it was also part of the estate that she had inherited, even if Carlos thought it was his. She took a deep breath to steady herself. "Yes, that's a good idea."

They all set out along the gravel road, which turned out to be wide enough for three people to walk abreast. It was surrounded by coffee plantation on both sides. Joaquín pointed out the newly-pruned trees that shaded the shiny green leaves of the coffee plants.

Patricia steeled herself as they approached the site of the house. But no trace of the Fuentes remained, nothing to bring up memories. The concrete building was low and windowless, every bit as ugly as her mother had suggested. A double door was secured with a large dead bolt lock. If World War III arrived, her brother would be ready.

There was no sign of Carlos's sports car. "It appears that we won't get a tour today," Eugenia said. "I can't say I'm disappointed."

Joaquín turned to Patricia. "While you're here, you should take a look at the valley."

They walked across a weedy lawn to the steps that descended into the valley. Patricia drew in her breath. An orchard spread out below her.

"Apple trees," Joaquín said. "Your father planted them. The apples are small and rather mealy, not good enough for export, but they can be sold locally."

"We had cider for a few years," Eugenia said. "And the cook learned to make apple strudel. Your father loved that. It reminded him of his childhood."

Patricia gazed at the rows of trees extending halfway across the valley. Just beyond them, a wooden structure with a corrugated metal roof was visible. Her heart skipped a beat. Pablo's tool shed. Beyond it, the dig was just a low plot of land overgrown with scrub. For some reason, her father must have chosen to leave the dig site uncultivated.

She thought of Pablo with his rakish beard, pacing the rim of the dig and of Demetrio with his blue Chicago Cubs cap. And of the other men, scraping away at the earth, uncovering a long-vanished town. Everything they had discovered was buried now. She had seen enough of the world to know that dreams often ended in failure, but the destruction of the dig still stung.

"Everything has changed," Patricia said. "Only the river and the mountains remain as they were." As they retraced their steps to Finca Baldt, Patricia addressed Joaquín. "I imagine you've made some changes since you took over management of Finca Baldt."

"Some. I've reinstated your father's sound business practices as much as possible. Although I have to say that your brother has been strongly opposed to any restrictions on his ability to draw money."

"I'm sure." And Patricia had no difficulty imagining her mother caving in to her demanding son.

"I've also suggested to your mother that she consider some limited diversification. Continue to plant coffee but expand to other export crops. Possibly invest in processing whatever the finca produces. That way, if coffee prices are low, or there's fungus or some other blight, the finca will still generate a steady profit."

"That sounds reasonable."

"I knew you'd come around," Eugenia said. "Now you understand why you need to sign over the estate to me."

They were nearing the house. "We can't cut Carlos out completely," Patricia said.

"It's what he deserves," Eugenia said. "Have you heard the way he talks about me?" Her face was flushed, and Patricia could see she was ready to start a rant.

"Eugenia," Joaquín said softly. The two exchanged a look, and she calmed down.

"We see no perfect solution," he said. "One option would be to give your brother a periodic payment consisting of some percentage of the profits."

"You think he'll be satisfied with that?" Patricia asked. It fell far short of what Carlos had in mind. Total control.

"It isn't for me to say," Joaquín said. "I'm just trying to focus on measures that would allow the finca to remain viable on a long-term basis."

Measures that would benefit Eugenia, who was his employer and very possibly his lover. But Patricia admitted that Joaquín's recommendations made sense.

They walked around the wall and into the courtyard. Joaquín excused himself and headed for her father's office. His office now, Patricia reminded herself. She and her mother ended up in the parlor, where they relaxed on Eugenia's comfortable new furniture. It was fortunate that coffee was selling high. Carlos wasn't the only one spending money.

"Sign the finca over to me," Eugenia said. "Do it now, before Carlos goes to court."

Patricia sighed. It was the best option. The plantation would be in good hands, and with a little luck, her mother would have a pleasant old age. But was it really wise? "Mama, even if I hand over the finca to you, you're still going to have a problem with Carlos. I'm afraid of what he might do if he doesn't get the place."

Eugenia narrowed her eyes. "He has threatened me. You can be sure of that. But I won't have my son controlling my life. I have a pistol, you know. I keep it by my bed. It's small, but I'm an expert shot. And besides, I won't be alone. Joaquín will be here to provide support."

"All right," Patricia said. "I'll sign over Finca Baldt to you." It wasn't as if she had a good alternative.

Eugenia beamed. "I'll call the attorney. We can drive to the capital tomorrow."

"It's only fair that I tell Carlos first," Patricia said. It was best that she get it over with.

"If you must. He's staying at our house in the capital."

A moment later, they were in the parlor, and Eugenia was dialing the number. She greeted Carlos, then passed the phone to Patricia.

"*Hermanita*, what can I do for you?" Carlos asked. In the background, a couple of men were talking, and Carlos hushed them.

"Look, Carlos, I've called to tell you that I've made a decision. I'm giving the Finca to Mama. But you'll receive—"

"Tell the old woman she'll be sorry. And so will you." Patricia jumped as Carlos slammed down the receiver at his end. She listened to the dial tone for a second before hanging up.

Eugenia was standing beside her, hands clenched. "I heard," she said.

"We may have made a mistake."

Several minutes later, Patricia was walking to the Land Cruiser with her mother. Eugenia's good humor had returned after she talked to her attorney in the capital. He could see them at four o'clock the next day, when he would have the legal papers ready for Patricia to sign. By tomorrow afternoon, Finca Baldt would belong to her mother.

"I'll pick you up tomorrow at one," her mother said. "It will be a delightful outing, just the two of us."

Patricia decided she shouldn't simply dismiss her mother's optimistic words. Eugenia seemed open to rebuilding their relationship. And perhaps there was reason for hope. Her mother had defended Meg against Alma's accusation, or at least she hadn't condemned Meg. And plenty of parents and children restructured their roles in later years.

Relief washed over Patricia as she climbed into the Land Cruiser—relief that her first visit to Finca Baldt in twenty-four years had gone reasonably well. But as she drove toward San Felipe and the clinic, even the sunny blue sky and cool breeze couldn't entirely dispel the dark mood left by Carlos. And Alma Tapia's hostility toward the Fuentes had surprised her. Anger still smoldered over events that had occurred decades earlier. She remembered her father's fury and sense of betrayal when he found out Pablo was giving away the valley of Los Ancianos. Some emotions died hard.

CHAPTER THIRTEEN

The clinic waiting room was half full when Patricia hurried through about 2:30. She was glad to be there after her challenging trip to Finca Baldt. As usual, when her life felt out of control, it helped to focus on work.

At four o'clock, Patricia took a break between patients and went to the office to call Meg. "I'm afraid I don't have much to report," she said once she got Meg on the phone. She summarized her conversations with Beatriz, Gustavo, her father's workers, and Alma Tapia, leaving out the unsavory bits. "They were all dead ends, I'm afraid."

"Oh well," Meg said, "I was hoping, of course, but I can't say I'm really surprised. So tell me, what about your inheritance? Have you settled that?"

"I'm giving the finca to Mama."

"And your brother? Is he satisfied with your decision?"

"Not at all. But I know that Mama will take better care of the place."

They signed off after Patricia promised to call as soon as she heard anything of interest.

At six o'clock, as Patricia's last patient of the day left, Leti appeared at the door of the examining room. "You have a visitor," she said with a mischievous smile. "My Uncle Sergio. He says he knows you from years ago."

The man who walked in looked vaguely familiar. He was an attractive guy in his mid-forties, with light brown hair and wire rim glasses that magnified his hazel eyes. He was dressed in jeans, with a tan blazer over a white shirt.

Her attention was drawn to his left cheekbone. It had clearly been broken, leaving a concave space underneath. The outer edge of his eye tilted slightly downward. It gave his face an asymmetrical look, not so different from her own, although more pronounced.

"I'm Sergio Velasco," he said. "I don't know if you remember me."

As they shook hands, recognition swept over her. "Of course," she said. "What a pleasure to see you. Please sit. Didn't we once watch a procession together during Holy Week?"

"At my aunt's house, yes," he said, lowering himself onto the molded plastic chair. "As I recall, we walked to the park together."

"I remember. And later, you came to the hospital to visit Meg. You and Ernesto Guevara."

"That's right."

"Did Leti tell you I was here?" she asked.

"She has told everybody. You're sort of a celebrity, you know."

"Ah yes. The girl who drove off a cliff."

He smiled. "And lived to tell the story. That's the important part. In fact, if I may say so, you look great."

"Thanks. I had a good plastic surgeon." Her facial scars were faintly visible but not disfiguring. It could have been much worse. She touched her cheek at the spot corresponding to the place where his own face appeared fractured. "You look like you had a run-in."

He pointed to the concave spot. "This? It's from an interrogation with a lead pipe."

She winced. "After the coup?"

He nodded. "While I was in prison."

"We wondered what had happened to you. Meg's father tried to get information, but he was never successful."

"The Guatemalan army doesn't excel at record keeping. Are you still in touch with Meg?" Patricia said she was, and he pulled out an envelope from inside his blazer and placed it on the desk. "I thought you might be, so I wrote her a letter. It's nothing exciting. I thought she would want to know what had happened to some of the PROC members she knew. You can read it if you like."

"I'll make sure she gets it," Patricia said. So, it was PROC that Meg had hung out with. She'd never named them specifically.

"How is Meg?" Sergio asked, and Patricia explained that she was married with two daughters.

"Her husband is a labor organizer," she said. "He works for a union."

"So," he said, "she married a rabble-rouser. Good for her."

Patricia remembered now that Sergio had once been a political organizer. "If I'm not mistaken, you were a troublemaker once yourself."

"Yes, but no more. And you? My niece says you're here on some kind of mysterious business. Does it concern your father? I know he passed away not long ago. I'm sorry."

"We weren't close."

He cocked his head. "Come to think of it...didn't you try to shoot your father once?"

"What? Who told you that?"

"Ernesto."

"Of course," she said with a wry smile. "I'd completely forgotten." She pictured her younger self standing in the bell tower high above the capital city, Ernesto Guevara at her side. She had pointed her imaginary gun at her imaginary father. Pulled the trigger. Several times. "I think it was Ernesto's idea of emotional therapy.

But no, I'm not here about my father. At least, that's not the main reason." She explained about the letter Meg had received.

"J.J. was a sweet little boy," Sergio said. "I was sad when I learned that he had died in the fire. You think he might truly be alive?"

"Personally, I doubt it, but as long as there's a chance, I have to keep looking." She hesitated. Sergio was an old friend of Meg's and a guy who would know his way around San Felipe. "I've been interviewing people, but I've just about run out of leads. Actually, I could use some help."

"What kind of help?"

"I'm not sure exactly. Maybe someone who could accompany me to places where young men congregate. See if anyone looks like he could be an adult version of J.J."

"You think you'll recognize him?"

"Maybe not, but I don't know what else to do. And I'd rather not walk into bars by myself. I don't want people to think I'm on the prowl."

Sergio's brow furrowed. "Let's see. You want me to help you search for a boy who probably died twenty-four years ago. In a town of twenty-two thousand people."

"That's about it."

He shrugged. "Sure. Why not. I've always been a supporter of lost causes. When do we start?"

"How about after we close up here?"

Leti said good evening with a knowing smile as Patricia and Sergio left together a few minutes later. It was six o'clock, time for a bite to eat, so Sergio guided them to a large, well-lit café a few blocks away. The place looked clean, although the Formica tables showed signs of hard use. Most of the tables were occupied, including a few where young men talked, laughed, and drank bottles of Gallo, the beer that Patricia remembered from her youth.

While they waited for ham and avocado sandwiches, Patricia peered over her glass of Sprite at the guys at the next table. They looked like tradesmen winding down after a long day.

"See any likely prospects?" Sergio asked.

"Well, there is one possibility. The fellow in the black jacket." The guy was probably late twenties, around the age that J.J. would be. He was attractive, with brown hair and a golden tan, and his laugh was good-hearted, like Pablo's had been. She felt no intuitive spark for this man, but then she couldn't count on getting one.

Sergio took a quick glance. "I know his family. His mother is from San Felipe, but his father immigrated here from northern Spain, the Basque country, I think. The father is light-skinned, almost blond."

"So the guy isn't J.J."

"Sorry. When my mother was alive, she kept track of all the old families around San Felipe. And now my sisters do. They gossip about everybody. If there was anything strange about the family, I'd know. Or could find out. But I don't see much point to delving into his history."

The food arrived, and they both started eating. It was pleasant sitting here, having a sandwich with Sergio, and for a moment she imagined she was just joining an old friend for a meal, not on a mission to appraise strange young men.

"I'd forgotten you were a teacher," she said. "English, right?"

"In a past life. Now I work for my older brother, Leti's father. He manufactures molded plastic stuff—buckets, chairs like the ones at the clinic. We gave the place a good price on those chairs."

"She's a good worker. And friendly."

"I'll tell her you said so."

Patricia took a swallow of her soda. As usual, she'd asked for no ice, not trusting the water. "Have you ever heard from Ernesto?"

"The year after the coup. He wrote from Mexico. He'd married Hilda, his Peruvian lover, and they were expecting a child. But I didn't write back. I was drinking pretty heavily then, and I didn't have anything good to say. Did he write to you?"

"No. We didn't exchange addresses. And anyway, he saw me as bourgeois. But we had a long conversation once, and he encouraged me to become a doctor. A revolutionary doctor maybe. Sometimes people ask me how I decided to become a physician. I used to tell them that Che Guevara talked me into it. But no one ever believed me."

Sergio arched a brow. "And have you? Become a revolutionary doctor?"

"Not really. There isn't much call for it where I live. Iowa has a kind of socialized medicine, although we don't dare call it that. But the poor have access to decent medical care." She took a last bite of her sandwich. "So, I never became a revolutionary doctor, but then neither did Ernesto. Maybe he should have."

Sergio nodded. "That would have been better than getting gunned down by Bolivian soldiers." He gave her a long look. "You know, there are plenty of opportunities for doctors here—revolutionary or not."

"No doubt. But I have a good life in the States. My patients need me."

Sergio paid for their meal, over Patricia's protest. Then they walked to a smoky bar a couple of streets down. They ordered beer, and Patricia nursed hers while people came and left. None of the men at the tables or at the bar leaped out at her as a possible J.J. When she started yawning, Sergio offered to walk her home.

They ambled up Oriente Street, the sidewalk dimly lit by street lamps, past shops that were closed for the night. A cool breeze came and went, lifting her bobbed hair. She still couldn't get over the miracle of balmy weather in February. "Do you mind if I ask about what happened to you after the coup?"

"There isn't a lot to tell. The Army arrested everyone with any ties to the left. Lots of my friends disappeared—members of PROC, other organizers. The week after Arbenz resigned, soldiers came to the house where I was staying. It was the middle of the night, and they dragged me out."

"How long were you in prison?"

"Three months. Ten of us were jammed into a filthy little cell. Then one day, one of the guards came and told me I was free to go. My older brother picked me up. When I got home, I discovered that my mother had died of a heart attack shortly after I was taken."

"Oh no."

"My brothers and sisters still blame me for her death."

"I hope you don't blame yourself," she said.

"Maybe a little. I used to, anyway. I've given up politics, but the government still keeps an eye on me. I'm even forbidden from owning a radio, if you can believe that." They turned onto a side street. "How about you?" he asked. "How did you end up in the States?"

She explained about the plastic surgery, then staying in the U.S. for college and medical school and eventually going to New Bergen.

"You never thought about coming back?"

"Too many bad memories here," she said. "And I guess I got comfortable. I have my own clinic and a group of friends. Besides, New Bergen isn't bad—for a small town in the middle of nowhere. Kind of like San Felipe, in that sense."

"A group of friends," he said. "Anyone in particular?"

"Like a boyfriend? Actually, yes." She thought of Hank and smiled.

"Ah. He must be good."

"He is. But unfortunately, he wants to get married, and I don't." She must be a little tipsy, she thought, spilling the intimate details of her life to this guy she hardly knew. As if to confirm it, the heel of her sandal caught in a crack in the sidewalk, and she pitched forward. Sergio caught her arm and steadied her.

"Thanks," she said. They resumed walking, but she kept her eyes on the sidewalk. "How about you? Did you marry?" He wore no wedding ring, but then some married men didn't.

"No wife. But I do have a sixteen-year-old daughter, Lucinda. Her mother thought we should get married years ago when she got pregnant. But it would never have worked. I was a mess in those days. Too much drinking, too much bitterness. I guess she thought she could reform me, but that was a lost cause. She ended up marrying someone else a few years later, a former classmate of my sister's. He's a pretty good stepfather, from what I can see."

"Do you see much of your daughter?"

"Now and then. Mostly when she wants money. I spent a lot on her fifteenth birthday party. That made her happy. I don't blame Lucinda, you know? Kids are ingrates. Real gratitude comes later."

They arrived at the gate to El Patio, and she dug her key out of her purse. "Thanks for going with me. I'm afraid we weren't very successful."

"It's just a start. Do you want to try again?"

"Sure," she said. It was probably useless looking for J.J. this way. She really had no idea what he would look like or sound like. But she liked being with Sergio, and there was always a chance they would uncover some lead to Meg's son. "But I'm not sure when I'll be free. I'm going to the city with my mother tomorrow to visit her attorney. Then Friday night is Beatriz's opening at the Cultural Center. I was thinking about going to that."

"Would you like an escort?"

She smiled. "I'd love one." They arranged to meet at El Patio at seven on Friday evening. He kissed her on the cheek, and she opened the gate, then hesitated, turning back to Sergio. "You said gratitude came with age. Are you grateful now?"

He flashed her a lopsided grin. "Some days I am."

CHAPTER FOURTEEN

Patricia walked with Fiona to the clinic the next morning. Actually, raced was more like it. For a small person, Fiona had a rapid stride, and she never ran short of breath. For Patricia, it was pleasant listening to Fiona's lively chatter about patients and the marimba lesson she was going to that evening.

At the clinic, Leti arrived late and seemed preoccupied. At one point in the morning, she handed Patricia the wrong patient folder. "Oh, sorry," she said.

"Is anything wrong?" Patricia asked.

"Just some family stuff. Nothing important," Leti said, handing Patricia the correct file.

Arturo called while Patricia was with a patient, and she returned the call at break time.

"I've received two letters in response to the newspaper ad," he said, "but neither seems like a good prospect." He had compared the responses to the original letter, and the new letters bore no resemblance to the original one. One letter was handwritten, with a few spelling errors. The other was typed, but the characters were uniform, with no flying capital letters.

"Did they say anything about J.J. or his whereabouts?"

"Neither refers to Juan José by name or identifies him any other way. Both writers have post office boxes in Guatemala City."

"Treasure hunters, I suppose."

"Exactly," Arturo said. "I'll write back to them and ask for a meeting, but I'm not optimistic."

"This is so frustrating," Patricia grumbled. "Why doesn't our 'friend' show himself? I'm tired of being in limbo." She needed to get back to New Bergen. To her patients and to Hank, who would be returning from Barbados soon. "By the way," she said, "I'm going to sign the finca over to Mama."

"Good idea. I'm sure she's more trustworthy than your brother. But I hope she knows she may still be in for a fight."

"I'll pass on the message." They talked for a minute about Arturo's daughter, who had won a school prize for an essay, before they hung up.

By one o'clock, Fiona, Leti, and the remaining patients had left for lunch, leaving Patricia to nibble on a bag of plantain chips while she waited for her mother. She hoped the visit with the attorney would be quick and uneventful.

Eugenia arrived, wearing the stylish gray dress she'd worn to the airport, her face shaded by sunglasses. But instead of breezing in, she immediately sank into a waiting room chair.

"Mama, are you all right?" Patricia asked, sitting beside her.

"He's gone," Eugenia said in a shaky voice. "Joaquín has left. He's gone to stay with his son in the States."

"What happened?"

Eugenia removed her glasses, revealing red, puffy eyes. "He received an anonymous phone call. Some man told him he was on a death list. If he stayed, he would be killed."

"Oh no." Patricia thought back to her earlier conversation with

Arturo. He had been fairly certain that Carlos wouldn't attack her or her mother. She'd been so relieved, she hadn't thought about what kind of collateral damage her brother might inflict.

Her mother's face dissolved into misery. "Just once," she wailed, "just once I thought I might have a little happiness. After all those years with your father." She mopped her eyes with a lace-trimmed handkerchief and glared at Patricia. "Do you have any idea what it was like living with him? Especially the last years. He blamed everything on me. Every business setback. Every problem with Carlos or the servants. It was all my fault. As if I were conspiring against him. He made my life hell."

"I'm sorry, Mama." She was. Her mother had clearly borne the brunt of her father's mental problems.

Her mother held out her hand, palm down. "Look. See the wrinkles? And that brown spot? I have the skin of an old lady. Who knows how many attractive years I have left. I wanted a little love, a little sweetness in my life. Was that too much to ask?" She dabbed at her eyes.

Patricia gazed at her mother, unsure of what to do. She had never seen her so teary and out of control. If this were a friend in distress, Patricia would have hugged her. But she and her mother had never shared much physical affection. "We'll figure out something."

But what? Could her mother manage the finca on her own? Had she learned enough from Joaquín? And what sort of retaliation would Carlos take if she tried to run Finca Baldt? His father had burned down an Indian town. What might the son do? A situation that had been precarious now looked close to hopeless.

"You know, Mama, maybe we should wait and see the attorney tomorrow or the next day. After we've had a chance to think about what this will mean."

Her mother's shoulders sagged. "I suppose you're right."

Patricia went into the office and called the attorney's office, canceling their appointment. When she came back to the waiting room, her mother was looking more composed, her lipstick reapplied.

"Have you had lunch?" Patricia asked.

"No. I couldn't eat. I was too upset."

Patricia suggested that they go to the restaurant at the Bella Vista Hotel, and her mother conceded that a bowl of *sopa de mariscos* didn't sound bad. And maybe a cocktail.

Eugenia drove them across town in her Buick LeSabre, although Patricia had offered to drive. "I'm upset, but I'm not an invalid," Eugenia said.

The Bella Vista Hotel was posh by San Felipe standards, with an airy reception area staffed by attractive employees in business attire. Eugenia led the way through a side door, which opened into the restaurant. The place was cheerful and airy, with watercolors of volcanic mountains, lakes, and colonial cities decorating the walls. The seafood soup, served on china, was tasty. As they were finishing their meal, a couple of well-dressed, middle-aged fellows stopped at their table. They told Eugenia how lovely she was looking and said how glad they were that she was out in public again. Eugenia introduced Patricia to the businessmen, referring to her as "my daughter, the physician."

"I hope we will be seeing more of you both," said the older of the pair, a man with a trim mustache and liquid brown eyes. After that, Eugenia visibly perked up.

Patricia decided that she might as well work at the clinic that afternoon if she wasn't going to the capital to visit the lawyer. As Eugenia drove them back to the clinic, Patricia noticed that her mother looked downcast once more. They stopped in front of the building, where Patricia turned to her mother.

"Mama, did Joaquín say anything about your joining him in the States?"

"No."

"Maybe once he's settled..."

Eugenia shot her a disdainful look. "We both know that I am no longer part of his life."

Patricia said nothing. At least her mother was being realistic.

"Under the circumstances," Patricia said, "maybe it would be best if Carlos took the finca. He might ruin it, but at least he would no longer be a threat to you."

"No!" Eugenia banged on the steering wheel. The horn blared, causing a man walking along the sidewalk to jerk and almost trip. "No," Eugenia repeated sullenly.

"Look, Mama, maybe you could find an apartment near Claudia. You always enjoy being with your sister."

Her mother glowered. "Oh, I can just see it. I would be the poor widow whose children abandoned her. And I couldn't depend on Carlos for an income. Not the way he goes through money."

Patricia took a deep breath. "You are welcome to come and live with me in New Bergen." Had she really said that? It could mean spending the rest of her life with her embittered mother. What would Hank say? Well, they would just have to make the best of it.

Her mother shook her head, her eyes fierce. "In that appalling little town? What would I do all day? Dust the furniture? No, thank you. I'll find a new manager. I'm keeping the finca."

"If that's what you want. We can talk again tomorrow." Her mother might feel differently after a night's sleep. Patricia reached for the door handle.

"I think I'll come in too," Eugenia said. "I've been wondering what the clinic is like."

"Sure. You're welcome to look around, but I'll be busy. I'm afraid I won't be able to spend time with you."

"I wouldn't expect you to," Eugenia said.

Patricia introduced her mother to Leti, who brought a chair over so that Eugenia could sit beside her. After that, Patricia washed up, then examined a five-year-old boy whose face and hands were covered with sores, one of several cases of impetigo that she'd treated at the clinic. Next came a young man with a machete wound on his leg that had become infected. He sat stoically as she cleaned the wound, dressed it, and prescribed a course of antibiotics, explaining that he must finish every last pill. He left limping but looking more upbeat than when he arrived.

When Patricia opened the door to signal she was ready for the next patient, her mother appeared, file folder in hand. "Señora Fernandez is here to see you," she said, handing over the file. "Eye infection."

"Mama, what are you—"

"Leti had to leave," her mother said and ushered in a small wiry woman in a faded dress, who appeared a little unnerved at being attended by this well-dressed lady.

By four-thirty, when Fiona and Patricia stopped for coffee and crackers, Leti had still not returned and Eugenia had taken charge. "Leti's brother came for her," Eugenia explained. "Some kind of family emergency."

They closed up the clinic a little after six. "You saved the day," Fiona said to Eugenia.

"I was happy to help," Eugenia said. "I'm not as useless as my daughter thinks I am."

Patricia accompanied her mother to the spot where Eugenia had parked her car.

"You were terrific," Patricia said. In fact, she was amazed, not just that her mother had helped out, but at the respectful way that she had treated the patients, even the shabbiest ones. "You handled all the patients very well."

"They seemed like good people," she said. "And poor things, they needed a little comfort. I know how that feels. Besides," she said, straightening up to her full height of five foot two, "I can be professional if I need to be."

"I'm proud of you, Mama," Patricia said. For the first time since she'd come home, she had a sliver of hope for her family. "I'll call you tomorrow. We can talk about the finca then."

Her mother remained planted on the spot. "I don't want to spend the night alone. Now that Joaquín is gone, the house will feel too sad."

Patricia hesitated. The thought of driving up to Finca Baldt and spending the night in her old room was unappealing. "Stay with me here, if you like," she said. "My bed is a double."

"Maybe I will," Eugenia said. "I brought an overnight bag, just in case."

Patricia suggested they have sandwiches at the café where she had eaten with Sergio, and her mother agreed. But Sergio wasn't there, and he didn't come in later, although Patricia kept watching for him. It would have been pleasant to see him, even just to say hello.

The light was fading by the time Patricia got into her mother's car and directed her to El Patio. Eugenia parked next to Patricia's Land Cruiser.

Lights were on in three of the cottages, giving the tiny neighborhood a homey glow. The faint sound of marimba music emanated from Fiona's apartment. One of her cassette tapes probably.

They entered Patricia's cottage, and Eugenia scanned the place. "Well, it's adequate," she said. Her mother had arrived with half

145

a bottle of brandy, and Patricia poured some into juice glasses. She handed one to her mother, who had seated herself at one end of the rustic sofa, her gray pumps dropped on the floor. Patricia pulled off her sandals and sat beside her. She was tired, but the time had come for some honest talk.

"Tell me about Papa," Patricia said. "When did he first start acting crazy?"

Her mother swirled the brandy around the glass, then took a sip. "Your father? Who can say? He was always jealous. When we were courting, he became enraged if any man looked at me. I was flattered. What did I know? I was only sixteen."

Patricia remembered a photo from her parents' wedding. A girl in a white satin dress held a bouquet of flowers, her innocent face alight. What a young bride her mother had been.

Eugenia's voice softened. "Oh, but Otto was so terribly handsome. And a good dancer too. He was ten years older than I was, but that was fine with me. I suppose I wanted a husband who would protect me. Mama didn't care for him, but Papa wanted the match. Otto's parents had a large coffee finca in Alta Verapaz and banking connections in Europe."

"So you got married."

"Yes, and everything was all right at first. You were born, and we had good coffee harvests. I started remodeling the house. You should have seen it when we moved in. What a horror. Rotting beams. No electricity—"

"And Papa? When did he start acting strange?"

Eugenia stared at her brandy. "I'd say it was later, when the war in Europe started. Guatemala sided with the Allies, you know, but a lot of German families maintained their German citizenship, even if they were born here. Otto's parents did, and they were declared enemy aliens. It was very sad. The government took away their property—all that good, coffee-producing land—and they were deported to a prison camp in Texas. Thank God Otto had renounced his German citizenship earlier. My father had insisted."

Patricia had no real memory of her grandparents on her father's side, only an image of them from a sepia wedding photo that her father had kept on his bureau. A handsome young man wearing a dark suit with a stiff white collar sat ramrod straight. Behind him stood a young woman in a full-length white dress with puffy sleeves and a tiny waist. Perched on her head was a wide-brimmed hat tilted at an angle and set off by a long feather. As a child, Patricia had always admired that hat. Both young people had light hair and eyes that stared out at the world somberly.

"What happened to them?" Patricia asked. "I don't remember their coming back."

"That's because they didn't. We got a letter from some American bureaucrat at the camp. Otto's father had died of a heart attack."

"And my grandmother?"

"She passed away too, but it was later. When the war ended, she insisted on going to Germany to look for her family members who were still there. I think there might also have been some art objects she wanted to track down. She had always claimed that her family was wealthy. Otto tried to dissuade her from going, but she was stubborn. Later, we received a letter from some cousin saying that your grandmother had died of pneumonia."

Her poor father, losing both parents and any claim to their property. "I don't remember any of this."

"We decided not to tell you and Carlos. You were too young to understand, and it was all quite upsetting."

Eugenia paused, apparently in thought. "Looking back, I think something must have broken in Otto when his parents were deported. He started warning me that we must be vigilant. He was convinced that everybody wanted to steal our property. It frightened me, thinking we were surrounded by enemies, but after a while, I stopped taking his predictions so seriously.

"Then several years later, that socialist Arbenz became President. It was as if your father had been right all along. People did want to take away our land. Otto was enraged. Well, we were all convinced that Arbenz was the devil incarnate. You remember."

Patricia remembered the hysteria, all right. But not everyone had seen Arbenz as the devil. Not Sergio, who had been imprisoned for supporting the President. Or Ernesto, who had been willing to take to the hills to defend Arbenz, even though he himself was Argentinian and had no stake in the struggle.

Her mother sipped her brandy. "Then a few years ago Otto's mind seemed to deteriorate. That's when he accused me of infidelity. And declared that Carlos was a bastard. I kept your father's condition as quiet as I could. For years, I never invited anyone to the house. I was too embarrassed."

Patricia looked out the window to the courtyard with the potted bougainvilleas. It seemed that the situation at Finca Baldt had gone from bad to worse. "It's horrible that Papa turned on you and Carlos. But it still seems strange that he left me the finca."

"It is odd. I suppose if you'd been around, he might have concocted stories about you too. But you were far away. At some point, he started talking about how you would return, and then everything would be all right. I let him rave on. It was the least of his delusions. Of course, he didn't mention he was leaving you his entire estate."

"I wish he hadn't," she said. "Oh, Mama, what are we going to do about Finca Baldt? I don't see any good means to protect it."

"We will find a way," Eugenia said resolutely, and Patricia reminded herself that her mother had always been good in a crisis.

CHAPTER FIFTEEN

Patricia awoke at six-thirty and slipped out of bed, trying not to awaken her slumbering mother. It wasn't until Patricia had fried a couple of eggs, made toast from her loaf of white bread, and heated water for instant coffee that Eugenia emerged from the bedroom.

Her mother ate without complaint, which must have required an effort. She offered to help out at the clinic again, but they both decided that it would be wise for her to go home and demonstrate to everyone that she was in charge of Finca Baldt.

Patricia saw her mother off in the Buick, reminding her to call if anything came up and fervently hoping that nothing would. Then she strode down the street, heading for the clinic.

It was Friday. This was her sixth day in Guatemala, and she was no closer to finding J.J. than when she arrived, unless she wanted to consider an elimination of possible leads to be progress. At any rate, she didn't see any way she could fly home to the States on Sunday. She would need to call Anita at the clinic in New Bergen.

Leti was already at work when Patricia arrived a few minutes later. The girl apologized profusely for running off the day before.

She'd had a family emergency—something about a missing nephew who finally showed up. "I only left because your mother offered to look after the patients," Leti explained. Patricia reassured the girl that Eugenia had successfully ushered patients around. The paper work could be another story.

A minute later, Patricia was in the office, phoning the clinic in New Bergen. Anita answered and reported that everything was going smoothly there.

"I need to spend another week in Guatemala," Patricia said. "Let me speak with Dr. Bergit."

"Arne? He hasn't come in yet. But I don't think he'll have a problem staying. He's made himself right at home, even put up his diplomas. And he knows a lot of the families he treats—you know, from growing up here. I'll tell you what. When he gets here, I'll ask him if he can work for another week. If he says no, I'll start looking for someone else to be on call."

"Anita, you're the best. Any word from your father?" Hank would be flying back the next day from a week of vacation on Barbados. *Their* vacation.

"Actually, he called last night. I couldn't believe it. You know how tight he is with money. I think he mostly just wanted to check up on Judy, make sure she hadn't had the baby while he was gone. She hasn't. So far."

"How is Judy doing?"

"Fine, I think. She complains about not being able to get comfortable, of course. But all her vital signs are good, and the baby's heartbeat sounds strong."

"Good. Tell her I said hello." Patricia had thought she would be the one delivering Judy's baby, but if she didn't get home soon, it might be Arne Bergit. "And your father? How did he sound?"

"Great. He found a woman from the tour group who was also on her own, so they sort of teamed up. Dad says she's a history buff, so they've toured some of the historical sites."

"That's wonderful," Patricia said. She was happy for him, of course, although the idea of Hank running around the island with another woman was a little unsettling.

Anita admitted that Hank hadn't left any messages for Patricia. "But he didn't know you were going to call. I'm sure he misses you."

The rest of the morning went smoothly. At break, Fiona said she was having a friend of hers over for dinner—Claudette, a Peace Corps worker—and suggested that Patricia join them. They were planning to eat, then go to Beatriz's reception at the Cultural Center.

Patricia accepted the dinner invitation but explained that she had arranged to go to the reception with Sergio. Fiona lifted an eyebrow in question. "No, it's nothing like that," Patricia said. "We're old friends, and he's helping me to look for J.J."

A little before noon, Leti told Patricia that she had a phone call. She sat at the desk in the office and picked up the receiver.

"I hear the old woman's lover has left the country," Carlos said gleefully.

"So I'm told. Did you make the death threat? Or did one of your disgusting friends make it for you?"

He chuckled. "What does it matter? Anyway, now we know what a coward Joaquín is."

"For God's sake, the man's life was threatened." She picked up a pencil and tapped it against the desk. "Mama is heartbroken."

"*Pobrecita.*" Poor little thing. "And did he invite her to go with him? Since they're so much in love?"

"You'll have to ask her," Patricia said, not wanting to pass on any more information than necessary.

"Let's talk about happier things," Carlos said. "I'm planning a party at Los Ancianos to celebrate my inheritance of Finca Baldt. I'll let you know the date. It should be soon."

After work, Patricia stopped at a small liquor store and bought a bottle of wine to contribute to dinner. Fiona and her guest were setting the table when Patricia arrived. The scent of onion and peppers filled the air.

Fiona greeted Patricia. "This is Claudette. She's the Peace Corps volunteer I was telling you about."

"Hi," Claudette said, pausing from setting the table. She was a slender young woman with a narrow face and bright blue eyes. Her hair—a rich honey brown—was pulled back in a low pony tail, and the tips of her bangs brushed her eyebrows.

Dinner tasted as good as it smelled, a stew with garbanzos mixed with squash, peppers, onion, and tomato, all served over rice. As they ate, Claudette explained that she was living in Santa Catarina, working with the local women on health and hygiene. But she spent her weekends in San Felipe with her boyfriend, Quique, who was a striker on the city's football team. Clearly, Claudette had made the transition from calling the sport "soccer" to referring to it as "football." A striker, Patricia remembered, was a forward who scored most of the goals.

"Claudette's an unusual name," Patricia said. "Is your family French?"

"No, my mom's a big Claudette Colbert fan. She was hoping I'd grow up beautiful and chic. Afraid it didn't work."

Her mother wasn't far off the mark, Patricia thought. Claudette was wearing a cobalt blue tee shirt and a floral wrap-around skirt that tied in the front, resembling a sarong. The outfit gave her an exotic, arty look. And when Claudette got up to fill the pitcher from a big jar of filtered water, Patricia noticed that she moved with the grace of a dancer.

"What kind of work does your boyfriend do?" Patricia asked.

"He's a mechanic, works for López Automotive."

"I know his boss," Patricia said.

"Don Gustavo. He's a sweetie, but he doesn't pay Quique what he's worth. I keep telling him he should ask for a raise. You'd think he could do it. I mean, Gustavo is like an uncle to him. He even calls him *tío*. Anyway, you'll meet Quique tonight. He's escorting his mom, Beatriz. It's her big night."

"I didn't realize Beatriz had a son," Patricia said. "How old is he?"

"Twenty-eight," Claudette said. "Apparently, I broke some hearts when I started dating him."

Twenty-eight? Had Beatriz given birth to him while she was at Finca Baldt? Odd. She didn't remember hearing about him. And she had never seen a small child at Los Ancianos, certainly not a son of Beatriz's. He must have lived elsewhere. Well, that wasn't so unusual for the child of a maid, especially if he was born out of wedlock. He might live with a grandparent or other family member if the employer didn't want him around.

After supper, Patricia changed into her black dress with its bolero jacket, brightening it up with her gold chain necklace and matching earrings. She wore a pair of black pumps that were too plain to be very stylish but allowed her to walk in comfort.

Sergio arrived about six-thirty, looking handsome in a casual tan suit with a shirt that was open farther down than Hank would have left it. He gave her an appreciative look. "You are a vision," he said, and escorted her to a brown Chevy sedan with "Plásticos Velasco" painted on the side.

Patricia settled into the passenger seat, relieved to know that for an evening she could set aside thoughts of searching for J.J. and of dealing with Carlos. She would celebrate Beatriz's well-earned success and do it in the company of a good-looking old friend.

CHAPTER SIXTEEN

Patricia drove with Sergio to a part of town that hadn't existed two decades earlier. The main street was lined with a movie theater, a few shops, and the Cultural Center, which was a modern, one-story concrete building. They parked, then followed a well-dressed couple—the woman in a satiny red dress with three-inch heels—through the double doors and into a high-ceilinged foyer, where a sign stood on a tripod:

The Art of Embroidery
The Works of Beatriz Aguilar Soto

A hum of conversation came from the room on the right, and they stepped into the exhibit hall, where some twenty of Beatriz's embroidered creations were arranged on the walls. A dozen people wandered among the pictures, chatting in soft voices, punctuated by an occasional quiet laugh. The hall itself was austere, with stark white walls and fluorescent lighting, but the vibrant colors of the embroidered pictures combined with the bright hues of the women's dresses gave the place a festive feeling.

At the opposite end of the hall stood a long table with glasses and bottles of soft drinks beside a platter heaped with biscuit-like cookies—a local delicacy—and a platter of crackers and cheese. The Cultural Center, which undoubtedly ran on a tight budget, had made an effort for this event, probably helped out by Tienda Beatriz.

Beatriz was standing near the center of the room, in a small group. She looked elegant in a burgundy dress with a softly draped cowl neckline. Her thick black hair was swept up in a sophisticated coif, and she wore filigreed silver earrings. Patricia had to give her credit. Beatriz had come a long way from her days working as a seamstress and cook. Few people ever managed to make that social leap, and in spite of her seemingly limited social skills, she had done it. At her side stood a distinguished man in a tailored suit, his dark hair turning gray at the temples. Some new guests came in, and he greeted them with a handshake and an invitation to help themselves to refreshments. She realized he must be the director or some other Cultural Center official.

While Sergio went to get drinks, Fiona and Claudette arrived. Patricia noticed that Claudette had let her hair down, and the honey-brown locks cascaded below her shoulders.

"I should join Quique," Claudette said and headed for the small group with Beatriz. A handsome young man with a golden tan turned and beamed at her, then planted a kiss on her cheek.

"That's Quique, I take it," Patricia said.

"He's not too hard on the eyes, is he?" Fiona said.

"Not at all." If he weren't Beatriz's son, she would have considered him as a possible J.J. He was the right age, and his coloring was more or less what she was looking for.

Sergio returned with two glasses of Coke. Fiona spotted her marimba teacher and excused herself to talk with him.

"We were just admiring Quique," Patricia said, before sipping her drink.

"He's a fine football player," Sergio said. "You know he's one of the strikers for the San Felipe team?"

"So I heard. Any idea who his father is?"

Sergio gave Patricia a long look before answering. "He goes by Aguilar, his mother's last name. But most people think his father was someone close to you—Otto Baldt."

She gasped. "You're kidding." She gazed at the young man standing between Beatriz and Claudette. Her father had another son?

Sergio cleared his throat. "You're staring."

"Oh, right." She broke her gaze.

"The family's always the last to know," Sergio said. "It's a shock, I know. Do you want to step outside? Get a little fresh air?"

"No, no, I'm okay." But she sneaked another look at Quique. It occurred to her, if her father had an illegitimate son, that could be one more complication in the distribution of her father's estate.

"Maybe we should join Gustavo," Sergio said, taking her arm. "He looks a little out of his element." They ambled over to Gustavo, who was standing against the wall by the refreshment table, looking ill at ease.

The two men almost immediately launched into a discussion of cars. Patricia tried to keep an interested look on her face, but she couldn't stop thinking of Quique and glanced at him from time to time. Was it possible that he was her half-brother? She didn't see how. After all, Beatriz had lived at Finca Baldt, and Patricia had never heard any mention of a child.

Then she remembered. One summer, when Patricia was home from school on holiday, Beatriz had brought a small child, a one-year-old maybe, to stay with her at Finca Baldt. A cute little boy. But Eugenia, who was usually tolerant of children, took an instant dislike to this one. Patricia went back to school and when she returned on vacation, the boy was gone. Shortly after that, Beatriz went to work for the Fuentes.

Patricia gazed at Quique. Was this the same little boy? And if so, was he her half-brother? She could only see his profile, and that didn't tell her much. He didn't seem to look much like her father, but then, she and Carlos didn't resemble their father closely either.

Sergio broke off the conversation with Gustavo, suggesting that he and Patricia take a look at the pictures. They wandered across the room, ending up in front of a landscape featuring a stream embroidered with various shades of blue, gray, and white, suggesting sunlight and rock. Near one end of the stream, three women knelt on rocks, washing their laundry.

"It's not bad," Sergio said, "especially if you stand back a little. She did a good job with the water."

"Yes, the colors are pretty." Patricia couldn't help glancing across the room at the group with Quique and his mother. Should she go over there and congratulate Beatriz? Introduce herself to Quique? How uncomfortable would that be? Sergio moved on to the next picture, the one of Beatriz's father in the schoolyard. Patricia trailed him.

"Okay," she said, "enough embroidery. I need to meet my brother."

As if on cue, Claudette and Quique broke off from the group and started walking in their direction.

Sergio and Quique shook hands and greeted each other in a friendly, familiar way.

Quique addressed Patricia. "Claudette tells me you're helping out at Fiona's clinic, Doctora Baldt." He seemed perfectly at ease.

"Yes, for a couple of weeks. I'm lucky to be here for your mother's opening. I especially like the pictures of Santa Catarina."

"They're beautiful," Sergio said. "I must admit, I haven't been to the town in years. I suppose the place has changed."

"It's Claudette who's the expert on Santa Catarina," Quique said. "I was born there, but I've never actually been back to see the place." How odd, Patricia thought, then remembered her patient's comment about Beatriz never returning to visit.

"I doubt if it's changed much," Claudette said. "Well, actually, the government has graveled the road from San Felipe. I think that's recent." Patricia noticed that Claudette's Spanish was fairly fluent, although of course, she spoke with an American accent. "What else? Oh, and they have electricity. Except not in the house where I'm living. The rats ate the wiring."

Patricia winced. Well, at least Santa Catarina had a decent road now. When she was a girl, the dirt road had been virtually impassable in the rainy season and not a whole lot better in the dry season.

"I heard the town has a progressive priest," Sergio said.

"Father Apolonio," Claudette said. "Yes, he's helping to set up a local co-operative." But her voice was guarded.

"You don't care for the priest?" Patricia asked.

"No, he's great. It's just..."

Quique placed a hand on her arm. "A priest was killed recently in Baja Verapaz, a friend of Father Apolonio's. People say that an army death squad murdered him. Claudette is afraid the same thing could happen to Father Apolonio."

Sergio shook his head. "Killing priests. God help us."

"The government here scares me," Claudette said and shot a look at Quique.

"I know, but we must stand up for what's right, *mi amor*," he said. "We can't just close our eyes to injustice."

If this was her father's son, Patricia thought, her father must be turning over in his grave. She glanced at Sergio. If anyone should understand the price of standing up for principles, it was he. But he was silent now, his face betraying no emotion, aside from a tensing of the jaw.

"I just want you to be safe," Claudette said to Quique.

The Director appeared at Quique's elbow. "Excuse me," he said, "your mother is asking for you."

"I'd better go back," Quique said. He kissed Claudette on the cheek and crossed back to his mother's group of admirers.

"Typical Beatriz," Claudette muttered.

A tall young man with a handsomely sculpted face appeared in the doorway, wearing the black suit and white collar of a priest. He crossed to Beatriz's group, where Quique greeted him heartily.

"Who is he?" Patricia asked.

"Father Gerard," Claudette said. "Of course, a guy that good-looking has to be a priest. He's French-Canadian, but his Spanish is really good." She said it with a hint of envy. "He has a little church in Colonia Las Américas."

"Las Américas is a new barrio in San Felipe," Sergio explained to Patricia. "Most of the residents are poor, and the city has been slow to provide utilities."

"Quique has a house there," Claudette said. "Actually, he has water and electricity, but they keep going off. Father Gerard has organized a football team for the kids in the parish. Quique helps with that."

A hush descended over the room, and they all turned to the center, where the Director was standing with a hand raised. He thanked everyone for coming, then introduced Beatriz, explaining that she was the artist who had embroidered the beautiful pictures in the exhibition.

Beatriz stepped forward. "I wish to dedicate this artwork to my father, Teodoro Aguilar Belén," she said. "He was a teacher and a man who loved beauty and learning. It was his mission to instill this passion in his pupils. And in his stubborn young daughter as well." A low chuckle rippled through the audience.

"Over the years," she continued, "my father's flame kindled my own, and I dreamed of becoming an artist. Unfortunately, my father died when I was fifteen, and I was convinced that my dream had died with him." She paused. "I hope you will forgive me if I don't reveal how many years have passed since that day." A patter of laughter followed. "I will only say that my dream has at last come true. For inspiration, I have drawn on many scenes from my humble childhood. I hope my pictures will bring back memories of your own early years. I am grateful to the Cultural Center for giving me this opportunity, and I thank you all for coming."

Her face suffused with happiness as the audience broke into applause. Patricia had never seen Beatriz so happy or so beautiful. And her eloquence was a surprise. She had always been so quiet and intensely private. Who would have guessed she would become a well-known local artist?

Patricia tried to picture Beatriz as she was at fifteen, when she had first come to Finca Baldt. She must have been pretty and very vulnerable. What had happened back then? Had Patricia's father seduced Beatriz? Patricia shuddered. It wasn't the kind of thing a daughter should have to think about. But she could hardly turn her back on past injuries now. Beatriz had become pregnant with a child by Otto Baldt, a child that he had refused to recognize. Or so it would seem. Patricia understood now why Beatriz had been ready to leave Finca Baldt and go to work at Los Ancianos.

"Ladies and gentlemen, dear friends," the Director said, raising his hand. "I have an announcement to make while you are all here." He extended his arm to Beatriz, and she moved to his side. "This lady, whom I have come to admire deeply—Beatriz Aguilar Soto— has consented to be my wife." Small gasps of excitement rose from the crowd. He took her hand and she beamed up at him. "We intend to marry within the year."

The announcement was followed by a hum of approval, and Beatriz and her fiancé were quickly surrounded by well-wishers.

Patricia spotted Quique, who looked calm and a little amused. He must have known about the announcement in advance. Claudette moved beside him, and he put his arm around her waist.

Then Patricia spotted Gustavo standing in the corner, a look of disbelief and misery on his face. He hadn't known, she thought. Beatriz's old friend and supporter, the man who had once loved her, had not been informed of the betrothal.

Patricia found herself a little overwhelmed by all the news. Sergio excused himself and joined a group of three men, business acquaintances, he said. She exited the double doors to find Fiona and Claudette standing together near the entrance.

"I needed a little distance from Quique's mother," Claudette said.

"Let's sit on the bench," Fiona said, pointing across the street to a small park. It was dark now, and a street lamp cast a mellow light, filtered by the leaves of a nearby tree.

"I have good news," Fiona said as they sat. Her face had the happy expectancy of a kid at show and tell. "There's going to be a big marimba recital in six weeks, and the teacher asked me to perform in it. I'll be playing with Julio." She grinned. "He requested me."

"Julio?" Patricia said. "The guy from Chayaka?"

"Yes. He's a brilliant musician. And I'm a pure beginner. I can't believe he asked for me."

Patricia and Claudette congratulated her. "I only wish I could be there," Patricia said. She would love to see Fiona perform.

"Come back for the recital," Fiona said. "Or bide awhile. We can always use your help at the clinic."

The idea didn't seem quite as crazy as it would have a few days ago.

"Oh, and Julio is going to Chayaka tomorrow," Fiona said. "He'll ask about the watchman at Los Ancianos. But he said he couldn't promise anything."

"Thanks," Patricia said. The watchman was the last on her list of potential interviewees. With a little luck, she would soon be finished with that task.

Claudette took a pack of Belmonts and a matchbook out of her bag. "I'm quitting when I get back to the States," she said as she lit up, then passed the pack to Fiona.

"Just one to celebrate," Fiona said, taking out a cigarette and lighting it from Claudette's.

"What the hell," Patricia said, reaching for the pack. It wasn't every day she gained a brother. She lit up, inhaled, and coughed. "I can't believe you smoke these things."

"I'm on a budget," Claudette said.

They sat companionably, smoking in the shadows. It reminded Patricia of her teen years—smokes shared behind the Country Club pool.

"Sergio seems nice," Claudette said. "Quique said he's a hero. From the old days."

"He paid a price for his activism," Patricia said. "But I'm glad people remember what he did." She flicked ashes onto the ground and felt the soft evening breeze waft through her hair. The bolero jacket felt good now. "I was lucky to run into him here."

Fiona turned to Claudette. "How are things with you and Quique?"

"Who knows? We've sort of dropped the idea of getting married. Just as well, really."

Patricia stared up at the night sky. She'd just learned she had a half-brother, and already she was learning about his love life.

Fiona clicked her tongue. "It's hard when you're far from home. You're lonely and homesick, and you need someone to befriend you and explain how things work. It's easy to fall for someone, even if you're not well suited." She shifted on the bench. "Oh. Not that you and Quique aren't grand together."

Patricia glanced at Fiona. What kind of unsuitable fellows had come into her life? Could Julio, the Chayakan guy, be one of them?

"It's okay," Claudette said. "I know what you mean."

"So, you were thinking about marriage?" Patricia asked her.

"We'd tossed the idea around. I even thought about staying here in San Felipe. But what would I do? Teach English? I have a degree in microbiology, and I worked my tail off to get it. This was going to be my two years of adventure before I got a real job. Besides, his mother hates me."

"Could you both go to the States?" Patricia asked. "This doesn't seem like a very safe place to live right now."

"No kidding," Claudette said. "We talked about getting married and going to the U.S. But Quique is happy here. He likes working for Gustavo, and he spends hours coaching football with Father Gerard's kids. Besides, he's very rooted here, you know? Wants to make things better. He belongs to some left-wing political group. He refuses to tell me which one, for my own safety, he says. When he was younger, he actually considered joining the guerrillas."

Patricia's breath caught. Her brother, a guerrilla. Her father would definitely turn over in his grave.

"Oh, I don't think he was serious," Claudette said. "I imagine he was rebelling against his mother. She's very protective. Stifling, really. I think it helped their relationship when he got his own place to live."

For a brief, happy moment, Patricia thought of handing over Finca Baldt to Quique. Based on their short acquaintance, he seemed like the most stable member of the family, even if he had contemplated becoming an armed insurgent. But leaving the estate to Quique would be impractical in every way.

"Look," Claudette said, "you can't tell anyone about this guerrilla thing. I told Quique I'd keep it a secret, and here I am blabbing it to both of you."

"It's safe with me," Fiona said.

"And me," Patricia said. But given the current political situation, Quique was clearly taking risks—belonging to a left-wing organization and hanging out with a priest who was committed to social action.

"How much longer will you be here?" she asked Claudette.

"Six months."

"A lot can happen in six months," Patricia said. Or even a week. One dizzying week.

It was late by the time Sergio dropped Patricia off at El Patio. She was tired and didn't invite him in, but they made plans to meet for lunch the next day at the Chinese restaurant.

She got ready for bed, then lay awake on the lumpy mattress, her mind spinning. Did she really have a second brother? Or was she putting too much credence in popular gossip? The sad fact was, she'd rather have Quique for a brother than Carlos. Tomorrow she would talk to Beatriz, see what she had to say about her son's father.

CHAPTER SEVENTEEN

Patricia awoke the next morning to the knowledge that she might have a friendly, bright, good-looking half-brother. She also remembered that it was Saturday, which meant the clinic would be open until noon. But the clinic could wait. Patricia had a quick breakfast, stopped by Fiona's place to say she would arrive at work a little late, and hurried down the street to Tienda Beatriz. With a little luck, she would soon find out if Quique was indeed her brother.

After the big opening the night before, Patricia didn't really expect to see Beatriz in the store, but there she was, clipboard in hand, looking over shelves of cans in the back. No wonder she was a successful shopkeeper. Beatriz looked up when Patricia approached.

"Congratulations on your exhibition," Patricia said. "It was a great success."

"You are very kind," Beatriz said. "Is there something I can do for you?"

Patricia asked if they might talk in private, and Beatriz ushered her into her parlor, where they sat on the sofa, and Beatriz instructed a maid to serve coffee.

"The reception was well attended," Patricia said.

"Yes. My fiancé and I have many friends in the area. I noticed you were with Señor Velasco."

"He's an old friend," Patricia said. "I believe he's also a friend of your son, Quique."

"Very possibly. The Velasco family is prominent in San Felipe."

Patricia thought it was probably a commitment to social justice that formed the basis of Sergio and Quique's friendship, not the social prominence of their families, but she held her tongue. "I was pleased to hear of your engagement," she said. "And I'm sure that Meg will be glad to hear it too."

"Thank you," Beatriz said. The maid served cups of coffee and withdrew. "If you will excuse my directness, Doctora, I don't think you dropped by this morning just to congratulate me."

"You're right," Patricia said. "I met your son Quique for the first time last night. He seems like a fine young man."

"I think so," Beatriz said.

Patricia hesitated. "I'm not sure how to say this. What brings me here is, I'm told that my father was also Quique's father."

"People talk," Beatriz said.

"Is what they say true?"

Beatriz sipped her coffee. "Since you ask, yes, Quique was Otto's son. But your father never recognized him. I gave birth to Quique in Santa Catarina and left him with my mother so I could go back to work. A year later, I took Quique to Finca Baldt. I was sure that once Otto saw our son, he would love him. But he hardly spared Quique a look. His own child was nothing to him."

"I'm sorry," Patricia said. She took a swallow of the heavily sweetened coffee.

"And of course, your mother didn't like to have Quique around," Beatriz said. "He was a reminder of her husband's infidelity, I suppose. So I sent Quique back to my mother in Santa Catarina. When I moved to Los Ancianos, I intended to take Quique with me. But by then my mother didn't want to part with him. So I left him with her."

"Does Quique know who his father is?"

"I told him that his father had died in an accident on the coast before he was born. So, you see, he has no reason to think of Otto as his father. Or to think of you as his sister." She laid her cup on the saucer with a small clatter. "Now you know. I ask you not to share this information with my son. It would upset him, and I would deny the story."

"I understand. Thank you for telling me," Patricia said.

"Many people in San Felipe believe that Otto was Quique's father, so it isn't exactly a secret. And you were always an obstinate girl. I imagine you would have kept sniffing around until you found the truth."

Patricia winced. It wasn't a very flattering picture of her, but it was one her mother probably would have agreed with. "I hope to get to know Quique while I'm here in San Felipe."

"Yes? Well, don't expect too much. Quique has never cared for the Baldt family."

The bustle of the clinic was a relief after sitting in Beatriz's parlor. There was something toxic about that woman, Patricia decided, although she was grateful for her honesty. By mid-morning break time, Patricia was only too aware that Claudette's Belmonts had revived her desire for nicotine. It was not a failing she wanted to give in to, so she walked to a small shop down the street and bought a pack of Juicy Fruit, which she chewed as she strolled back to the clinic. The day had turned partially overcast. Formations of light gray clouds crossed sedately eastward, dimming the bright highland sky. It was the first time in the seven days she'd been there that anything resembling a rain cloud had crossed overhead.

"You have a letter," Leti said a little after noon, when Patricia's last patient of the day had left. "It's in the office."

At last, Patricia thought. Phone calls were fine, but when she hung up, the person was gone. She'd been wanting mail, something that she could hold onto and re-read when she wanted to feel connected to the person. A postcard from Hank would be welcome, even though he should be flying home from Barbados today. She was looking forward to calling him tomorrow and talking over all the craziness here.

The letter lay on the office desk. Patricia's heart pounded as soon as she saw the envelope. It was addressed to Doctora Patricia Baldt Contreras, and it was typed with the same peculiarities of the anonymous letter—some letters dark and others light, with flying capital letters, all the marks of an inexpert manual typist. Even the blue envelope was the same.

Trembling, she ripped it open. The letter was brief. The Spanish words read:

> Esteemed Doctora Baldt,
> Please do me the favor of meeting me at the Central Park across from the Cathedral at 1700 hours tonight. I will tell you about Juan José Fuente then.
> A Friend

Patricia clutched the letter and gave a small cheer. Could it be true? Did this mean that J.J. was alive? She would find out at five o'clock. She had an urge to call Meg. No. It would be better to wait until after the meeting. She read through the letter again. How could she possibly wait that long? Couldn't the jerk have asked to meet her for lunch?

Fiona appeared at the door. "What's up?"

"A letter from the secret writer," she said and handed it to Fiona.

Fiona read it, giving a little gasp. "It's true, then. Your friend's son is alive. Or is he? It's not really clear, is it? Do you fancy company? Shall I go with you?"

Patricia considered it. "I should probably go alone. I don't want to do anything to spook the guy." She peered at the envelope again. No stamp. It must have been hand delivered. Leti appeared in the doorway. "Good news?" she asked.

"Possibly," Patricia said. "Where did this letter come from?"

"I don't know. It just showed up on my desk. I took a patient to Fiona's examining room, and when I came back, there it was."

More mystery, as if there weren't enough. Fiona guided Leti out of the room, leaving Patricia to stare at the letter. Suddenly, she remembered Sergio. When he had dropped her off at El Patio the night before, they had agreed to meet for lunch at the Chinese restaurant today.

The Golden Dragon was busy, the air thick with the aromas of fried foods, but Sergio had snagged a table along the far wall. Patricia slipped into the chair across from him and passed him the letter. "Go ahead. Read it."

"*Ay dios*," he mumbled as he read.

"How can I wait until five o'clock?" Patricia moaned.

"Let's eat, then go to a movie," Sergio suggested. "A two o'clock matinee. It will take your mind off the meeting. Then I'll take you to the park."

They ended up at a movie theater down the street from the Cultural Center. According to Sergio, the old theater that Patricia had visited as a child had suffered structural damage during the earthquake, and the owner didn't want to invest in repairs, so it was being torn down. This theater was nicer, with reasonably comfortable seats and a large screen. Plus, it lacked the bats that used to fly around and leave shadows projected on the screen in the old theater. Actually, as a child, Patricia had always enjoyed the bats' swooping antics.

The movie that they sat through, *How to Steal a Million*, was a comedy starring Audrey Hepburn and Peter O'Toole. Patricia recognized that the story was about an art heist, but that was as far as she got, since her mind kept drifting off to her appointment in the park, and she was thankful when the movie ended. She and Sergio emerged from the dark theater into the late afternoon light, and they drove across town, then strolled around the downtown area for about twenty minutes, Patricia's nervousness steadily rising, as they waited for five o'clock. At the entrance to the Central Park, Sergio gave Patricia's hand a reassuring squeeze, then hung back.

Patricia crossed the park, scanning its occupants, trying not to be too obvious about it. A group of young guys lounged on a wooden bench, ogling a bunch of teenage girls who hurried across the park. A scrawny boy sat by a small pile of newspapers, and nearby a fellow with a spidery mustache sold lottery tickets. At the far end, a tattered old man slumped on a bench, his eyes closed.

Patricia sat down on an empty wooden bench, still warm from the day's heat, and set her shoulder bag beside her. The Cathedral was to her back, across the street, and she faced the spot where the microbuses—micros, they were called—pulled up. Overhead, a breeze rustled the leaves of a mimosa tree, dappling the bench and sidewalk with alternating areas of sun and shadow.

She peered across the park to the far end, where Sergio had seated himself by the dozing man. He was smoking a cigarette, his legs crossed. Why hadn't she thought to bring cigarettes? Something to still her hands, which were tapping against her navy skirt.

Her bench faced the market, quiet now that the vendors had left for the day. A crowded micro, belching diesel fumes, darted into the buses' loading zone. A stringy young man leaped out the door. "San Pablo, San Pablo, San Pablo," he called in a high sing-song voice, beckoning riders. Patricia tensed as two passengers climbed out of the small vehicle—a paunchy, balding man and a woman carrying a baby mostly covered by a blanket. Both proceeded down the street. Patricia exhaled. It was still early. Maybe the next bus would bring the letter writer.

It occurred to her that the last time she was here, she had also been with Sergio. It was Holy Week of 1954. The Fuentes had been with them, and as she envisioned J.J. with his red balloon, her eyes began to fill with tears. Stop it, she ordered herself. A glance at her watch. Five minutes after five.

Another micro arrived and deposited several passengers. A young woman in a peach-colored cardigan got off, her gaze scanning the park. Patricia's heart raced. Was she the one? So young. And a woman. Patricia had been expecting a man. She began to stand. But the woman smiled and quickened her steps as she approached a young man across the park. They walked away, hand in hand. Damn.

The scrawny newsboy approached her. Was he just a vendor, or could he be carrying a message for her? He offered her a copy of La Prensa, and she paid for it. But he just took her money and moved away.

Patricia looked down at the newspaper while staying alert to movement around her. She scanned headlines and glanced at the accompanying photos. A summit of finance ministers was meeting in San José. A town near the capital was getting potable water, and the First Lady was at the ceremony, flanked by army officers. An empty room littered with trash was claimed to be a site where children had been held before their internal organs were removed and sold in the U.S. Patricia shuddered. This newspaper was such a rag, she thought. According to the story, the abductors had not been apprehended, nor had the children's bodies been found. She wondered what kind of fear was at the bottom of this sensational garbage. Fear of some looming power, embodied in the U.S.? Fear of losing one's children? It was a nightmare that had actually come true for Meg.

Another micro dropped off a few people, all hustling away. A quarter past the hour. Surely her "friend" would be here soon.

She read her horoscope for the following day. A business opportunity was in the offing, and she should grab it. She looked at Hank's sign: Gemini. There was a possibility of romance or the deepening of an existing relationship. She thought of the female tourist Hank had buddied up with in Barbados. By tomorrow, she would be out of the picture.

It was all rubbish of course. She'd never believed in astrology. Nevertheless, she checked the horoscopes for her mother and Carlos. Her brother's wasn't bad, but her mother might as well stay in bed tomorrow. She wondered when Sergio's birthday was. And Fiona's. She glanced at her watch. Five twenty-five.

Her rear was getting sore. Where was the guy? Was it possible he wouldn't show up? No, she cautioned herself, don't even think it. She stood and stretched. In her peripheral vision she saw Sergio lighting another cigarette. Should she ask him for one? No, she thought, just stay where you are.

At six o'clock, Sergio sat down beside her.

"Don't tell me it's you," she said. He looked confused, then burst into laughter at the absurdity of the idea that he was the writer. Half-hysterical chortles bubbled out of her, her hilarity feeding on Sergio's. She bent over, arms wrapped around her middle, the laughter turning to tears. After a while, her outburst subsided, and she rummaged in her bag for a tissue, wiped her eyes, and blew her nose. "I wanted so much to find J.J.," she said.

"I know," Sergio said, and put his arm around her shoulders. "Let's go get a drink. There's a quiet bar near here."

"I guess it wasn't a total waste of time," she said as they walked down the street. "At least I know a few things I didn't know before."

"Like what?"

"Well, the writer is probably in the vicinity of San Felipe. Not only that, but he knows who I am and that I'm working at the clinic. He also knows I'm looking for J.J."

"Right."

"And one more thing," she said. "The fellow is still invested in this interaction in some way." She sighed. "If only I knew why he set up this meeting and then failed to show up." She halted and looked around, up the street and down. Was he here? Watching her? Following her? The idea gave her goosebumps. "Did you notice anyone in the park who was acting strangely?"

"Not really," Sergio said. "Sorry."

They resumed walking and ended up in a small bar with a picture on the door of what looked like a barn owl next to the name *La Lechuza*. Inside, well-dressed men and women sat around darkly polished tables, sipping mixed drinks. A recording of Spanish classical guitar played in the background. Patricia recognized two older couples she had seen at Beatriz's opening the night before. This was the bar for the well-to-do of San Felipe, Patricia realized.

A young waitress with shiny dark hair took their order: a vodka tonic for Patricia and a mineral water with lime for Sergio. The drinks came right away, plunked down on coasters embellished with a picture of an owl.

Patricia took a drink and felt her tension begin to slide away. "Maybe I should place an ad in the paper," she said. "It will read: I was in the park. Where were you? Signed: A Pissed Off Friend."

"Here's another idea," Sergio said. "The San Felipe team has a big football match tomorrow. Every young man in San Felipe will be there. We could go and see if any of them look like a possible J.J."

"Sure. Why not," Patricia said. It wasn't as if she had anything better to do with her Sunday afternoon. And there was always a tiny possibility that someone would look like Meg and Pablo's son. It occurred to her there might be another reason to go. "Will Quique be playing?"

"He should be. You'll enjoy watching him. I should warn you, though, it's likely to be a rough match. We're playing the Metro Sports Club. They're a team from the capital, a bunch of rich guys. They always play dirty and get away with it. Our team invariably ends up with injuries." He paused. "Now that I think of it, your brother is on the Metro team."

"Not one of the dirty players, I hope," she said, but she was pretty sure of the answer.

Sergio shrugged.

Did she really want to watch Carlos playing against Quique? She wondered what kind of player Carlos was. She hoped he had some skills besides an ability to injure other players and get away with it.

"It's up to you," Sergio said. "If we go, and the game gets too brutal, we can always leave. I'm not a football fanatic."

"Let's go then," she said. "I haven't watched a real football game for years."

CHAPTER EIGHTEEN

The next morning Patricia awoke feeling the effect of the three vodka tonics that she'd drunk with Sergio the night before. In New Bergen, she drank very little, never knowing when a medical emergency might arise, so it had felt like a luxury to get tipsy. When they left the bar, Sergio had taken her arm and guided her back to his car a few blocks away. At El Patio, they had said good night with a friendly kiss on the cheek and a promise to meet up the following afternoon.

Fiona dropped by around ten to announce that she and Claudette were going to the football game that afternoon. "Come with us if you're free," she said. Patricia explained that Sergio had offered to take her and suggested they could make it a foursome. The outing with Sergio wasn't a date, after all, just one more attempt to find J.J., and probably a futile one. Only yesterday she'd been so sure the search would be over by now. It was hard to work up any hope.

Patricia dressed in her khaki slacks and a short-sleeved blouse and dropped by Fiona's apartment about one-thirty, where she found Fiona dressed similarly, in slacks and a blouse. In contrast, Claudette could have passed for a college student, in jeans and a

University of Michigan t-shirt, her long hair pulled back in a pony tail. Fiona had a thermos of coffee and cups in a bag.

When Sergio arrived, he seemed content to join the group, apparently amused by the idea of going to the game with three women. They all piled into the clinic van, which Fiona drove to the edge of town, where the football field was situated.

As they approached the field, Patricia saw a line of buses and microbuses, many of them crammed full, with two or three young men hanging half way out the door. Each vehicle pulled up to the entrance and discharged its lively football fans. Fiona drove by and parked the van on the shoulder of the road, a couple of minutes' walk past the field.

Once inside the entrance, Sergio led the way to a long, grassy embankment where several hundred people were milling about and sitting in groups spread across the hill. An excited din filled the air. The high-pitched noise of vendors hawking drinks and snacks rose above spirited conversations. Patricia and her group made their way slowly through the crowd, pausing periodically to greet Fiona's patients and Sergio's friends and relations, some of whom kidded him about his bevy of beautiful friends.

"You're boosting my reputation," he joked to Patricia.

She noticed that Gustavo, Beatriz, and her fiancé, the director of the Cultural Center, were all seated together on folding chairs not far from the San Felipe team's bench. Gustavo must have come to terms with Beatriz's engagement.

Sergio led the group to the top of the embankment, close to center field, where they spread out their blanket and sat. Patricia looked around to get her bearings. The fence around the other three sides of the football field was plastered with advertisements—for Gallo beer, Coca Cola, and various businesses, including López Automotive, Gustavo's place.

It was a fine day for a football match, Patricia thought. An expanse of wispy clouds covered much of the sky, keeping down the glare. To the west lay a low, thin band of darker clouds, possibly portending a little rain later in the day, a rarity for February. In the distance, the mountains rose up, their silent presence contrasting with the clamor of the football fans.

Patricia barely recognized Leti when she appeared beside their blanket. She was wearing skin-tight jeans and a peasant blouse with a plunging neckline. Gray eyeshadow and heavy mascara gave her brown eyes a sultry look. Leti greeted everyone, including her Uncle Sergio, who wisely said nothing about her appearance. Claudette made room for Leti on the blanket, and they started chatting about their football-playing boyfriends. It turned out that Leti was also dating a striker.

Sergio descended the embankment to say hello to a few friends, while Fiona and Claudette went off to buy popcorn and chips, leaving Patricia and Leti on the blanket. Several of the San Felipe players jogged onto the field in faded-looking jerseys striped with sky blue and gold, their shorts a matching blue.

"Look," said Leti excitedly. "There's my boyfriend, Tino. He and Quique are the two best strikers." Leti pointed to a slim, muscular young man entering the field. He had an open, cheerful face, and his hair and skin color suggested African roots.

"He's nice-looking," Patricia said.

Leti smiled contentedly. "I think so too. He played for a team on the coast before he moved to San Felipe. He works construction, and it keeps him in good shape."

The rest of the team soon joined him. The oldest player was probably near forty, with the start of a paunch. He grinned at someone in the audience, and Patricia noticed that he was missing a couple of front teeth. "That's Dago," Leti said. "He's a truck driver. They say he has kids in all the towns around here."

One small, wiry player looked about sixteen. He moved with frenetic energy, dribbling the ball back and forth between his feet, first in one direction, then another. He reminded her of a squirrel. "That's Pepe," Leti said. "He was in school with my younger brother."

Looking across the field, Patricia saw that a couple of the players had the facial structure and solid build of Indians. She wouldn't be surprised if their parents or grandparents lived in Indian towns.

Quique was the last San Felipe player to jog onto the field, and Patricia was impressed again at how handsome he was, with his slender, muscular frame and golden tan. Her good-looking kid brother. Or so it seemed.

Sergio returned and sat next to Patricia, followed by Fiona and Claudette, who passed out bags of popcorn and plantain chips. Leti caught sight of an old friend and hurried off to join her.

A minute later, the happy buzz of the crowd quieted.

"Look," Claudette said grimly. "It's the Metros."

The first members of the Metro Sports Club jogged onto the field and began warming up. They looked striking, with their team's name emblazoned across dark red jerseys over charcoal gray shorts. No one looked Indian, and from what Sergio had said, she guessed that they got their muscles from working out at a private gym or country club. Certainly not from manual labor.

A tall Metro with a bald head was dribbling a ball near the San Felipe team when he stopped, foot atop the ball. He looked with disdain at Dago, the paunchy, gap-toothed San Felipe player. A sinking feeling came over Patricia.

"Does San Felipe ever win against the Metros?" she asked.

"Never," Claudette said. "But they're dying to."

Sergio nodded. "The whole town is eager for a win."

Patricia spotted Carlos as he jogged onto the field beside a guy with the hefty build of an NFL linebacker. Not your typical slim soccer player.

Carlos looked up to the crowd, and even from a distance, Patricia could see a sneer on his face. "There's my brother Carlos," she said. "Over there by that huge fellow."

"The big guy is Muro," Sergio said. "He's too slow to be a very good player. But when a Metro player commits a foul, he's right there, blocking the referee's view." His name was apt, Patricia thought. "Muro" meant "wall."

A young man walked across the embankment in their direction—Father Gerard, wearing chinos and a clerical collar over a black shirt. Claudette greeted him and introduced him to everyone. "Please join us," Sergio said.

"Just for a minute," Father Gerard said, sitting on a corner of the blanket. In Spanish with a French-Canadian accent, he remarked that he remembered seeing everyone at Beatriz's reception. Their conversation turned to her engagement to the director of the Cultural Center.

"Did you meet the director's family?" Patricia asked. None had been pointed out to her at the Opening.

"He has two adult children, but they live in the capital," Father Gerard said. "Unfortunately, they were unable to attend."

"They don't approve of the match," Claudette said. "They're social climbers. Quique told me."

Sergio turned to the priest. "I understand you're coaching a football team."

"That's right. I brought a couple of the boys today." Father Gerard pointed to two kids around twelve years old, who were mock-punching each other farther down the hill. "They've been helping out with repairs at the Church. Keeps them out of trouble. This is their big reward."

"Quique is their idol," Claudette said.

"He's an excellent role model," Father Gerard said. "A fine man and a superb athlete." He talked about the team and his hopes for building a sense of community in the barrio. "And how about you, Dr. Baldt?" he asked, facing her. "Have you come back to practice medicine?"

"I'm only here for a couple of weeks. I have a clinic in the U.S."

"Maybe you should reconsider. The need here is enormous. I'm sure you see that."

"My patients in the States also require care."

"But you can be replaced there. Here you would fill a need that wouldn't be met otherwise."

"I'll keep it in mind," she said dryly.

"I'd better go join the kids," Father Gerard said and made his way down the embankment.

"He's rather pushy," Patricia said.

"Are you irritated because he's rude or because he's right?" Sergio asked.

"Very funny."

"Don't mind Father Gerard," Claudette said. "He's a good guy. But he has strong convictions. It's probably just as well he's a priest. Imagine being married to him. You know, it's like, he won't drink Coke because the company is greedy and unscrupulous. He's right. I know that, but sometimes I just want a Coke."

"How close are he and Quique?" Patricia asked.

"Quique admires him. I think they both feel a little wounded. Quique grew up without a father, and Father Gerard was adopted as a small child. They share that bond."

Adopted. Patricia remembered Jonathan's plan to look into adoptions from Guatemala to the States. She wondered if children had gone to Canada too. Maybe she should mention that to him, as a last resort.

On the field, the players retreated to the sidelines, where they clustered around the coaches. A moment later, they were back on the field, now spread out in their positions. "Oh, look," Fiona said. "We've got the ball."

On the field, Tino kicked the ball diagonally to Quique. As the fans cheered, Quique dribbled it up the left sideline, ever closer to the Metro goal, dodging their defensive players, who instantly converged on him. Tino began to streak forward to the right, and Quique managed to kick the ball to him through a second-long opening in the Metro ranks. Tino stopped the ball with his foot, and a moment later sent it rocketing toward the goal. But the Metro goalie leaped forward, catching the ball in his gloved hands. He threw it to a teammate, who began moving it back toward the San Felipe goal.

After several minutes, Patricia recognized the pattern of this game. Quique and Tino repeatedly moved the ball within a few yards of the Metro goal, a grueling task. But the goalie blocked every kick, no matter how skillfully positioned.

"Damn, he's good," Sergio said as the goalie blocked another shot. "The guy seems to know where the ball is going before the kick is even made." He shook his head. "That's the problem. Our offense is better than the Metro's, but their defense is solid."

Patricia soon realized, to her relief, that Carlos was part of that strong defense. He was a central defender who often managed to place himself between the ball and the goal. He was small and persistent, and a couple of times he captured the ball from San Felipe players who had let their guard down for an instant.

Although Patricia couldn't help cheering on the San Felipe team, it was a relief to see Carlos do something well. After all those years of dribbling the ball around the courtyard at Finca Baldt, he had developed into a skilled player.

But the best moments were provided by Quique. At one point, a Metro player sent a ball in a high arc to a teammate half-way across the field. In a flash, Quique leaped high into the air, his right leg thrust above his head. His foot hit the ball and deflected it down to Tino. Patricia gasped, then applauded along with the crowd, although the Metro guards quickly encircled Tino.

"Quique's quite an acrobat," Patricia said.

"He's very agile," Claudette said. "Plus, he's crazy about kung fu movies. I swear, he watched *The Game of Death* half a dozen times."

"I guess it paid off," Patricia said.

It didn't take long to figure out how the Metros compensated for their weak offense. Twenty minutes into the game, a San Felipe midfielder suffered a dislocated jaw after a Metro player's elbow slammed into it. No foul was called.

And a striker limped off the field after he was shoved to the ground, tumbling over another player. The Metro player who'd pushed him received a cautionary yellow card, but San Felipe fans grumbled. It should have been a red card, throwing him out of the game.

"Are the referees blind?" Patricia asked.

Sergio snorted. "Money may have changed hands. Or maybe they don't want to antagonize the rich kids."

Shortly before half-time, a collision occurred as the bald Metro player and Dago, the gap-toothed truck driver, simultaneously tried to head-butt a ball that was descending between them. Dago thudded onto the ground, cradling his gut and gasping for air.

It had to be a foul. The bald Metro player had clearly kicked or punched Dago. Patricia waited for the referee to hold up a red card, tossing Baldy out of the game, but none came. Little Pepe helped Dago to his feet. Baldy said something, then threw back his head and guffawed. Pepe's face contorted with fury, and he punched Baldy in the face. Baldy staggered backwards, hand on his nose, as the San Felipe fans cheered and stamped their feet in approval. The referee ousted the unrepentant Pepe with a red card, as the fans continued to applaud him.

Unfortunately, the referee also awarded Metro a penalty kick. One of their strikers stepped up to take the shot. The man stood motionless, his eyes focused on the ball a few yards away. Then he ran toward the ball and kicked it low and to the left, just inside the net. A goal.

Patricia exhaled deeply, hardly aware she'd been holding her breath. The goal was a blow. But San Felipe had plenty of time for a comeback, if they could just keep enough players on the field.

At half-time, the score was still San Felipe zero, Metro one, and the mood among the San Felipe spectators was gloomy. People got up and grumbled about the "cowardly refs" and the "damn Metros."

Patricia and Sergio walked down the embankment and strolled along the bottom, Patricia scanning the crowd as if she were looking for someone, which she was—a grown-up J.J. It occurred to her that the letter writer might also be there, and she found herself suspicious of anyone who looked her way.

After several discouraging minutes, she halted. "Okay. I give up," she said. "Let's go back." There was no way she could pick out J.J. without some kind of clue. And it was creepy to think of someone watching her. They climbed the hill and sank down beside Fiona and Claudette.

Sergio had brought a flask of brandy, and as Fiona passed cups of coffee, Sergio fortified them. Leti joined them, fingering a small locket with the image of St. Sebastian. Patron saint of athletes, she explained. She and Claudette agreed that they hardly cared who won. They just wanted Quique and Tino to finish the game uninjured.

The second half of the game felt sluggish, with both teams laboring for each yard gained.

"Trench warfare," Patricia said. "That's what it feels like. But only one side is getting hurt."

By the fourth quarter, the sun was lower in the sky. Through most of the game, it had remained partially obscured by the feathery clouds. Now it dipped behind a band of low gray clouds, and the air turned chilly. A San Felipe infielder kicked the ball to Tino, who was in the open several yards ahead. Tino rushed up the field, dribbling the ball, as three Metro players converged on him.

Sergio groaned. "Look at Muro." Sure enough, the Wall had hung back, positioning himself between his teammates and the closest referee. Just then, one of the Metros charged up behind Tino and slid into a back tackle, feet first. The crowd gasped as Tino went down, tumbling forward.

The tackler stood, brushing dirt off the back of his shorts as a whistle shrieked. Tino lay still, a limp figure in blue and gold. Even from the hill, Patricia could see that his left leg protruded at an angle below the knee. "Oh no," Patricia murmured. She and Fiona both stood, ready to take action, but a doctor hustled onto the field, black bag in hand. Tino tried to lift himself but sank back onto the ground. Patricia looked down to the foot of the embankment and saw Leti standing there, her hands raised to her face.

Two men jogged forward, carrying a stretcher, and the players, who had gathered around Tino, divided to let them through. Tino, his face contorted in pain, was carried to the sidelines, where Leti appeared beside him.

Claudette turned to Patricia, her face flushed with anger. "A back tackle. That's illegal. Not to mention, incredibly dangerous."

A second referee joined the first one in the middle of the field, where they conferred, both looking uncertain.

"Hey, Ref, where are your balls?" shouted a man several yards away. "Give him a red card."

"Ro-jo, Ro-jo," shouted another man in a deep voice that carried across the crowd. 'Red, Red.' Quickly, the chant was picked up by every man, woman, and child in the crowd. They shook their fists and stamped their feet. "Ro-jo, Ro-jo," they shouted, until the din shook the stadium, like a temblor. The first referee shot a furtive glance at the crowd, his expression nervous. Then slowly, he pulled out a red card and raised it to the Metro player who had toppled Tino.

The crowd cheered and clapped. The tackler scowled and walked off the field, practically plowing into the referee, who jumped back at the last minute. The referee blotted his face with a handkerchief, then awarded a free direct kick to San Felipe.

"I only wish they'd thrown out Muro too," Sergio muttered.

Quique strode to the middle of the field, a few yards behind the ball. He stood motionless, then rushed forward and kicked the ball high, above the straining arms of the goalie, just inside the net. A perfect shot. As the crowd cheered, Quique turned to the sidelines and saluted Tino, who was still on the stretcher.

The score was tied at one to one, with four minutes to go. Patricia turned to Sergio. "Are ties allowed, or could this go into overtime?" There was no way she wanted this game to continue. It had already lasted too long, with too many injuries.

"Relax. We don't have overtimes."

Patricia turned back to the game just as one of the Metro players kicked a high pass to a teammate. But a San Felipe midfielder sprang forward and intercepted it with a header. The ball hurtled toward Quique, who was a few yards from the Metro goal. He corralled the ball with his foot and started to move forward but was immediately halted by Carlos, who nimbly positioned himself between Quique and the goal. Patricia held her breath as Quique dribbled the ball back and forth, feinting in one direction, then the opposite, trying to find a way to pass to a teammate. But Carlos checked every move.

Quique started to charge around Carlos, but Carlos moved swiftly with him, arms raised, legs wide, his body blocking the goal. In a flash, Quique saw his opening and kicked the ball between Carlos's legs. It flew in a low diagonal, beyond the goalie's hastily outstretched arms, straight across the goal line.

Goal! Quique raised his arms in triumph as a roar broke from the crowd, and the fans rose as one to their feet. Claudette whooped, bouncing up and down.

Carlos swung around, shock and disbelief on his face. *Ay dios,* Patricia thought. Her poor brother. How humiliating to have the ball kicked between his legs.

Quique's teammates piled around him as the fans laughed and cheered.

"Oye, Carlitos," a drunken man called, "where'd you learn to spread your legs? From your whore?" A woman near him turned to shush him, but several people laughed.

Across the field, Carlos's expression had turned from disbelief to fury. Murderous fury. Patricia's stomach clenched. If only someone other than Quique had kicked the ball. Anyone but their half-brother.

The ball was put back into play, but it stalled midway down the field as the clock ticked down: 20 seconds, 15, 10, then 5, 4, 3, 2, 1. The whistle blew, and the stadium erupted in ecstatic cheers. The game had ended with San Felipe 2, Metro Sports Club 1.

On the field, the San Felipe players jumped and shouted and thumped each other on the back. Patricia's face felt warm, and she realized that the sun had moved below the band of gray clouds to a strip of clear sky. Its bright rays slanted across the rejoicing San Felipe players and their fans.

A hush fell over the crowd, as everyone turned toward Quique. He pulled off his San Felipe jersey and waved it high over his head. "Go, Quique!" shouted one of the men. And with a whoop, he ran around the field's perimeter, waving the blue and gold-striped shirt like a flag. Patricia stood in awe. Quique looked for all the world like an Olympic champion, the sun reflected off his damp, wavy brown hair and his tanned body. Finally, he came to a halt and was absorbed into the mass of happy San Felipe fans. Patricia glanced beside her at Claudette. Tears were running down her smiling face.

The rich boys have been defeated, Patricia thought. By an auto mechanic, a truck driver, and a Black kid from the coast, as well as several other humble guys. It had to be a sweet moment for the people of San Felipe. But Carlos Baldt, the presumed heir to Finca Baldt, had not only been defeated, he'd been humiliated in front of everyone. There would be a payback. Of that she was sure.

Patricia sat with Sergio on the back seat of the clinic van. In the front seat, Fiona and Claudette chatted happily while they waited for the buses to collect their jubilant passengers and move out.

Patricia felt anything but jubilant. She turned to Sergio. "I'm afraid for Quique," she said. "Did you see the look on Carlos's face? After that last goal?"

"Yes. Pure hatred. I regret to say this, Patricia, but your brother has a bad reputation. I believe you have good reason to think that Quique is in trouble."

Darn it. She had hoped that Sergio would tell her she was over-reacting. It was just a game, he'd say. Carlos was irritated, but he'd get over it. Instead, Sergio had confirmed her fears.

Her brother was going to want revenge for his public humiliation. And he had his militia behind him, men who had no scruples about kidnapping or murdering people. Now that she thought of it, Quique's life could actually be in danger. He might receive an anonymous phone call threatening death, as Joaquín had. Or Carlos might omit the nicety of a warning. The idea sent a chill through her. Quique needed to know that he had a dangerous enemy. She thought back to her conversation with Arturo. People on death lists sometimes went into hiding. Was that an option for Quique? Where would he go?

"Do you think Quique would agree to hide out for a while?" she asked Sergio. Maybe he could disappear until this all blew over—assuming it ever did.

"I doubt it," Sergio said. "Quique doesn't seem like the kind of guy who turns and runs, at least not without strong cause. But somebody has to warn him, tell him to be careful. And his friends need to watch his back. Do you want me to talk to him?"

"No," she said, "I'll do it." Carlos was her brother, after all. It was time she took some responsibility for her family. Claudette said she had talked to Quique about the possibility of going to the States. He wasn't willing to leave then, but maybe now he'd reconsider. Now that his life might be at stake.

CHAPTER NINETEEN

"Patricia Baldt is in San Felipe."

Noemi drew in her breath, stunned by Julio's announcement. It was Sunday afternoon, and all the family was gathered in the patio behind their house in Chayaka. Noemi and her daughter knelt on reed mats, weaving brown thread into cloth on their backstrap looms, while Julio and his father sat on low wooden stools, drinking herbal tea.

"Humph," her father mumbled in response to Julio's information.

"Isn't that the woman who drove her car off the cliff?" Natividad asked. Her loom hung from the wall, beside her mother's. At twelve, Nati was already becoming a skilled weaver.

"Yes, daughter," Noemi said. It had been years since Noemi had seen Señorita Baldt, not since the day that she had arrived at their aunt's house with the envelope full of money for Demetrio. And there had been little news after her accident, only that she had miraculously survived and then disappeared from Finca Baldt. She turned to Julio. "Did you see her?"

"No. She's a doctor now, working at a clinic in San Felipe. A friend of mine works as a nurse there. She told me." He flushed, causing Noemi to wonder if the friend was someone special. "The Doctora is only in San Felipe temporarily," he said. "On an errand for Margarita Fuente."

For Doña Meg. Noemi had only a vague memory of her, from the day the Fuentes arrived in Chayaka to recruit workers for the dig. Noemi had been ten at the time, and she was intrigued by the tall gringa with the pale face and the yellowish hair. After Demetrio went to work for the Fuentes, he had mentioned Doña Meg many times. And she had given him books, some of them with colorful photographs that Noemi had pored over. They were her first real introduction to a wider world. And, of course, Doña Meg had sent the money for Demetrio, which the Señorita delivered. The Señorita who was now a physician, a doctora.

"What's the Doctora's errand?" Noemi asked.

Julio explained about the letter that Doña Meg had received and the Doctora's search for Meg's son. "She wants to talk to everyone who was at Los Ancianos the night of the fire." He glanced sideways at his father. "Including the watchman."

His father scowled.

"Does she know that the watchman was Domingo?" Noemi asked.

"No," Julio said. "She wants to find out who he was."

"That's easy," their father said. "Tell her no one remembers."

"Father," Noemi said, "what if Domingo knows something about the boy?"

"He doesn't," her father said. "He never mentioned anything about a child."

She remembered that night well, although it had been twenty-four years ago, when she was twelve, Nati's age. She had awakened in the darkness to hear Domingo, a young man then, calling outside their door, his voice panicky. He told Demetrio and her father about the fire at Los Ancianos and the need for the Fuentes' workers to flee town. And all because that devil, Otto Baldt, blamed them for the fire. "Domingo was terrified that night," she said. "He might have forgotten to mention the child."

Her father's voice hardened. "He would have said something, and he didn't."

Julio nodded. "I'll tell my friend that no one remembers the watchman."

Noemi went back to her weaving. She and Nati worked quietly, the only sounds the periodic thump of the wooden rod that packed down the threads on the loom and occasional half-hearted barks from their hound, Warrior, who was lounging beside a young lime tree that Noemi had been coaxing along.

Noemi thought of the knots on her necklace. The last one recorded the earthquake two years earlier, a heartbreaking catastrophe. And the knot to the left of that recorded two other terrible events, closely aligned in time—Pablo Fuente's unfulfilled promise to return the valley to the town and Otto Baldt's burning down the houses in Chayaka.

But there was no mention of the fire at Los Ancianos. Even though the fire was connected to the loss of the valley, her father had not woven the tragedy at Los Ancianos into the story behind the knot. In fact, Don Pablo, the owner of Los Ancianos, had died in the fire, voiding the new deed to the valley. But her father's version of events indicated only that the valley was promised to the people of Chayaka, but the promise was broken. Then, in an act of senseless cruelty, the neighboring Ladino landowners had arrived in the night and burned down the people's homes. It was the story that Noemi had told at her womanhood ceremony many years earlier, and it had remained the same through every ceremony since then, as each girl recited the history of her people, passing from one knotted thread on her necklace to the next. The destruction of the Fuentes' house had not entered her people's history.

Well, maybe that was all right, Noemi thought as she pro-pelled the shuttle across the loom. Her people had no claim to the house at Los Ancianos. What truly bothered her, she realized, was that they still had no idea how the fire at the Fuentes' house had started. People in the neighboring towns all believed that the Chayakans were responsible. In San Felipe, people had accused Julio of coming from a town of cold-blooded murderers. That lie had certainly become engraved in the local Ladinos' history.

Now that she thought about it, she realized that if anyone had insight into how the fire started, it would be Domingo. He had been the watchman, after all. He had never returned to Chayaka after he left on the night of the fires, and he had never passed on information about what happened. Or had he? None of the elders would speak of the fire at Los Ancianos, but that didn't mean they didn't know anything.

Noemi looked at her daughter, who was focused on the fabric she was weaving. Soon she would be a woman with her own ka-kepi, her own knotted necklace. Noemi wanted her to know the whole story of the night of the fires. Nati should grasp what really happened and understand that her people were blameless.

"I'd better get back to San Felipe," Julio said, rising from his stool.

"I'll walk with you to the bus," Noemi said, and a minute later they were walking down the dirt road that led past their neigh-bors' houses to the bus stop in front of the municipal building. Julio would take the last bus of the day out of Chayaka, heading for San Felipe. Up ahead, a few men had gathered, all preparing to return to the capital after a weekend visit home. Noemi slowed. "I've been thinking," she said, her voice low so that no passersby would hear. "I would like to help the Doctora search for the boy."

Julio shot her a stern sideways glance. "You heard our father."

"I know. And I don't want to stir up trouble. But Domingo might remember details of what went on that night. Clues that would help lead to Doña Meg's son."

A young man hurried past them on the way to the bus stop, and they paused in front of a concrete block house, one of several constructed after the earthquake with help from a Dutch relief organization.

"Father is right," Julio said sharply. "It's best to leave the past alone."

Noemi cast a surprised look at her brother. What was this? Noemi could hardly remember a controversy when Julio had sided with their father. "You know I respect our father's beliefs," she said, "but this time I think he is mistaken. If I take the Doctora to see Domingo, we can inquire about the boy. But we may also discover what happened at Los Ancianos that night, how the fire started."

Julio scowled. "That's what you really want, isn't it? To dig up the past. You and our brother are the same. But see where it led him. Where it led us all."

Julio's words stung. And they were unfair. It was true that she was interested in the history of their people, but she certainly didn't dig around for it. Except maybe in this case. She heard the anger in Julio's voice, and she recognized the resentment he had always felt against Demetrio. It had not been easy for Julio to live in the shadow of his older brother, who had always seemed so perfect.

And she heard a hint of dread in Julio's voice. A fear of the past. Not a decades-old fear, but a more recent one. Two years earlier, Julio had been living in San Felipe, working as a shoemaker and married to a young woman from Chayaka. His wife was pretty, but in Noemi's opinion, not very mature. The girl felt lonely and miserable in San Felipe, and after she gave birth to a son, she had taken the infant and moved back to live with her parents.

Then the earthquake struck. It was the middle of the night when Noemi awoke suddenly, terrified at the maniacal shaking of the earth under her sleeping mat. She had leaped up, grabbed Nati, and shouted to her father. They all staggered out of the house seconds before the building collapsed. They were thrown to the ground as the earth continued to heave, but in the end, they only suffered cuts and bruises, most of them from trying to dig people out of the debris. She still had nightmares about that night, of the heaving earth, of the crash of houses collapsing and screams from her neighbors, of the smothering dust that rose high into the air. Of the thirst and hunger that followed.

Noemi's husband Martín had been in the capital then, where the earthquake wasn't as severe, and he had also survived without major injury. But her brother Julio's family hadn't been so lucky. Although Julio survived unharmed in San Felipe, his wife and small son were crushed under his father-in-law's house in Chayaka. It was a fate shared by many people there. The earthquake had leveled the town, leaving dozens dead and many more injured. Noemi could understand why Julio didn't want to think about the past. Guilt gnawed at him for being far from his wife and child when they died. And there would be no hopeful search for Julio's child. The boy was dead beyond any doubt.

They resumed walking. "Listen to me, Julio. You were very young at the time of the fire, but I still remember. Señorita Baldt came to warn us that her father was going to burn down the town." She too must have been young, Noemi realized, but she had crossed the ridge in the middle of the night to warn everyone. "And later, the Señorita brought us the money from Doña Meg. The money that paid for you to learn shoemaking. Now the Señorita is a doctor, and it is our turn to help her and Doña Meg." She paused, cocking her head. "Don't you think so?"

Julio looked away. He would come around, she knew. She was, after all, his older sister. She had looked after him when he was a boy, and she had supported his intention to move to San Felipe and study a trade, despite their father's misgivings. After the earthquake, she had grieved with him, accompanying him in the rites for the dead.

"I don't know," Julio said. "It all sounds foolish to me. What makes you think that Domingo will tell anything to the Doctora?"

"Maybe he will. Maybe he won't. We won't know until she tries." In fact, she wasn't sure that Domingo would confide anything to the Doctora. The Baldt family, aside from Patricia, had never been friendly to the people of Chayaka. But Noemi was related to Domingo by marriage. And after the earthquake, she had kept an eye on his elderly parents, a service that Domingo had appreciated. He might talk to her.

Domingo had fled to Guatemala City twenty-four years earlier, fearing for his life after the fire at Los Ancianos. Apparently, the threat of Otto Baldt had kept him there. He was fortunate to have carpentry skills, and after a number of years, he had opened his own shop in the city.

"And if Martín is at Domingo's place when you arrive?" Julio asked.

Noemi hesitated. Her husband Martín had left Chayaka four years earlier to make some money. His Uncle Domingo had given him a job and a place to live in his family compound. At first, Noemi had accepted Martín's decision to work in the capital. The fact was, he and her father didn't get along well, and the household was less tense without Martín there. The first month or so after her husband left, he had come home every weekend. Then the visits came every few weeks. Martín urged Noemi to bring Nati and join him in the city. But how could she leave her father? And uprooting the old man wasn't possible. Chayaka was his world.

Martín had been gone for over a year when Noemi learned about his infidelity. Domingo had visited Noemi during one of his periodic visits to Chayaka, and he confessed with regret that his nephew was spending time with a Ladina girl. Noemi could imagine what that meant, especially as Martin had begun sending less money home to her. Then a few months ago Noemi learned third-hand from her cousin Pilar that Martín was now the father of a baby boy. It was a knife in Noemi's heart, and she'd said nothing to Nati about her new half-brother. She'd also revealed nothing to her father, but he probably knew already. The old men had their own sources of information. She told Julio about her husband's second family, and he had started giving her small sums of money when he went home, enough to tide them over.

Now that Noemi was contemplating a trip to the capital, she had to admit that she didn't want to see Martín with his new wife and child. She needed no reminder of her pitiable status as an abandoned wife. But neither did she want to let the Doctora down.

"There's another thing," Julio said, although Noemi could tell his resistance was weakening. "You haven't seen the Doctora for years. What if she's changed? What if we can't trust her?"

"You're right," Noemi said. "That's a concern. But we can listen to her and observe her, see what she's like. If we think her heart is sound, I'll offer to take her to Domingo. If not, I'll say nothing."

"All right then," Julio said. "We'll talk to her together and come to a decision."

Noemi smiled at her little brother, now a full-grown man in his thirties. "Yes. We'll do that. I'll take the first bus to San Felipe on Tuesday morning. We can go to the clinic together."

CHAPTER TWENTY

Patricia put on her cream-colored cardigan sweater and strode to the clinic to make her long-awaited call to Hank. It was Sunday evening, and he should be home from Barbados by now. It had been hard watching him go off on his Caribbean vacation without her, but hopefully his week in the sun would help energize him to make it through the rest of the cold, snowy winter. That had been her intention when she'd planned their vacation—a brief but glorious reprieve from winter. She was getting her own reprieve, but it was feeling less than glorious.

She opened the clinic's side door with her key, turned on the hall light, and made her way to the office. It seemed like she'd waited forever to tell Hank all her news—about Quique and Carlos, and working with Fiona at the clinic. Sitting at the desk, she dialed the country code for the U.S., then Hank's phone number. The phone rang once, twice, and kept on ringing. After twelve rings, she hung up.

Where was he? Probably with his daughters, regaling them with stories about the trip. She could hardly fault him for going out on a Sunday evening instead of staying home, as he usually did. And he couldn't have reached her at the clinic earlier, even if he'd tried. So, no problem. She would try again tomorrow.

She locked up the clinic, then walked briskly back to her apartment in the cool evening air. She had been looking forward to hearing Hank's deep, resonant voice, the voice that always assured her that all was right with the world. At the moment, her world did not feel even remotely all right. Even so, she had to admit that here in her home country, she felt a certain heightened awareness that she hardly ever felt in New Bergen. Maybe it was because the situation was so volatile, and the stakes were so high.

The next morning, the clinic was still buzzing with news of the San Felipe team's triumphant win at the football match on Sunday. Leti came in a few minutes late and reported that Tino was in the hospital, recovering from early-morning surgery on his broken leg. His surgeon expected him to make a successful recovery, and he was in reasonably good spirits, having been inundated with wishes for a speedy recovery from his family, teammates and seemingly half of San Felipe.

At one point, Patricia walked through the waiting room and heard a couple of old guys chortling as they relived the moment when Quique kicked the ball between Carlos's legs. Clearly, they thought it was hilarious. She hoped that Carlos wasn't being subjected to such ridicule.

Patricia's third patient was a nervous woman in a shabby dress and dusty flip flops. She had a cut on her arm that had become infected, and Patricia dressed the wound and gave her an injection of antibiotics.

"You should see improvement in a few days," Patricia said, but the woman continued to look fearful. "Is anything else wrong?" she asked. "Anything you'd like to talk about?"

The woman clasped her work-roughened hands in her lap. "It's something I saw," she said in a low voice. "On my way here from Las Américas."

Patricia tensed. That was the neighborhood at the edge of town where Quique lived. "There was a disturbance?"

The woman shook her head, then spoke just above a whisper. "A body. In the ditch." She crossed herself and shuddered. "They had slashed him. It was terrible."

Patricia froze. Could it be Quique? Was it possible that Carlos had already taken his revenge? "Did you know the man? What did he look like?"

"I didn't recognize him. He was an older man, a campesino maybe."

Patricia exhaled. It wasn't Quique.

The woman got up to leave. "No one is safe these days," she said.

A little before noon, Patricia drove to López Automotive. She would invite Quique for lunch, warn him about Carlos, and tactfully suggest he apply for a visa to the States. The farther he was from Carlos, the better.

In the garage, she spotted Quique working under the hood of a pick-up. Although she had been quite certain he wasn't the corpse in the ditch, it was still a relief to see him.

He looked up as she approached him. "Doctora. How can I serve you? Does your car need work?"

"Actually, I'd like to buy you lunch. There's something I want to discuss with you."

"That sounds mysterious."

"No. It's all straightforward. We just need a chance to talk."

"There's a café not too far from here. It isn't fancy, but the food's okay."

Quique cleaned up, then they walked up the street and around the block, Patricia passing on Leti's news about Tino.

At the restaurant, they took a table off to the side. Quique ordered a beer and Patricia ordered a Coke. They both requested ham sandwiches, which Quique said were pretty good. Three young guys at a nearby table spotted Quique and gazed at him admiringly. Quique seemed unaware of their adulation. He must be used to it.

She waited until the drinks were served, then took a deep breath. "Look," she said, "I'm not sure how to say this, so I'll just say it. My father is Otto Baldt, and I believe that makes me your half-sister. I didn't realize it until about a week ago."

He looked puzzled, then shook his head. "Oh, I see. You think that Otto Baldt was my father. Lots of people seem to believe that. But he wasn't. So you can't be my sister."

"I was told that—"

"Look, Doctora, Claudette said you were helping Fiona at the Clinic. So I imagine you're a good person. But you and I are not related."

What had she expected? She couldn't blame him for rejecting her, given that her father had rejected *him*. "My father was a foolish man in a lot of ways. No one knows that better than I."

"Your father was nothing to me, Doctora. I never even met him." His eyes narrowed. "Oh. Are you here about the inheritance? Claudette said you were working on that. Don't worry. I don't expect anything."

"No, actually, I came to warn you about my brother Carlos. I'm afraid he may try to take revenge on you. And I also want to make you an offer."

"Revenge?"

"For the football match. For that last goal."

Quique threw back his head and laughed. "Oh, that. One of my best shots. But look, every player makes mistakes. We all look like idiots from time to time. Why should your brother be any different? And anyway, there's nothing to get upset about. It's only a game."

"I think it's more than a game to Carlos. I suspect he wants to kill you." There. It was out. Welcome to the family. Your brother wants you dead.

"Doctora, please. I'm sure the entire Metro team would like to see me dead. But I can't start looking over my shoulder every time I score a goal." He paused. "I've heard about your brother, though. And I appreciate the warning."

The food arrived, and Quique dug into his sandwich. Patricia stared at hers, trying to think of a new tack. Quique had no idea just how much Carlos detested him or how out of control Carlos was.

"You said you wanted to make me an offer," he said.

"I wanted to suggest that you apply for a visa to the States. I could help you get it."

He raised an eyebrow. "Did Claudette put you up to this?"

"No. It's my idea. The fact is, I'm afraid for your life. Carlos has a militia, you know. And frankly, I think he may be crazy. He has threatened both my mother and me. And he put a family friend on a death list. The fellow left the country."

"Even if I wanted to go, visas are hard to come by."

"Not if I claim you as my brother. I have an influential friend in Chicago. I think he could pull some strings and arrange a visa for you. Fast."

"That's generous of you, but you have no proof we're related, right? Anyway, it seems pretty drastic." He started to pick up his beer bottle, then put it back down. "Just out of curiosity, why do you want to help me? You don't know me at all. And even if it turned out that I was your half-brother, well, most families want nothing to do with their illegitimate kin."

She looked down at her half-eaten sandwich. It was a fair question, and she wasn't sure she had a good answer. Why had Quique become so important to her? Of course, there was the risk to him from Carlos, and that was huge, but it was more than that. Quique was a miracle to her. He was the strong, good-natured brother she'd always wanted. All those years she was growing up at Finca Baldt, he had been right here in San Felipe, and she'd had no clue. But now he was part of her life.

She met his gaze, aware she couldn't tell him any of those things. "I like your kung fu kicks," she said.

He grinned, his brown eyes crinkling. "Yeah, Claudette does too."

Patricia heard a booming voice and saw a large, muscular man enter the café and head for an open door in the back of the room. It was Muro, she realized. And at his side was Carlos. He spotted her and lifted his chin in recognition. A second later, he halted. His gaze locked on Quique, and his handsome dark eyes glazed over with loathing. Her breath caught, and she turned to Quique, who had gone pale. Carlos disappeared through the back door.

"How fast can you get a visa?" Quique asked in a low voice. "I mean, just in case."

Thank God Carlos had shown up, she thought. That one hateful look was more persuasive than anything she could have said.

"Pretty fast, I think." She took a notepad and pen out of her bag. "I'll need some information—your full name, for starters."

He nodded. "Enrique Aguilar Soto. My father worked for the fruit company on the coast. I don't have his name because he died unexpectedly, before I was born."

"And your date of birth?"

"July 10, 1950." He frowned. "I suppose you'll need a birth certificate. That could be a problem. I was born in Santa Catarina, but there was a fire at the mayor's office several years ago, and a bunch of the old records were destroyed. They told Mama that all the information from 1950 burned up."

"I'll handle it," she said. It was just one more obstacle, besides the formidable one that her father had never formally recognized Quique as his son. No matter. One way or another, she was going to get her brother away from here.

Back at the clinic, Patricia went into the office, opened her purse, and pulled out the sheet of paper with the phone numbers that Jonathan Cabell's assistant had compiled for her. There it was: "American Consulate," right under "American Embassy." She dialed the number. A moment later, a woman with a brisk manner answered in Spanish and explained to Patricia that no, she could not talk to a consular officer. However, she could make an appointment to do so. "I have an opening on May tenth," she said.

"May? This is February. That's months from now."

"We're very busy. You're not the only person applying for a visa."

"I understand that," Patricia said, "but this is urgent. Please let me speak to your superior."

"I'm sorry, Dr. Baldt. There are no consular officers available. Would you like the appointment for May tenth, or should I give it to someone else?"

Stuff it, she wanted to say. Instead, she politely declined the appointment.

Jonathan's Cabell's phone number was on the same list, and she dialed it. As she waited for the call to go through, she pictured Jonathan sitting at his desk overlooking Lake Michigan. On the opposite wall would be the photograph of Dwight Eisenhower, standing beside Jonathan in a stream, both men in waders, holding rods and reels.

Jonathan's assistant answered the phone, and a minute later Jonathan was greeting Patricia warmly.

"Any news?" he asked, and she could hear the guarded hopefulness in his voice.

"I'm sorry. Nothing about J.J. Actually, I have a favor to ask." She explained that she had a half-brother in San Felipe, and she'd like to help him get a visa to the States.

"You have another brother?" Jonathan said. "You've been holding out on us."

"I just found out. Believe me, it was a surprise. He doesn't actually claim my father as his, but everybody in San Felipe knows he's Papa's son."

"Well, that's the best news I've heard in a long time. A brother you never knew about. Tell me all about the boy."

Patricia discovered she was happy to describe Quique—his good looks, his work as a mechanic, his skill at soccer, his volunteer work with the Canadian priest, his American girlfriend. Briefly, she explained about the explosive political situation in the country, including the presence of death squads. She didn't mention that Carlos was involved with one. None of the information seemed to surprise Jonathan.

"Let me see what I can do about Immigration," Jonathan said.

At five o'clock Patricia took a phone call in the clinic office. She thought it would be Hank, at last, but this time it was Meg. "Dad told me about Quique," she said. "Oh, Patricia, that's so exciting. Are you pleased to have a new brother?"

"As a matter of fact, I am," Patricia said. "But I'm sorry to put Jonathan to so much trouble with Immigration."

"Are you kidding? He's happy as a clam. And so am I. You realize of course that Quique is as good as my brother too, since we're all family."

Family. The Cabells had been her adopted family for years, in loyalty if not law. It was only natural that when Quique arrived in the U.S., he would be welcomed joyfully, as a long-lost family member. In fact, she mused, maybe she should have tried to pass him off as J.J. As eager as Meg was to have her son back, she might not have examined him too closely.

When the last of the patients had left, Patricia sat at the desk in the clinic's office and called Hank. He picked up on the fifth ring.

"Hullo?" It was his familiar deep voice, sounding a little tired.

Patricia smiled, buoyed at the sound. "It's me. How are you?"

"Patty? I was just thinking of you. How are things in...what's the name of the town? Sorry. I guess my brain's still on the island."

"San Felipe."

"Right. Any news from the anonymous writer?"

She explained about waiting at the park for the meeting that never materialized.

"Sorry to hear it. That must have been frustrating."

This whole damn trip has been frustrating, she thought. "How was your vacation? Did you like Barbados?"

"Oh, it was great. Toured the island. Swam in the ocean. Went snorkeling. Saw all these fantastic tropical fish. You would have loved it."

"Sounds like fun." She twirled the phone line around her finger. "Anita said you found someone to hang out with."

"Oh, yeah. Irene."

Had his voice softened? "I'm glad you made a friend."

"Yeah. We were lucky. Say, I have good news. Judy had her baby. Michael John Ericsson," he said, his voice swelling. "Six pounds, four ounces."

"Oh, Hank, you're a grandfather! Congratulations."

"Thanks." He sounded pleased and a little smug.

"Who delivered Michael?"

"Anita mostly, from what she said. But Dr. Bergit was there to help out. She said it was his first delivery since medical school, so he was happy to have her do most of the work."

"How are they doing—Judy and the baby?"

"Both doing fine. Mike has a good pair of lungs and a head of blond hair. A real Norseman. Irene said her grandkids were all born bald."

Irene knew before she did? "Oh? Where is Irene?" She tried to sound casual.

"Back in Montana. She has a ranch there, lives with her son and his family."

"So, she found out before I did?" She tried to say it lightly, teasingly.

"She asked me to call her as soon as Judy had the baby. So I did."

"It's nice that you're staying in touch."

A pause. "Actually, Irene has invited me to visit her in Montana next month."

Not us, Patricia thought. Just him. "Oh? And what did you tell her?"

"That I'd think about it." A pause. "I told her about you, of course."

"Oh? And what did you tell her?" Had the two of them sat around raking over Patricia's failings?

"Just that we've been together for a while. That you don't want to get married. Not to me, anyway." They were back to this issue again, his desire to marry and her unwillingness.

"The fact is," Hank said, "Irene and I have a lot in common. We both had a real good first marriage. We have grown kids and grandkids, and we're both ready to start again. Look, I was going to wait until you got back to bring this up. But maybe now is a good time to say it." He cleared his throat. "If you want to marry me, then I'll call Irene and tell her I won't be going to Montana. But if that's not what you want, I'll plan to visit her."

Patricia felt like she'd been punched in the stomach. Just what she didn't need, on top of everything else in her life. An ultimatum from Hank.

"You can think about it, tell me when you get back," he said, his voice softer. "When will that be? Saturday?"

"Not that soon. The end of next week, maybe." Actually, she had no idea when she'd get everything taken care of. She still had to figure out what happened to J.J., if that was humanly possible. Beyond that, she needed to find a way to keep the finca, her mother, and now Quique safe from Carlos. The end of her visit was not yet in sight.

"That will give you time to consider your decision," he said.

"Yes. I'll do that."

"Well, talk to you later," he said. She waited, expecting him to say "I love you" or "I've missed you." But he didn't say it.

"Yeah, talk to you soon," she said.

They hung up, and she stared, unseeing, at the shelf of medical texts in English and Spanish above the desk. Hank's demand was badly timed, but she couldn't really blame him for making it. She sank back on her chair. Marriage to Hank. It wouldn't be so bad, would it? In New Bergen, they were practically living as a couple already, considering all the evenings and weekends they spent together. And Hank was easy-going and affectionate, not to mention sexy in a mature way. Certainly, fifty-three wasn't that old. She'd met his relatives. They were vital and hard-working well into their eighties.

She wondered where they'd live as newly-weds—her house or his? His, no doubt. His place was full of years of accumulated junk, and she couldn't see him parting with it. He might be willing to give her up, but he would be hard pressed to let go of the broken-down Chevy he kept in the barn or his vast assortment of vintage tools and the lumber he'd collected over the years.

Besides, the house was where his girls had grown up. She didn't want to take the place away from them.

Patricia continued sitting at the desk, staring into the void. Then she remembered that she needed to tell Anita that she was extending her stay in San Felipe. She looked at her watch. A quarter to six. Anita might still be at the clinic, finishing up. Mondays tended to be long, with patients having accumulated medical problems over the weekend. Patricia called the clinic number, and Anita picked up the phone after a few rings.

"When are you coming back?" Anita asked after they'd greeted each other.

"That's what I called to tell you. I'm not sure."

"Arne will probably stay on if you want him to," Anita said. "He's been moping around, telling me he's going to miss being the country doctor when you return."

She'd never really thought she was indispensable. Here was proof. "It's good to know I'm so easily replaced," Patricia said, trying to sound light-hearted.

"Oh no," Anita said. "The patients all ask about you. And I can hardly wait till you're back. Arne's wife is a sweetheart, but she brings home-baked pastries every day. Today it was these darling little apricot-walnut muffins. I must have eaten half a dozen. I tell you, my slacks are already feeling tight." She laughed. "If you don't get back soon, I'll need a new wardrobe."

"Sounds dire," Patricia said. "Say, I hear you're an aunt."

"We're all so excited. And did you hear? Mikey arrived two weeks early, right on Mom's birthday. I know it's crazy, but it feels like a sign. Like Mom is still with us."

Patricia remembered what a terrible blow Betty's death of cancer had been to Hank's two daughters five years earlier. "I don't think it's crazy. She's probably keeping an eye on you." Who knew?

Betty had always watched over the girls—unlike her own mother, who had taken little interest in her children.

"Do you think so?" Anita asked, her voice cracking. A pause, then a laugh. "In that case I'd definitely better cut back on the muffins."

She and Anita talked for another minute, then said good-bye. After Patricia hung up, she stood up, gathered her purse, and left the clinic, locking up behind her. As she walked down the street, her thoughts returned to Hank's phone call. It was decision time, or soon would be. Did she want to marry Hank? And was she ready to step into the role of grandmother? She'd never even been a mother.

An empty feeling settled in her gut. She would never be the grandma that Betty would have been—still was, in her daughters' hearts. Patricia thought of her life in New Bergen. It didn't vary much, aside from the occasional cross-country ski trip. She worked hard at the clinic, shopped for groceries at the Jack and Jill, accompanied Hank to potlucks in the basement of the First Lutheran Church, had pizza with her single female friends, went to a movie now and then.

And always, always she was the foreigner, the outsider. She'd become resigned to it. But would she also be the outsider in Hank's family? Not just an in-law, but the woman who tried to take Betty's place. She was sure that Hank didn't feel that way about her. But there were things he didn't see.

CHAPTER TWENTY-ONE

A little before eight, Patricia strode along the streets of San Felipe, joining the Tuesday morning bustle of people hurrying to work. She thought of Hank. The uncertainty that she'd felt the night before about his ultimatum had turned to irritation. Couldn't he have waited until she got home? He must have recognized that she was under stress. Still, as he said, there was no rush in making a decision. She had other things to think about, and at least for the moment, she was still maintaining her position one step above Irene.

By the time Patricia reached the clinic, the cool morning air and her brisk walk had evened out her mood. As she strode across the waiting room, her breath caught. At the back, Fiona was talking to a woman in a brown huipil and skirt, the unmistakable clothing of Chayaka. The woman appeared to be in her thirties, as did the man beside her. His features were Indian, but he was dressed in Ladino-style slacks and a white shirt. As Patricia approached them, she realized there was something familiar about the Chayakan woman with the round, solemn face and almond-shaped eyes. She appeared uneasy, although of course, that was a common reaction to being in a clinic.

Fiona turned. "Patricia," she said in her Scots-accented Spanish, "I would like to present my friend, Julio Quespe. And this is his sister—"

"Noemi," Patricia said, breaking into a smile. "Oh, my gosh, it's been so long."

Noemi smiled in return, looking relieved. "I am glad to see you, Doctora," she said. She spoke in Spanish, but her voice had the Chayakan lilt, its sound bringing back memories of Demetrio and the other workers at the dig. At first, Patricia had found their speech ugly, she remembered. But over time she had become comfortable with it. What a terrible little snob she had been. It was a wonder that Demetrio had put up with her. Or that Pablo had let her into the dig at all.

"You know each other?" Fiona asked.

"From years ago," Patricia said. "Noemi was just a girl when we met. And Julio was even younger." She thought of her long-ago trip to Chayaka to deliver Meg's letter. The Chayakans had regarded her with suspicion, but not Noemi. She had disobeyed her aunt in order to talk to Patricia.

"I'd best attend to patients," Fiona said, "but you all should have a proper chat."

They crowded into the office, taking the three available chairs. "How is your brother Demetrio?" Patricia asked. "I've thought of him often."

Noemi and Julio exchanged a look. "I have sad news," Julio said. "Our brother is dead."

Patricia rocked back, a gasp escaping her. Demetrio dead? How could it be? A memory flooded her—of Demetrio cradling the pot shard with the bands of birds. All this time she'd thought of Demetrio as alive. Now she would never see him again.

Her eyes filled with tears, and she blinked them back. However deeply she might feel his loss, it must be far worse for Noemi and Julio. "I'm so sorry," she said. "When did he die? During the earthquake?"

Julio shook his head. "A few years before that. He was working in the countryside. When he came home, he was sick. And then he passed away."

Patricia thought back. Demetrio had been only a couple of years older than she was. So he must have been in his mid to late thirties when he died. "Did he have a wife? Children?"

"No, Doctora," Noemi said.

How sad, she thought, for a man so devoted to Chayaka never to marry and have kids.

"Our brother traveled a lot," Noemi said. "He lived in many places."

"I see." Patricia felt a tug at her heart as she realized that Noemi and Julio shared not only Demetrio's dark oval eyes but his quiet dignity too. "I have never known a finer man than Demetrio," she said. "I can see him in you both."

Noemi and Julio exchanged a look, ending with a small nod from Julio.

Noemi turned to Patricia. "Fiona says you want to find the watchman who was at Los Ancianos the night of the fire."

So that's why they had come this morning, because of her request to Fiona. "Yes. I'm looking for information about Meg's son, Juan José. She received an anonymous letter. It said that he was alive." She hoped that her words would spark a sign of some knowledge, but she saw nothing beyond concern in their expressions. "I've spoken with everyone I could find who witnessed the fire," she continued. "The only person left is the watchman. I understand he was from Chayaka. Do you know him?"

"Yes," Julio said. "But he doesn't live there now."

"He lives in the capital," Noemi said. "I can take you to see him. But he may not want to talk about that night. It was a painful time for our people. We can see what he says." Her voice was gentle but authoritative, the voice Demetrio had used with the workers at the dig when he had important information to convey. Demetrio was gone, but his younger sister had a force of her own.

"Shall we go now?" Patricia asked.

Noemi nodded. "I am ready."

Patricia took Fiona aside and explained that she and Noemi would be driving to the capital.

"No problem," Fiona said. "Leti and I will carry on here."

Julio approached them. "I have to go now."

"I'll see you at the Cultural Center," Fiona said. She clasped her hands. "I'm excited about the marimba concert. And a bit nervous."

"You will be fine," Julio said. By the time Patricia and Noemi were ready to leave, he and Fiona were busy planning a series of practice sessions. How natural they look together, Patricia thought. Fiona and Julio, both of a similar age and height. And it hit her that they were fond of each other.

Patricia and Noemi set off for El Patio, where the Land Cruiser was parked. The sidewalks were less crowded now that people had arrived at work. Patricia began to greet a middle-aged man standing in front of a house, but she halted, shocked, when she realized he was staring at Noemi with open distaste. Patricia shrank under the malign gaze, as if it had been directed at her as well, but amazingly, Noemi appeared to ignore the man. But could she really? Had centuries of hostility from Ladinos taught Indians to block out the hatred? Or had they just learned to mask their feelings?

At El Patio, they used the bathroom in Patricia's apartment, then climbed into the Land Cruiser, settling in for the three-hour drive. Patricia steered the car across town, finally pulling onto the boulevard that led out of San Felipe. It was better not to be too optimistic about the meeting with the watchman, she warned herself. So far, nothing had come of her inquiries. Still, she couldn't stifle that small hope that this would be her big break, that the watchman would have the key to J.J.'s whereabouts.

Outside of town, pines studded the hills surrounding them, the branches forming patterns in the shadows that crossed the road. Noemi gazed out the window, seemingly transfixed, and it occurred to Patricia that Noemi had probably never made this trip in a car. But her Spanish was good, for an Indian woman. Maybe her world wasn't too circumscribed. "It's a nice day for a drive," Patricia said.

Noemi turned to face her. "Yes." She seemed to hesitate. "Doctora, do you think Doña Meg's son is alive? Is it possible?"

"That's what we've been asking ourselves," Patricia said. "All I know is, Pablo Fuente and his son never left the burning house. At least no one saw them. So we assumed they had both died. Later, the police found the charred remains of a man and a child, and everyone assumed they were Pablo and J.J."

Noemi seemed to ponder that. "So, the boy is probably dead. But we cannot be sure. Not one hundred percent sure. In that case, we must look for the boy. No, for the man. If he lived, he is a man now, maybe with a wife and children."

"Exactly," Patricia said. "Thank you for coming. It's very kind of you to help."

Noemi lowered her eyes to the woven bag on her lap. "I too have a reason to go. I want to know what happened at Los Ancianos that night. You see, people in other towns say...they say the people of Chayaka burned down the Fuentes' house. Julio heard them say this. They said it to his face."

"That's awful," Patricia said. She thought of her father, who had not only spread the story but started it in the first place. She wished it was only his ignorance at fault, but she knew that malice had played its part. It was always easy to blame Indians. And he had a special dislike of Chayaka. He couldn't bear the idea of Indians owning the valley at Los Ancianos. By the end, he probably believed his own lies about the arson. Maybe he had believed them from the start. "What do the people in Chayaka say about the fire at Los Ancianos? Do they have any idea how it started?"

"No one in Chayaka talks about that night. It was a terrible time. First, the fire at Los Ancianos. Then our houses burned down. And finally, we lost the valley. People do not want to remember."

"But you want to?" Patricia asked.

"I have a twelve-year-old daughter. I want her to know the truth. Not to feel shame."

"I can tell you a little," Patricia said. She explained about her father and his workers driving to Los Ancianos to put out the fire. "One of the workers thought he saw a man in Chayakan clothing running away from the house. My father decided that the man must have started the fire. That's what he told Javier Tapia, and later he said the same thing to the police. I'm sorry. I tried to tell Papa that he was mistaken, but he wouldn't listen to me."

"What about Doña Meg?" Noemi asked. "Does she believe that my people burned down the house?"

"No, and neither did her parents. Meg's mother thought the electrical wiring might have been at fault. It was old and dangerous. Or maybe somehow the propane tanks had exploded. Her parents never believed the workers were responsible. They knew how fond Pablo and Meg were of the men. Especially Demetrio."

"I'm glad," Noemi said.

"And anyway, the idea was absurd. Your people had no reason to burn down the house. Pablo had signed the papers giving the valley to your town." Of course, she thought, Chayaka had soon lost the valley, just as the towns that had received land under Arbenz's land reform had lost theirs. From what Arturo had told her, the laws were annulled after Arbenz was deposed. The people in power didn't want Indians and peasants to own good land.

They rode in silence for several minutes, as the car passed the remains of harvested cornfields, the stalks burned to the ground.

"You say that Domingo was the watchman," Patricia said. "Do you know him well?"

"He is my husband's uncle."

That should help. "So, was your husband in favor of this trip?"

"My husband works in Uncle Domingo's shop in the capital." She paused. "I haven't seen him for over a year."

They were separated then. Had Noemi's husband abandoned her? That could make this trip more complicated, especially if the husband was there.

"Have you been to the shop?" Patricia asked.

"No, but Julio has. He told me how to find it. It's just off the Avenida Bolivar in Zone 3. On Second Avenue, past Rosita's bakery and across from the Torres Pharmacy."

"That shouldn't be too hard to find. I just hope your uncle will be willing to talk about Los Ancianos with us."

"We will try."

They drove on, lapsing into silence once again. Patricia's thoughts turned to Demetrio. The shock of learning about his death had partially subsided, and now questions bubbled up. "You said that Demetrio traveled a lot. Did he move around to find work?"

Noemi nodded. "He worked at digs around the country for many years. Usually for gringos. Dr. Herrero recommended him to archaeologists, and they hired Demetrio."

"They were lucky to get him."

"Yes. He came home with lots of good stories. And he learned many languages, so he could talk with the workers. He was smart that way."

"I remember."

"He was happy excavating," Noemi said. "He told me so. He helped to uncover wonderful things. Tall pyramids hidden in the jungle, beautiful masks decorated with jade, caves with ancient paintings. He had a good life."

"I'm glad to know that," Patricia said. It wasn't difficult to imagine Demetrio in the thick of the excavations. She remembered him at Los Ancianos, standing in line with her for coffee, telling her about the small discoveries of the day. He had taken pleasure in them all.

If only she could have said good-bye to him. And then she remembered that they had said good-bye. It was after the elders forbade the Chayakan workers from digging at Los Ancianos. She and Demetrio had walked across the valley together, stopping at the base of the hill that led to Chayaka. She still remembered the warmth of his handshake. The work ban hadn't been permanent, and Demetrio had returned to the dig, but it was never the same after that. She'd had virtually no contact with him, and not long after, her father had dragged her away from the excavations.

Now that she thought of it, that long-ago farewell had been the final one. So, she had been able to say good-bye to Demetrio after all. She was grateful that he had come into her life. He'd been a friend and mentor. And now she had the chance to get to know his siblings and niece. When life gave you a second chance, even by way of a long detour, you were a fool not to take it.

CHAPTER TWENTY-TWO

I t was easy enough for Patricia to find Domingo's business, the Excelsior Carpenter Shop, after stopping at a gas station to fill up the tank and ask for directions. She parked in a space just beyond the shop on a street lined with small businesses.

She and Noemi walked into the office at the front of the shop and stood at the counter. Through a side door they heard hammering and the intermittent buzz of a saw. The smell of fresh wood and a haze of sawdust permeated the air.

A young man with Indian features appeared at the door, his long apron littered with wood shavings. Noemi took charge, explaining who they were and asking to speak with Señor Domingo Chombe, the proprietor. The man disappeared into the shop, returning a moment later to escort them to a door at the other end of the workroom. Patricia wondered if Noemi's husband might be among the workmen, but Noemi looked straight ahead, showing no sign of recognizing any of them.

The door opened, and Patricia and Noemi were taken to a room furnished with a wooden table and an assortment of rustic wooden chairs with faded cushions, all facing a TV set topped with a

V-shaped antenna. Under the low ceiling hung a framed picture of an ethereal-looking Jesus.

Patricia and Noemi sat, and a minute later, Domingo joined them. He was middle-aged, with a paunch that no doubt signaled his financial success. When he saw Noemi, his broad face opened into a grin, displaying widely-spaced teeth. In Spanish, he welcomed them both to his home.

Noemi introduced Patricia, and Domingo stiffened when he heard the name Baldt. She explained that Patricia lived in the U.S. now, but she was volunteering at a clinic in San Felipe.

"Is that right?" Domingo said in a carefully neutral tone. This interview is going to be hard, Patricia thought. Then Noemi mentioned that she had dropped in to visit with Domingo's parents the day before, and they sent their greetings. Domingo inquired about Noemi's father and brother, and she replied that her father was well, cantankerous as always, eliciting a smile from Domingo. He seemed interested that Julio was learning to play the marimba and would be participating in a concert.

A middle-aged woman with frizzy brown hair and a light complexion entered with cups of coffee and a plate of store-bought sandwich cookies. Domingo introduced her as his wife. So, Patricia thought, he had married a Ladina, not a woman from Chayaka or even an Indian. Mrs. Chombe served the drinks, her reserved smile revealing a chipped front tooth. Before leaving, she cast a quick, sweeping look at Noemi. Patricia suspected that this was the first time that Mrs. Chombe had seen her nephew Martín's Chayakan wife. She didn't appear pleased.

"Uncle, I have come to ask you a favor," Noemi said after her aunt had withdrawn.

"I will help you if I can," he said.

Noemi faced Patricia. "Please excuse us, Doctora," she said, then turned to Domingo and began speaking in their Indian language.

Patricia had learned a little in her time at the dig, but mostly she relied on a few Spanish words and names that she recognized—Pablo Fuente, la gringa, Los Ancianos—to get a clue as to what Noemi was saying.

Noemi spoke softly, her tone friendly but serious. Domingo frowned a couple of times, and his responses sounded terse. At one point, pain flooded the man's deep brown eyes, and Noemi lowered her gaze for a moment. They spoke for another minute, then Domingo nodded.

Noemi sat back. In another room, a baby cried and a woman hushed it with soothing sounds. For a moment, Noemi's gaze shifted in that direction. Patricia realized that the infant could be her husband's second child, the one he had by the Ladina.

"I will tell you what I remember, Doctora," Domingo said in Spanish, his gaze fixed on a distant point, so that his eyes didn't meet hers. "But what I relate is for your ears, and for the ears of Señora Fuente. Not for the police or for others."

"You have my word," Patricia said. She hoped the word of a Baldt counted for something, that her father and brother hadn't completely destroyed the family's credibility. Noemi had vouched for her, and apparently that was sufficient. Patricia would have to guard the information well, whatever it turned out to be.

Domingo sat upright, hands clasped in front of him. "As you know, I was the watchman at the Fuentes' house. The family had left for a week and their employees had left too. I was a serious young man, and I knew I was in a position of responsibility. I walked around the property, making sure everything was as it should be.

"Then, when it was near midnight, I heard the sound of a Jeep. It was the Fuentes, returning early. I helped them unload their things. Then Don Pablo took me aside and said that he'd signed the papers transferring the valley to Chayaka. I was very excited.

I asked Don Pablo if I could go down to the valley, to check on it. I had told Demetrio that I would keep an eye on the place, if I could.

"Don Pablo agreed, and I walked around the valley, listening and watching. Nothing seemed amiss. When I got to the dig, the area was covered with plastic sheets, but I could see the outline of the place clearly in the moonlight. I sat down outside the shed, and I must have dozed off. I awoke to the smell of smoke. Not the smoke of our hearth fires. This had a strange smell, a sick smell.

"I got up and looked across the valley, toward the Fuentes' house on the cliff at the far end. Flames were rising into the air. I was horrified. I was the watchman, you see, and I'd let the house catch on fire. I was sure that Don Pablo would blame me. I began to run across the valley to the house. Then suddenly there was an explosion, and enormous flames rose into the air. The fire was like some kind of monster devouring the house."

The propane tanks, Patricia thought. Evelyn, Meg's mother, had said they were too close to the house.

"In the light, I made out a green truck near the house. One of the Finca Baldt trucks."

So, Gustavo was there already, Patricia thought. He must have arrived shortly after the fire started.

Domingo hesitated. He looked at Noemi, who nodded encouragingly. "I was running when I saw something out of the corner of my eye," he said. "Something moving across the ridge above me to the south." He paused, looking uncertain.

Patricia sat forward, barely breathing. Could it be J.J.?

"Please tell us what you saw, uncle," Noemi said.

"The problem is, I'm not sure. It was a strange creature. A hooded figure like a man, but it was running on four legs. With an awkward gait."

What in the world? Patricia exchanged a confused look with Noemi.

"It is difficult to see things in the dark, and from such a distance," Noemi said. "Is it possible you saw a horse under a blanket? Or maybe some crippled animal?"

"No," Domingo said, his voice lowering. "It was not like any living creature I know. It was a spirit, an omen of evil. I stood there, without moving. I was terrified that the creature would see me. It would fly down and suck out my soul. But it continued running across the ridge, and finally it disappeared into the darkness."

Patricia breathed out. Domingo had seen some kind of imaginary phantom, when she'd been hoping he'd spotted a four-year-old child.

"Then I started running to the house again," Domingo said. "But I was nervous about who might have come in the truck. So, instead of taking the steps up from the valley, I followed a steep path that led to some trees not far from the house. When I was almost at the top, I spotted a man. He was standing with his back to me, watching the fire."

"What did he look like?" Patricia asked.

Domingo's brow creased. "A worker maybe. He had wide shoulders, but his legs looked short and skinny. That's all I remember."

"That must have been Gustavo, my father's mechanic," Patricia said. "He had seen the light in the sky over the Fuentes' house. He drove over to check it out." But it seemed odd that he was just standing there, observing the fire. Of course, Gustavo was a practical man, and maybe at first, even he had felt helpless before the ferocious flames.

Domingo took a sip of coffee and put down the cup. "That's when I realized that I hadn't seen the Fuentes since the fire began. Of course, I became very frightened. What if they were inside? But just then, the man started walking around the house. He must know where the family is, I thought. They're behind the house, and he is going to join them there."

Domingo paused, his gazed lowered. "I am ashamed to say that I stayed where I was. I had to face Don Pablo. I knew that. But what could I say to him? I could not tell him I had fallen asleep. He had trusted me to look after his property. Then, after a while, I heard a loud rumble, and another truck arrived. Men jumped down. I heard one of them call, 'Don Otto,' and a man answered—a tall, blond man. This must be Otto Baldt, I thought. The men got to work immediately, trying to put out the fire. I could see that Don Otto was in charge, so I stayed out of the way."

Domingo stopped speaking. Patricia opened her mouth to say something comforting, but Noemi shook her head, and they both waited silently.

Finally, Domingo turned to Patricia. "I never knew your father, Doctora, but with all respect, I heard that he was an angry man, and he did not like Indians. I was afraid he would see me, and he would blame me for the fire. So, I watched from behind a tree."

"You were right to avoid my father," Patricia said.

The tension in Domingo's face eased a little. "I didn't know if I should stay or leave. Then a man walked over near the tree where I was hiding. I started backing away, but he saw me, and I ran into the trees that led down to the ravine. I heard him shouting, 'Hey! I saw an Indian. The guy who set the fire.' I wanted to turn and defend myself, but I was scared. So, instead, I ran farther into the ravine. When I was at the bottom, I heard voices above me. 'Who was it?' a man asked. And another man said, 'A guy from Chayaka. Probably one of Fuente's workers.'

"Please believe me," Domingo said. "If I had known that Don Pablo's family was still in the house, I would have remained. I would have done everything I could to save them."

"I understand," Patricia said.

Domingo sighed and swept a hand through his short, black hair. "I knew I had to get to Chayaka." He turned to Noemi. "I raced to your father's house and told him everything. Then we went to the mayor. He and your father agreed that Don Pablo's workers weren't safe in the town, not if Don Otto thought that they had set fire to the house. Besides, we knew that the Ladinos would be furious when they found out that Don Pablo was giving the valley to Chayaka. If Don Otto knew about it already, he would have one more reason to punish the town. He was a violent man, and he would choose a violent means of taking revenge on us, maybe even killing Don Pablo's workers."

Patricia flinched. Her horrible father. The Chayakans seemed to know him well.

Domingo turned to Noemi and continued. "Your father wanted to tell everyone to escape into the forest, but the mayor said no, that wasn't necessary, at least for now. So, we only went to the houses of the men who had worked at the dig. The men gathered a few possessions and fled. I was the last to leave. After several weeks, some went back to Chayaka. But not me. I stayed here in the capital and worked for my cousin."

In the patio, a child's high-pitched voice shrieked, then burst into tired sobs.

"And the Fuentes' boy?" Noemi asked gently. "Did you ever see him?"

"No," he said mournfully. "I never saw the child."

Noemi and Domingo exchanged a few more utterances in their language, then they all stood.

"Thank you," Patricia said. "I know these memories are heavy ones."

"I am not proud of my actions that night," Domingo said. "I should have put out the fire when it started. Or at least awakened the family. I was a coward to run away."

"You were young," Patricia said. "Who hasn't made mistakes in his youth? Besides, you were right about my father. He might have killed you if he'd found you at Los Ancianos."

Domingo nodded. "Please tell Doña Meg that the workers from Chayaka never turned on the Fuente family."

"I'll tell her," Patricia said.

"And I'm sorry I have no information about her little boy."

They turned to leave, and Noemi suddenly halted. A nervous-looking Indian man in his thirties stood in the doorway. "May I speak with you?" he asked her quietly. It must be her husband, Patricia thought. The rat.

Noemi straightened. "Very well. But I only have a minute. I'm here with the Doctora."

Patricia offered to wait outside, and Domingo escorted her through the workshop and out to the street while Noemi remained inside. "Thank you for talking with me about Los Ancianos," Patricia said.

"There was evil there that night. I can still feel it in my bones. But it was long ago. I am glad to put it behind me now."

"Yes," she said. "I would like to do that too." Maybe someday, when this was all finished. They said good-bye, and Domingo went back into the shop.

She ambled over to her car, but her thoughts were turbulent, and she ended up traversing the street, going over the conversation with Domingo in her mind. He had been her last real hope for information, and she still had no idea if J.J. had survived the fire, or even how the fire had started. On the other hand, she had a better picture of what happened at Los Ancianos that night. And she had the sense that Domingo's confession had been cathartic for him. That was worth something.

She paused at a cramped storefront where magazines displayed photos of Mexican TV stars. For ten centavos, she bought a little bag of plantain chips that she munched on as she waited for Noemi. She hoped that Noemi's conversation wasn't too painful.

As Patricia was approaching the car, Noemi appeared, her face flushed, and they both climbed into the vehicle.

"That was my husband, Martín," Noemi said, but volunteered no further information. She gazed out the side window as Patricia started the car and maneuvered it into the street. "You know," Noemi said, "I would never want to live here. It is no place to raise children—with the dirty air and all the thieves and other villains. And no one here knows the old ways. My father says that sooner or later they lose their souls." She seemed to ponder that. "Yes," she said finally. "I think it's true."

CHAPTER TWENTY-THREE

Noemi sank onto the passenger's seat of the Doctora's car. It was a relief to have the conversation with Domingo over. And she had to admit, she was glad to have seen Martín. He still cared for her, he said, and for Nati, the daughter he hadn't seen for over a year. Nor had he wanted to leave Chayaka, he said. It was her father who was the problem. Martín could no longer live under the same roof as that cantankerous old man.

Noemi thought back to the last months before Martín left for the city. Her father had been especially irritable, criticizing everyone around him. She was used to it and let his words slide off her. But Martín was sensitive to his father-in-law's slights. She should have defended Martín better, Noemi realized. If only she'd known how. At least, it wasn't her own flaws that had sent her husband away, not her stubbornness or the way she became absorbed in things of little importance. She was glad for that.

Now that Martín had another family, Noemi supposed she too might remarry, but she couldn't think of any likely prospects in Chayaka. When she was a young woman, two boys had tried to court her, but they had given up when they realized they would have to move in with her father if they married her. And there was no alternative. Someone had to look after her father, and it fell to Noemi. Martín had been the first man willing to wed her under the circumstances. They had married without a priest, but with a traditional Chayakan ceremony and the blessings of the town. Noemi wondered if Martín had married in the Church this time. The Ladina girl might have insisted on it.

Noemi thought of her secretive, irascible father, the source of her marital problems. He had never been affectionate, but he had always been respectful of his children, never striking them, and she had always had the sense that he cared for them in his own way. She would never forget the hours that she and her father had spent sitting side by side on her aunt's patio, where he had taught her the history of their people. That knowledge was now part of who she was, and what's more, it gave her a position of respect in the town. But just as importantly, Noemi would always look after her father in order to honor her sweet and caring mother, who had greatly admired her husband.

It was after one o'clock by the time the Doctora announced that they were approaching Zone Four, where the city market was situated. Noemi admitted to being hungry, and they parked near the market, then made their way inside to a large, airy dining space, filled with delicious smells and the chatter of people seated around long plank tables. She and the Doctora sat on a bench near a vendor selling hot stuffed peppers and plantains filled with beans, a feast that they hungrily gobbled down.

A couple of Indian men in new-looking straw cowboy hats approached and sat at the same table. Noemi greeted them in Spanish, and they revealed they'd come from Momostenango and had just delivered a load of woolen blankets to a market vendor. It was pleasant talking to them, Noemi thought, these men from another Indian town with their own ways of dressing and talking. She'd been taught that outsiders were dangerous, and interaction with them was to be avoided, but from what she'd seen, it wasn't always the case. The men finished their meal and got up, wishing Noemi and the Doctora a good day.

"How did your conversation go with your husband?" the Doctora asked.

"It went well. Martín intends to visit Chayaka soon—maybe this weekend. He wants to see our daughter, Natividad."

"Well, that's good news," the Doctora said.

Back on the road, Noemi stared vacantly out the window as they entered the stream of cars leaving the capital, some heading for the mountains and others for the coast. On the way into the city, she had watched the changing scenery with interest. Over the years, she'd visited the place a few times, once to visit the Museum of Anthropology with Demetrio—an exciting trip. But that was years ago, and the city had altered since the earthquake, with vacant lots and new buildings. Now, however, her head was full of thoughts about their visit to Domingo's shop, and she paid little attention to what was outside the car windows.

She was disappointed that Domingo had told them nothing to help understand how the fire had started at Los Ancianos, although it was clear, of course, that no Chayakan was involved. And she now understood why Otto Baldt thought that it was a Chayakan who was guilty of setting the fire. His worker had seen Domingo running away and thought he was responsible.

The sad thing was that they were no closer to finding Doña Meg's son. Noemi thought back to Domingo's description of the four-legged creature on the cliff. It was very odd. She'd grown up hearing stories of spirits taking different forms, sometimes human, some-times animal, but none had taken the form of a hooded man with four legs. Unless...she glanced at the Doctora, who was focused on maneuvering among the vehicles that streamed around them.

"Do you remember the creature that Domingo saw on the cliff?" Noemi asked.

"Sure. What about it?"

"I don't think it was a spirit. I think it was something else."

"Like what?"

Noemi hesitated. Was her idea even worth bringing up? She decided to take the chance. "What if Domingo saw two people under a cloak?"

"Two people?"

"A tall person and a short one. Maybe an adult and a child. You know, one head, four legs."

Patricia faced Noemi, wide-eyed. "A child? You mean...you think that J.J. might have been under the cloak?"

Noemi gasped as the car began to swerve into the next lane.

The Doctora jerked it back as a car horn blasted, and she pulled the car off the road into the parking lot of a pharmacy. "Sorry," she said, her hands gripping the wheel.

"Doctora, are you all right?" Noemi asked. She too was feeling a little shaken.

"Yes, yes. It's just...it was a shock. To think that the apparition might have been J.J."

"It's only an idea," said Noemi.

"But it's a possibility. And it's the only one that's come up so far. We have to consider it." She tapped a finger on the steering wheel. "If the short legs belonged to J.J., the next question is, who did the long legs belong to? Who was the man under the hood?"

"They say there are people who steal children," Noemi said. "And sell them to gringos."

"I've read those stories too," Patricia said, "although I'm not sure I believe them all. Supposedly, the child is sent to the U.S. or some other wealthy country. He's adopted by a family with money. It's hard to believe anyone could be that greedy and cruel, but then, there are all kinds of people. Meg's father is looking into that possibility, just in case."

The Doctora steered the car back onto the highway. After a while, they took the turn-off leading into the mountains, and the road became narrower and steeper. Noemi kept juggling ideas in her head. Was it possible that someone had burned down the Fuentes' house in order to kidnap their son? Even for a Ladino, that seemed crazy. She thought of the hooded figure. Domingo said it looked like a man. But could he be sure? "The person in the cloak," she said, "it might have been a woman, no?"

"I suppose so," the Doctora said. She steered around a rickety truck belching fumes.

"Maybe the woman was lonely," Noemi said. "I have heard of such things. A woman is childless. Or maybe her child dies. So, she looks for a child—an orphan or a sister's child. Of course, she wouldn't just steal him. Not usually."

The Doctora nodded. "It's possible, I suppose. A grief-stricken woman becomes a kidnapper or agrees to take a stolen child."

Noemi lowered her gaze to her lap. She had raised the idea that it might have been a cloaked woman that Domingo saw, but she truly hoped it wasn't the case. Some things were too unnatural. Many mothers lost a son or daughter, sometimes more than one, but they would never steal another woman's child.

CHAPTER TWENTY-FOUR

I t was a little after five when Patricia dropped off Noemi at the shoe repair shop where her brother Julio worked, and a few minutes later, she pulled into the parking area at El Patio. She felt drained of energy after the long drive and the intense conversation with Domingo. Trudging to her apartment, she went in and lay down on the bed in the tiny bedroom, pulling a woolen blanket over her. She awoke to a tap on her front door.

"Patricia?" came Fiona's voice. Patricia rose and padded to the door.

"Fancy some stew?" Fiona asked.

A few minutes later, Patricia sat at Fiona's table, breathing in the rich aroma of beef stew.

"I'm keen to hear about your trip," Fiona said as she joined Patricia. "What did you learn?"

Patricia prepared to launch into a description of the trip to Domingo's shop but abruptly halted, remembering her vow of confidentiality. "There's not much to report," she said. "The watchman didn't remember seeing J.J."

"That's a pity," Fiona said.

Patricia longed to ask Fiona what she thought of the apparition. Instead, she described her lunch at the market with Noemi. "She reminds me of her older brother, Demetrio," Patricia said, then described how she and Demetrio had met and worked together at the Fuentes' excavation.

"I wish I had known him," Fiona said. "His brother Julio is a very fine person," she said, her cheeks flushing. "And he's a very talented musician. We've set up a practice schedule to prepare for the concert."

After supper, Patricia walked to Beatriz's shop to buy shampoo. She'd finished the sample-size tube she'd packed for the trip. Besides, it felt good to stretch her legs after the filling meal.

Beatriz was behind the counter, apparently working the late shift. She was conversing with Father Gerard, the handsome French Canadian priest.

"How is your search for the child going?" Father Gerard asked after they'd greeted one another.

"Actually, I may have a lead," Patricia said. As soon as she said it, she realized that she should have kept her mouth shut, but the words had spilled out.

"I'm delighted to hear it," Father Gerard said, his brown eyes crinkling in a smile.

"What kind of lead?" Beatriz asked. "Was it from someone you trust? Lots of people like to tell stories, whether they're true or not."

A feeling of disquiet crept over Patricia. This shop was probably a hub for San Felipe gossip, with dozens of people coming and going. It would be easy for the news of Patricia's possible discovery to leak out to someone with a stake in the outcome of her search, possibly even an arsonist or kidnapper. She needed to be more careful. "Really," she said, "it's not even a lead. Probably just wishful thinking."

"Either way, my prayers are with you," Father Gerard said.

"And mine," said Beatriz.

Patricia thanked them both and went to look for shampoo. She paid for her purchase and left quietly.

Sleep came slowly that night as Patricia lay in bed. She wanted very much to believe that Domingo had spotted J.J. that night, that the boy had survived. But was she deceiving herself? She might be giving too much importance to a wispy shred of memory, one that could have been distorted by time. Domingo's sighting was, after all, nothing more than a brief glimpse of a ghostly figure lit by the light of moon and flame.

Patricia awoke the next morning feeling a certain lightness, and it took her a moment to realize why. Being with Noemi had been like being with Demetrio. His sister had the same gentle demeanor, the lilting voice, the insightful intelligence. It had felt good to be with her.

Now that she was getting to know Noemi and Julio, it would be too bad to lose touch with them. There was always mail, although it was slow and not entirely dependable at the Guatemalan end. Once she got back to the States, she could look for ways to be supportive of Noemi's daughter, Natividad.

Patricia put an egg on to boil, then dressed in a pink, short-sleeved blouse and navy skirt. Fiona's laundry woman had consented to wash Patricia's clothing also, and the woman returned her clothes clean and neatly pressed, looking far better than they did back in New Bergen, where Patricia usually neglected to haul them out of her dryer until they were wrinkled.

When Patricia arrived at the clinic, the waiting room was half full, and the time went quickly. At break, she peered out to see how many more patients had come in, and she spotted Gustavo, who was slouched in a chair, shoulders hunched and eyes gazing downward, a picture of misery. She hoped his ailment was nothing too serious.

She flashed back to Domingo's memory of Los Ancianos in flame and of Gustavo standing immobile before the fire. It must have been right before he found Meg. If only he'd turned and looked across to the cliff. He might have seen J.J. being hurried away by the cloaked figure. If such a thing actually happened. She pushed the thought aside. While she was at the clinic, her mind needed to be on her patients.

Patricia headed back to her examining room, and Leti handed her Gustavo's file. "He insisted on seeing only you," she said. The sheet on top said: "No problem stated." Leti shrugged.

"Okay," Patricia said. Gustavo must be feeling sensitive about his condition, maybe a genital or urinary tract problem. He might have been too embarrassed to describe the problem to Leti, an attractive young woman.

Gustavo entered the examining room a moment later. After exchanging greetings, Patricia sat down beside a small table with a few supplies—gloves, tissues, thermometers—while Gustavo took the patient's chair across from her. "How can I help you?" she asked, trying to sound both friendly and professional.

Gustavo gazed at the door longingly, like a prisoner desperate for escape. Then he lowered his gaze to his worn brown leather shoes, his hands clenched. "I have made a terrible mistake."

Venereal disease? It wouldn't be the first case she'd seen here. "Yes? You can tell me. We are in confidence."

"I wrote the letter."

"The letter," she repeated. "What letter was that?"

He stared at her, his lips smashed together.

Then it hit her. "*Ay dios mío*. It was you. You wrote to Meg Fuente, didn't you?"

He nodded.

"Is J.J. alive?"

His pained expression told her even before he shook his head.

A cry rose in her throat. Dead. J.J. was dead. She felt something wither inside her.

"I am very sorry," he said. "I was stupid to write the letter."

She wanted to scream at him, but she kept her voice level. "Why did you do it?"

Gustavo met her gaze, his dark eyes a pool of anguish. "Ever since that night, I've felt guilty. Because I didn't go back for the boy and his father."

That night. The night of the fire at Los Ancianos. "How could you have gone back for them? The house was in flames. It was collapsing. I saw it."

"I know but...." His shoulders sagged. "That night lives with me. I just wanted to comfort Doña Meg. I wanted her to know...to think...that her boy was alive."

Patricia raised a hand to her brow. This was too much. "Gustavo, do you have any idea how much pain and trouble you've caused?"

He hung his head, silent.

"You know what this means, right? Now I'll have to tell Meg that her son is dead." Unless you'd like to do it, she wanted to say, but she wasn't quite that heartless.

He flinched and met her eyes. "If only I could take back the letter. Please believe me. I never meant to hurt her."

"I know," Patricia said, feeling a tiny shred of compassion for this idiot. Then a thought occurred to her. Last night at Beatriz's shop, she'd said she had a lead. Could Gustavo have heard about it? Did he realize he needed to stop the hopeless search before it went any farther? "Gustavo, did you tell Beatriz about your letter?"

He nodded. "She said I had to talk to you today. So I came."

At least Beatriz had some sense.

Gustavo stood. "Thank you for your understanding, Doctora," he said. "You are a good person." Then he slipped out the door, closing it behind him.

Patricia stared vacantly at the wall in front of her, with its poster urging parents to vaccinate their children. J.J. was dead. Ever since Meg received the letter, Patricia had held this little seed of hope that he was alive. Now it was gone. Whatever Domingo had seen in the firelight, it wasn't J.J. Tears welled in her eyes, and she took a tissue from the box on the table.

A knock on the door. Leti's face appeared. "Are you ready for your next...oh." She gently closed the door, and a minute later Fiona came in and sat across from her in the patient's chair.

"Tell me about it," she said.

"Oh, Fiona, he's dead. J.J. is dead." Her voice broke. "He died in the fire."

"Ach. The poor wee thing."

"I didn't expect it to hurt so much. Not after all these years."

Fiona stood and laid a comforting hand on Patricia's arm. "It's just the way of it. You're mourning him all over again."

The tears flowed, and Patricia mopped them up with the tissue. "I wanted so badly to tell Meg that J.J. was alive. I wanted it more than anything."

Fiona clicked her tongue. "I'm that sorry. Look, stay here or go for a walk, whatever helps. I'll be here if you need me."

Patricia trekked half way across San Felipe, setting a brisk pace. She wanted to wear herself out, be so exhausted that she felt nothing. What a fool she'd been, thinking that she could find J.J.

On her way back to the clinic, she arrived at the Central Park, then crossed the street and climbed the stairs leading up to the white stone cathedral. Inside, she made the sign of the cross, more out of habit than conviction, before sitting in the back row of dark wooden pews. The place was as she remembered it from visits during her childhood, with its white walls, high vaulted ceiling, and the front altar trimmed in gold. Saints clothed in fine fabrics kept watch over the congregation from alcoves along the walls. Above the altar stood a statue of Jesus bleeding on the cross, reminding the faithful that they weren't alone in their suffering. Patricia closed her eyes and let the spicy aroma of incense and the deep, cavernous quiet sink into her.

When she opened her eyes, she rose and made her way forward, her joints stiff from the long hike. She entered a side chapel with a statue of the Virgin Mary and rows of votive candles. An ancient-looking woman, bent over in a black dress, was lighting a candle and mumbling a prayer. For a husband or friend? Maybe even a son or daughter, at her age. Life was a vale of tears. She'd heard that often enough, growing up. Expect to suffer until you die.

Patricia paid for three votive candles, one for Pablo, one for J.J., and one for Demetrio. "You are in my heart," she whispered as she lit each one. As she walked down the side aisle, she passed familiar saints in the alcoves—San Miguel, San Juan Bautista, San Pedro, and her favorite—Santa Teresa, all silent observers of innumerable broken hearts. By the time she left the church, she felt scoured out by grief, but the tears were over.

It was a little after six when she spotted the clinic sign half a block away. Thank goodness. Besides having sore feet, the air had turned chilly, and she hadn't taken a wrap. But she was ready, or at least as ready as she would ever be, to take on the next hurdle—phone calls to Meg and Jonathan. The work day would be over in Chicago, and with luck, Meg's husband Charlie would be home.

The clinic door was locked, but Fiona let her in. "I was just tidying up," she said. "Are you all right?"

"Yes, mostly." She explained that she was going to call Meg.

"I don't envy you," Fiona said. "Oh, by the way, you have a phone message from the American consulate." She handed Patricia a note saying she had an eleven o'clock appointment the next day to discuss a visa for Enrique Aguilar Soto—Quique.

So, Jonathan Cabell had come through. "Thank you," Patricia said. "I needed some good news."

Patricia sat at the office desk and dialed Meg's number. Meg picked up at the other end, and Patricia said hello, trying to keep her voice calm.

"There's something wrong, isn't there?" Meg stated.

"I have news. I'm afraid it isn't good. Is Charlie there? He should hear this too."

Meg called Charlie, her voice wobbly. "It's Patricia. She wants to talk to both of us." A moment later Patricia heard the click of another extension, and Charlie greeted her.

"Okay, tell us," Meg said softly.

"It's just as we feared," Patricia said. "J.J. died in the fire."

Silence. Then a long, barely audible "Oh."

"I'm sorry," Patricia said. "I can't tell you how sorry I am."

"It's okay," Meg said before her voice dissolved into muffled sobs.

"Did you find the writer?" Charlie asked.

"Yes. It was Gustavo, my father's mechanic. The fellow who

rescued Meg from the house." She explained that he had felt guilty about not being able to rescue J.J., and he wanted Meg to have the comfort of thinking that her son had survived. "He feels terrible about the letter."

"He should," Charlie said.

"The girls will be disappointed," Meg said.

"I'll tell them," Charlie said. "We're grateful for all you've done, Patricia. Do you know yet when you'll come back?"

She hadn't thought of that. Her original reason for coming to Guatemala was now over. "Let's see. I have an appointment at the Embassy tomorrow. And a few things to take care of. I suppose I'll fly back next week, maybe around Wednesday." That would give her a few days to transfer Finca Baldt to her mother and see that the visa application for Quique was underway. She felt a knot in her stomach. Could she really leave then, while Carlos still posed a danger to Quique and her mother? "I'll let you know," she said, and they hung up after a round of thanks and goodbyes.

The call to Jonathan wasn't quite as hard. "We can't really hate Gustavo, can we?" he said. "After all, he saved Meg's life all those years ago. He sounds unbalanced to me."

Patricia could imagine what a psychiatrist might say. Something like, "Gustavo has past traumas that he's never fully integrated." Very similar to what a psychiatrist had once told her when she was doing her psychiatry rotation in medical school and underwent a short, compulsory analysis. She had chosen to disregard the diagnosis.

After Patricia and Jonathan hung up, she continued to sit at the desk, her gaze traveling idly over the shelf of medical books above the desk, most written in English, a couple in Spanish. One thing was sure, she didn't want to be alone with her thoughts to-night. Over the last few years, she'd become accustomed to talking through her problems and disappointments with Hank, but that

241

was now out of the question. Fiona had mentioned earlier that she was going to spend the evening practicing the marimba with Julio, so she wasn't available. And anyway, Patricia felt like she'd dumped her problems on Fiona too much already. She contemplated calling Arturo, but she didn't need lawyerly advice, and besides, she had a feeling he wanted to further their relationship in a way that wasn't appropriate for a married man. She would call him tomorrow to let him know that the search for J.J. was over.

Sergio had given her one of his business cards, and she pulled it out of her purse and dialed the number of the plastics company where he worked. By luck, he was still there.

"Can I buy you dinner?" she asked.

"Sure. Where would you like to go?"

"Someplace out of the way." If she fell apart, she didn't want to do it in front of a crowd.

"I know a place that should work," Sergio said. Ten minutes later he drove up to the clinic. She was standing in front, her mind in some kind of limbo, and she climbed into the car, settling into the passenger's seat.

"You okay?" he asked. She knew from an earlier glance in the bathroom mirror that she looked washed out, her eyes rimmed in red.

"J.J. is dead." She'd said it so often now, the words were a little less wrenching.

Sergio's face fell. "Oh no. I'm sorry." He reached over and squeezed her hand. "How did you find out?"

She recounted her conversation with Gustavo while Sergio listened, nodding occasionally.

"Poor Meg," he said. "Have you told her?"

"I called her. And her father too."

"How was she? Did she seem all right?"

"Not really. But her husband was there with her."

"That's good," he said. "She wasn't alone. And now the worst is over, no?"

Sergio drove them to the Café Europa, a restaurant on the other side of town. It was cozy in a low-budget, old-fashioned sort of way, with tables arranged around a small circular dance floor. Travel posters with scenic European sites hung on the walls, and the tables each had a squat wine bottle with a drippy candle stuffed in it. Patricia and Sergio sat beside a poster of the Roman Coliseum. Only three other tables had customers. Apparently, business was slow during the week.

As Sergio perused the menu, Patricia couldn't help noticing that he looked good in his camel-colored suit. A sage green shirt, unbuttoned part way, brought out the green in his hazel eyes.

When the waiter arrived, Patricia asked for a vodka tonic, hoping it would numb the pain. Sergio ordered a beer.

The waiter returned with the drinks, and they both ordered lasagna. Patricia took a long swallow of her drink and felt herself relax. An aromatic basket of French bread arrived.

"Have some," Sergio said. "Vodka doesn't make a wholesome dinner. I should know."

She took a piece of the warm bread. The hollow feeling in the pit of her stomach wasn't just misery, she realized. It was also hunger.

A few minutes later, the waiter served the lasagna. After a few bites, Patricia set down her fork. "There's one more piece of news. Hank wants to leave me for a lady rancher in Montana. Her name is Irene."

"Nice name. Is she rich?"

"Maybe, but I don't think that's the attraction. He wants a wife with grandkids."

"A grandmother. That's a new one. Usually men go for someone young and sexy. Like you."

She ignored the compliment. "He gave me a choice. Either I marry him when I get back, or he dumps me for Irene."

"That's easy," said Sergio. "Send him off to Grandma. And you stay here."

"I'd have to be crazy to remain here," she said.

"Why?"

She sighed. "Think about it. My brother detests me. And he's really going to hate me when I sign over the finca to Mama."

"You've decided?"

"Yes. At least, I think so." She thought of her mother, who had been surprisingly friendly lately. Almost sisterly. When Patricia left, Eugenia would be on her own, pitted against her son, the monster Carlos.

"Your family is difficult," Sergio agreed. "But you could live in San Felipe. They rarely show up here. I imagine it's too provincial for them."

Sergio was right. The Baldts were snobs. She probably still was, although living in New Bergen had tempered her snootiness. Actually, the idea of staying in Guatemala had been lying at the back of her mind, but she'd mostly ignored it, assuming it would disappear of its own accord. It wasn't just her family that stood in the way, or even the idea of abandoning her patients and friends in New Bergen.

"I find the political situation here frightening," she said. "If my brother doesn't murder me over the finca, some right-wing death squad could decide it doesn't like me."

"Very true," he said, "and I don't take the situation lightly. There are lots of good reasons to leave. But stay anyway."

She peered at him to see if he was joking, but he didn't seem to be. "Why should I?"

"Because this is where you belong."

She took a forkful of lasagna, chewing it slowly. It was presumptuous of Sergio to think he knew what was best for her. But oddly enough, she wasn't irritated. And she had to admit, Hank's ultimatum had put New Bergen in a different light.

"Would you like another drink?" Sergio asked, when they'd finished their meal.

"I'd better not. I'm going to the capital early tomorrow morning." She told him about Quique's agreement to let her look into a U.S. visa for him, and her success in getting an eleven o'clock appointment at the consulate.

"Why don't we go together?" Sergio said. "I need to visit our company's banker. I can drop you off at the embassy and take care of my business. It shouldn't take long. Actually, I would be happy for the company." They arranged to meet at El Patio at seven and take Patricia's car. Sergio offered to drive, saying he wanted to try out a Land Cruiser. Besides, he knew his way around the capital.

Across the room, a skinny young man put money in a juke box in the corner, and a lively merengue came on. The rhythm of the tambora set her foot tapping. The young man and his slender, long-haired girlfriend stepped onto the dance floor and began moving to the music, their eyes locked on each other.

"Let's dance," Sergio said.

"Thanks, but I'm too tired."

"It will revive you."

"It's been years since I've danced merengue. I probably can't even do it."

"I bet you could do it in your sleep." He stood and extended his hand to her.

Why not? She rose and let him lead her to the dance floor. A pleasant tingle went through her when she felt his hand on the small of her back. His other hand clasped hers lightly.

And then they danced, her body picking up the syncopated beat, leaving behind the tensions of the day. He led her expertly, and soon their bodies were in sync—feet, hips, shoulders, arms. His lips curved into a knowing smile. In response, she affected the aloof but subtly teasing look she'd perfected as a teenager. His eyes flashed, and he guided her into a graceful turn, her body moving in the sensuous Latina way. She was alive, vibrant and sexy.

They sat down at the end of the song. "You're not a bad dancer," she said.

"I have three older sisters. They made sure I wouldn't embarrass myself on the dance floor."

"They did a good job. And you were right. I could dance merengue in my sleep." She laughed. "In fact, I think I just did." All this time, she had hungered for the dance and didn't even know it.

He grinned. "Next time we'll try the cumbia."

CHAPTER TWENTY-FIVE

Patricia woke up at first light, with sore muscles from her walk across San Felipe. The news about J.J. had been hard to bear, but the uncertainty was now over, and that was a good thing. Today she could look forward to driving into the city with Sergio. He had dropped her off at El Patio the evening before with a kiss that sent a tingle up her spine and promised better things to come.

She stood up and stretched, aware she must gather her strength to take on an American consular officer later that morning. Walking over to her small closet, she eyed her limited wardrobe critically. In addition to one of her blouse and skirt combinations, she chose her tomato-red blazer. It would provide her with a little power boost. She half wished she'd packed heels to give her a couple more inches. Her low black pumps would have to do.

Sergio was at her door at seven o'clock. He looked like a businessman, but not a stodgy one, in a slate-colored suit with a lavender tie. His brown hair was wavy in back where it brushed his neck.

"Okay, tell me," he said a few minutes later, when they'd left San Felipe and were on the highway. "How are you going to convince the American government that Quique Aguilar is your brother?"

"Good question." She ran her hands through her hair. She hoped the short bob would look okay when they arrived. It had still been wet when she left her apartment. "I wish I had someone to back up my claim."

"Like Quique's mother?"

"Exactly. But I can't count on her."

"You're right," Sergio said. "Claudette made it sound like Beatriz had a tight grip on her son. I can't see her letting go of him without a struggle." He swerved the car to avoid a bicyclist with a load of firewood on the back. "What about your own mother? She's a lady of wealth and status. Maybe she could say that your father claimed Quique on his death bed."

"My mother would die first." Or would she? Eugenia resented Beatriz, for reasons that were now clear, and she'd banished Quique from Finca Baldt when he was a toddler. But what if Patricia made a deal? "Now that I think of it, I could offer to sign over the finca to Mama if she testifies that Quique is Papa's son. I was planning to give her the estate anyway." Her mother might gag on the words, but she would probably do it if it meant getting Finca Baldt.

There was also the problem of Quique having no birth certificate, but she could deal with that later. People lost birth certificates. There had to be a way to get around it.

By ten-thirty, Sergio was driving through the streets of the capital. He turned onto the Avenida Reforma, which bordered Zone Ten. She noticed that he tensed as the American Embassy came into view.

She could understand his feelings. The embassy must have unhappy associations for him. It was the place from which the CIA had supposedly transmitted Radio Liberation twenty-four years earlier, sending its lies over the airways. It was also the place where the American ambassador had conversed with President Arbenz, knowing all the time that the U.S.-backed invasion force would soon arrive to depose him. And since then, the U.S. government had continued to support dictators who had no interest in the welfare of the common people. The Arbenz regime had been the first and last chance for the poor, offering them an opportunity to acquire a little land and gain workers' rights. And the U.S. was instrumental in crushing those reforms.

Sergio let Patricia off in front of the multi-story concrete building housing the embassy and consulate. It was surrounded by a tall fence, and young marines guarded the entrance. As an American, if an adoptive one, Patricia couldn't help wishing that the embassy looked more welcoming.

"I'll come back when I finish at the bank," Sergio said as he dropped her off. "But let's meet outside the Chinese Embassy down the street. I'm allergic to this place."

Patricia strode through the gate. Once in the lobby, a receptionist sent her to a lounge where anxious-looking people waited in rows of chairs. A few minutes later, a middle-aged Guatemalan woman in a tailored suit escorted her through a set of doors and up an elevator to the second floor, where Douglas Bostian, Vice-Consul, awaited her.

Bostian greeted Patricia with a smile and handshake, motioning her to sit in the comfortable leather chair on the other side of his desk. He opened a manila folder—Quique's dossier, she supposed. "You'll be pleased to hear that we are prepared to move forward expeditiously with your half-brother's visa."

"I'm very grateful," she said. Maybe this would be easier than she'd anticipated.

Bostian's good humor vanished, however, as Patricia explained the obstacles: her father had never formally recognized Quique as his son, and it might be difficult to obtain Quique's birth certificate.

Bostian tapped a fountain pen on his green blotter. "If your father failed to recognize Mr. Aguilar, I assume you have other evidence that he is your brother."

"Certainly," Patricia said. "My father declared on his death bed that Mr. Aguilar was his son. My mother, Eugenia Contreras de Baldt, will testify to that."

"Were you present?" Bostian asked.

"No, but two of the servants were, and they will also testify." It wouldn't be difficult to persuade a couple of maids to comply. "And frankly, Mr. Bostian, it is common knowledge that Enrique is my father's son. Everyone in San Felipe knows."

"That may be, but I'm afraid it doesn't qualify as proof." He skimmed through the sheets of paper in the file before him, then sat back. "Actually, Dr. Baldt, it appears that Jonathan Cabell is prepared to sponsor Mr. Aguilar, so it may not be necessary to establish that he is your half-brother. We should be able to issue him a work visa on the strength of Mr. Cabell's sponsorship. I understand your request has a certain urgency. The work visa will get him into the U.S. without further delay."

"Really? That's marvelous." Patricia felt her whole body relax. She wouldn't have to coerce her mother into telling a lie. And Quique had not been eager to join the Baldt clan. Now he wouldn't have to. At least for now.

Bostian frowned. "But we still need some proof of his birth." He tapped his pen on the blotter again. "You'll need to get a properly authenticated statement from the mayor of the town where he was born. Santa Catarina, isn't it? It should affirm that Mr. Aguilar was born there on—what was the date? July 10, 1950. Your brother can bring the document when he comes for his personal interview. My secretary will arrange that."

Patricia thanked Bostian, whose genial smile had returned now that the negotiations were concluded. She stopped at the secretary's desk and made an appointment for Quique with a consular officer for the following Tuesday. How smoothly things were accomplished when Jonathan Cabell's influence was brought to bear. The secretary escorted her back to the reception area downstairs. Patricia felt jubilant as she headed for the exit. Quique would get a visa without having to change his identity. Now she just needed the mayor's cooperation.

Sergio had parked in a small lot around the corner from the Chinese Embassy—actually the embassy of Taiwan. They drove to a nearby French restaurant, where they dined on seafood crepes. Sergio was in a good mood. The bank had approved a loan for expansion of the plastic factory. His older brother would be pleased. And Sergio was happy to hear about Patricia's success with the consular officer.

"I wish the gringos would treat everyone that well," he grumbled.

"Would you mind if we stopped off at Santa Catarina?" Patricia asked. The turnoff for the town was on their way, about half an hour south of San Felipe. They could be there by four o'clock, time enough for Patricia to get a certificate attesting to Quique's birth.

"Why not," Sergio said. "I haven't been there for years, not since I was an organizer. I can look up an old friend. I heard he's been active with a new co-operative."

As they drove out of the capital, Patricia thought back to her last trip to Santa Catarina. She had been eleven at the time. Three of her cousins had come to Finca Baldt for a visit, and they all decided to go to Santa Catarina for its saint's day celebration. Her teenage cousin had maneuvered a Finca Baldt truck over the winding, pot-holed dirt road. It was slow going. Patricia remembered little of the town—just a dusty plaza, a Catholic church with a spire, and a few tents with vendors selling religious ornaments and snack foods. It was a Ladino town, and not surprisingly, she'd seen no Indians.

After two and a half hours of driving, Sergio steered the Land Cruiser onto the road to Santa Catarina. Fortunately, as Claudette had reported, the road was now gravel.

The town square looked more modern than it had the last time Patricia was there. The municipal building, a cement block struc-ture, was on one side of the square. An elementary school with a wide veranda took up half of the adjoining block. Sergio turned onto a side street and parked near a tiny Pentacostal church. From what Patricia had heard, these small evangelical churches were taking hold in lots of remote places like Santa Catarina. She wondered where Claudette was staying. Too bad they wouldn't have time to visit her.

As soon as they got out of the car, Sergio threw his suit jacket and tie on the back seat. It was a warm day, a good reason to dress light, but Sergio appeared uneasy as he rolled up his sleeves.

"You look fine," she said.

He grinned sheepishly. "Last time I was here I was a young revolutionary. I don't want people to see the dressy clothes and think I sold out."

For the first time, Patricia realized that Sergio was a little un-comfortable with what he'd become, a manager in his brother's prosperous plastics company. She didn't see how that made him a sell-out, but what did she know? The closest she'd come to being a revolutionary was the night she spent in the bell tower with Che Guevara. And her task had been to make sure people turned off their lights in order to keep American planes from bombing the city. It had been a patriotic duty in her opinion, even if her team members were mostly Communists.

She reached up and tousled Sergio's hair lightly. "There. Now you're a little unkempt. Better for your image." She had an urge to kiss him on the cheek, but she resisted the impulse. Everyone in this small town would soon be talking about them as it was. And gossip traveled, maybe even to the clinic in San Felipe.

They walked back to the plaza, exchanging a greeting with a middle-aged woman wearing a faded polyester dress and carrying a woven basket. Sergio suggested to Patricia that they meet at the car when they were finished, and he headed across the square. She entered the municipal building and found two men sitting in the main room behind rustic wooden desks. One of them was a potbellied fellow with an air of authority. The other fellow, who sported a scanty mustache, sat behind an old-fashioned black typewriter. The two men had been laughing, but they quickly sobered. Behind them, a wrinkled, bird-like woman was sweeping with a twig broom.

"Excuse me, Gentlemen," Patricia said. "I am Doctora Patricia Baldt." They both straightened. "I hope I'm not disturbing you."

"No, Doctora, it's not a problem," said the potbellied man. He introduced himself as the mayor of Santa Catarina and his companion as the town secretary. "How can we serve you?"

"I am here on behalf of Señor Enrique Aguilar Soto. He was born here, I believe, and he has asked me to look for his birth records."

The mayor exchanged a guarded look with the secretary, then invited her to sit down on a wooden chair.

"Señor Aguilar was born in July of 1950," Patricia said. She expected the mayor to explain about the fire that had destroyed the records from that year.

"Do you know his date of birth?" the mayor asked.

"July 10."

The secretary rose from the desk and stepped into a side room, returning with a gray fabric-bound book. A hand-written label read "Births and Deaths: 1950-1954." He laid it on his desk and leafed through the book. "Here it is," he said and turned the book so that it faced Patricia. His finger pointed to an entry under July 10. Born: Enrique Aguilar Soto. Mother: Beatriz Aguilar Soto. Father: Otto Baldt.

She couldn't believe it! Not only was the birth record here, but Beatriz had identified Otto Baldt as the father, even though she hadn't given Quique his name. At the time of Quique's birth, she had probably still hoped that Otto would recognize their son. Was this why Beatriz had told Quique that his birth record was destroyed? Maybe she didn't want him to see Otto Baldt listed as his father.

"Could you give me a letter providing this information about his birth?" Patricia asked.

"Certainly," the mayor said. "Don Felix, take care of it please. I'll sign the document." The secretary cranked a sheet of paper into his typewriter and pecked away at the letter.

A few minutes later, Patricia paid for the letter, complete with an official town seal, and she exited the building, exuberant, the folded document in her hand. She had been extremely fortunate today, succeeding first at the consulate and then in Santa Catarina. She walked to the corner of the street where they had parked, but Sergio wasn't at the car yet, probably having a beer with his pal.

As she wondered what to do next, the woman who had been sweeping appeared beside her. She was tiny, her head just reaching Patricia's shoulder. Her gray hair was parted in the middle and pulled into two scrawny braids. "Quique was a sweet little boy," she said.

"You remember him?" Patricia asked.

"Yes. His grandmother and I were good friends." She tilted her head. "*Ay*, how she adored that child."

"I can imagine."

"Would you like to see his grave?"

Patricia startled. "You must be thinking of another child, Señora. I came to find the records for Enrique, the son of Beatriz Aguilar Soto."

The woman nodded, her small black eyes alert. "Quique, we called him. He was just a little guy when he died, *pobrecito*. Two years old maybe."

"Really." This was going nowhere, Patricia realized. The old woman had clearly confused Quique with another child.

"It was August of 1952. I remember because my little granddaughter died then too. A terrible sickness went through the town. We lost three children in a single week. *Ay*, it broke our hearts. I can show you his grave."

Why not? Patricia thought. She didn't mind humoring this old lady. If Sergio was talking over old times with a friend, he could be a while, and a walk would feel good after sitting in the car for hours.

They crossed the plaza and followed the street beside the church, walking for three blocks until they came to a hill. The old lady started climbing up a path, Patricia behind her. At the top they halted, and Patricia looked out over a wide, flat cemetery strewn with weeds. A shadow crossed the graveyard, and she raised her eyes to see a swallow with a long tail. A messenger, Demetrio might have said. The old woman led her past gravestones, many small and worn down by the elements. Several of the newer-looking markers shared the same year of death—1976. Two years ago. They were earthquake victims, she realized. This town had seen its share of suffering.

The maid stopped at a group of three gravestones near a tall pine tree. The one on the left was for the schoolteacher, Teodoro Aguilar Belén. That must be Beatriz's father, Patricia thought. And the one beside it was for Mercedes, his wife. Below them was a smaller marker, for Enrique Aguilar Soto.

255

Patricia stared in shock at the small headstone. Enrique's birth date matched that of the town records—July 10, 1950. What she couldn't understand, what set her mind reeling, was the fact that there was indeed a date of death—August 23, 1952.

It wasn't possible. How could Quique Aguilar, Beatriz's son, have died in 1952? He was living in San Felipe today. Unlikely explanations rose in her mind. Could the boy have had a twin, who for some reason was given Quique's name? Was it possible that another child was buried here? Or no child at all? She walked over to the maid, who had wandered away to peer at a nearby grave.

"Tell me, Señora," Patricia said, "were you here when Enrique was buried?"

"Certainly. I came with his grandmother. Then a week later, we buried my own granddaughter."

"I'm so sorry," Patricia said. "Did Beatriz have other children?"

The old woman shook her head. "Only the one. They say she adopted a boy later, but I never saw him. She didn't bring him here. Well, that's the way, isn't it? The young people go off to other places and forget about the old people at home."

Patricia thanked the maid for her help, and the old woman headed back across the graveyard. Patricia remained, trying to make sense of the headstones. She noticed that Mercedes had died in September of 1952, two months after Enrique. Poor Beatriz. To lose both her mother and her son. If that's what really happened.

But if the first Quique was buried here, who was the second Quique, the one in San Felipe? Noemi's comment flashed through her head. A woman who had lost a child might try to replace him. Beatriz lost her two-year-old son in 1952. Had she somehow tried to replace him with another child?

A chill coursed up her spine. She knew. The second Quique was Juan José Fuente—J.J.

No. That was crazy. Or was it? Could Beatriz's son actually be Meg's son? Only moments before, she'd been so certain that the Quique in San Felipe was her half-brother. Now everything had been thrown into doubt. Suddenly, she remembered Domingo's vision of a cloaked figure with four legs. The child could have been J.J. after all. And the adult? Beatriz or some other kidnapper.

She tried to picture Quique. Did he look anything like Meg or Pablo? She'd assumed that Quique had inherited his light complexion from her own father, Otto Baldt. But he could just as easily have inherited it from Meg. And the dark hair and brown eyes could have come not from Beatriz but from Pablo. As for Quique's features, it was hard to say. She would have to look more closely for family resemblances now that she was almost certain he was a Fuente.

Slowly, she walked across the cemetery. Be careful, she cautioned herself. No false hopes. No rushing to conclusions. This time she had to be sure, really sure. She began taking stock of what she knew. The first Quique, her father's illegitimate son, had died at the age of two in 1952. Then, two years later, after the fire, Beatriz moved to San Felipe, where she was joined by a four-year-old boy who carried her dead son's name.

Patricia came to the edge of the hill, where it sloped down to the town below. She gazed out over Santa Catarina, with its church spire reaching above the straggly streets, some of them little more than dirt paths. She made out a figure next to her car. Sergio, waiting for her. In the distance, the sun hovered over the mountains, now in partial shadow, and the air was turning cool. She turned around to catch a last glimpse of Enrique's grave. Family members were moving through her life quickly. Her father had died, and now, apparently, she had lost her half-brother, dead at the age of two.

Patricia hurried down the hill and back to the plaza, where Sergio was leaning against the car, smoking a cigarette. He ground out the remains with his shoe. "There's something you need to know about Beatriz's son," he said.

"That he died?"

Sergio nodded. "Who told you? The Mayor?"

"The maid. She showed me his gravestone."

On the drive to San Felipe, they traded information. According to Sergio's old friend, everyone in Santa Catarina knew that Beatriz's son had died. They also knew that she'd adopted a boy later, at the time that she opened a store in San Felipe. Most people believed that the boy came from some impoverished family, distant relations maybe. No one could figure out why she had given the child her dead son's name, but then everyone in Santa Catarina thought that Beatriz was a little crazy. Smart and ambitious, but also crazy. There were rumors that Beatriz had bribed local officials to remain silent to outsiders about her son's death. It occurred to Patricia that the bribes might be the reason the mayor hadn't mentioned Quique's death when she asked for information about his birth. Beatriz said she had never returned to Santa Catarina to visit, and Patricia remembered Quique saying he'd never seen his birth place, even though it was close by.

"Okay. Consider this," Patricia said. "Meg's son J.J. is four years old at the time of the fire. Everyone believes he died in it. Then not long afterward—I'm guessing a few weeks or months—a four-year-old child shows up with Beatriz in San Felipe."

Sergio peered at her. "Wait a minute. You think that Quique is really J.J.? That Beatriz stole him?"

"I'm not sure. Maybe. Something like that, anyway."

Sergio's eyes remained on the road. "I don't know, Patricia. This is a little hard to absorb."

"Do you have a better explanation? Because I would love to hear it."

He seemed to consider it for a minute. "Okay. Maybe you're right. But it seems very odd, that Beatriz would burn down the house, abduct J.J., and transform him into Quique, her own son."

"Maybe that's not how it worked. Who knows? If only we could ask Beatriz. But I don't trust her to tell us the truth. Besides, I don't want to alert her that we suspect her son is really J.J."

"Gustavo might know something."

"Yes," she said, "but I don't trust him either. He's almost certainly in Beatriz's pocket." Who else might have relevant information? "Maybe I should call Meg, see what she can tell us about Beatriz's son. I won't tell her why I'm asking."

Sergio slowed the car for a curve ahead, the last one before San Felipe.

"I guess I should talk to Quique too," she said. "See if he has any memories of Los Ancianos from when he was little."

"Hold on, Patricia. From what I can see, your first priority is to get Quique away from your brother. Before something bad happens. So, get him the work visa and take him to the States. You can figure out the rest later."

Sergio was right. For now, caution was the best course. If Quique was really J.J., a lot of people would be affected, and not just Beatriz. J.J. would be the rightful owner of Los Ancianos, both the coffee finca and the valley, land that now belonged to her own family. Carlos didn't need one more reason to murder Quique.

For now, she would report to Quique about her progress at the Consulate with his visa, and she would ask Meg if she knew anything about Beatriz's son, the one who died in Santa Catarina. The rest could wait.

Back at El Patio, Sergio parked Patricia's car next to his brown Chevy.

"I'd better report to my brother on the trip to the bank," Sergio said. He kissed Patricia on the cheek and climbed into his car. "We'll talk tomorrow."

"Right."

"Everything will work out," he said before driving away.

Patricia plodded to her apartment, where she guzzled a bottle of Coke and ate a chunk of cheese with the last of her crackers. A nap would have been nice, but she was eager to talk to Meg, so she headed for the clinic. It was after six and closed for the day, but Patricia let herself in with her key and headed for the office. Seated before the telephone, she realized that this could be hard—asking Meg about a child who had passed away. They hadn't spoken since Patricia broke the news that J.J. was dead.

But Meg sounded glad to hear from her and didn't mind answering questions. Beatriz had had a son, Meg remembered. He had lived with his grandmother in Santa Catarina. But he had died. A respiratory illness, she thought.

"Do you remember when he died? Was it in 1952?"

"Let me think. It was during our first year, not long after Beatriz came to work for us. So yes, that would make it 1952. In August. I remember because we took a quick trip to Mexico that month. We'd given Beatriz a few days off to visit her mother. But we came back from our trip and she didn't return. So finally I drove over to Santa Catarina. Beatriz was at her mother's house, and they were both sitting like statues, all dressed in black. They'd buried her son a few days before. He was only two." Her voice cracked. "The same age as my J.J."

Patricia would have been at school in the capital at the time of the toddler's death, oblivious to it all. Had her father felt anything at the death of his son? It was impossible to know now. "Do you remember the boy's name?"

"Let's see. Quique, I think. Short for Enrique. Oh, you know that. It's your half-brother's name, isn't it? Anyway, Beatriz came back a few days later. After that she was even more closed off than before. It was understandable, of course. She stayed that way for a long time. Now that I think of it, she started to revive when she got it into her head to buy the grocery store in San Felipe." A pause on the line. "Patricia, what's this all about?"

"Oh, I'm just trying to get a clearer picture of events, you know, tie up loose ends. Did Beatriz ever talk about another child? Someone else she was responsible for? A nephew maybe? Or a boy she wanted to adopt?"

"Not that I recall. No one that she spoke of anyway. Why? Do you think Beatriz was looking after another child? That seems odd."

"Oh, no, it was just a rumor I heard," Patricia said. "Probably nothing to it." She thanked Meg for the information, then they chatted for a few minutes about Meg's girls and about Patricia's mother helping out at the clinic. Meg chuckled at Patricia's account of Eugenia ushering the patients around. Patricia was relieved to hang up on a light note.

But that feeling soon faded. She picked up a pencil and rolled it between her thumb and index finger. So, she thought, there was no other child in the picture. Not in Santa Catarina or at Los Ancianos.

She had considered the idea that Beatriz might have rescued the waif in the ravine, but from what Meg had said, that child was older than four. Six or seven maybe.

Patricia set down the pencil. From what she could see, Quique was almost certainly J.J. For now, it was a secret she must guard from Quique himself and from Meg and Jonathan, a piece of infor-mation known only to herself and Sergio. And of course, to Beatriz and Gustavo. And therein lay the danger. Those two must not find out she had discovered the truth about Quique. Who knew what they might do to avoid having their deception exposed?

Tomorrow she would go to Gustavo's shop and give Quique the letter from the mayor of Santa Catarina attesting to his birth. She now realized it was a certificate of birth for a child who had died twenty-six years earlier, but she didn't need to tell Quique that. She counted on him to remember the deadly stare that Carlos had fixed on him at the restaurant. It was certainly seared into *her* memory. If everything went according to plan, Quique would go the consulate with her on Tuesday, and his visa would come through quickly, maybe even in a few days. She would fly with him to the U.S., and there, one way or another, he could learn his true identity.

CHAPTER TWENTY-SIX

It wasn't until the next morning, while Patricia was waiting for an egg to boil, that the realization finally hit her. She had done the impossible. She'd found J.J.—or at least, she was pretty sure she had. There were still some big gaps in her information. Like how J.J. had ended up in Beatriz's care. For now, she had to set those questions aside. Her immediate goal was to convince Quique to go to the States. At lunchtime, she would drive over to López Automotive for a chat with him.

However, her plans changed when her mother showed up at the clinic shortly before twelve.

"Let's have lunch at the Bella Vista," Eugenia said in a tone that didn't brook argument. She drove them to the hotel, where she requested a table in the corner.

"Carlos is up to no good," Eugenia said as soon as they had ordered drinks—a mineral water for Patricia and a glass of wine for her mother. "He's been looking pleased with himself for the last few days. Then this morning he and that Muro fellow strolled into the house all sweaty and tracking dirt. They wouldn't say what they'd been doing."

Carlos certainly wasn't planting a garden, Patricia thought. As a child, her brother had never eaten anything green, at least not by choice. Anyway, manual labor was beneath him. She leaned toward her mother and lowered her voice. "Let's hope Carlos isn't burying his victims." She meant it as a joke, then realized there might be too much truth to it.

"Nothing is too dreadful for your brother," Eugenia said. "But he's lazy. He would never go to the trouble of burying anyone." Eugenia glanced around the sparsely populated room. "You know, I'm having second thoughts about taking over the finca."

"You want me to give it to Carlos?"

"Of course, I don't want you to. But what choice do I have?"

Patricia sipped her mineral water, aware that her brother might end up getting what he wanted, or what he thought he wanted.

At a little after four, Patricia left the clinic and drove to López Automotive. She found Gustavo in the garage, working on a sorry-looking black sedan. He flinched when he saw her, no doubt thinking of the shameless letter he'd written.

"Could I borrow Quique for a few minutes?" she asked.

"He isn't here. He's at Finca Baldt, with your brother."

Finca Baldt? She stiffened. "What's he doing there?"

"I don't know, Doctora. Your brother came here looking for Quique, about an hour ago. He told Quique he must go to the finca immediately. He said Claudette was there. There had been some kind of accident, but he wouldn't say what had happened, only that it was urgent. Quique left right away."

Her mother had said that Carlos was up to something. This must be it. Quique would be at Finca Baldt by now, up to his neck in whatever nasty business Carlos had cooked up.

Gustavo frowned. "Doctora, do you think that Quique is in some kind of trouble? Maybe I should drive up there."

"Don't bother. I'll go and find out." She considered calling the finca from Gustavo's garage, but she didn't want him listening in on the conversation. Gustavo had always been loyal to her father, and he might feel some allegiance to Carlos. Besides, he was unreliable. He'd made that clear when he confessed to being the anonymous writer.

She hurried out of the garage and back to the car. She would call her brother from the clinic and find out what had happened to Claudette. Then she would drive to Finca Baldt.

At the clinic, Patricia was both surprised and relieved to see Claudette sitting in the patients' area, reading a paperback.

"I'm meeting Quique here," Claudette said, "but he seems to be running late."

"You haven't been to Finca Baldt?"

"No. Why would I?"

Patricia reported what she'd learned from Gustavo. Leticia came over. "Your brother phoned, Doctora," she said. "He wants you to return the call."

From the office, Patricia dialed the Finca Baldt number, Claudette standing beside her.

Her mother answered, sounding shaky. When she heard Patricia's voice, she lowered hers. "Come quickly," she said. "Your brother is—"

Carlos came on. "Patricia, I was about to call you. You're missing the celebration."

"What celebration is that?" she asked warily.

"We're marking my ownership—my rightful ownership—of Finca Baldt."

"Really?" He had talked about a lawsuit, but she didn't think the courts would have worked this fast. Had her mother told him he could have the finca? "I hadn't heard you were taking over."

"No? Come, and I'll tell you all about it."

He hung up.

"I'm driving to Finca Baldt," Patricia told Claudette. Something bad was going on. Even if her brother had managed to gain control of Finca Baldt, why did he want Quique there?

"I'll go with you," Claudette said.

Patricia considered the offer. She wouldn't mind having an ally, but she didn't want to involve one more innocent victim in Carlos's scheme, whatever it was. Besides, her mother was at the finca, and she could lend Patricia a hand. "Thanks, but it's better if you stay here. I'll call when I find out what's going on."

Twenty minutes later, Patricia pulled up to the finca gate. Carlos was standing there, talking to Muro, both men in their Club Metro jackets. Muro had a rifle slung over his shoulder, one that looked a lot like her father's Austrian firearm. Muro glanced at Patricia, not bothering to acknowledge her, then gave Carlos a jaunty salute and disappeared inside the courtyard.

She got out of the car. "I'm here, Carlos, as you requested. Where is Quique Aguilar?"

Carlos ambled over. "You're in luck. He's joining us for my little celebration. I'll take you there." He motioned to a green pick-up truck, the Finca Baldt transport.

"Where are we going?"

"Los Ancianos."

To the concrete bunker? That should be a fun party. If she was right about Quique, Carlos had taken him to the site of his boyhood home. She supposed that seeing Los Ancianos might jog Quique's memories, although both the house site and the valley below it had changed a great deal in the last two decades.

"I'll follow you in my car," she said.

"I'll drive us," he said, motioning to his truck, his voice leaving no doubt that it was an order.

Just then, Eugenia hurried out the gate toward them. She looked stylish in her embroidered vest and linen slacks, but her cheeks were flushed, and she appeared nervous.

"Go back inside," Carlos ordered.

"Can't a mother greet her daughter?" Eugenia said as she rushed by him. She kissed Patricia on the cheek. "Be careful," she whispered, then stepped away. "Come back, and we'll all have coffee together." The anxiety in her eyes belied the casual words.

Patricia climbed into the truck beside Carlos. The vehicle was dusty, and the gears ground when Carlos shifted into first. Her father had always made sure his vehicles were in good repair, but Carlos was probably too lazy to bother with that kind of detail. Carlos drove to the narrow road leading to Los Ancianos. It was the one she'd walked several days earlier with her mother and the unfortunate Joaquin, who was now someplace in the States. Tree branches scratched the passenger side of the car, the metal shrieking in protest.

"What's Muro doing here?" Patricia asked. "Wasn't that Papa's rifle he was carrying?"

"He'll see to it that no one disturbs us," Carlos said.

A minute later they pulled up to his bunker.

Patricia got out of the truck and walked toward the building. No windows were visible, at least from this side. Was Quique being held hostage inside? "You could use some balloons for your party," she said.

"That's my militia headquarters," Carlos said. "The celebration is this way." He headed for the steps leading down to the valley.

What kind of game was this? "Where is Quique?" she demanded. Was he even here?

Carlos smirked. "Settle down. You'll join him shortly."

The old steps leading down to the valley had been replaced, but the present ones were wobbly and a few jutted out at strange angles. The black pumps she was wearing were comfortable enough, but she wished she were wearing slacks instead of a skirt. At the base, they strode along a path between rows of her father's apple trees. A breeze had come up, rustling the leaves.

"Let me guess," she said, striding beside Carlos. "You lured Quique here, telling him that Claudette was in trouble. And now you're holding him here against his will."

He chuckled. "Something like that."

"You know, Carlos, you can't just take revenge on anyone who beats you at football."

He snorted. "You know nothing. Aguilar is a Communist, he and that priest he hangs around with. If he disappears, no one will object."

She started to say that every football fan in San Felipe would object, but halted. "What do you mean—if he disappears?" An icy chill ran through her. "What are you saying? That you're planning to kill him?"

"That depends on you, Sister. You sign over Finca Baldt to me, and the bastard goes free."

Her father's finca for Quique's life? She felt like laughing. It was a trade she would make in a minute. Whether Quique was J.J. or her half-brother, she would take him to the States. Let Carlos destroy Finca Baldt. It would be hard on her mother. But even if Patricia had signed the estate over to her, it would only have been a matter of time—days, weeks—before Eugenia surrendered it to her son. Even her mother seemed to realize that now.

"We should be able to come to an arrangement," she said.

An open space appeared at the end of the rows of apple trees, and a moment later Pablo's shed stood before them. It listed forlornly, its wood grayed with age. Only its metal roof looked solid. Carlos opened a padlock and the door creaked open.

Patricia stepped into the shed and was assailed by stifling heat, the result of the closed room and the afternoon sun beating down on the corrugated metal roof. Dust filled her nose and throat, and she sneezed.

The room was dark inside, except for the light entering from the door and from a dirty window. She made out a figure tied to a chair at the far end of the shed, his mouth covered with tape. Quique. Or was he really J.J.?

Quique raised his eyes to her. Relief flooded them, quickly replaced by distrust.

"As you can see, he's alive," Carlos said, "at least for now."

Patricia glanced around. The shed was larger than she remembered, probably because the last time she'd entered the room, it had been filled with archaeological supplies. Now all she saw was a coil of rope on a shelf and two shovels encrusted with dirt. A small, dusty table sat under the window. Probably the same one that Demetrio had once used.

She strode over to Quique. Ropes pinned down his arms and chest and encircled his ankles. One eye was swollen nearly shut, and his right hand extended at an odd angle below the sleeve of his mechanic's coveralls. A fracture, no doubt. She swore under her breath. What a monster her brother had turned into.

She bent down to Quique's ear. "I'll get you out of here," she whispered, then straightened and faced Carlos. "Untie him. I need to examine his arm."

"As soon as you sign over the finca."

"Forget it. I am not signing anything until he's free and I've looked after his injuries. And for God's sake, take that tape off his mouth."

"Anything you say, sister." He ambled over to Quique, grasped one edge of the tape, and ripped it off. Quique yelped in pain, then moved his jaw back and forth.

Patricia flinched. "Give me a hand here," she said to her brother as she attempted to untie the rope.

"Sure. Just to show you how reasonable I can be. When I'm in a good mood." He took a pocketknife out of his jeans and sawed at the rope encircling J.J.'s chest. It fell to the floor, leaving Quique free, except for his feet, which were still bound. Carlos closed the knife and returned it to his pocket, then turned to Patricia. "Done. Now look him over and be quick about it." He reached under his jacket and removed a pistol from a shoulder holster. "And no tricks. Understand?" He stepped to the door, re-holstered his gun, and lit up a cigarette.

Patricia knelt beside Quique. "My wrist is broken," he said in a scratchy voice. "Not that it matters. Your brother is going to kill me."

She flinched. Stay calm, she told herself. They would get through this. "Don't worry," she said. "Carlos is using you as a pawn to get the finca from me. I'll sign it over to him. Then he'll let you go."

"No. When Muro was tying me up, he said I'd pay for that winning goal at the football match. Your brother is a lunatic. He wants me dead."

"I won't let that happen," she said. "If Carlos wants to kill you, he'll have to kill me first." Quique raised a skeptical eyebrow, then winced as she unbuttoned his sleeve and examined his wrist.

The bone was fractured, all right, but it hadn't broken through the skin. "This doesn't look too bad. I'll find something to stabilize your wrist. I can set the bone once we get back to San Felipe."

"You've had long enough," Carlos announced from the doorway.

She stood and faced him. "I need some kind of splint. A hard stick would do. Something about as long as his forearm."

"Later," Carlos said. "First, you sign."

She glanced at Quique, who shook his head in a barely perceptible motion. Don't do it, his eyes said.

"Finish untying Quique and find a splint. Then I'll sign."

"You'll sign now. I have the document right here." He pulled a folded paper out of an inner pocket, strode to the table, and flattened the paper on it.

"No." Once Carlos had her signature, he could do whatever he wanted with Quique. With her too, for that matter. Somehow she had to convince her brother to untie him. After that, they would play it by ear. "Don't you see, Carlos?" she said. "If I sign this way, I'll be doing it under duress. The contract will be worthless."

"I'll take that risk."

"No. I want to do this properly. I'm signing over the estate because I want to, not because you've threatened me. I had already decided to give you the finca."

"Too bad you didn't tell me sooner," Carlos said.

"Now I have. Look. Once I've signed, Quique and I are going to get on a plane and go to the U.S. It's as simple as that. We will pretend this little episode never occurred. You'll have everything you want. Just untie him."

A shadow crossed the room, and Patricia looked toward the door, where her mother stood. She'd added a billowing taupe-colored coat and a long paisley scarf to her outfit. She scrunched her nose. "It stinks in here," she said.

"I'm signing over the finca to Carlos," Patricia said.

"Good," her mother said. "I'll sign as a witness." She turned to Carlos. "*Hijo*, untie the young man—this instant."

"I am in charge here," Carlos snarled. Then a sly smile crossed his face. "But just to demonstrate what an obedient son I am, I will untie the bastard." He removed the knife from his pocket and cut the rope binding Quique's ankles. Quique moved his legs stiffly, flexing his calf muscles. "But you'll stay right there," Carlos said, pressing his knife against Quique's throat. "We don't want any unnecessary bloodshed, do we?"

"Don't we need another witness?" Eugenia said. "This fellow can sign and make it all official."

Patricia flashed a grateful look at her mother, then turned to her brother. "That's right. You need a second witness."

Carlos scowled but finally relented. "Sure. Why not?"

"Mama, could I borrow your scarf for a sling?" Patricia asked.

"Of course," Eugenia said.

Patricia fashioned the scarf into an improvised sling and slipped Quique's arm into it. "I hope you don't mind signing as a witness," she said.

"Why not," he mumbled. "I trust you know what you're doing." If only I did, Patricia thought. She could only pray that her brother would act rationally and uphold his end of the bargain. If he didn't, she wasn't sure what she would do. All she knew for sure was that she had to protect Quique.

Eugenia brushed off her coat and eyed Carlos. "You surely can't think I'm going to sign anything in this dreadful place."

Patricia faced her brother. "Mama's right. This is an important event. Why don't we go up to the house?"

"Forget it," Carlos said.

"Well then, we can at least move the table outside," Patricia said. It would give them more space, more opportunities for escape.

Carlos balked, but his mother cajoled him, and a moment later he and Patricia carried the table to a spot outside the shed. She straightened and breathed in the fresh air, a relief after the dusty, stifling shed. In the distance, the sun was low over the mountains. Darkness wasn't far off.

Carlos positioned the document on the table, anchoring it with a rock. Patricia eyed the stone. It might work as a weapon, if she needed to throw something at Carlos.

Eugenia approached Patricia and took her hands. "I am so happy that you want to help your brother." She kissed Patricia's cheek, whispering, "I have a gun."

"Very touching," Carlos said. "Let's get started."

Quique emerged from the shed, his stride a little off balance from his disabled arm. He stood next to Patricia, glancing toward the orchard that lay several yards behind them. The ever-vigilant striker.

"Let me adjust the sling," Patricia said, moving close. "Mama has a pistol," she whispered. He nodded.

"No talking," Carlos snapped. He removed a pen from his jacket pocket and placed it on the paper. "Go ahead," he said, turning to Patricia. "Sign."

She stepped forward and read the document. Carlos must have employed a proper attorney. It was written in flowery, nineteenth century legalese. In short, she was giving the finca to Carlos and renouncing any further claims to her father's estate. With her signature, she would disinherit herself forever. She felt a pang of regret—ridiculous, given that she'd cut off ties to her family years before. And she'd never imagined that she would inherit Finca Baldt. Her brother was supposed to do that. Even so, by signing the paper, she was giving up her home.

"Hurry up," Carlos said.

Patricia picked up the pen and signed her name—Patricia Baldt Contreras. She hardly ever used "Contreras," her mother's last name, in the States. And her professional signature had become more of a scrawl. This signature looked strange, like something written by her younger self.

She stepped back, next to Quique.

"You're next," Carlos said to Eugenia, who walked sedately to the table. She took the pen and signed with a flourish.

He turned to Quique. "Now you." Quique stepped forward and scribbled a wavy line with his left hand.

"Done," announced Carlos. "I'm now the owner of Finca Baldt."

"Congratulations," Patricia said. "I wish you peace and prosperity." As if that were likely. "We'll be going now," she said, and turned to Quique, who was already backing away.

To Patricia's horror, Carlos reached under his jacket and drew out his pistol. Thrusting her out of the way, he lunged for Quique, grabbing him by his injured arm. Quique groaned, and by the time Patricia had regained her balance, Carlos had his pistol in Quique's back.

Damn. She had waited too long, hoping that Carlos would let them go. Next time she had to do better. Be more alert, move faster. Another opportunity had to present itself.

"I thought we'd take a walk," Carlos said, as if this were a casual tour of the grounds. His voice lowered. "Go up to the car, Mama. Wait for me there."

Eugenia looked uncertain.

Carlos's face darkened. "Go on. I have things to discuss with my sister."

Eugenia put her hand into her coat pocket, and Patricia held her breath. Would her mother pull out the gun? But she turned and started moving toward the orchard.

"Mama, wait," Patricia called, dashing toward her mother. She had to retrieve the pistol.

"Stop!" Carlos shouted. "Or I'll put a bullet in the bastard's back." Patricia froze.

"That's better," Carlos said. "We're going to the old dig. What's left of it. You first, sister."

Patricia trudged the few yards from the shed to the dig site, her heart beating in her ears. With each step, she tried to calm herself. It was no good letting Carlos see her fear. She glanced backward, but there was no sign of her mother. Damn.

She stopped at what had once been the rim surrounding the pit. The dig itself was now a wide weedy area, sloping down a few feet, then more or less level. Half way across lay a large rectangular hole that looked newly dug. She estimated it was inside the boundaries of the ceremonial center—the burial place of the ancient priests of Chayaka. Why would anyone be digging there now?

"Down the hill," Carlos ordered. "Keep going."

She looked back, fear constricting her throat. Quique was behind her, Carlos's pistol still thrust into his back.

"Go on," Carlos barked.

She scrambled down the slope. This was insane. Surely her brother wouldn't actually kill them. What kind of lunatic would kill his own sister? She plodded across the sunken field where she had walked so often, back when she was an archaeologist-in-training, or so she'd imagined herself. The ground had been several feet lower then, before the dig was filled in. She hesitated a moment, then stepped onto the land that must be directly above the ceremonial center. Goose bumps rose on her arms. Demetrio had excavated here, under the watchful eye of the elders. This was sacred space.

Patricia halted at the edge of the freshly dug hole. It appeared to be about six feet long and four feet wide. Maybe four feet deep. Her stomach clenched. She knew what this was. Carlos had marched them to an open grave, one deep enough for two bodies. Or more.

"Stop there," Carlos shouted. He shoved his prisoner forward, so that Quique and Patricia were standing side by side, overlooking the empty pit. They exchanged a glance. Like her, Quique was clearly scared, but she also sensed a watchfulness in him. A readiness to move. Carlos stepped behind them, his Metro jacket rustling.

"They say there was a graveyard here," Carlos said. "Appropriate, don't you think?"

Had this always been his plan? To march them to their grave and kill them both? "All right, Carlos," she said, turning to face him. "You've had your fun. Let's go back."

"I'm afraid not." Carlos kept his pistol trained on Quique. His face bore a look of twisted amusement. It was an expression she'd seen before, on the face of his ten-year-old self, when he was about to torture a lizard. "My poor, unfortunate sister," he said. "You had your chance. You could have turned over the finca to me earlier. But you were stupid, and now it's too late."

Patricia's heart was racing. How could she get through to him? She took a deep breath. "Carlos, listen to me. I know I wasn't a good sister to you. I should have come back for you. But I was young and made bad decisions. I'm sorry."

"Spare me," Carlos said. "You're only saying this because you're afraid of me. And you should be."

"No. I mean it." She hesitated, searching for words. Speak from the heart, she told herself. "I would like us to make a fresh start, to be a true family—you, Mama, and I. It's what we always wanted, even Papa, in his own way."

Carlos snorted. "That's what you think. The old man didn't give a damn about me. I was his only son, and he despised me."

"He never really knew you, Carlos. He couldn't see what a great football player you were. He never gave you credit for your strength." A strength that had become warped, she thought. But even she had to admit her little brother was a force to be reckoned with.

His arrogant look eased.

"Papa didn't know me either," she said. "Did you know I got kicked out of school my last year? Mama made up a lie to cover for me. Otherwise, Papa would have gone into one of his rages."

"Well, she never covered for me," he grumbled.

"Papa intimidated her too. I can see that now. Besides, you know that Mama was really more interested in decorating the patio than she was in us."

Carlos laughed, but it was a clean laugh, untouched by scorn or malice. He was coming around. She could feel it.

"Now that Papa's gone, Mama is changing," she said. "I've seen it the last several days. She's even helped out with patients at the clinic. Who could have imagined her doing that? She's becoming kinder, more loving."

Carlos snorted. "I haven't noticed it."

"I know, but you will. Now that Papa is gone and you have the finca, we can start again, be a real family. You can come visit me in the States. Go skiing. Or tour Chicago. We can do it."

His expression softened, and she glimpsed the little boy she had once known, the one who had longed for approval.

"Put away the gun, Carlos. Please. We'll go back to the house and be the family we were always meant to be."

He hesitated, then his face hardened. "Good try."

She heard footsteps and caught sight of her mother hurrying across the rim of the dig, her coat billowing around her.

"Son of a bitch," Carlos mumbled.

Eugenia ran down the slope until she was a few feet away, then stopped and dug into her pocket. She pulled out her pistol and held it at arm's length, one hand supporting the other. The barrel pointed at Carlos. "Drop your gun, hijo," Eugenia said. "I'm not afraid to shoot."

"Don't make me laugh," Carlos said, barely glancing away from Quique. "You're not going to shoot your own son. What would your friends say?"

"Drop the gun," she repeated. "Now." But her voice was unsteady, and Patricia's hope sputtered out. Carlos was right. Her mother wasn't going to shoot. Not even a lousy bullet to his foot.

Eugenia lowered the gun. "*Ay, hijo,*" she cried. "What have I done? What have I done to deserve such a son?" She started to wail in long, high-pitched shrieks. "Ay-ee-ee-ee! Ay-ee-ee-ee!"

"Shut up! Just shut up!" Carlos shouted, whirling to face his mother. "Get out of—"

In a flash, Quique stepped toward Carlos, and his foot shot up in a kung fu kick. It connected with Carlos's hand, and the revolver hurtled, somersaulting, into the air. Carlos shoved Quique to the ground. As the gun fell, Patricia lunged for it. But Carlos crashed into her, ramming an elbow into her gut. She thudded to the ground. Gasping for breath, she watched as Carlos grabbed the gun and raised it triumphantly.

Patricia struggled to sit up. Damn it! It was their big chance, possibly their last chance, and she'd failed. She watched helplessly as Carlos strode over to Eugenia and demanded her pistol, which she handed over meekly. So much for her mother as an ally. Patricia turned behind her, to see Quique rising to his feet, slowed by the sling. He had landed just above the open grave.

"No more delays," Carlos declared, raising his pistol and aiming it at Quique.

"No!" Patricia screamed. The sound of a gunshot sliced the air, and she braced herself for the sight of blood and torn flesh. But a second later, Quique was still standing upright, unharmed. He was staring wide-eyed at Carlos. When Patricia turned, she saw her brother teeter backwards, then collapse, his chest bloody.

Her mother's scream pierced the air.

Patricia grimaced in pain as she staggered over to her brother. He was on his back, blood gushing from his chest right over the heart. His eyes were open but vacant, seemingly staring in disbelief.

She dropped to her knees and placed her fingers against the carotid artery in Carlos's neck. No pulse. Nothing. A sick feeling came over her. The bullet had struck her brother's heart and destroyed it.

She looked up in the direction from which the bullet must have come. There, on the rim of the dig, stood Gustavo, holding a rifle, his face stricken.

Her mother knelt beside her, looking terrified. "He's dying, isn't he?" she said. "My son is dying." She crossed herself and took Carlos's hand in hers, tears rolling down her cheeks.

Patricia reached over to close her brother's eyes, then laid a hand on her mother's shoulder. "I'm sorry, Mama. There's no pulse. He's gone."

Her mother's face contorted, and she collapsed over her son's body, sobbing.

Patricia sat back. Two days ago, she had thought she had two brothers, Carlos and Quique. Now she had none. Slowly, she stood, feeling stiff and heartsick. Later she would cry. But not now. There was too much to take care of.

Gustavo approached. In his hand was her father's Austrian rifle, with its elegant vine and leaf pattern.

Otto's beloved rifle had just killed his son.

"I'm sorry, Doctora," Gustavo said. "I couldn't let Carlos kill J.J."

CHAPTER TWENTY-SEVEN

The sun had dropped behind the mountains, leaving a golden glow, when Patricia, Eugenia, Quique, and Gustavo formed a small circle at the edge of the apple orchard. Patricia shivered and tried to ignore Carlos's body, which lay several feet away, his head and chest covered by his mother's coat. She was cold, exhausted, and her midsection ached where Carlos had thrust his elbow into her. Her companions all looked equally spent.

"We have to come up with a story," Patricia said. "A convincing one."

"I'll confess to the police," Gustavo said. "It's right that I should pay for my sins."

"No, tío," Quique said. "The police will arrest you and put you in jail. And Carlos had powerful friends, people who will want to see his killer dead. No one should die for shooting Carlos Baldt."

Patricia winced, but this was not the time to indulge in hurt feelings. "Quique's right," she said. Carlos's right-wing friends would want revenge. And even if they didn't, things could get messy. If Gustavo was arrested for Carlos's murder, she and her mother would undoubtedly become ensnared in nasty media coverage.

"We need a story that's good enough to satisfy the police but will cause minimal harm to everyone."

Silence ensued as they looked from one to the other. "I suppose we could blame Carlos's death on the guerrillas," Patricia said.

"No," Quique said. "I've seen the way the army works. They'll kill innocent people in retribution. Lots of them probably."

It was true, Patricia realized. She'd read of massacres of supposed guerrilla sympathizers by the army, and she didn't want to set off that kind of violence here. "Look. Let's say the death was an accident. I was carrying Papa's rifle. I tripped and it went off. The police probably won't arrest me."

"No, *hija*," her mother said. "I can't allow it. Your reputation would be ruined. I'll take the blame. I can say I was walking around the property. I suspected there were intruders, so I'd taken Otto's rifle with me. I was clumsy and it fired."

Patricia gazed at her mother. "Oh, Mama, you can't. Just think what people would say."

"I know. I will be an object of pity—the mother who killed her son. But you see, don't you? It's the best of our miserable options."

Patricia considered the idea. Of all of them, her mother, the matriarch of a prominent family, was the least likely to be harrassed by the police. They would never have the audacity to arrest her.

She looked at her co-conspirators. Gustavo's eyes were fixed on the ground. Quique met her gaze and nodded. No one mentioned that Eugenia had, in fact, aimed a pistol at her son and threatened to shoot him. "All right," Patricia said. "Mama had a shooting accident."

"Wait. What about Muro?" Quique said. "He will never buy the story." He looked around. "I'm surprised he hasn't shown up."

Gustavo raised his eyes. "I left Muro tied up at the house."

"How did you manage that?" Quique asked. "In fact, what are you doing here?"

"Carlos was acting suspicious when he came to the garage looking for you," Gustavo said. "Then, when the Doctora came looking for you, I began to suspect that something was wrong. So I closed the garage and drove up here. When I got to the finca, I parked my car out of sight and sneaked up to the house. No one was around, except Muro and some man. They were talking in the courtyard. I stayed out of sight and listened. Muro told the guy that Carlos had taken you to the valley, and you would soon be out of the way—permanently. I knew I must do something, but Muro was carrying Don Otto's rifle, so I had to be careful. After the stranger drove away, I picked up a flower pot, crept up behind Muro, and smashed it over his head. He collapsed, then I tied him up and took the rifle."

"That was quick thinking," Patricia said.

"I was a soldier before I was a mechanic," he said. "I learned a few things."

"Is Muro alive?" she asked. They didn't need one more corpse.

"He came to, but he wasn't in a good mood."

"Muro's fingerprints must be on the rifle," Quique said, "along with Gustavo's. If we testified that it was Muro who killed Carlos, he would be in real trouble."

"You want to accuse Muro?" Patricia asked. "I don't know. We would all have to lie to the police. And we might have to deal with the other members of Carlos's militia."

"Actually," Quique said, "I was thinking we could use his fingerprints on the gun as a threat. You know. We give Muro two options. He can accept our story of the accident and leave quietly. Or we will see that he is arrested for murder."

"That might just work," Patricia said. "Let's go up to the house and find out."

Quique faced Gustavo. "Then, I want to know what you meant when you said you couldn't let Carlos kill J.J."

"All in good time," Patricia said. "I need to wash up and make a few phone calls. And I could use a strong cup of coffee."

Patricia scrubbed herself at the bathroom sink, trying not to think that it was her brother's dried blood she was rinsing down the drain. Her emotions were a muddle of sorrow, relief, and jangled nerves. Soon, she would hear from Gustavo what had happened at Los Ancianos, and she looked forward to knowing at last, but she dreaded his confession as well. She only hoped they could control any repercussions, especially for Quique.

She went into her father's former office and made three phone calls. The first was to the clinic, where Fiona picked up on the first ring. She assured Patricia that she and Claudette would wait there for Quique, and she would look after his broken wrist. They would also find a safe place for Quique to stay. It would be important to keep him out of sight. Even though Muro had left quickly, eager to avoid a murder charge, he could have second thoughts. And there was always the risk that Carlos's militia might want to complete Carlos's final mission against Quique.

The next phone call was to Patricia's Aunt Claudia. "I'll stay with Mama tonight," Patricia said, after explaining that Carlos had died from an accidental gunshot wound. Eugenia could present her own version of events later. Claudia assured Patricia that she would drive up from the capital the next morning and stay with her sister as long as Eugenia needed her.

Last, Patricia called the police station in San Felipe and reported her mother's tragic accident with the rifle. Patricia said that she had just given her mother a strong sedative, which was not true, but it gave Patricia an excuse to hold off the authorities. They would be welcome to arrive the following day, she explained, if they wished to make inquiries. The officer in charge expressed his condolences and said that under the circumstances, he expected the visit would be a mere formality. Patricia hung up, realizing that soon all of San Felipe would hear about her family's misfortune.

She left the office and followed the walkway to the dining room. As she passed the parlor, she saw that two older women—wives or mothers of finca workers probably—were already laying out Carlos's body.

As a medical student, Patricia had become familiar with cadavers, and she'd seen more death since then. She was sure that by this time, her brother's body would be merely a cold shell, his spirit departed. After all the madness, she hoped that his spirit rested in a peaceful, loving place.

Patricia paused at the door to the dining room. Her small group of co-conspirators sat silently around the table, Quique and Gustavo on one side and her mother across from them. All three appeared wrapped in private thoughts or shut down by exhaustion. Quique's left eye was swollen shut, and his arm was still in the sling, although she'd stabilized it with a splint. Eugenia had insisted on joining the group. For too many years, she explained, Otto had seen to it that she knew nothing about what went on at the finca.

They all looked up when Patricia sat down at the head of the table. A maid had left a pot of coffee, and Patricia poured herself a cup. The aroma and warmth cut through her fatigue. When she set down the cup, everyone's gaze was fixed on her.

"Gustavo," she said, "please tell us what happened at Los Ancianos on the night of the fire."

"Yes," Quique said, "and if you would be so kind, *tío*, I would like to know what the devil this has to do with me."

In a barely audible voice, Gustavo said, "I burned down the Fuentes' house. I have lived with the shame for twenty-four years."

Patricia gasped. "It was you who set the fire?"

Gustavo nodded. "I didn't want to. It was an order from Don Otto."

Patricia's heart sank. But it wasn't a complete shock. For a long time, she'd harbored a tiny suspicion that her father was implicated in the fire. She eyed her mother. "Did you know?"

"No. Your father did not confide in me. I suspected he was up to something...but I didn't know what it was."

"Believe me," Gustavo said, "Don Otto assured me that the Fuentes would be away. And the servants as well. That's the only reason I agreed. Because I was certain that no one would be hurt."

Patricia had a flash of memory. It was late May of 1954, and she was sitting across from her father in his office, informing him that the Fuentes were going to Costa Rica the first week of June. She had been surprised at the interest he took in the family's activities, since he despised them so. Now she understood. She had inadvertently provided him with a window of opportunity to burn down the house. In a way, she too was implicated in the crime.

"I don't understand," Quique said. "Why did Otto Baldt want to destroy the Fuentes' house?"

"It goes back to the valley at Los Ancianos," Patricia said. "Pablo Fuente was planning to give it to Chayaka, part of a bargain he had made with the town earlier. My father was furious when he found out. You have to remember, the whole country was in an uproar. The finca owners were all terrified that the government would take away some of their land. When Pablo gave the valley to the Indians, I think Papa saw it as a huge betrayal."

"Believe me, Quique," Gustavo said, "Don Otto never meant to kill anyone. He only wanted to scare off your family. He thought if he burned down your house, your family would leave."

"My family?" Quique said. "What are you talking about?"

Gustavo lowered his eyes.

"Go ahead, Gustavo," Patricia said. "Tell us the rest. You set fire to the house. But you weren't alone, were you? Who was with you?"

He looked up, his eyes beseeching. "Doctora, you told me that Doña Meg didn't want revenge. That you wouldn't bring charges against anyone."

"You have my word."

"Beatriz was with me," Gustavo said.

"What?" Quique's eyes widened. "Mama was with you?"

"She worked for the Fuentes, so she had a house key," Gustavo said. "I set up a fuse leading to the propane tanks, and Beatriz splashed gasoline from the tanks into the house. I was worried about the watchman, but he wasn't there. We were very lucky, I thought. The fire started perfectly, spreading through the house. When the tanks exploded, the whole house went up in flames.

"I remember standing in front of the house, watching the flames. When I looked for Beatriz, she was several yards away, but she wasn't alone. She was holding on to the Fuentes' little boy, Juan José. The next thing I knew, the two of them were running away, along the cliff's edge. Beatriz had worn a long cape, and it covered them both."

Domingo's apparition, Patricia thought. "Quique," she said, "do you remember any of this? Does it seem familiar?"

He looked at her quizzically. "How could I remember it? I wasn't there."

Patricia turned back to Gustavo. "What happened next?"

Gustavo's face flooded with anguish. "At that moment, I realized that the family was at home. It was a terrible blow. I ran around the house and saw Doña Meg standing at a second-story window. She looked like a ghost, with smoke swirling around her. And then she disappeared. I found a ladder and climbed up to the second floor. I broke open the window and carried her out."

It must have been difficult, Patricia thought, carrying Meg out of the burning house, but Gustavo had somehow managed it. She pictured Meg lying on the ground in her white nightgown, with the doctor beside her and Eugenia looking on. Patricia had barely been aware of Gustavo hovering in the background. The whole scene had altered for her, now that she knew that Gustavo was not only the hero but also the villain.

Gustavo started coughing, his thick, smoker's cough. When he stopped, he took a swallow of coffee. Then he resumed, his voice raspy. "I wanted to go back for Don Pablo, but by then the flames were too high. The house was falling down. I told myself, maybe Don Pablo got out. Maybe he is safe somewhere. But I learned later, he wasn't."

"I must have arrived around that time," Eugenia said. "I can testify that Gustavo went to the hospital with me and returned to Finca Baldt the next day."

Gustavo nodded. "I expected to find Beatriz at the finca with the boy, but they weren't there. Then I thought maybe she had taken J.J. to the hospital where Doña Meg was staying. But no, she hadn't done that either. All I could do was wait for her. It was the worst time of my life." He went silent, his hands clenched on his lap.

"When did you finally see Beatriz?" Patricia asked.

"A month later. I heard that she had bought the grocery in San Felipe. I went to visit her in her apartment behind the shop, and when I excused myself to use the toilet, there was J.J., standing in the hallway. He looked very sad, very lost. Beatriz sent him to his room and acted like nothing was wrong. I told her we had to return the boy to his family. She looked at me like I was crazy. 'You are mistaken,' she said. 'That is my son, Quique.' She had had a little boy, you see. A child named Quique. He'd died two years earlier."

"None of this makes sense," Quique said. "I don't remember any boy staying with us. Certainly not a kid with my name."

Gustavo looked down, his jaw muscles working, but he said nothing.

"Look," Patricia said, "I know this is hard to believe, but here's what I think happened. Beatriz found J.J. at Los Ancianos and took him to live with her in San Felipe. At her new store. She told him that he had a new name, Quique. It must have taken a while, but eventually the boy forgot that he had ever been Juan José Fuente. He came to believe that he was her son, Enrique Aguilar Soto."

Quique had turned pale. "What are you saying? That Mama isn't my real mother? That I'm this...this Juan José Fuente?"

Patricia nodded. "I see no other logical explanation."

"I don't believe it," Quique said. "It isn't possible."

"That's what I thought," Patricia said. "Until yesterday, when I went to Santa Catarina. That's when I started to unravel the threads. You see, there was a record of a child's birth at the town hall. Enrique Aquilar Soto was born on July 10, 1950, just as Beatriz told you. The father was listed as Otto Baldt."

"What?" Quique said. "That can't be. He wasn't my father."

"You're right," Patricia said. "He wasn't. He was the father of another child. A child with your name, who died on August 23, 1952. I saw the gravestone in the cemetery at Santa Catarina. Enrique Aguilar Soto is buried next to Beatriz's father and mother."

Quique shook his head. "This is crazy. Who is the kid buried in Santa Catarina?"

"Beatriz's son."

"So, she had two sons, me and this other kid."

"No," Patricia said. "She only had one, the child in the cemetery."

Quique raised his uninjured hand to his forehead, looking like he had a massive headache.

Eugenia shook her head. "Ay, Gustavo, if only you'd told my husband about J.J on the night of the fire, none of this would have happened."

"I have told myself that a million times," Gustavo said. "But I was afraid of Don Otto, of what he would do when he discovered that J.J. was alive. I knew he wouldn't want a witness to the fire. So I said nothing."

"You could have told me," Eugenia said. "I would have contacted Meg's parents."

"I know. I wanted to tell you in the car, on the way to the city. But I was confused. So I decided to wait and talk to Beatriz first. Then later, when I saw her, it was clear that she adored the boy. I could not betray her."

The maid came in with a fresh pot of coffee and refreshed everyone's cups. Patricia stretched. They were almost finished, the threads unraveling further, the truth revealing itself. She took a sip of the hot coffee. "Tell me, Gustavo, why did you finally write to Meg?"

"My sins weighed on me, and I made a promise to myself. If Don Otto passed away before me, I would write to Doña Meg and tell her that J.J. had survived."

"So, after my father died, you wrote to Meg," Patricia said.

He nodded. "Just to let her know that J.J. was alive. I didn't sign it or leave an address, so I thought that would be the end of it. But the advertisements started in the newspapers. Doña Meg was looking for me. I finally broke down and told Beatriz about the letter. She was furious, screaming at me, calling me terrible names. She said that Quique was her son. And if I told anyone about the fire at Los Ancianos, I would be sorry. So I agreed not to respond to the ads."

"But you did later," Patricia said. "You left a note for me at the clinic. I waited for you at the park, but you never showed up."

Gustavo shook his head forlornly. "It was a mistake. You see, the night before, Beatriz had announced her engagement at the Cultural Center. It was a shock to me. I knew she liked the director, but I had always thought that someday she and I...well, I wanted to let her know that I wasn't some fool that she could take for granted. I was going to tell our secret."

Patricia looked away. Poor unhappy Gustavo. He had been in love with Beatriz for as long as she could remember. He must be in his sixties now, but he still acted like a smitten teenager. "Then why didn't you show up at the park?" she asked. "I waited for an hour."

"I know, and I felt bad. But after I sent the note, Beatriz dropped by the garage and apologized for not telling me about the engagement. You see, her fiancé had insisted that she keep it a secret. She invited me to sit with them at the football match the following afternoon. After that, I felt ashamed for defying her. So I didn't go to meet you. I'm sorry."

"*Por dios, tío*," Quique mumbled. "Is there anyone you haven't deceived?"

"There's something else I want to know," Patricia said. "Why was Beatriz willing to burn down the house? My father couldn't have ordered her to do it. She was working for the Fuentes at the time."

Gustavo sighed. "I only know that a few weeks before the fire, Beatriz got it into her head that she had to buy the grocery in San Felipe. It was all she could think of. She was sick of being a servant and wanted to be her own boss. Doña Meg had given her some money, and I gave her some too, but she was still short of what she needed. I told Don Otto, thinking he might lend her the money. And he did, but there was a condition. The next time the Fuentes were gone from their house, she would help to burn it down. In return, he would give her the money for the shop."

A pact with the devil, Patricia thought. Beatriz had sold out Meg and Pablo for the price of the shop in San Felipe. Across the table, Quique looked stunned. "I'm sorry, Quique," she said. "I can imagine how hard this is for you."

He stared at her. "Can you? I doubt it. I have no idea who I am. I have no memory of being this little boy, this Juan José Fuente. But I can't be Enrique Aguilar either. From what you told me, he's dead. My whole life has been a lie. So, who am I?"

CHAPTER TWENTY-EIGHT

It was almost nine o'clock, and Patricia stood at the front gate of the Baldt house, watching with relief as Gustavo's truck rumbled down the road. Quique was in the passenger's seat, his broken wrist in a sturdy sling. They were on their way to the clinic, where Fiona and Claudette would welcome them.

At first, Quique had balked at driving with Gustavo, but Patricia had taken him aside. She reminded him that the old man was guilty of terrible things, but he had committed them out of love or loyalty, however misguided. And in fact, he had saved Quique's life a few hours earlier. If Gustavo hadn't shown up, Quique would be dead.

"I do owe him for that," Quique had said. "And he taught me a lot about cars."

Patricia exhaled a long breath as the truck vanished into the darkness. It had been an eventful day. Among those events, she had gone back to the old tool shed at Los Ancianos, where Quique was held prisoner. Not long after, she had signed away her rights to the estate, and she'd nearly been murdered by her brother. Then she had knelt, helpless, beside Carlos's lifeless body. Finally, she had learned the truth about what took place at Los Ancianos all those years ago. And Quique had learned it too, although he might not be able to accept it right away.

Patricia walked back through the gate, and as she entered the courtyard, she saw light under her mother's bedroom door. Eugenia had suggested that Patricia share her double bed, and Patricia had to agree that it wasn't a good night to be alone.

Crossing to her mother's room, Patricia knocked at the door and entered. Eugenia was sitting up in the bed, wearing rose-colored pajamas, her dark hair framing her face. She looked younger, the forgiving light of a candle softening her faint age lines. Her mother had always liked candles. And sherry. A stemmed glass of honey-colored liquid sat on her bedside table.

"I put out a nightgown for you," Eugenia said. "And help yourself to a drink."

On the far side of the bed lay a cotton gown, pale aqua in color. Patricia removed her clothing and slipped on the gown, which fell to her calves. She crossed to her mother's dressing table, the wood floor cool on her bare feet. A cut-glass decanter sat to the side of the mirror, light flickering on its faceted surfaces. She poured half a glass and took a sip. The sherry's warmth melted away the outer layer of her fatigue.

This was the first time she had been in her parents' bedroom since she was a teenager. A walnut four-poster bed and carved armoire still dominated the room, but yellow curtains at the window and a matching coverlet on the bed gave the room a lighter feeling.

Patricia set her drink down on the bedside table, plumped up a pillow, and set it against the headboard. The bed creaked as she climbed in beside her mother, pulling the covers over her lap.

"I miss Carlos," her mother said.

"I know. I do too." It was the little boy that she missed, whose memory caused her heart to ache.

Tears welled in her mother's eyes, and she dabbed them with a handkerchief bunched up in her hand, then lowered her hand to the coverlet. "Did you call the police?"

"Yes. The officer seemed satisfied with our story. Somebody will come tomorrow morning. Just a formality, he said."

"I picked up Otto's rifle," Eugenia said. "So now my fingerprints are on it. In case the police look."

Patricia was amazed that her mother had thought of it. It couldn't have been easy—handling the gun that had killed her son. "You were brave."

Eugenia shrugged.

Her mother's maternal instincts were not the best, Patricia mused, but she had surprising amounts of grit and endurance. She had held herself together through the showdown at the dig and the discussions that followed. She had also directed her maid to fetch women to prepare Carlos's body for burial. In the U.S., that would have been considered destruction of evidence. But this was not the U.S. Anyway, her mother's confession and her fingerprints on the rifle, if the police cared to look, should forestall any official investigation.

Patricia thought back to the scene at the dig. "You know, Mama, I wasn't sure you would come back after Carlos sent you to the car."

Her mother looked at her in surprise. "Did you imagine that I would abandon you? Of course not. I hid behind the shed to watch and listen. Then Gustavo showed up with your father's rifle. I've never been so happy to see anyone." Eugenia sipped her sherry. "Of course, at that point, I still hoped it would all end peacefully. Anyway, Gustavo and I came to an agreement. I would do my best to disarm Carlos. But if I wasn't successful, he would do whatever was necessary to keep you and Quique alive."

"I didn't see Gustavo until after it was all over."

"That's because I drew your attention away from him. While I was telling Carlos to put down his gun, Gustavo was crawling to the rim of the dig. Unfortunately, your brother guessed that I was bluffing. So, when that tactic didn't work, I started wailing like a banshee."

"I have to admit, you put on a good show," Patricia said.

"Well, I had to do something to give Gustavo time to get into position. And I hoped that if I distracted Carlos, you and Quique would find a way to overpower him."

Patricia thought of Quique's kung fu kick and her desperate lunge for the gun. "It almost worked."

"Yes. Almost." They sat quietly, sipping their sherry. Outside, an owl hooted twice.

"What do you think?" Eugenia asked. "Can Quique really be Juan José Fuente?"

"It certainly looks that way."

"Well, at least Meg will get her son back, after all these years." Eugenia drained her glass. "Pour me a little more sherry, will you?"

Patricia refilled her mother's glass, then plumped her pillow again and climbed back under the covers.

"There is one thing I can't understand," Eugenia said. "How could your brother even think of killing you? His own sister."

"I know. I didn't truly believe he would shoot me until I was looking into the grave."

"What a horror," her mother murmured.

"I suppose that murdering me made sense to Carlos. He thought that if he let me go, I would reveal his crimes to the world. I suppose I might have—although I was fully prepared to just get on a plane with Quique and keep my mouth shut. But how could Carlos trust me? I was the sister who abandoned him years ago. According to his rules, I had to disappear."

Patricia stared into the middle distance. Was there another reason that Carlos was prepared to shoot her? Maybe her real crime was being the favored child when they were growing up, even though she was a girl. Her father had proven it by leaving the estate to her. And to top it off, Carlos had caught her in a treasonous act—having lunch with Quique, a man who had humiliated him in front of half of San Felipe. Motivations for murder could be complex.

The candle flickered, and its reflection from the dressing table mirror sent shadows dancing on the wall.

"You know, I've changed my mind," Eugenia said glumly. "I wanted the finca so badly. But now I don't want it at all. Not at the price of my son's life."

"Don't blame yourself, Mama. Carlos was unfit to run Finca Baldt. You know that. You were right to fight him for it."

"He never had a head for business. But he seemed interested in politics."

Sure, Patricia thought. She could imagine Carlos rising in the ranks of some horrible right-wing party. One that condoned murdering its opponents.

"Ay, what's to become of me?" Eugenia moaned. "Maybe I'll enter a convent. I remember you were planning to do it once."

Was she? She vaguely remembered wanting to be a sister in a medical mission in Africa. She eyed her elegant, materialistic mother. "You know, you'd have to wear your nails short, and no polish."

Eugenia looked down at her dark red nails, now chipped in a couple of places. "Not even a pale shade? No, I suppose not. The sisters would spot it in a minute." She sighed. "Maybe I should go back to the States with you, live in that little town."

Patricia stifled a groan. "Mama, you hated New Bergen, remember? And you were there in the summer. Believe me, the winter is far worse."

"I don't know how you stand it," Eugenia said.

"It helps to stay busy." And to have a lover, which she would no longer have, unless she changed her mind about marriage.

They finished their sherry, and Eugenia blew out the candle before they settled into the bed. "Carlos was a beautiful baby," her mother said as they lay side by side. "He had those lovely, long eyelashes. Remember?"

"Yes," Patricia said. She'd been eight years old when he was born, and she'd been fascinated by her baby brother with the luminous brown eyes and chubby arms and legs. "I thought he was marvelous."

It wasn't long before Patricia heard her mother's slow, humming breath. Somehow, she'd managed to fall asleep. How could she do that? Nothing weighed too heavily on her mother, she decided. Eugenia dealt with what she needed to and harbored little remorse for what she did or didn't do. Maybe that was as it should be.

Patricia lay still for several more minutes before she too slipped into sleep. But she awoke at four in the morning, according to the bedside clock. It would have been nice to fall asleep once again, but she knew there was no chance. She was fully alert. In the darkness, she got up, slipped on her shoes, and wrapped herself in a woolen shawl that her mother had left draped over the foot of the bed.

She paused at the bedroom door, conscious of stiff muscles and a tender gut, then headed across the courtyard, out the gate, and onto the gravel drive. As she walked, she was aware of the Spanish cedars on both sides—tall, shadowy wraiths that perfumed the air and whispered softly in the breeze.

What day was it? Saturday. She'd been in Guatemala for nearly two weeks, although it felt more like two months. She would need to stay several more days, long enough to attend Carlos's funeral. And to sign over the finca to her mother. Even if Eugenia was no longer so eager to own the plantation, Patricia doubted if she was truly ready to leave the place, especially given all her efforts to furnish the house to her satisfaction. And at least now her mother could take over the finca without fear of reprisals. But transitions were always bumpy. It would be good to stay a little longer to see that her mother was making a good start. An additional week or maybe two.

She turned and faced the house, taking in its graceful Spanish architecture. The place was quiet now under the velvety sky, thick with stars. They were the same stars that shone over New Bergen, but different somehow—brighter. Everything here seemed more intense, more compelling.

And then it hit her. She wasn't going back to the States. Something had shifted inside her. And it wasn't just her father's death that was responsible. Or her brother's. No. She no longer needed the refuge that New Bergen had provided. She was firmly rooted here, in this place. The finca and the countryside were as much a part of her as she was of them. For better or worse, their fates were entwined.

A breeze came up, and she pulled the shawl around her. She knew that it was unwise for people to make major decisions when they were in emotional turmoil. But she felt surprisingly steady after everything that had gone on. Still, she needed to be realistic. If she left New Bergen, what would be the cost to herself and to others?

New Bergen had definite advantages. The town had its share of drama, but early morning walkers didn't discover mutilated corpses in roadside ditches. And death squads didn't murder Catholic priests. It would be difficult to give up the relative safety and political sanity of an Iowa town.

And of course, she had become fond of people there. Her patients mattered to her, but realistically, the town could find a doctor to replace her. Anita would continue to work there as a nurse, and people would gradually become attached to the new physician. She would miss her circle of friends who met for pizza and movies. And there was Hank. He was a sweet, intelligent man and a fine lover, but she didn't want to marry him. Not really. He and Irene would be a better match. She could picture them going on cruises and displaying photos of grandchildren around the house. They would have a good life.

Oddly enough, one thing that she would truly miss was cross-country skiing, gliding over the snow-covered hills around New Bergen. She remembered one breathtakingly cold day, when she and Hank had gotten up early to ski. It had snowed the night before, and the sun sparkled on smooth sheets of snow. As they propelled themselves up hills and swept down them, the only sounds she heard were the shushing of their skis and her own heavy breathing. They paused at the top of a hill. Below them, farmhouses were dotted across the land, with smoke swirling up from their chimneys. A feeling of deep peace filled her, a sense that all was well with the world. That, she would miss.

But it wasn't enough. Slowly, she began walking back toward the house. Everything was falling into place. She would take over the finca. That would remove the responsibility from her mother, who was strong in many ways, but was getting older and was inexperienced as a planter. The Baldt-Contreras family had an obligation to keep the finca going, not just for themselves, but for the laborers and their families—good, hardworking people, who cared for the coffee plants through the long cycle of growth and harvesting. She'd known many of them since she was a girl.

She thought of Noemi and Julio, Demetrio's younger brother and sister. And of Natividad, Noemi's daughter, whom she had yet to meet. And Fiona. How often did one find such a genuine friend?

If she stayed, she could attend Fiona and Julio's marimba concert. The thought lifted her spirits.

And of course, there was Sergio—the idealist, the survivor, the skillful dance partner who evoked the sexy, Latina side of her. She had to admit, it would have been very hard to say good-bye to him.

She stopped walking. In her mind, she pictured Demetrio, the day he had decided to leave the dig. She saw him striding toward Chayaka in his Chicago Cubs hat, his cloth bag hanging down from his shoulder. He had just given up his chance to become an archaeologist, to get a real education. All because Pablo had decided to dig in the Ceremonial Center, and the elders in Chayaka had forbidden the workers to do so. For Demetrio, there had been no choice. If the elders said he must leave the dig, then he must leave. His people came first. Demetrio would have understood her decision to stay.

Patricia woke the next morning to full sunlight filtering through the lemon-yellow curtains of her mother's bedroom. She had crept back into bed the night before and miraculously had fallen asleep. Now she was alone. And, *gracias a dios*, she was alive. And so was Quique. The two of them had stood over their open graves, seemingly doomed, but in the end, they had both walked away. Unlike her little brother Carlos. At least he would have a decent burial, something he would have denied them. She was pretty sure that if Carlos had succeeded in his plan, she and Quique would have just disappeared, like so many people taken by the death squads.

She thought back to her late-night stroll. Even in the light of day—especially in the light of day—her decision seemed sound. She would stay and take over the family plantation.

Her mother was in the dining room, drinking coffee. She looked up. Her eyes looked dull, but her hair was clean and styled, and she had applied a little lipstick. Her stylish black blouse and pencil skirt reminded Patricia that she would have to get hold of some proper mourning clothes. Something fashionable if she was going to be seen with her mother.

"Have some breakfast," Eugenia said. "The police will be coming soon. Then the priest. And God only knows who else."

Her poor mother. Two deaths so close together. Her husband, then her son. A maid appeared with coffee. Patricia asked her to bring a plate of fruit and cheese. "Aunt Claudia will be here this afternoon," she said to her mother. "She'll help."

Eugenia made a pouty face. "And you? I suppose you will be leaving as soon as you can."

"No, I'm staying."

Her mother brightened. "Oh? For how long?"

"Permanently, I hope. I'd like to try my hand at running the finca."

"Hija!"

"I'm hoping you'll help me," Patricia said.

"With great pleasure. I learned a lot from Joaquín, you know." She took Patricia's hand. "I heard what you said to your brother yesterday, that wc could be a true family. Did you really mean it?"

Patricia gave her mother's hand a squeeze. "Sure. Why not."

After breakfast, Patricia shut herself in the office and dialed Jonathan Cabell's number. The truth was, she wasn't ready to talk to Meg. Besides, Jonathan was calm and level-headed, and he was working on Quique's visa, so it made sense to call him first.

Jonathan greeted her warmly. "What's up?"

"Are you sitting down?"

"That sounds ominous. What's this news that might knock me over?"

"I think I've found J.J." A long silence. She'd been too abrupt.

"I'm sitting now," he said, his voice tight. "Tell me more."

She related everything she had learned in the last two days about Enrique Aguilar's birth and death and what she'd learned from Gustavo's confession. Patricia left out Carlos's death and the circumstances that surrounded it. And her decision to stay in Guatemala. Those could wait until another day.

When she finished, there was another long silence. "I don't know, Patricia. I surely value your judgment, but this whole search for J.J. has been a carnival ride. Up and down. Now up again."

She'd expected more excitement, but maybe that was unrealistic. "It's a lot to take in."

"What about Quique? Does he remember any of it?"

"No. But he was only four, and maybe the whole experience was just too traumatic."

"Well," Jonathan said, "you don't have proof that the young man is J.J., but you do have very strong evidence. What does your gut tell you? You're convinced that Quique is really J.J.?"

"Yes. That is, I see no other explanation. But Quique isn't really comfortable with the idea. He's pretty confused at the moment, not sure exactly who he is."

"Well, that's understandable. It's been a long time since he was J.J. We can take it slowly. His visa is being expedited, and it will be ready soon. Then you can bring him here. We'll get to know him, and he'll get to know us."

Jonathan's measured approach was comforting after all the recent chaos. "That sounds good," she said. "But there is one possible obstacle on this end. Quique isn't fond of the U.S. I'm not positive he'll agree to go."

"I guess that part is up to you, then. Talk to the lad, convince him to come. I can fly down if that would help."

"Let me see what I can do first." At least she should have some credibility now that she and Quique had stood side by side facing their shared grave. And she was pretty sure she could count on Claudette to help convince Quique to go to the States, since she was already concerned about his safety.

"But let's not tell Meg right away," Jonathan said, "not until we learn what Quique wants to do. I know my daughter pretty well. Whatever the boy decides—whether he wants to become part of our family or not—she'll accept it. But you know she's going to want to see him immediately, and that might not be a good idea. He'll need a chance to get used to the fact that he has another family."

"Sure. We can wait," Patricia said, although the truth was, she was tired of waiting. She was ready to bring her quest to a close, to see Quique reunited with Meg and Jonathan, and to start her new life. But Jonathan was right. It was better to find out where Quique stood. If anything went wrong, Meg didn't need another precipitous dive on the roller coaster. Actually, Patricia thought, for her, this whole hunt for J.J. had been more like an excursion through a fun house, one with hidden doors and distorting mirrors. She'd been stymied and confused repeatedly before finally reaching the end.

"I'll call back when I know something," she said. "Soon, I hope."

"I'll look forward to it. And Patricia," Jonathan said, his voice breaking, "thank you."

CHAPTER TWENTY-NINE

May 15, San Felipe

Patricia entered the sunny Café Roxy on Poniente Street and sat at her usual table near the front window. The café was quiet today, aside from the noisy whirring of a blender and the murmured conversation of a young couple sitting in the back.

She had passed Beatriz's shop, where the "For Sale" sign that had been there for the last several weeks was now gone. Beatriz must have found a buyer. Patricia could understand her need to leave town. The day before Quique's departure for the U.S., Beatriz's fiancé had broken off their engagement. Then gossip had mushroomed about Quique being Juan José Fuente. That's when the "For Sale" sign had appeared on the shop. According to rumor, Beatriz and Gustavo were moving to Escuintla, a steamy, lowland town, where presumably they would start their lives over. Somehow, Beatriz must have found it in her heart to forgive her old friend for betraying her. Gustavo had saved Quique's life, and that must have helped.

It was hard to feel much sympathy for Beatriz after all the suffering she'd caused. Still, her early life had been sad, and Quique had turned out well in spite of everything. Beatriz had undoubted-ly loved him in her own way.

A pretty, dark-skinned waitress in a low-cut peasant blouse stopped at Patricia's table. "A banana milkshake?" she asked.

"How did you guess?"

The waitress smiled. It was what Patricia had ordered at the Roxy every Thursday for the last month. Her stop there had become part of her Thursday routine since she'd taken over the finca two and a half months earlier. She would drive to San Felipe, run a few errands, and pick up mail—most of which she would read while drinking her milkshake. Then she'd spend the afternoon working at the clinic. Usually, she and Fiona had supper, relaxing and trading news.

This was her break from running the coffee finca, which was challenging work, but surprisingly satisfying, especially now that she was gradually gaining in expertise. She enjoyed walking among the trees with her overseer, an intelligent, observant man who had worked as a laborer for her father for years. The rainy season had begun two weeks earlier, with its afternoon showers. It meant the beginning of a new growing season. She looked forward to watch-ing the cherries bud, then ripen into coffee beans.

Patricia and her mother had developed a working relationship that veered between affection and irritation. So far, their disagree-ments had been few and were all negotiable. As her mother was fond of declaring: "Now we are truly family." In addition to man-aging the plantation and working in San Felipe on Thursday after-noons, Patricia spent most weekends with Sergio. At the thought of him, she felt a little tug of desire. For a change, they were driving to the capital that weekend to have dinner with Arturo and his sister, Ceci. She wondered if Arturo's wife would show up.

A pile of her mail sat on the table before her, and she started looking through it, drawing out a large manila envelope from Meg.

Opening the packet, she found four glossy Polaroids and a hand-written letter on several sheets of Meg's cream-colored stationery.

The waitress arrived with the banana shake, and Patricia took a sip through the straw, savoring the cold creaminess, before she started looking through the photos. In the first one, Quique and Jonathan stood in front of a pale gold station wagon, Quique's hand on the hood in a proprietary stance. Both were grinning. Patricia flipped over the photo. "Quique and Dad bonding over Quique's new Volvo."

Patricia smiled. She had felt an enormous relief when Quique agreed to go to the U.S. and meet Meg's family. Patricia and Claudette had both put their best efforts into convincing Quique to go to the U.S., but in the end, it was Sergio who did the job. He and Quique had drinks together one evening, and at the end of it, Quique announced that he would visit Meg. Neither Sergio nor Quique ever fully divulged what they'd talked about, but Patricia got the feeling that Sergio knew Meg better than she'd realized.

After that, Quique, Meg, and Jonathan had come to an agreement. In the U.S., Quique would remain Quique, and he would play the role of the twins' newly-discovered cousin.

Patricia picked up the second photo, in which Quique was sandwiched between the twins on the sofa. He was laughing as the girls posed, grinning, with their hands hovering over a huge bowl of popcorn that was sitting on Quique's lap. On the reverse side: "Amy, Quique, and Laura. Popcorn and movie night."

The third photo showed Quique and Meg sitting next to each other at the dining room table, books open before them, smiling wearily. On the other side: "Tutoring Quique for his Illinois driver's test. He passed it last Friday. In English!"

The last photo featured Claudette and Quique in jeans, plaid shirts, and sneakers, standing in front of the station wagon. On the ground beside them were sleeping bags, backpacks, and other camping gear. Quique's arm was around Claudette. He was beaming. She had a wry smile. On the back: "Quique and Claudette starting their western adventure."

She opened Meg's letter, written in cursive in blue ink, in a graceful style very similar to that of Evelyn, her mother.

April 30, 1978

Dear Patricia,

It was wonderful to hear from you. Thanks so much for the charming photo of Noemi and her daughter at the park in San Felipe. And I love the picture of Julio and your friend Fiona at the marimba recital. I'm very pleased that you have become friends with Demetrio's family. They are attractive people, aren't they? It's not surprising, of course, given what a handsome young man Demetrio was.

Things are fine here. The doctor says I'm making an excellent recovery from the fracture. He must be right because I'm hobbling around well.

I've been busy with our Oak Park residents' association. We have found a nice Black family who are going to move in down the street from us. So far, our plan for neighborly integration seems to be working, and I like hanging out with the good people in our group.

I'm sending pictures. As you can see, Charlie's new Polaroid camera is being put to good use.

Claudette has been at our house for the last week. I'm grateful that Peace Corps decided to send her home early. It sounds like the political situation in Santa Catarina was pretty grim. She and Quique have been taking the L all around Chicago. She confided to me that they're experiencing a little stress. In Guatemala, he looked out for her, and now it's often the other way around. Still, they are sweet together. (He calls her "mi amor.")

The two of them left on their big trip west this morning. (See the photo.) Right now their itinerary includes Mesa Verde, the Grand Canyon, Zion National Park, and Rocky Mountain National Park. It sounds like a great trip, although it will still be cold in the mountains. Beautiful, but cold. I thought I'd be brave about Quique's departure, considering they'll only be gone a few weeks, but I burst into tears as soon as their car turned the corner.

Quique and Dad surmounted all communication problems in the course of searching for Quique's Volvo. They are now plotting to buy a used Maserati with a bi-turbo engine, which I understand is quite the thing. They're going to fix it up together. I noticed that Quique has taken to calling Dad "Abuelo." It tickles Dad no end to be his Grandpa once again.

As you noticed when you were here, Quique and the girls hit it off immediately. They have introduced their handsome cousin to their friends, never failing to mention that he was a famous soccer player in Guatemala. He's started working out with a pick-up soccer team not too far from us. Some of the players speak Spanish, which works out well for Quique. Both of our girls now want to study Spanish over the summer. I suspect it's partly so they can talk to Quique's good-looking teammates.

Charlie has been on the road quite a bit. Quique thinks it's cool that Charlie is a union organizer, and Charlie respects Quique for his political views and his experience coaching soccer with barrio kids. It appears to be a good foundation for a relationship.

It seems like Quique and I have been slowest at building a relationship. He has always been very respectful to me, and he even helps me with laundry, but there has always been a polite distance between us.

Then, a few days ago I was cleaning up in the kitchen, and he walked in, and out of the blue he said he was sorry that he couldn't be J.J. for me. I didn't know what to say, so I floundered around and finally said not to worry, that I liked the person he was, and I was glad he was in the family. He said that he liked me too, and he liked having someone to speak Spanish with. And this was a good home, even though nobody made tortillas. So I offered to buy him a comal and let him practice on the grill in back. He thought that was pretty funny, and we joked around for a while. The conversation wound down, and he started to leave the kitchen. But then he came over and kissed me on the cheek and said, "I'm glad you found me."

I tell you this, Patricia, because it was you who found him. And I know that you risked your life to bring him back. No one ever had a better friend and sister than you.

You know, I've wondered off and on how J.J. could have survived the fire, and I think it's possible he went to check on his tree house that night. It was new, and he was dying to visit it. I had told him he had to wait, but maybe he climbed out of bed in the middle of the night and snuck over there. So, he disobeyed me, and it saved his life. There is probably a moral in there somewhere, but I'm not sure I want to know what it is.

By the way, I have a new hobby. I've begun fashioning knotted necklaces for our family, just simple ones, nothing as complex as the Chayakan quipus. I'm using *brightly colored yarn, so they're rather pretty. The knots stand for people we love and who have helped us in our lives from the time we were little, so the quipu is a personal history of gratitude. Let me know if you would like one, and we can figure out who should go on it.*

I wish the news from Guatemala were better. It sounds like the violence is continuing.

Please say hello to your mother and to Sergio.

I hold you in the Light, always.

Love,

Meg

P.S. Our daffodils are blooming, and they are glorious.

Patricia sat for a moment, drinking her banana shake. Then she looked at the photos again, smiling at each one in turn. She pictured Meg sitting at the dining room table, working away on the family's necklaces, a labor of love. Okay, she thought. Tomorrow, she would start a list of people to whom she was grateful. It would be a reminder of all the goodness in her life, besides providing Meg with the material for a quipu.

She placed the stationery and photos back in the envelope, took a final slurp of her drink, and paid the waitress. A minute later she was striding along the street to Fiona's clinic, an island of healing in a turbulent world. Fiona would definitely get a knot, a large one in a beautiful color. Bright blue perhaps, for highland skies and for peace.

ACKNOWLEDGMENTS

I am grateful to readers who have expressed their enjoyment of *Reading the Knots*, and I hope this sequel will satisfy their wish to know about what happens to Patricia, Meg, and Noemi. My deep thanks go to members of my on-line writing group: Carrie Bedford, Maryvonne Fent, Gillian Hobbs, and Diana Corbitt. They smoothed out numerous rough spots and encouraged me along the way. I am grateful to Mary Ann Hendrickson and Tyler Hendrickson for the improvements they made to the final draft. Many thanks to my ever-supportive husband, Jan Michael, who read through the final draft and formatted it. And thanks to Gordon McClellan and Suanne Laqueur at Canoe Tree Press for carefully guiding this book to publication.

ABOUT THE AUTHOR

Susan Garzon is a retired anthropologist, linguist, and teacher of English as a foreign language. She lived for eight years in Latin America, where she taught English and carried out anthropological field work. During her two years of field work in Guatemala, she spent much of her time in a Mayan town. Following a university career, she currently lives in Oklahoma with her husband and three cats.

Visit her at www.susangarzon.com